D1562749

ALSO BY L.E. THOMAS

Star Runners

Star Runners: Revelation Protocol

Star Runners: Mission Wraith

Star Runners: Scorpions

Star Runners: Dark Space

For the latest information on Star Runners,

visit www.StarRunners.net

STAR RUNNERS: REVELATION PROTOCOL

L.E. THOMAS

STAR RUNNERS

REVELATION PROTOCOL

A novel by L.E. Thomas

Edited by Monique Happy Editorial Services

www.moniquehappy.com

Cover art by Andrei Bat.

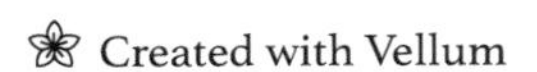
Created with Vellum

For Mom and Dad, who taught me to fly.

PROLOGUE

"I'm going home."

The man sitting next to Josh Morris revealed yellowing teeth under a bushy mustache. He appeared to be in his mid-forties with weathered skin splintering into wrinkles at his eyes. His black eyes glazed over under heavy eyelids as he leaned back in his seat, preparing for a nap during the flight to Earth. His perfectly pressed navy blue suit showed no creases as he settled into the chair.

Josh smiled. "Me, too. It's been a while."

"How long?"

"Little over a year." He thought of what it would feel like to leave Base Prime and see the California sun. "Not sure what I'm going to do back in the 'real' world."

"Wear sunglasses." The fellow passenger studied him. "If it's only been a year, that's nothing. You in Fleet?"

Josh nodded. "I'm a pilot, yes. You?"

"Transferring to the EIF."

"EIF?"

The man grinned. "You *are* new here, aren't you? Earth Intelligence Force. Was in the CIA, but quit when I was recruited. I served on several forces throughout the Legion in recent years, from planets to the Fringe. I even worked at the capital's location for a year. Been a while since I was back home, too. Lot longer than a year. When this position came open, I jumped at the chance."

Josh shook his head. "I didn't realize the Legion recruited cops from Earth."

The man frowned. "Not just any cop on the beat, but yeah, they recruit who they can. Name's Mike Fischer."

He offered his hand. "Josh Morris."

"How long you been a Star Runner?"

"Just finished flight school, but I've been in space since the beginning of last summer."

"Flight school as tough as they say?"

Josh paused, thinking about his months on Tarton's Junction. The studying and flight training seemed more like two lifetimes. The endless days of seeing nothing but the nebulae for natural light. What had started off fun and amazing had become a chore. He had only wanted to go to school. A free scholarship for playing Star Runners seemed like a great way to do that—even easier than playing on a football team like Dad wanted. The reality turned out to be more demanding and dangerous than he could have fathomed.

He sighed. "It ain't easy."

The freighter *Saber* rocked as it prepped the curvature drive. The space outside the viewport glowed, a bright mix of fire red and emerald green.

Fischer grumbled. "I guess nothing ever is. You going on leave?"

"That's the plan. Probably going to be my last time home for a while. I've been told I'll get my assignment when my leave is up."

"Been told that's a big deal for you flyboys," Fischer said, closing his eyes.

"They haven't said much about it. Any guess where they'll send me?"

Fischer sighed, his eyes remaining closed. "Time was, a Star Runner fresh out of flight school could be sent anywhere. I've heard stories of you boys being assigned to science vessels and studying the void along the Fringe, doing real exploration like the old days. But those days are long gone, I'm afraid."

"Why's that?"

His brow furrowed. "Been a long time since the big boys went at it. Rumor has it, it's coming again."

"I see."

Josh thought of the fragile peace between the Legion and the Zahl Empire. He wondered if there was any truth to what Fischer had heard. Rumors on Tarton's Junction traveled with about as much weight as a feather in a hurricane. If he believed every rumor he heard on the station, Austin would be dating one of his flight instructors. Besides, Josh had learned little about the Zahl Empire during his studies, other than how to recognize their fighters. Other than a brief overview of the previous time the two forces went to war, the detailed Zahl history had been left out of any discussions.

Deciding to change the subject, Josh cleared his throat. "You get any break while you're on Earth?"

"I wish. Been ordered home to join a task force."

"A task force?"

"That's all I know. It's probably training. Every now and then, Command sends us to a backwater planet like Earth to tighten up our counter-espionage efforts. That's probably what this is."

Josh snorted, shaking his head. "I'm still learning about this world."

Fischer stretched into his seat. "They want you to know your fighter inside and out. That's more important than the ins and outs of this world. Believe me, you don't want to know about the politics of a territory as large as the Legion. Not to mention the constant crap going on between our government and the Zahl Empire." He sighed. "Where are you from?"

"Marietta, Georgia."

"Never been there. I'm from Saint Louis myself. Or I used to be. I got picked up at a Legion school in the suburbs. Legion's a big place. I move around."

"I'll bet. Where all have you been?"

He shrugged. “All around really.”

“I haven’t been to another planet, yet.”

“You will. They aren’t all that different really. Just people trying to make ends meet, trying to take care of their families, give their kids a decent shot at life. That’s true on the dark worlds and on the open Legion planets.”

“You serve on mostly dark worlds?”

“Served on all kinds. The Fringe, now, that’s a different story.”

The *Saber* passed through the curvature drive. Josh's stomach dropped, but he had grown accustomed to the gravity swells that occurred during a curve. He sighed, waiting for the feeling to pass.

His parents would be excited to have him home. Dad had already bought tickets to the Braves game. Hot dogs and fireworks for Independence Day. It was like a dream. The transition staff had briefed him on the story he would provide his parents. They’d also created a plethora of doctored photographs depicting constructed schools for villages on islands in the south Pacific. Josh had even contracted a "fever" the last month, which was supposed to explain why his skin was pale and why he had lost weight. The officers insisted that the goal of the deception was to supply too much information for family members in order to maintain the illusion. He took his orders. If this was the price to visit home again, so be it.

Austin would have loved to come with him; too bad they couldn't have started flight school at the same time. Josh's performance in Rockshot had earned him enough points to graduate. Austin would be right behind him. Soon they would be on opposite sides of the galaxy, flying for the Legion. He might not see his friend for a long, long time. Try as he might, the thought of being away from everyone and everything he loved nagged at the back of his mind.

But the same could be said for his friends on Earth. He would have to check in with Kadyn, see if she would be home for summer as well. Perhaps he would finally find the time to tell her how he felt, use this one last trip home to throw it all out there and see if she felt the same way.

He had written Kadyn regularly or as often as he could since he’d spent most of the past year on Tarton's Junction. She seemed to be enjoying art school in Savannah, and rarely mentioned Austin at all. Josh had always thought Kadyn had a thing for his best friend. Maybe he had been wrong about her feelings this entire time? Who knew? But if he had the opportunity on this two-week trip home, he had to see where it could lead. She had to know. If anything happened, he'd talk to Austin before it led anywhere. That's the least he could do.

The *Saber* altered its course. A stack of magazines slid off an empty seat across the aisle.

"Is that normal?" Fischer asked. "Never happened to be me before, but you're the pilot. What was that?"

"Probably a course correction to maintain a position directly behind the moon while the shroud warms up," he offered. "Truthfully, I don't know."

He gazed at the faint stars peppering the black space.

The interior lights flickered, shifting to blood red.

"Attention, this is your captain speaking," the speakers buzzed. "Two unidentified craft have launched from the dark side of Earth's moon. They are inbound and have not responded to our hails."

Josh swallowed. Space craft on the dark side of the moon? That made no sense. The pilot had to be mistaken. Suddenly, the freighter banked harder than it had been designed to do, the space outside his window shooting past. Earth's moon moved across his view, filling his window with the black and gray of the surface. The incoming craft flickered in the starlight as they bore down on the *Saber.*

"Protocol says we must turn back," the pilot continued. "We are prepping the drive. Please remain in your seats."

Josh leaned against the window, studying the incoming craft. Two smaller modified Trident fighters with wings bristling with weaponry.

Tyral Pirates.

He squinted at the third larger vessel. Thick black tentacles extended from the base like a jellyfish. A cold feeling burrowed into his gut like stomach rot.

"See anything?" Fischer asked, leaning over his shoulder.

He turned. "They plan to board us."

"Board us?" His dark eyes widened. "Who?"

He swallowed, his mouth dry as a sandbox. "Tyral Pirates."

“Pirates?” Fischer barked. “Here? How in the world did they manage this?”

“I don’t know.”

After leaning over Josh’s shoulder and staring out the window for a long moment, Fischer stood and produced a laser pistol from inside his black coat. He checked the charge. "You gotta sidearm?"

Josh nodded.

"Good," Fischer said. "Once we know their entry location, we need all the civies as far away from the access point as possible. They’ll probably try to rip open an emergency escape hatch, or they could just blast through the hull."

Josh blinked several times, gripping the cool steel of his laser pistol. His breathing increased. "Yes, sir."

Fischer grabbed his shoulder. "Listen, keep your cool. We need to work together. I don’t know how this filth has managed to stage an attack on the dark side of Earth’s moon, but that doesn’t matter now. If that scum is truly coming on board, they are the worst of the lot, the lowest of the low. They’ll come for blood. They have no mercy, so show none. What's your rank?"

"Lieutenant."

"Right." Fischer turned to the rest of the passengers who spoke in hushed, harsh tones. "All right, listen up! These pirates might try and board us to steal this freighter. I want everybody with a weapon to come over here and meet Lieutenant Morris at the front of this cabin. The rest of you gather at the rear. The most likely place of entry will be close to the cockpit so they can take control of the ship."

Three Star Runners wearing the red uniforms of Excalibur Squadron came to the front of the cabin, while Fischer led the other passengers to the rear. The Star Runners nodded and checked their weapons, a grim look on their faces.

The freighter rumbled, laser fire thumping against the rear shields.

"All right, this is real," the tallest Excalibur pilot said, his face growing pale. "I had hoped the freighter captain was a moron. I thought Earth was safe."

"So did I," Josh said. He glanced at the pilot who looked older than him, the skin around his eyes laced with lines like road map. "You heading home?"

"I *was*."

Josh looked up as the freighter rocked.

"We're trying to open a curve," another pilot said.

"They'll follow us," Josh said. "I've seen this happen."

"So have I," the older Excalibur pilot said. "Too many times."

Light flashed from the windows like lightning. His stomach revolved around his core, his vision skipping. The laser fire momentarily halted.

"Now it depends on where the curve opened and where we came out," the pilot said. "If we're too far from the Junction, the alert fighters won't get to us in time."

Laser fire blasted the *Saber's* shields. Josh leaned over his seat, peering out of the window in search of the welcome sight of Tarton's Junction. He saw nothing but space and the glowing edge of the nebulae.

"We're too far," he said.

The outer walls of the freighter behind the cockpit burst, the white light blinding him. Women screamed. The Excalibur pilots tumbled to the ground. Josh fell behind his seat. The vacuum of space howled for two seconds before an energy field from the Tyral boarding craft sealed off the opening.

The tallest Excalibur Star Runner cried out, tumbling behind the seat onto the ground next to Josh, a blackened burn sizzling his eye socket. Another pilot returned fire. Two bolts struck his chest, sending him flying back across the seats. Pirate fire blasted across the cabin, filling the air with blue light and the smell of burning electronics. Josh risked a glance over the seat, his heart pounding in his ears.

Six pirates wearing all black flight suits and carrying massive rifles marched with purpose through a jagged hole in the hull as they rained fire across the cabin. Passengers dropped, laser fire mowing them down like grass. Four pirates faced toward him while the other two concentrated on the cockpit door. Laser bolts blasted the seats as Josh took cover. He gripped the pistol hard, his palms sweating. The onslaught ignited the seat's fabric, starting a fire. The interior lights flickered and dimmed.

The surviving Excalibur pilot crawled toward him, his chest covered in a smoking patch of blackened flesh. Josh yanked him behind the seat.

"We-we cannot let them take the cockpit," the pilot said, his teeth chattering.

"You're in shock!" Josh yelled, firing into the aisle without looking. He glanced down at the man's wound. He never knew a laser rifle could incinerate a person's body in such a way.

"Th-that won't matter if they take the ship," the pilot said, grabbing Josh's arm with his good hand. "Nothing will! Stop them!"

Josh stuck his pistol over the top of the seat and fired. When he looked back to the wounded man, he stared back with lifeless eyes. A frigid chill shot down his spine.

"Morris!"

Remaining close to the floor, Josh glanced down the aisle toward the rear of the ship. Fischer crawled toward him, his pistol drawn.

"Are you all that's left?" he asked.

Josh nodded.

"Pirates have also boarded in the rear and the front group has already taken control of the freighter." Fischer snapped his fingers. "Are you with me?"

"I am." Josh closed his eyes. "What do we do?"

With his free hand, Fischer pulled from his jacket pocket a small disk the size of a hockey puck. Laser fire shot over their heads, the chaotic sounds of battle surrounding them. A shower of sparks fell down.

"This is a flash bang!" Fischer yelled. "I throw it down there and distract them. We try and take them out before they recover. Got it?"

Josh gripped his pistol hard, his knuckles turning white. "Do it."

Fischer pulled his arm back and hurled the flash bang. He held three fingers in front Josh's face, two, one.

The cabin pulsed with a hot white light. Screams from the pirates joined those of the passengers.

"Now!"

Fischer stood up and fired, his pistol burning blue like a pilot light. Josh raised over the seats and added his pistol fire to the mix. Four pirates remained in a rough line at the head of the cabin, their hands over their eyes. Two on the right dropped to the ground as Fischer's bolts exploded into them. Josh hesitated and then killed one of the other pirates with a lucky shot to the face, sending sparks flying as the man crumbled.

The surviving enemy swung around, his rifle spitting a wave of bolts into the seats, walls, and ceiling. More seats caught fire. A white gas shot down from the ceiling, the fires activating the repression systems. The walls blackened. Fischer yelled as a bolt sizzled into his left arm, sending his gun to the floor. Josh dropped to one knee as a bolt zipped over his head. He took aim, squeezed the trigger, and dropped the final opponent.

He exhaled and turned to Fischer. "What now?"

Fischer glanced at the red gash splitting the fabric of his coat, the laser burn eating away at his skin. He slapped a fresh charge into his pistol. "Grab their weapons. Watch the rear."

"But there's still two in the cockpit!"

"I'll get in there!" Fischer yelled. "Cover me!"

Josh ran among the bodies in the forward cabin behind the cockpit, taking care not to allow his gaze to linger on the carnage littering the floor. He grabbed a pirate rifle and knelt down in the aisle as Fischer went to work on the barred cockpit door.

His heart raced as he gasped for breath, trying to steady the large weapon. He imagined the pirates rushing toward him through the white gas and black smoke. He tried to envision dropping each of them with one shot as he maintained his cool. Austin would tell him to stay frosty, but flying in the cockpit of a Trident was different than shooting a man in front of him.

Or would the pirates try to move quietly?

The *Saber* had to be closing in on Tarton's Junction. Where were the alert fighters? How much longer until they arrived? He thought of Austin watching him leave from the mess hall and hoped his friend wasn't there anymore.

Stop it, he told himself. Stay frosty.

"Hurry up, Fischer!" he yelled without turning, his attention aft.

"I'm trying to bypass the lock so—wait!"

Laser fire sliced through the inferno. Josh spun around, his finger resting on the rifle's trigger. Fischer fell to the ground, hands clutching at his stomach as two pirates emerged from the cockpit. Josh aimed and squeezed the trigger.

Nothing happen.

He squeezed again and again, but no fire burst from the weapon. He couldn't verify if it were out of charges or the rifle was simply broken. Standing in the aisle, he hurled the weapon at the pirates and yanked his pistol from its holster.

His world flashed with light like he stood inside a lightning bolt, pain searing at his back. His muscles burned as if they ignited in gasoline. He tumbled to the deck, his body refusing to respond to his commands. His muscles twitched. His head smashed into the base of a seat, fire raging around him.

"Wicked little toy, isn't it?" the pirate said as he stood over Josh. "You can't fire another man's weapon."

The pirates roared with laughter. Josh glared at the pirate who had spoken, the man's face concealed by black fabric. He only saw one bloodshot, watery eye, the other covered in a metal patch.

"Your muscles are incapacitated," the pirate sneered. "You are our prisoner. You will regain control of your body if we decide to let you live. For now, it's lights out."

Before Josh could speak, the butt of the pirate's rifle smashed into his face.

The world went dark.

1

The freighter came apart, the Tyral Pirate fighters firing with lethal precision. Josh's body floated through a burning gap in the hull and into the vacuum of space, his hands reaching out as he stared with eyes as black as eight balls.

"Help me!" His face twisted in pain.

Austin Stone jolted, kicking the seat in front of him. Blood pumped through his ears with the force of a cannon shot. A bead of sweat dripped down his cheek.

"You okay?"

The passenger next to him turned, the tablet in his hands momentarily forgotten. He wore a green flight suit with the Lobera patch.

Austin blinked and shook his head. "Sorry."

"Bad dream?"

He nodded. "Yes."

"They pass."

Austin leaned forward and rubbed his face. Outside his window Earth's moon passed, the blackened craters drifting past his view. The freighter's engines whined as the shroud activated, hiding the vessel from any instruments on Earth. It had been a year since he had seen the moon's surface. He remembered Bear and Skylar pressing against the window, their excitement something tangible and real. Their anticipation of what would happen next mixed strangely with the professional boredom of Captain Jonathan Nubern.

He smiled.

Before he boarded this freighter for his anticipated flight home, Nubern said the Legion recruited medical personnel. His stomach churned whenever he thought about the impending conversation with his mother. She wouldn't believe him at first, would probably accuse him of doing drugs while he had been at school. He wondered how he would even begin the discussion, and then somehow tell her she might have the opportunity to join him.

It wasn't something he would bring up right away. He hadn't been home in a year, so he wanted to soak in the next two weeks of leave. He needed to make each day count, maybe even each hour.

A cold twinge struck his heart. Josh's parents had been notified by now of their son's disappearance. The Legion had an Expiration Protocol for missing pilots and crewmen who hailed from dark worlds like Earth. The families would be told a story of their loved one's disappearance, but Austin dreaded facing the Morris family. He thought of avoiding them for the entire two weeks, but knew it was an impossible task since his mother had probably told Mrs. Morris he was coming home.

He thought of Josh every day since the Tyral Pirates had taken the *Saber* within sight of Tarton's Junction. Josh had probably been killed along with the other several hundred passengers. From what he had gathered from the scuttlebutt around the station, the pirates were not known for their humanitarian gestures toward prisoners. In fact, most pirates would either kill the prisoners during interrogations or work them to death through mining, farming, or whatever other work they required. He glared out the window.

"Don't fight the battles of the past," the passenger said as if he were telepathic.

"Excuse me?"

"Your nightmare. It's best to try and let things go."

Austin sighed. "You didn't lose your best friend."

"No," the man admitted, "but I've lost comrades. It comes with the territory. For what it's worth, I'm sorry. Are you headed home?"

He nodded. "You?"

"Same." He extended his hand. "Lieutenant Ryan Bean. I'm from Bozeman, Montana."

"Austin Stone. Atlanta, Georgia."

"Nice to meet you, Austin. Been flying long?"

He glanced at the shiny wings on his chest. "Just got these, actually."

"Ah, going home on the reward leave. Enjoy it. It won't come again for a while."

"Have you been gone long?"

Ryan looked out the window. "Three years on a carrier, and one year planet side for training. It's been long tours of nothing broken by brief sessions of crazy. I've been told most tours are like that on the Fringe."

"I see," Austin said.

In his courses, he learned about the boundaries of Legion and Zahl space. However, the infinitely more interesting aspect was the broad regions at the edge of known space, a location the Star Runners referred to as the Fringe. The sparsely populated worlds struggled with marauding bands of vicious pirates, conniving smugglers, and oppressive warlords. The Fringe was a boundary the Legion needed to patrol just as aggressively as the border with the Zahl.

"Have you received your orders, yet?" Ryan asked.

"Not yet. I'm supposed to get them after my leave is up."

Ryan smiled and gazed at the ceiling. "I remember my first trip home. My cousins and I went camping in the Spanish Peaks. We sat around the fire for hours. They wanted to know about my travels, but I had to give them the script of helping people. It's true, I guess, just not the people they thought I was helping. It was hard, but I knew it was important to keep the secret." He exhaled slowly. "That was four years ago."

Austin looked at Ryan, who was not much older than himself, but the tone of his voice seemed different than that of his classmates, aged and without emotion. Ryan's mind seemed to be elsewhere, lingering on a memory. "I bet you've seen some things out there."

Ryan didn't blink. "I've seen things you wouldn't believe."

"Like what?"

He shifted in his seat. "I don't want to disappoint you. I remember when I was in your shoes."

The tone of Ryan's voice once again sent a chill straight through Austin's gut. "Go ahead."

Looking over his shoulder before he spoke, Ryan leaned closer. "Just be sure, when your term is up, that you really want to continue being one of the Legion's 'Star Runners.'"

Austin frowned as Ryan held his fingers over his head in mock quotes with the words Star Runners. "What do you mean? Why wouldn't I want to do this?"

Ryan lowered his voice. "Some people love it—I'm not denying that. But let's just say they don't exactly tell you the entire truth during flight academy. Everything's not puppy dogs and ice cream out there."

Austin shook his head, his blood pressure rising. "You don't know what I've seen. The pirates—"

"Pirates," Ryan said shaking his head, "they're nothing."

"They killed my friend."

"No offense, Stone, but your friend is just one of the million pilots recruited off these Legion backwater worlds. You ever wonder why they recruit from a video game? I mean *really* wonder about it? And why everything's set up like a happy flight academy with sim pods and Rockshot competitions? You're being indoctrinated. They want you *so* into this that you'll be willing to go anywhere."

Austin thought of Nubern and the entire recruitment process. "I don't believe that."

"It's why they recruit so young. They identify you have talent, but they are also looking for dreamers; people who want to get out of their current situation."

Pausing, Ryan eyed him. "You'll be sent so far away you won't even remember what Earth looks like." He looked down at his hands. "Or what it smells like...feels like. This galaxy's a big place. There are rumors of factions setting up for another galactic war, who knows if it's true. Then there are the pirates, warlords, slavers, and the endless vigil of what might come from the Fringe or Dark Space beyond. And we have to patrol all of it. It's why the Legion desperately needs pilots. You're giving up the best years of your life for this and they know it."

Austin didn't know what to say. What if Ryan was right?

The Legion had him locked into service for the next five years until he was allowed to re-enlist or leave. He was so focused on going to college and getting a degree because he knew it was what Dad had wanted for him. He didn't stop to ask questions and when he did have questions, he just shook them from his mind. Then his wildest dreams came true once the video game he used to escape reality *became* his reality. Maybe he was too deep into the trees to see the forest for what it was.

"Look," Austin said after a long pause, "I want to do this."

Ryan held up his hands in a mock surrender. "I just wanted to tell you the truth. Some people love this, are born for it."

Austin decided to turn the tables. "So you aren't? Are you going to re-up?"

Ryan rubbed his chin. "I'm coming home to think about it. I'm due next year. I just don't know. I was recruited when the game was brand new. I was so excited."

For the first time, Ryan's eyes softened. Austin relaxed a bit, listening to the other Star Runner speak.

"Four of us left the school in San Francisco. I remember seeing Atlantis for the first time." He shook his head. "It was like having the blinders pulled off. And the first time I saw a Trident? Forget it, man. I was hooked."

Ryan fiddled with his hands. "I left my girlfriend for this. At first, they don't tell you how long the tours are going to be—or maybe I just didn't really get it. You just give the mission trip speech over and over."

His face grew rigid. "But right after you are rewarded leave home after flight school and you sign your papers for that first assignment, months turn into years. Command knows you don't need any cover story after that. Your friends and family give up on you, figure you're just some reclusive freak because you've had to live with vague stories about why you've been away so long. They think you just don't like people or that your antisocial. My girlfriend even said I was agoraphobic because I was always gone and didn't want to do anything in public when I was home. I got so tired of lying to people with these ridiculous stories."

Austin looked at him. "What happened to your girlfriend?"

"Same thing that happened to all my friends," he said softly without looking away from the deck. "Sometimes I wish the Legion would take a page from the Zahlian playbook."

Austin frowned. "Like what? I thought they are our enemy."

Ryan exhaled. "That's what I'm told. I just know there are no dark worlds in Zahlian space; they have no need for the lies...the secrets." His eyes bore into the back of the seat in front of him. "I might still have Vanessa if it weren't for the secrecy."

"I thought the Legion didn't reveal itself in hopes of protecting the systems in their territory and providing natural freedom to progress."

Ryan closed his eyes. "I know the line just fine, Stone. They taught me, too."

The moon passed out of view. Austin sighed, the dream images of Josh reaching for him searing into his mind once again.

"We made it," Austin breathed.

"Made it where?"

"Past the moon."

Ryan nodded. "I heard about the *Saber.* Getting pretty ballsy, those Tyral Pirates. I've never heard of a vessel attacked so close to Earth. I don't know how they plotted a curve this far out. I've heard agents from the Zahl Empire work on Earth all the time, but not pirates."

"Why not?"

"Can't afford shrouding tech and no pirates are going to risk revealing themselves to a dark world unless they have an invasion force."

"But the Zahl Empire sends agents to Earth? For what?"

"Spying, stealing technologies, disrupting our operations." Ryan shrugged. "All unofficially of course."

Austin thought of Earth's history. "Sounds like the Cold War."

"It *is* the Cold War, just on an infinitely larger scale. There's so much space with so many planets in Zahl and Legion space, I doubt there will ever be a full scale war again. It'd be the end of us all." Ryan placed his tablet in his lap. "Did you lose someone on the *Saber*?"

Austin looked out the window, craning his neck for a view of Earth. "My best friend was on board."

"And you saw it?"

He nodded. "Once they passed back through the curve at Tarton's, I saw the fighters bearing down on the freighter, the other transport craft attached. It happened too fast for the alert fighters to respond. And then they were gone."

"He could still be alive."

Austin sighed and cracked his knuckles, knots forming in his stomach. "Thanks, but I've heard stories about what pirates do to prisoners. If he was taken alive, I hope it wasn't for long. I don't want to think of Josh living as a slave."

"No, you definitely don't want that." Ryan turned back to the tablet in his lap.

They rode in silence, the hum of the engines lulling him to sleep. Despite the lingering doubt brought on by Ryan's words, Austin focused on reuniting with Mom and Kadyn. It would be good to see them again.

When he opened his eyes, the blue-green of Earth filled most of his window. The cloudless sky over the Pacific revealed Australia and New Zealand. Passengers started picking up their belongings and Ryan tucked his tablet into a black satchel.

"Stone," he said, pushing Austin's shoulder, "we should grab a coffee in San Francisco. I didn't mean to be such a drag. I just have too much on my mind. You need to think about these things now so it's not such an ordeal when your reenlistment time happens."

"I will," he said. "Thanks. I thought you had to get back to Montana?"

"I have an old friend in the city I want to see first. See if they remember me. Then I'll head out tomorrow."

Austin thought about traveling back to Georgia. "So do we just take the tubes back to our schools?"

Ryan peered over Austin's shoulder out the window. "Once you're home, you can take any transport you want. I'll be taking a company car home, though. I've been away from here so long, I'd like to drive when I'm back."

"Oh."

"Don't worry, man. They'll have someone there to talk you through. Just ask when we're going through de-con."

"De-con?" Austin asked. "Decontamination?"

"They told you about that on the station, right?"

"They mentioned it, yeah." He frowned. "Didn't know I'd have to go through it again."

"It's no big deal," Ryan said. "It's pretty standard on all Legion ports."

The freighter rumbled into Earth's atmosphere as it descended. His head rocked. He closed his eyes, the sound of the engines growing.

"Ladies and gentlemen," the pilot announced over the intercom, "we're starting our descent to Atlantis and should arrive in the next thirty minutes. Please remain seated and we hope you enjoyed your flight." The pilot paused before adding, "Welcome to Earth."

Austin watched the atmosphere burn against the freighter's shields, pulsating flashes of orange and yellow throughout cabin.

THE FREIGHTER DESCENDED into the blue deep waters of the Pacific, the light outside the window transitioning from the bright to dark blue like a bruise before going black. When the bubbles disappeared, the view outside his window could have passed for the darkness of space.

As the vessel descended into the blackness, conversations lessened, the tones softening. Austin glanced around the cabin. The occupants appeared much the same as his first trip when he departed Earth; a mix of civilian clothes and Legion uniforms. The image of the *Saber* flashed in his mind once again. Josh never made it this far on his first trip home. His mind wandered, picturing Josh in his final moments with the pirates. Had he fought until the end? Did death come quickly?

He shuddered.

Austin hadn't been gone as long as Josh, but he earned the right to go home following the incident on Flin Six. Ryker was on her way to a Legion world of Oma for rehab on her leg. Skylar and Bear continued their flight training on Tarton's Junction. Austin found himself alone, again.

But it was different this time.

He glanced at Ryan, a fellow Star Runner, who had fallen asleep during the final moments of the descent. Austin had earned his place in the brotherhood of Legion pilots. He was a Star Runner. No one could ever take that away. He would make Josh proud.

The descent slowed, awakening the dozing passengers. Bubbles flickered past the window. A soft blue light pulsated from below. The freighter banked into a slow turn, revealing the circular dome of Atlantis. They made their way towards the four large saucer-shaped hangar doors. Another freighter, just visible in the low light provided by the landing buoys, drifted away from a hangar door on its way to the surface. He watched the other freighter depart the underwater facility, wondering if any passengers on board were seeing this for the first time. He shook his head, amazed at the clockwork efficiency of Earth's largest and busiest Legion star port.

"Makes you think, doesn't it?" Ryan asked.

He turned. "I didn't know you were awake. Yeah, it does." He gazed back out the window. "I've never seen it before—at least, not from up here. On the trip out, it's all dark and you go straight up."

Ryan nodded. "I remember. Seems like a long time ago."

Austin pressed against the view port. “I thought I'd be gone longer than this, but I finished up flight school in about a year.”

"Really?" Ryan sat back, his jaw dropping open. "How'd you manage that? Wait, are you the newbie from the Flin Six mission?"

Austin's face warmed. "Yes, that was me."

"Oh, man, we all heard about you just before I was dispatched to Tarton's Junction for leave. That was crazy."

"Yeah."

"You scrapped with pirates *and* rescued two superior officers. Man. You know, someone said you were the fastest newbie through flight school in decades. You feel like talking about it?"

Austin bit his lip. "Not much to say. Scorpion was down and I had to save her."

Ryan raised his eyebrows. "A her, eh? Now I see."

"It wasn't like that."

"Sure it wasn't." He smiled. "I'm just messing with you. If you ever need a thing, man, don't hesitate to ask. If I decide to stay in the service, I hope we get to serve together sometime."

Austin gestured toward Ryan's green uniform. "Not likely."

"Squadrons are stationed at the same places all the time. You can forget that squadron hatred out on tour. All that rivalry stuff's a bunch of crap anyway. They like to cook it up during flight school for the competition of it all, but when you're out, we're all Star Runners. With everything and everyone in the galaxy gunning for us, we better be on the same side when were out there." He grinned like a salesman. “And you could always transfer.”

"Not a chance. I don't think Tizona would let me live that down."

"Probably not."

The sound of water flowing through pipes filled the air as the hangar's outer door shut above them. The freighter rocked and came to a stop on the landing pad. Passengers stood and stretched, some grabbing bags from overhead compartments while others spoke with one another.

"Well, we're here," Ryan said, standing and reaching his arms far over his head. "Weird to be back?"

Austin nodded. "It is."

As they gathered their belongings, the freighter taxied from the hangar air lock and into the row of other vessels. Spacecraft of different types, from massive bulky freighters to sleek cutters, were parked side-by-side. Hanging from suspension wires and harnesses, crews swarmed over the vessels to begin maintenance and repairs. Circular burn marks covered the freighter directly adjacent to their own, the crews focusing on the concerned areas. Sparks and wielding tools flashed from a hundred different locations in the massive hangar. The expanse stretched into infinity, the view obscured by the rising smoke of the workers' wielding torches.

"I forgot how big this hangar was," Austin said, leaning closer to the window.

"Come on," Ryan said. "We have a tube bound for San Francisco with our name on it."

A five-car trolley hovered over the steel grating outside the freighter. Passengers boarded like they traveled to an amusement park. Austin hesitated, staring at the space where he should see wheels.

“Let's go,” Ryan said.

"So how does the wheel-less technology actually work? Is it a thruster of some kind?"

"It's not," Ryan said as he took a seat in the second car. "You ever play with magnets as a kid?"

"Yeah," he said as he sat down. "Why?"

"It's the same thing. I was told it all has to do with magnetics. You haven't traveled to any other Legion worlds, yet?"

"No."

"The magtech negates the need for wheels. It's a lot cheaper too when you think about how much people waste on tires. Magtech uses metals found in whatever it is hovering over."

Austin looked at the metal grating of the hangar floor. "Guess it doesn't work on water?"

"Not that I know of."

The trolley beeped twice before zipping away from the freighter. A hot breeze hit Austin's face as they passed between the lines of massive starships. His first time in the hangar had been rushed and on foot, so he didn't have time to take in the sights. The trolley moved fast, but he relaxed and marveled at the variety of spacecraft located in the hangar.

"I thought there were mostly military freighters in Atlantis?" Austin asked.

"This is the only Legion port on Earth not monopolized completely by the military. All manner of ships come through here."

"Like what?"

Ryan stifled a yawn. "Officers on a pleasure cruise, businessmen with clearance to conduct business on Earth, Legion agents conducting counter-espionage. You'd be surprised how much traffic comes through here and no one in the dark has any idea."

The trolley pulled into a roundabout. The speakers beeped twice.

In one wave of motion, the passengers left the trolley and marched up the wide, steel stairs leading to three arches. Two veered left, bringing passengers to a business or pleasure destination. Two Legion Marines flanked the arch on the right, laser rifles resting over the chests. They wore black battle dress uniforms and combat helmets. Both surveyed passengers as they filed past, staring through their thick, clear goggles. They appeared ready for a riot to break out at any moment.

Ryan approached first, his ID card in his right hand. Austin followed his lead. They passed without incident.

"Are they always there?" he asked.

"Probably not when you came through the first time," Ryan said. "They try not to scare the fresh meat."

"Great."

He laughed. "Relax, man. They're just keeping the place secure.

When you're stationed on a carrier, you'll be around marines all the time."

"You know many?"

"Sure. We had a complement during my time fighting in the Orm Minor Rebellion. Got to know a bunch of the guys. Lost a few, too." Ryan waved his hand as if he wafted at a buzzing fly. "Anyway, no matter what else happens—you're home for the next two weeks."

The arch led to a pathway winding to the right and culminating in a steel wall. Without slowing, Ryan marched toward the gray obstacle. The wall dilated, revealing the Atlantis control room stretching several hundred yards. A massive Earth hologram hovered over the room, tiny points of multicolored light falling in and out of orbit. Radio traffic buzzed in countless conversations. Hundreds of Legion crew members wearing headsets sat at their stations, some reviewing personal holograms while others seemed engrossed in their transmissions. The dark "sky" above the bubble featured no luminescent creatures from the depths like they did on his first visit to Atlantis. Instead, one freighter ascended away from the port, disappearing into the blackness.

Ryan led him through the sea of terminals and moving crew members wearing light gray uniforms. Austin bumped into a desk as he studied the hologram of Earth. He marveled at the amount of shrouded traffic arriving and departing from all over the globe.

"How many ports does the Legion operate on Earth?" Austin asked, his gaze fixated on the hologram.

"I think there are four main ports and several smaller ones they wouldn't tell a lieutenant about. I'm probably not on a need-to-know status."

As they weaved between the lines of control stations, a bulky officer in a red Excalibur uniform stepped up to Ryan, who offered a crisp salute. Austin glanced at the bars over the officer's wings signifying the man was a commander.

"At ease, Lieutenant Bean," the commander said, smiling as he shook Ryan's hand. "Made it back from the Orm Minor, I see."

"Yes, sir."

The commander's expression darkened. "Tough as they say?"

Ryan shifted. "It wasn't easy, sir."

The commander studied Ryan for a moment, slowly nodding as he rested his hands on his hips. His eyes darted to Austin. "And who's this?"

"This, sir, is Lieutenant Stone, fresh from flight school."

Austin saluted, but the commander waved it off.

"I can see that from his shiny new wings. Where you from LT?"

"Around Atlanta, sir."

"Ah, North Georgia's some of the prettiest land this planet has to offer. Name's Commander Carv Wallace, now in my third tour here on Earth." He looked at Ryan. "You stick with Ryan here, okay?"

"Yes, sir."

"This guy's seen more of Legion space than most active Star Runners, that's for sure. Orm Minor was a tour...well, let's just say I'm glad to see you." Commander Wallace saluted. "Nice to meet you, Stone. Safe travels, Bean."

Once they had strolled out of earshot, Austin whispered, "That guy is a beast."

"Yeah," Ryan said, glancing at his tablet. "He took me under his wing on my first tour."

"Where was that?"

Ryan shrugged. "A backwater in Quadrant Four. We were patrolling the Zahl-Legion border for almost a year."

"See any action?"

"Yes."

Austin smiled. "That must be the tour where you got all your warm fuzzies about flying for the Legion."

"Right," Ryan said, allowing a crooked grin.

Austin knew he shouldn't press the issue. The experienced Trident drivers on Tarton's Junction never spoke about their tour experiences. Not in detail at least. This left Austin piecing together fragments of information and snippets of stories to form a disjointed narrative of life on tour in the Legion Navy. But maybe he could get some more detailed information from Ryan while they had coffee.

The door at the back of Atlantis control dilated, revealing the institutional white decontamination room he recalled from his first trip. Staff in tight-fitting white uniforms with silver trim led them to separate slabs floating above the deck. Austin did as instructed and allowed the attendant to begin the examination. They took a blood sample, examined his eyes, and typed his information into the tablet strapped to their arms. The exam took a few minutes.

"Enjoy your leave, Lieutenant Stone," the attendant said behind a white mask. "You are free to go."

"Thank you. I will."

Austin and Ryan jumped off their slabs and walked into the next room. A familiar hum droned inside. The shiny transport tubes lined the floors. Two Star Runners in Excalibur red flight suits stepped out of the nearest tube, nodded, and walked into the decontamination room.

"Let's get this over with," Ryan said, slinging his bag over his shoulder. He turned to the crew. "Both of us are bound for Base Prime."

The shorter crew member stepped toward Austin and motioned to a tube. He folded himself into the tube, the intensity of the hum increasing. The crew member slammed the tube shut. Austin had forgotten the gum Nubern gave him the previous time he traveled in a tube. He shut his eyes. The light surrounded him, flashed. He felt his stomach drop and twist, and then it was over.

The hatch slid open.

"Welcome to Base Prime," a voice boomed. "If you will please step out of the tube."

Austin opened his eyes, a migraine piercing his brain like a hot knife through ground beef. "My head's killing me. What happened?"

"You're still new at this, sir." Two hands gripped under his armpits and yanked him out of the tube. "It'll pass shortly."

With his eyes still clamped shut, Austin allowed the hands to lead him to a wall. He rubbed his temples with his index fingers. He could barely hear the roar of a crowd walking and talking as they passed around him. Distantly, he heard voices on speakers and the servos of a thousand machines.

"You look like hell," Ryan said.

"I feel like I'm going to puke."

"Did this happen to you the last time?"

He winced as he thought back. "Not this bad. I chewed gum the last time."

"Oh, someone was smart enough to tell you about that. Until your brain and body get used to the tube transport, keep chewing the gum."

Austin nodded and slightly opened his eyes. "I'll remember that next time. It's getting a little better."

Behind Ryan, people scurried in countless directions like a stadium parking lot after a game.

"This place sure hasn't changed. Come on, man," Ryan said, placing his hand on Austin's shoulder. "Let's get you through customs and out for some fresh air."

"Sounds good."

Ryan led him slowly through the crowd. Austin's stomach had ceased its tumbling and the pounding in his head lessened. They stood in line for ten minutes leading to customs. A man with thick brimmed glasses and a curved nose shaped like a vulture's beak sat behind the desk, asking Ryan a few questions Austin did not hear. Ryan turned over his laser pistol and stepped into what looked like a mobile fitting room. When he came out, the Lobera uniform had been replaced by dark blue jeans and a ratty T-shirt. He looked ten years younger.

"Next!"

Austin blinked and stepped forward. "Sorry. I have a headache."

The man looked down at him. "I don't care. Business?"

"No, I'm on leave."

The man sighed and looked at the ceiling. "What is your business here?"

Austin swallowed. "I'm a Star Runner on leave. I am returning home to Atlanta later today."

"Good for you. I need your weapon, wings, and any other identification marks linking you to your service with the Legion."

Austin slipped off the wings and unbuckled his holster.

"Are you carrying any other Legion or off world technologies and/or fruits, vegetables, living organisms, or drugs?"

"No. Nothing."

“Did you have any artificial limbs, organs, or other prosthetics installed while off world that you’d like to claim?”

“Are you serious? Sorry. No fake body parts.”

"Very well." He pointed to the fitting room. "Change there. Drop your uniform and other belongings into the silver box provided inside. It will be waiting for you upon your return. Next!"

"Thank you," Austin said.

He walked to the fitting room and shut the door behind him, placing his duffle bag containing the outfit he wore during his first day at Tizona on the bench. As he changed out of his uniform, he thought of Skylar coming to see him while he packed just before he left Tarton's Junction. She’d felt strange about him leaving. They had arrived at the same time, but now he had graduated before her. With what Ryan said, they could be sent to opposite ends of the galaxy within the next month.

He put on a dark green collar shirt Mom had given him and buckled his jeans. He took a deep breath and glanced in the mirror.

A familiar face looked back. The old reflection mirrored one from high school, although leaner with much shorter hair. He had worn nothing but Tizona blue for more than a year. The green shirt felt traitorous.

He dropped the uniform, wings, identification card, and pistol in the silver box under the mirror and stepped out into the flow of people.

“You look like a native again,” Ryan said as he walked next to Austin. "Let's go finish the rest of this and get that coffee."

———

"GOOD LORD, THAT'S GOOD," Austin said.

The delightful, bitter taste of coffee washed around his mouth, igniting his taste buds.

"What?" Ryan said, sipping on his own drink. "They don't have coffee on Tarton's Junction?"

He took another sip. "Not like this."

A cool breeze drifted past their table. The California sunshine beamed down, washing everything in a golden hue. Beautiful women clad in bikini tops skated past on roller blades and waved.

"With military bases all along the California coast, the local women hunt this area," Ryan said with a smile. "You have a girlfriend?"

Austin winced. He didn't know how to answer that question. He and Skylar shared an awkward kiss earlier in the year, but he had grown close with Ryker since the rescue on Flin Six. He thought of Ryker's rehab, wondered if she had reached her destination. When he had a moment, he would have to send her a message.

"Man, forget I asked," Ryan said. "If it takes you that long to answer, I'd rather not know."

"What?" Austin asked, hiding his mouth with his coffee mug.

"It's cool with me if you want to bat for the other side."

"It's not that. It's just a difficult answer."

"Don't worry about it." He glanced at his watch. "I need to catch a cab to Jason's house. I'll pick up my Legion ride in the morning. Decided how you're getting home?"

"Taking a tube back to my school and going from there."

"Cool." He handed over a stick of chewing gum. "For the trip. Hey man, stay in touch. I hope we serve together some time."

“I really want to hear more about your tours and what you’ve seen out there.” Austin thought of the limiting stay he’d had on Tarton’s Junction. “I don’t mean this in a bad way, but I feel like I don’t know anything about the universe after talking to you.”

“You don’t.” Ryan smiled and stood. “We’ll talk more soon.”

Austin shook his hand. "Really nice talking with you, Lieu—I mean, man."

"Yeah, being back takes some getting used to, but you'll manage. Bit of advice?"

"Sure."

Ryan looked at him. "I know I've already said it, but enjoy every minute you're here. I mean it; this will go by so fast. Soon, all of this will be nothing but a memory, a figment fading with the passage of time. They own you now, Stone. At least for the next five years." He looked up. "Out there will become your normal, your everyday life."

"Thanks, Ryan. I'll try."

He held the handshake a moment before scooping up his bag. He slipped on a baseball hat that might have been red at some point, and weaved through the sidewalk traffic. As Ryan waved to attract a taxi, Austin looked into his coffee and took a deep breath.

Ryan was right; he needed to enjoy the sunshine, relish every moment. The daylight warmed his skin. He would send emails to Ryker, Skylar, and Bear when he got home to let them know he made it. He missed them, all of them, and he felt like his heart existed in both places. He stared into the sky, his mind wandering.

An explosion ripped through the air.

Tables tumbled, crashing into splinters as a shockwave smashed into the sidewalk. Austin fell to the pavement, his cheek slapping the concrete. People screamed and cried. He blinked, his vision blurred. He touched his ear, saw blood on his fingers.

Slowly, he stood in the space formerly occupied by the coffee shop table. Police ran toward a fire raging in the street while the rest of the crowd ran the opposite direction. Austin squinted for a better view.

The inferno engulfed a twisted piece of metal in the shape of a car. The vehicle had no more doors; the paint had melted off the side. Black text bubbled and cracked in the midst of the flames.

The taxi.

Ryan's ride had exploded in the street.

He shook on weak legs as a hard lump twisted deep in his gut. A Legion Star Runner had just died on the streets of San Francisco. His eyes darted around the area, a sickening sense of paranoia engulfing him like a morning fog. Someone on this street had targeted Ryan, and Austin might be next.

He hurried through the chaos for the entrance to Base Prime, hoping safety awaited him. As he made his way through the flow of screaming people, he pushed away the image of Ryan smiling as he walked to the taxi to begin his leave.

2

A sweaty hand smacked his face.

Josh cringed, the side of his head flashing with pain. His vision blurred. Before him loomed a bearded man with a scar running from the corner of his eye to his chin. His attacker leaned in close. Hot putrid breath filled Josh's nostrils. The foul figure laughed, turned to the other pirates and said something in another language.

When he turned back, his lips curled back over his blackened teeth.

"Menga tow, Star Runner," he breathed.

He leaned forward and ripped the silver wings from Josh's chest.

Josh sprang forward in protest, but the pirate gestured with his pistol. Hanging his head, he leaned back and lifted his hands slightly.

As the wretched pirate attached the Star Runners' wings onto his own chest, Josh looked around the destroyed interior of the freighter. Other passengers formed a line, marching at gunpoint out of the vessel. Small fires popped, seats burning from the brief firefight.

Bodies, blackened and burned, had been shoved between the seats to keep the aisle clear for the exiting passengers. Among them, Agent Mike Fischer lay twisted in an unnatural shape between the chairs. Josh stared, unable to pull his eyes away from the man he had been speaking to hours before.

The foul pirate yanked Josh forward and shoved him into line. He laughed, pointing and making sure the other pirates saw him. Josh didn't understand, only obeyed and fell into line with the rest of the captives.

Josh fought against the nausea as he passed more destroyed bodies of men and women who died as the freighter had been captured. He tried to make sense of the situation. Hours before, he couldn't sit still because he would soon be home. Now, he would be at the mercy of a pirate gang.

A petite woman in line before him trembled as they passed the pirates. They touched her straight black hair, sneering and cackling like hyenas. Josh hit one of their hands away but received a blunt thump to the back of his head for his troubles.

Adding the growing lump on the back of his head to the other pains flaring around his body, Josh kept his eyes low and winced. The pirates led them through the hatch and into a large cavern in low light. The rocky interior stretched far enough to fit the freighter and several smaller fighters. Two openings to the cave flanked either side, both revealing a field of stars and asteroids.

They must have taken us to a hidden base somewhere, he thought.

A ragged group of prisoners worked on the far side of the cave, digging into the rock with pickaxes. Their skin appeared painted on their bones, their clothing nothing but tattered fabric linked by thin threads. Pirate crews brandishing rifles and menacing swords guarded the workers.

The pirate at the outer hatch pushed Josh down the ladder. They forced him into a line at the right of the ladder's base. Pirates stripped all the passengers, piling the clothing near the closest wall. The lady in front of him went to the left with the other women and the elderly. She glanced back at Josh, her dark eyes wide. Josh nodded, trying to project confidence, but the pirates quickly ripped apart their connection. They pushed her back into the group of crying women.

"What's going on?" the man closest to him asked.

A laser shot flashed, filling the cave with the sound of thunder. The man flew into the rock wall, sparks erupting from his chest.

Josh spun toward the direction of the shot. The repulsive guard sporting his Legion wings stood at the edge of the line, his rifle trained on Josh's face.

"Luctup!"

A voice boomed from the edge of the platform. All eyes turned to fall upon a well-dressed, middle-aged man. He stood with his hands on his hips, a flashy silver pistol in a black holster on his belt. He wore a red uniform with black trim and had his dark hair slicked back. The man, obviously the pirate leader, appeared in stark contrast to the other rabble in the cave as he took a few steps in their direction.

The leader paused, pointing at the line of the women and the elderly. He barked orders in another language.

The pirate rabble led the women and elderly away at gunpoint. Some screamed and wailed. Others moved away with a quiet resignation, either too tired or frightened to fight back. While they moved away, Josh glanced at the man who had been shot for speaking. Smoke still swirled and lifted from his chest.

The pirate wearing Josh's wings yelled back to the leader, gesturing wildly. The leader glanced in his direction and nodded. The eyes of the other prisoners looked toward him. Josh took a deep breath as his breathing quickened.

Were they going to kill him?

He focused on the end of the rifle, the same weapon just used to kill an innocent civilian. The rifle jerked toward the pirate leader. Josh took his steps as if he had great weights attached to his ankles.

He wanted to go home. It's all he had wanted since being brought to Tarton's Junction. He wanted to see his parents. He wanted to talk to Kadyn.

He shuffled between the other pirates. Their stench was overwhelming.

Two pirates stepped before Rodon.

One guard hissed in his ear.

"I don't understand," Josh whispered.

The man who had spoken laughed, holding his hand to his ear.

A hard object smashed into the back of Josh's leg. He tumbled to the rocks. A hand engulfed his skull and yanked him upright. Two pirates held Josh by the shoulders.

The leader took one knee in front of Josh and suddenly pulled out a yellow fruit that looked like an apple. He took a bite and stared. When he finished chewing, he smiled.

With the fruit still in his hand, he pointed at Josh. "Star Runner?"

Josh swallowed, hesitating. The man arched an eyebrow. He finally nodded.

The leader looked at his pirates and gestured with his free hand. The pirates placed a headset over Josh's head. The earpiece buzzed as the leader said something in their guttural language.

Josh shook his head. "What?"

The leader brought the back of his hand across Josh's face.

He tasted the salt of blood on his lip. It must be a translator.

"English," he said softly.

The buzzing in his earpiece ceased. When the leader spoke this time, Josh could understand.

"They tell me you are a Star Runner?" the translator buzzed.

He swallowed. "Yes."

"Welcome, Star Runner. I am Dax Rodon." He smiled. "We always revel in the chance to take a Star Runner alive and show him or her the light. Many of these you see around you were once sold the lie of the Legion."

Rodon finished the apple and stood, his hands once again on his hips.

"What do you want with me?" Josh asked through his teeth.

"Simple. Join us."

He recoiled. "Join you?"

"I need pilots," Rodon said with a shrug. "I also need laborers who will be worked to death. I think you would like to live, no?"

He glanced over to the workers on the far side of the cave. "I will never join you."

"Pity."

The pirates kicked Josh forward and began beating him. The rifles pounded his body until he spit blood. They turned him over, smashing the front of his face. Josh cried out, but they didn't stop.

He did not know how long they pummeled him. When they stopped, his eyes had nearly swollen shut. He dimly felt hands lift him to his knees. Through tears and blood, he saw Rodon kneeling down in front of him again.

"Now that you've had time to think about it," he said, "I ask again; will you join us?"

Josh wanted to say he would—he did not think he could survive another beating. But he faintly remembered his training and knew the pirates would only torture him to reveal weaknesses in the Legion forces. He would be forced to fight his own people.

"I ..." he breathed, his mouth filling with blood. "I...will not betray the Legion."

Rodon tossed what remained of his fruit at Josh's face. "Such a waste."

He folded his arms across his chest and said, "Do what you will with him. Help him understand what happens when he turns us down. If he survives, we can use him in the workforce. Come on! We have work to do."

A boot slammed into Josh's rib.

"Whoa!" Rodon yelled. For a moment, Josh thought he would be spared the torture. "Get my translator before you continue."

The pirates removed the headset. Soon, the beating continued. Josh lost consciousness, the world fading away into darkness.

THE WALLS LOOKED like rock covered in oil, the crumbled surface glistening in the dim light. Josh remained on his back, unmoving as he surveyed his surroundings. The small room prohibited him from completely stretching out, so he rested his legs on the walls. The surface looked like stone, but squished like a sponge under his bare feet. His muscles ached. His stomach twisted and turned, protesting the days he had gone without food. The green slop dropped yesterday at the opening slithered and crawled in the bowl. He tried to eat around the movement, focusing only on the thick snot broth. It tasted like a salty nosebleed doused with sour lemon juice. He had gagged, but swallowed the lukewarm liquid before it lingered too long on his tongue.

The floor chilled his skin. He had been forced to wear rags since his arrival. After beating him, Rodon's gang stripped him of his uniform, forcing him naked through a series of underground tunnels. Dozens of other prisoners marched with him, packed in so tight he rubbed against shoulders slippery with perspiration. The first night, he thought the pirates would kill him.

But they didn't.

Had it been weeks? Months? Mom and Dad definitely knew he had disappeared by now. The Braves' game had come and gone. His parents would have had to go by themselves, if they had gone at all. Soon, they would be told he was missing. They might never know the real reason he would not be coming home, only that he had been lost at sea. He swallowed, suppressing the urge to cry.

Why was this happening? What would be the pirates' end game? Starving hundreds of prisoners would serve no purpose, letting them live wouldn't, either.

Voices echoed from beyond the rusted metal gate of his tiny holding cell. With his translator gone, the conversations meant nothing, gibberish whispered by the goons of children's nightmares. Soon, he would be killed. *Please let it be fast.*

A man called, the voice closer than before, but in a foreign language. Josh sat up, resting on his elbows. The man called again.

"Hello?" Josh asked in a raspy voice, grunting as he pressed against the metal gate.

"Bley bak tara knee."

"I don't understand."

"Bley bak tara knee dulca."

"I am sorry. I can't help you if I don't understand."

He slithered toward the rusty gate and leaned against it, the rough surface scraping his neck. Heavy equipment rumbled from somewhere down the hall. An engine fired, rattling the walls as if a ship landed. After a moment, the engine ceased. Voices yelled followed by commotion of movement.

Josh stretched his legs in front of him as far as he could. His stomach ached. His head pounded. He crossed his arms over his chest and continued listening to the bizarre range of noises in this dreadful place...wherever it was. His mind wandered, drifting like a loose buoy in a restless ocean. He lost any concept of time.

He thought of his best friend. Austin had probably watched from Tarton's Junction when the *Saber* had been attacked. A memory flashed of Austin staring at the photo of Marilyn Monroe at the coffee shop when they were in high school. Kadyn, beautiful Kadyn, with her wild hair the color of sweet caramels, enjoying one of her fruit-filled, overpriced drinks.

Another memory came. Sunlight beaming through Kadyn's hair, radiating down from a cloudless spring sky. The smell of cheap popcorn filled his nose. She took one popped kernel at a time, chewing slowly as she watched Austin's baseball game unfold. She had said chewing slower forced her to eat less, and popcorn was nothing but empty calories. He sat quietly, nodding and listening to her voice. He had dated the cheerleaders, dated the so-called "hot" girls in high school, but his time with empty relationships had passed. Kadyn was special, following her own light. Whenever he could, he went to Austin's game with her because she was his best friend's only ride home. The game's lasted at least two hours, and he said little. During the game, he had a chance once.

"I'm going to the Falcons' game on Sunday," he had said.

Kadyn turned, staring at him under her red-rimmed sunglasses. "This weekend?"

"Yeah. My family's going. I haven't been in a while."

She had smiled at him. "Huh, I've never been to a pro football game before."

"Really?" he had asked, the memory hurting his heart. "You should go sometime. They're awesome."

A coldness shot through him.

He should have asked her then, opened up to her in the way he always did in his dreams. Everything had moved so quickly that final Christmas. He never told her anything, barely said goodbye before he left for San Francisco. He had always hesitated before, thinking Kadyn and Austin had something going on. Their relationship always seemed deep, but Austin never made a move. He should have asked Austin about his feelings toward Kadyn. Now, he would never get the chance to tell her anything.

His body ached worse than it had following the Gauntlet in the mountains of northern California. His joints complained with each movement, his muscles burning. Deep down, he knew his body was shutting down. He had not eaten a proper meal in at least a week. Or did it only feel that long? The clock fought him with each passing moment. Seconds became minutes, hours became days.

He allowed his mind to wander again, welcoming the sense of reliving the memories of Mom, Dad, and friends he would never see again.

"Bley bak tara?"

Josh jolted from a restless sleep. "I told you: I cannot understand your language. I can't understand you!"

"He wants to know your name," a different, rougher voice said.

The world stopped, the memories of his dreams snapping away like a shut-off light. Josh sat in silence, listening to his heart pumping blood into his ears with an impressive force. He must have hallucinated the voice.

"Well?" the voice asked again. "Your name?"

Josh swallowed, his throat dry as sandpaper. "Josh."

"Dosh."

"No. *Josh."*

"Ah, Josh. You speak Earth tongue very well."

The voice spoke in another language for a moment, apparently translating as a conversation ensued. Josh peered into the darkness as he listened for any clue as to the topic.

"Earth is a long ways from these space lanes," the voice finally said. "In fact, it's far from *any* space lanes. How did you learn this tongue?"

Josh thought a moment. Should he reveal everything to voices whispering in the dark?

"I spent many years there. You?"

"I have as well."

"You lived there?"

"Worked there."

Worked? How could someone work on Earth and end up a captive of the Tyral Pirates a thousand light years from anywhere? The man speaking from down the hall had to be either lying or there was more to this story.

"I don't know your name," Josh said.

"Delmar Wain."

"What did you do?"

"I transported things."

Josh waited for more explanation. When Delmar said nothing, he asked, "What? Like mail?"

"Sure. The mail."

Josh leaned his head against the rock. "You're a smuggler."

"Of sorts." Delmar paused before sneering, "Not all of us are fortunate enough to be a Legion Star Runner."

He tensed. "Who told you that lie?"

Delmar snorted. "I know everything that happens on this rock."

"How do you do that?"

"I listen."

In class, he learned about the dangers smuggling posed to the Legion space lanes. Legion agents struggled to root out corruption on core planets, but it was nearly impossible on dark worlds. He never considered that smugglers also operated on Earth. It had just never occurred to him.

“How long have you been here?” Josh asked.

“We’ve been in this spot for at least...how do you say it? A month?”

His shoulders deflated. “Have they done anything to you?”

Delmar paused. For a moment, Josh wondered if the stranger had gone to sleep.

“Not directly,” Delmar breathed. “Most of us have been waiting here. In the past, they’ve used me to help strip a stolen freighter or fighter, but nothing recently. It’s been quiet for us. Lots of machinery coming through this spot each day.”

“Machinery? Like what?”

“I’ve only heard it. Could be freighters. I don’t know.”

"Where are we now?” Josh asked. “Do you know?"

"No," he said, grumbling. “Doesn’t matter where, anyway. They’ll sell us to slavers soon."

Josh clutched his arms to his chest. "You think?"

"Yes. Or we will die here."

3

The energy beam shot into his right eye like a hot needle through butter.

"Ow!" Austin yelled. "I told you already-I'm fine!"

"We are just being careful, lieutenant, and this procedure is the quickest way to tell if you have a concussion." The nurse lowered the light and planted her hands on her hips. "You were very close to the explosion after all."

He glared at her. "No kidding."

With a bandage on his face where he had smacked into the concrete, Austin did not want to tell her about the ringing in his ears. He feared the admission would lead to more tests. He had enough. He wanted answers.

Two agents in plain clothes, claiming to be of the Legion Earth Intelligence Force, had arrived on the scene of the explosion and escorted him back to Base Prime. Once past security, the EIF took him into a compact room with bright florescent lighting and launched into a series of questions about the incident.

Did he notice anything unusual?

Did Lieutenant Bean seem distracted?

What was the last thing he said to you?

After forty-five minutes, they brought him to the infirmary where the nurse started poking him with laser sticks he didn't understand.

A tall, thin lieutenant colonel, with a tablet tucked under his arm marched in through the infirmary door. He scanned the room, seeming relieved when he looked at Austin.

"Lieutenant Stone, I am Lieutenant Roberto Ginn," he said in a deep voice as he approached. “I'm sorry, but your leave is going to be delayed. Will you come with me?"

Austin glanced at the nurse who nodded her approval. Ginn led him through two secured doors guarded by armed marines to a dimly lit control room. A dozen staff monitored holographic images. The cool blue light washed the area in a palette of neon colors emitting from the holograms. In addition to the twelve staff, two Lobera Star Runners sat hunched over holographic stations.

Ginn gestured to a computer station near the door. "You have a secure link. Please advise if you need anything."

Austin paused. "Pardon me, sir, but a link from what?"

“I'm not privy to that information. Please sit, log in, and find out. Your connection will be completed shortly."

As Ginn marched away, Austin slid into the cold, black chair as if it would explode. He put on the headset and glanced at the screens on the far side of the room. They displayed the local San Francisco news. Three stations showed images from the street of Ryan's taxi disintegrated into a burning wreck of metal. The caption indicated that officials thought terrorists had carried out the attack. *Perhaps that was true, but terrorists from where?*

The holographic projector at his station whined to life. The image materialized as if it was formed from water, and transformed into a familiar face staring back.

"Thank the Maker you're alright," Captain Jonathan Nubern said.

"I can't say the same for my traveling companion," Austin grumbled, his hands shaking. He balled them into fists and dropped them out of sight of the screen.

Nubern glanced off camera. "I know. Lieutenant Bean was a good man. We don't have much time, Austin. Since I am your CO, they asked me to make contact with you."

The image flickered as the visual message caught up with real time; the standard delay when conversing over light years. Austin had grown accustomed to the hesitation when he was on Tarton's Junction, but now it infuriated him.

"I have some disturbing news to share and I need to get to it," Nubern said. "I wish I had more time to educate you during flight school, but I thought there would be plenty of time."

"Educate me about what?"

"About the dangers out there." Nubern leaned into the camera. "There is much more going on in Quadrant Eight than I have been at liberty to tell you."

His stomach rolled. "Like what, sir?"

"Later." Nubern shook his head sharply. "You and your contacts are in danger. Here's what we know: An unknown force is targeting our Earth-bound Star Runners. The effort might be spreading to other planets, but we're not sure. Several incidents have occurred in recent days."

"My contacts? What incidents?"

"Yes. Lieutenant Bean was one of many Star Runners targeted in the past twenty-four hours. Any person you contacted while on Tarton's Junction could be a target. A few pilots have had family members die in bizarre accidents or simply vanish. Right now, we don't know why or even who is doing this. All your correspondence has been, and probably continues to be, hacked." He leaned off screen. "Your mother and someone named Kadyn, correct?"

Austin thought back, his mind racing as this new reality fell over him. He regularly sent messages to Mom and Kadyn during flight school. "Yes, sir."

"They need to be warned, Lieutenant," Nubern said, his eyes frigid as ice. "Not via phone or radio, but in person. They must be taken to safety. Command has provided all Star Runners currently on Earth authority to enact the Revelation Protocol."

A flush of adrenaline surged through his body. "I didn't know Command would ever give such an order."

"They just did."

Austin tightened his fists and bit down on his bottom lip. The Tyral Pirates killed his friend. Dax Rodon had slipped through his fingers after nearly killing his mentor and Ryker. Rodon had to be behind these latest terrorist attacks, but how? How was it possible that pirate scum continued to outwit and outfight the Legion Navy?

"Humor me, sir," Austin said through his teeth. "Do we know anything at all? Or are we at the mercy of these pirates? Again?" His tone revealed more sarcasm than he had intended. He took a deep breath, trying to calm himself.

Nubern glared at him. "Watch yourself, Lieutenant Stone. We don't know if this is the work of pirates, yet. Your concern should be warning your contacts as soon as possible. Time is not on our side."

Shaking his head, Austin realized he would have to immediately tell Mom *and* Kadyn the truth about his school, his new life, and the secret situation for the rest of the planet. All of it. After wanting more than anything to reveal everything about his new life for the past year, he now grew hesitant.

"Sir, how do I tell them?"

"You'll figure it out. For now, I want you to take a tube to the Tizona Academy Campus in Georgia and an officer will escort you to retrieve your contacts and bring them to a secure location. Once you and your people are secure, we will decide the next step. Be careful and keep your eyes open." He glanced at his watch. "Get moving, son."

"Yes, sir." Austin nodded and placed his hand on the headset.

"Lieutenant?" Nubern asked before he moved away from the desk.

"Yes, sir?"

"Be careful."

The screen darkened, leaving Austin alone in a bright sea of holographic images. He sat in silence, feeling as if he was rocking adrift in a canoe. His chest tightened as he realized his world and those he cared about on Earth were in danger.

I'm coming, Mom.

DESPITE NOW VIEWING his surroundings as a threat, nothing out of the ordinary happened on the tube trip to the Georgia swamps. Either the chewing gum worked this time or he finally had grown used to the process. During the entire journey, he continued thinking of his mom and Kadyn in danger. His skin felt clammy, his mouth dry.

The air stuck to his skin when the tube hissed open. Two security officers in Tizona blue rushed him out, grumbling something about the number of personnel coming through this junction.

Three Legion naval officers were waiting on an air boat at the dock alongside the wooden shack on stilts. The shack still appeared as if it had been in the middle of the swamp for a hundred years. The crumbling roof and split boards comprising the walls helped to disguise the tube station beneath.

Austin said nothing to the officers, only offering a nod as he sat down. The boat rocked as he boarded. He tried not to think about the car bombing that claimed Ryan Bean. The Star Runner had been there and then, a moment later, he was gone. He could still hear the explosion, smell the fire burning in the streets of San Francisco.

The boat's engine blasted the silence, sending birds cawing through the trees in the afternoon light. Austin jumped at the sound, his heart thumping into his ringing ears. He watched the black water pass by the boat, the hull splitting the green pond scum. The smell of rotting wood hung over the swamp. The sun cast long shadows across the familiar water Austin hoped he never had to taste again.

"Where you are coming from?" asked an older officer sitting across from Austin, his brow wrinkling beneath his white hair. His brown eyes focused across the boat.

"San Francisco."

"Where were you stationed?"

"Tarton's Junction," Austin said. "I was heading home for leave."

The older officer frowned. "I'm sorry."

"So am I," he said. "Where are you going?"

The man gazed out at the swamp. "Tizona Campus. I'm in Logistics. I was working deep cover in Brazil when I got the call to report here."

"Deep cover?"

"I'm a Legion officer working on Earth just like anyone else. I report to work, do my job, and go home." He turned back to face Austin. "I've never been called away from my home and family before. Do you know what's going on?"

"Just a little. They're recalling officers all over the planet."

"Not good."

"No, sir."

The boat nearly crashed into the dock. A security officer saluted when they stepped off the boat. Austin hurried over the short dock made of uneven wood planks. The officer gestured to a golf cart, and Austin and the three other officers boarded in silence. The security officers drove the golf cart along the rough path toward campus.

"Our newest arrivals are heading back to campus," the officer said into a radio on his shoulder.

"Copy," Security Chief Javin Sharkey's husky voice hissed from the radio. "We are waiting on the Grand Lawn."

The path meandered through the trees. Strands of moss tickled Austin's face as they moved past. The cart rumbled over wooden bridges swaying in the grim light. Despite the humidity, he folded his arms across his chest to fight off a shiver.

When the trees parted and revealed the Grand Lawn of the Tizona Campus, the Terminus Building looked smaller than Austin remembered. He saw the simulation pod building to the left, off by itself like a storage shack. Despite his feelings at the moment, he smiled slightly at the structure, remembering how he'd felt the first time he sat down in one of the pods. He saw the dormitories in the distance, and beyond them the physical training field stretched to the trees, all devoid of activity. He thought of Skylar and her desire to run regularly across the field. He owed her for the early training or he might not be here now.

Security lights flickered to life, beaming halos of light onto the trails winding through the campus. Just like the physical training field and the dormitories, the Terminus Building seemed deserted as the golf cart approached, passing the statue of the Tizona sword at the edge of the Grand Lawn. The cart's brakes screeched to a halt in front of the Terminus Building.

A stocky, muscular man stood at the base of the stairs, his arms behind his back, his face hidden in the fading light. Austin knew who it was before he heard the voice.

"Good evening, gentlemen. I am Security Chief Javin Sharkey. Classes are not in session at the moment. Feel free to move around the campus. Some of you are here to lie low for a spell until all of this is sorted out. Commander Pierce will provide a briefing now that you all are here. Lieutenant Stone?'"

Austin stepped off the cart and stood at attention. "Yes, sir."

"Our field agents here at the school are all on assignment at the moment," he said, his eyes narrowing. "Since your situation is time sensitive, I will be escorting you to Atlanta."

"You're going to drive me?"

"I was going to let you drive. It is about a five-hour drive, after all. We'll use one of the school cars at the gate. Before we leave, Commander Pierce would like to speak to you."

"Commander Pierce?"

"You know him as President Pierce." Sharkey looked at the other officers. "Officer Archer will look after the rest of you and lead you to your quarters."

Sharkey led Austin through the Terminus Building. The classrooms were dark and the floors had been polished to a high sheen. They entered the common area and Austin gazed at the high windows, the dwindling light revealing the tall trees beyond. Three officers sat at computer terminals. One woman, her hair streaked with silver, glanced at him as Sharkey led him up the stairs to the president's office.

When they entered, Pierce stood behind his desk. A fire roared in the fireplace etched with elaborate carvings. The book shelves sparkled in the firelight and the polished dog statues carved from volcanic glass glistened. Pierce remained engrossed in the papers on his desk when they entered.

"Commander," Sharkey said, "reporting as ordered."

"This is a mess," Pierce grumbled, not looking up from his papers. When he finally did so, Austin saw the bloodshot eyes of a man who hadn't slept in a while. "Stone."

He nodded. "Good evening, sir."

"Glad you made it safely. Word is you've been busy." Pierce looked at Sharkey. "Close the door. Get the windows."

As Sharkey closed the door and pressed a button on the wall to shut the outer windows, Pierce strolled over to the globe sculpture Austin remembered from his only other visit to the president's office; the night he'd left the Tizona Campus for flight school, although he hadn't known his final destination at the time. Pierce touched the sculpture of the three globes connected by a gold bar. A bright light shot from the middle globe, projecting a holographic image in the center of the room.

The images flashed blue. Two square photos, one of Mom and the other of Kadyn, emerged at the corner of a royal blue square.

"You've been asked to communicate with your contacts and evoke Revelation Protocol," Pierce said with a nod while the images transitioned to a map of Missouri. "While you were in transit to this campus, another accident occurred in Saint Charles, Missouri. A Star Runner was involved in an automobile accident while on his way to his family so he could carry out Revelation Protocol."

A video of the news came up on the hologram, displaying a story of a burning wreck on a rural road in Missouri. A twisted piece of blackened metal flared at the side of the two-lane road. Across the road from the fire, a crumpled truck had come to a stop on the shoulder. The television cameras were following the crying family members on the side of the road.

Austin shook his head. "An accident?"

Pierce motioned toward the hologram. "Another vehicle ran him off the road. The Star Runner was killed, as was the civilian who happened to be driving the opposite way. The pilot's entire family died an hour later in a house fire. The authorities have not been able to locate the vehicle that ran into our pilot, so we can only assume it is the work of these shadow forces currently targeting our pilots. If we keep losing our people, Atlantis won't be able to man the alert fighter squadron that is creating the umbrella over Earth."

"Earth has one squadron protecting it?" Austin wiped a droplet of sweat from his cheek.

"Earth doesn't need more support because it's a backwater planet. There has never been a need for more than one squadron at Atlantis. There has even been talk of removing the existing Tridents. This is just a minor incident to Command."

He took a deep breath. "I understand, sir."

"Okay," Pierce said, changing the holographic image to a map of north Georgia. "Once you have made contact with your mother and Kadyn, I want you to meet an EIF agent here at this outlet mall, about an hour north of your position, to receive your next instructions. Do not use any communication devices—any at all! Do you understand?"

"Yes, sir."

"We know we are being monitored. Talk to your contacts in person." He glanced at his watch. "You will arrive in the middle of the night. Do not let them know you are coming. By the time you meet with the agent at the rendezvous point, it is my hope we will know more about these attacks. Questions?"

Austin thought about the threat to Earth, wondering if the pirates had bigger ambitions than terrorism. "Sir, is it possible Earth is being softened up for an attack or, maybe, an invasion?"

Pierce jerked his head back and laughed. "Seriously? I heard you had impressed the officers on Tarton's Junction, but it obviously wasn't because of your studies."

He frowned. "Is it really that hard to imagine?"

"If you knew how many observation posts are scattered throughout Legion space," Pierce said, rubbing his chin, "you would never ask about the possibility of an invasion in Quadrant Eight. The only way a task force could even try it, is by curve hopping through our space. There isn't enough power in a ship for a curve of that distance."

"So it's not even possible?"

Pierce gazed into the holographic map still hovering over the center of the room like a spirit. "You shouldn't worry about these things. The only way it's possible is to use a power relay to boost your signals—they're like beacons. But no one could afford that except the military and that hasn't happened since the last war. I think it's safe to say Earth won't be invaded."

"And they said the Titanic wouldn't sink."

Sharkey cleared his throat and cast Austin a warning glance.

"Okay, moving on," Pierce said after a pause. "Chief Sharkey will accompany you on the trip to Atlanta. No Star Runners are to travel alone while this crisis continues. Get your mother, your friend, and meet the agent. Dismissed."

Sharkey snapped a salute and pulled open the door. Austin looked at Pierce and saluted. Pierce nodded and turned back to his work.

They marched down the stairs and into the common area. The other officers still focused on their computers. One typed and chewed on his fingernails. The Brazilian officer nodded as they strolled across the room.

"Who are all these people?"

"Tizona is a safe place," Sharkey said softly. "Some are officers who have no contacts or family here on Earth and are reporting to campuses across the globe, coming in to be safe until Command figures out exactly what is going on. Others are here to work during this emergency."

"I see." Austin looked at Sharkey. "And what do you think is going on?"

"I don't like speculating."

A blue Tizona golf cart was waiting for them outside the Terminus Building. Austin moved to the front seat and held on tight. Sharkey accelerated away from the building, sending gravel spitting backwards. He grabbed the bar for support so he didn't tumble onto the Grand Lawn.

"Chief?" Austin paused a moment to consider his words. "Has something like this ever happened?"

Sharkey negotiated a turn onto the wooded trail. "The action is usually far from Earth, but Command has placed everyone on high alert. No one has ever targeted Legion personnel on a backwater like here, at least not on this scale. Honestly, that's all we know. However, it appears Star Runners are being targeted throughout Quadrant Eight, not just on Earth."

"Who would do that?"

"Anyone. Zahl Empire. Pirates. It has happened before in the Quadrant, but long before my time. Class was thankfully not in session when we received word. It's a real pain evacuating the campus and dealing with parents."

"I'm sure."

The cart squeaked to a halt outside the main gate. Four Tizona-blue sedans were parked side-by-side in the lot.

"We going to drive all night?" Austin asked.

Sharkey rolled his eyes. "Well, they certainly don't fly."

IT FELT like it took an hour to reach the long stretch of Interstate 16 amid a world of endless pine trees broken up by gas stations and fast food restaurants. Sharkey spent his time engrossed in a tablet, furiously typing and swiping through documents while Austin drove. Driving the car felt odd after doing nothing but piloting a Trident fighter for the past few months. By the second hour, he battled fatigue as his thoughts wandered in the silence.

"Bathroom break," Sharkey barked, his voice pounding through the quiet like a jackhammer. He leaned over. "We could use some gas, too."

"Yes, sir."

"No need for that 'sir' crap anymore, Lieutenant. You outrank me and you earned it."

"Yes, sir."

Sharkey watched a transfer truck as they passed. "You know I was hard on you in school, but you understand now."

Austin thought of the hours Sharkey had spent yelling at all of them, of the time he'd spent teaching them survival training. "I do."

"Your training is what helped you save Scorpion and Talon."

He looked at him. "You heard about that?"

"The entire navy in Quadrant Eight heard about that." Sharkey stared forward for a heartbeat. "We're always briefed on the latest incidents with the Tyral Pirates. That's a situation that just keeps getting worse."

Austin felt his chest tighten at the mention of the pirates. "They all need to be destroyed."

He snorted. "I couldn't agree more. You know where they are?"

"Of course not."

"Well, that's the problem." Sharkey made a clicking sound with his tongue. "Still, you scrapped with them up close and personal. What was it like?"

Austin remembered Rodon's taunting voice over the gamma wave. He'd nearly shot down the pirate leader, even hit him with a laser shot despite the disadvantage of carrying Ryker and Nubern. The memory was so fresh, his heart raced, the adrenaline pumping through his veins. The final bolts crashing into Rodon's ship, ripping apart metal.

But he'd escaped. Some on board the Tarton's Junction thought Austin should be granted a kill for the effort, but there was no proof. Rodon was most likely still out there, waiting.

"Frustrating," he finally said. "I should've had him."

"Don't worry about Rodon," Sharkey said, folding his arms over his chest and reclining the seat backward. "He'll get what's coming to him."

"But how does he keep doing this?"

"I have no control over what he does. I can only control how I react. Right now, we're going to save your mother and friend. Let's worry about the task at hand, and right now, that task is making sure you don't fall asleep at the wheel. Let me just say I'm grateful you saved my old friend."

Austin blinked. "You mean Nubern?"

He nodded. "I served with Nubern years ago during his first command."

"You were a Star Runner?"

He nodded. "Until I lost my leg."

"Your leg? What?"

"Wonders of robotics, Lieutenant. One of the reasons I don't leave campus often, so I appreciate this diversion even if it is for unfortunate reasons."

Austin looked back at the road. If Sharkey was ever wounded or needed medical assistance, the discovery of an artificial leg would certainly turn heads in an emergency room.

"May I ask how, sir?" Austin asked, his eyes flickering from the road to Sharkey's leg.

"Line of duty," he grumbled, his head swaying toward the window as if he had drifted off to sleep. When he continued speaking, his drowsy voice made it sound as if he talked in his sleep. "I served on a carrier, long time ago. Boring tour at the border. Our task force got involved in preventing a rebellion on Lian; fighting got out of hand. A rogue Zahl warlord decided to take advantage, came in guns blazing, said we were invading the planet. He said he received a distress call and came in for the good of the Empire."

Austin swallowed, his eyes fixated on the lone road.

"The Zahl interceptors are fast," Sharkey continued, his eyes still closed, "faster than anything you'd believe. They swept in like a wave, crashing into our picket ships. I was on alert status, so I launched. Bandits filled the space around Lian like a fiery meteor shower. Never seen anything like it before, or since. I did what I could, but they blasted me out of the sky. Ship came apart, piece of metal ripped my leg to shreds. I had to eject, woke up on our ship. Nubern saved me."

He exhaled. "He's a good man."

"The best."

Austin had never heard anyone speak of a conflict with the Zahl Empire, he had only read about it in his required text. He definitely didn't know Nubern had faced off against Zahlian forces, not just pirates.

He shook his head, thinking about Pierce's vague orders. "Once we retrieve my mom and Kadyn, how do we know *who* to meet?"

"EIF agents can disappear in a crowd like no others. I have some instructions in my tablet. Remember, we're on strict radio silence—that includes internet. Make sure what you have is offline." He frowned. "Whole world's upside down right now, so I'm taking things one hour at a time."

"I understand," Austin said, his stomach growling.

"Let's get gas at the next stop," Sharkey said. "We need to move so we can get some coffee. We should get there in time for breakfast."

Up ahead, the massive lights of an exit ramp illuminated the black sky. Austin leaned over the steering wheel, fighting the sudden urge to use the bathroom.

"I never thanked you, Chief."

"Me?" Sharkey asked. "Why?"

"Your training. I wouldn't be here if it weren't for you."

Sharkey snickered. "No charge, Stone. I rarely get off that campus and I wouldn't be here if it weren't for you. We'll call it even."

4

The crash woke Josh. His joints popped as he folded his sore legs and propped himself against the damp wall. His teeth chattered and he clenched his jaw to stop, straining to decipher the chaotic sounds echoing through the dark corridors outside his cell. Men shouted in unfamiliar languages, the voices approaching.

"What's that?"

"They are coming," Delmar answered, his voice grim and rough like rocks rubbing together inside a burlap sack.

In the weeks since Josh's arrival, the area had been relatively quiet other than the silent guard bringing the same, inedible slop of slithering mucus. Several times, he wondered if the pirates had buried them inside this underground cavern because it was an inexpensive way to kill their prisoners. But the green-slop-carrying pirate continued to bring the food, so all he could do was wait. Before this moment, there had been nothing like this sound of yelling men and machinery.

The gate to his cell shuddered and a portion slid back into the rock. The guard barked in another language. An order apparently, but he had no way to know for sure. Josh hesitated before moving across the cell to the opening, his muscles aching. He poked his head through as a turtle would inch out of its shell, straining to see in the darkness. The smell of human waste and garbage hit him.

A metal object smashed into his forehead.

“Zaka tawa!”

Calloused hands coarse as sand paper clamped down on his throat. He gasped as his lungs ignited like a match on kerosene. His vision darkened. A metal object forced its way onto his skull, sharp fingers pressing into his neck and head. The incisive edges split his skin, and blood trickled down his forehead and cheeks. Salty blood tingled on his lips and tongue. Another cylindrical object was thrust into his ear. He cried out, but his voice was lost in a sea of shrieks.

"When I tell you to rise," Rodon's familiar voice cooed in his bleeding ear, "you will do so."

Josh nodded, not really understanding why or if anyone could see his response in the darkness. The mechanical fingers pressed into his head, and the grip tightened. Ignoring the discomfort, he risked a glance at his surroundings. Other prisoners lined the dim corridor. The crowded walkway stretched wide enough for two men to stand beside each other, but the ceiling was only about six feet high. Mysterious metal objects engulfed the heads of each prisoner like demented spiders. The rusted gear clamped over their skulls bumped into the rocks as they stood in unison. Guards in loose black fabric roamed between them, keeping their rifles aimed low.

This was it. They would be killed now. Delmar was right. The pirates had no need for them, so the executions would begin. He hoped they would be quick. He prayed for his parents to never know his true fate. But Kadyn, oh, how he wished he had said something during Austin's games—during any of the times he stared at her without speaking. He would never know if any part of her felt the same way.

The sound escaped the tunnel like a vacuum.

"You have been equipped with a translator to assist with today's duties," Rodon's words sizzled from a buzzing speaker attached to the device on his head. "You should all be able to understand me. Raise your hand if you understand."

A dozen yards to his front, a prisoner kept his hands down. A nearby guard kicked the his leg.

"Raise your hand!" the guard yelled.

When the prisoner did not comply, the guard pressed the rifle to his head and pulled the trigger. The laser blast filled the tunnel with red lightning. The doomed man tumbled to the ground, twitched twice, and fell still.

"Now, the rest of you should know the device you wear is also for security. At my command, the ingenious instrument will close on your head like a bear trap, effectively ending your service to me. My name is Dax Rodon. You are my prisoners. Time to get to work."

Josh's blood boiled, but he chomped on his bottom lip to calm down. He thought of all the Star Runners who had died because of this man, the innocent civilians killed. In his months on Tarton's Junction, the Tyral Pirates had always been lurking in the shadows. Officers whispered about the vague pirate threat, experienced Star Runners carried worried expressions, and mechanics grumbled as they repaired Tridents damaged during hit-and-run raids. Rodon had been leading them, growing bolder with each passing month.

And now Josh was his prisoner.

"Today," Rodon continued, "you will empty an acquired freighter and then strip it. Half of you will be sold off or killed at the end of the day. The best workers will stay. Guards! Move our workers into the hangar!"

With an agonized murmur, the mass of humanity lunged forward. Josh felt the hot breath from the man behind him on his neck. The guards packed them in like cattle. The metal spider on his head made him feel like he wore five football helmets. His body bounced and swayed along the uneven surface of the tunnel's floor.

"Stay close to me!" Delmar snapped from in front of him.

Having only shared whispers with Delmar in the darkness, Josh looked at his only companion for the first time. Delmar's head was shaved beneath the spider, and his robes, which might have been white once, were now covered in gray sludge. His tall, lanky body moved like a skeleton.

"We work together and we survive this," he hissed.

The group snaked through the passage lit only by crude flash lights. The guards beat stragglers with the butts of their rifles. Those unfortunate enough to trip and fall received the worst treatment. Trying to block out the sounds of suffering, he kept his eyes on the back of Delmar's head.

The tunnel opened to a colossal cavern illuminated by florescent lights hanging from the rocky ceiling. A metal floor littered with spacecraft and scrap metal stretched for hundreds of yards. At least a dozen stolen Trident fighters had been parked in no discernible pattern, each craft a desecrated memorial to a fallen Star Runner. He glanced to his left, then to his right.

The cavern opened on both sides to reveal an asteroid-filled star field. A massive hunk of rock spun slowly. Beyond, asteroids stretched into infinity.

So the Tyral Pirates hid in an asteroid field? No nearby planet or moon of any kind was visible, just the blackness of deep space. At least he was certain the pirates hadn't taken him to another planet. However, how far had they transported him? Was he on the other side of the galaxy? Would he ever see his family or friends again? Or Kadyn?

"Move it!" a guard yelled, smacking Josh in the back of the head.

A battered merchant freighter filled the majority of the makeshift hangar. Laser blasts had scorched the hull. Jagged cracks covered the freighter's hull, the metal blackened and burnt. There was a hole in the ship near the bridge.

That must be how they took the freighter, Josh thought. *Just like they had with the Saber.*

Tyral Pirates swarmed around the freighter. The base of the landing platform was covered in steel grates. Three pirates dumped tools down into the second level. Josh saw no control tower or crew quarters. If he could send a distress signal somehow, perhaps he could limit his stay...

"These passengers should be sorted," Rodon's voice hissed in his ear-piece. "All able-bodied men and women will be sent with Tatos on the left of the hangar. The sick, elderly, or otherwise useless will follow Simex on the right and be led to the airlock for release."

Josh looked to his right. The airlock door was the size of a two-car garage. Rodon planned to force the innocent passengers in there to die. He had to do something.

"You are brave," Delmar said without turning around, "but ultimately foolish. Do you really think you could take them all?"

He surveyed the hangar. At least twenty heavily armed guards stood in multiple locations throughout the hangar, all focused on the line of prisoners.

He leaned closer to Delmar. "We have to do something."

"We are," Delmar said. "We're surviving. One day we will stand, but today is not that day."

The freighter's cargo bay doors slid open. The first two passengers rushed out with steel crow bars cocked back in attack position, ready for battle. They screamed, unleashing a wavering battle cry of civilians who had never been in a fight. A flurry of laser blasts ended the rebellion before it even began, the guards laughing as they murdered the passengers. Josh winced. He wanted to turn away, but remained focused on the grisly scene. The two slain passengers fell to the hangar floor with a dozen candle-flame-sized fires burning on their bodies. The closest guard walked over to the men and fired a shot into each of their heads.

The following passengers had no fight in them; their feet dragged on the floor as guards marched them out. Their eyes focused on the ground, and some sobbed as they walked. A child gripped their mother's hand, only to be ripped away. Both the mother and the child screamed. Josh looked away, unable to watch any longer.

Some prisoners helped sort the freighter's passengers into their appropriate lines. Josh and Delmar were too far back in the line and were ordered to wait. Their task would be stripping the freighter for salvage once the passengers and crew had been removed.

The passengers shouted for their families as the guards separated them. Josh's eyes fell on Rodon. He strolled past the passengers like a used car salesman checking out his product. Rodon's dark hair tumbled onto his shoulders, which were clad in fine black silk. The passengers he deemed worthy disappeared into a tunnel on the far side of the hangar, probably bound for cells like the one Josh had just left. Rodon smacked his hands together and rubbed them as if he had just finished counting his money. He spun around and marched to a door across from Josh's position.

"Time to eat!" he yelled, gesturing for two minions to follow him.

As Rodon passed through the door, Josh glimpsed a room full of work stations and an operational hologram.

A control room.

"We need to get in there," Josh said, rubbing his nose to cover his mouth.

"Quiet," Delmar whispered. "Do you have a death wish?"

The guards ordered the remaining unfortunate passengers into the airlock. When the final passenger passed through, the door began sliding shut on the room full of people. A woman sitting on the floor cradling her baby looked at Josh. He held her gaze, not wanting to look away, as if he could stop the door from closing by sheer willpower. Their eyes locked until metal hit metal, blocking their connection in a chorus of hissing gasses.

Once the airlock closed, a guard yanked down on a red lever. Josh held his breath, glancing around the asteroid hangar in search of a resolution. He sighed. A brief yelp followed by a whooshing sound, and it was over.

5

The radio discussed nothing but the recent car bombing in San Francisco; angry voices argued over the lack of preparation of law enforcement and whether or not the U.S. government had adequately protected the city. Austin turned it off just after they passed Macon.

The skyscrapers of downtown Atlanta glowed on the sides of the interstate, stretching high into the night sky. Traffic was mercifully light. After passing through the city, he took the exit for Marietta and for home. New gas stations had been built during his absence, continuing the erasure of green space in the growing suburb. He smiled as they passed the coffee shop, though, happy it still remained. Josh and Kadyn would be glad to know that they could meet for coffee again once they all were in town.

His stomach dropped.

Josh would not be coming home, and his parents had undoubtedly been notified of his mysterious disappearance in the Pacific Ocean. Austin knew it was a lie, sure, but it sounded better than the truth: His friend had been murdered by the Tyral Pirates along with every other passenger on board the freighter.

"Watch it, Stone," Sharkey said, his eyes still closed as he tried to nap.

He adjusted his path slightly, pulling the car back from the edge of the road.

THE FLOODLIGHT over the garage sent a white beam through the late-night fog. The haze magnified the aura, filling the air in front of the house with a cloud-like vapor. A flurry of insects twirled around the light, fighting to get closer to the bulb. Beneath the gutter, the garbage can stood at the side of the house. The grass had been cut and no weeds crept over the edge of the sidewalk.

Mom had been keeping the house in good shape since he had been gone. Austin pulled the car past the house as Sharkey had insisted, driving down the deserted streets. The sun would not rise for several hours, and the house was dark.

Sharkey rested his hand over the holster beneath his blue jacket. He glanced around the road, his eyes darting from house to house.

Austin touched his chin, his fingertips cold.

"Do we turn back now?" he asked, his voice louder than he expected in the silence.

"Looks clear." He turned back from the window. "Let's go."

Austin turned around in the cul-de-sac and drove back to his house. He pulled into the driveway, killed the lights, and stretched. The fatigue of the long, boring drive fell over him.

"She's probably asleep," he said, yawning.

"I'm sure," Sharkey said, "but we need to wake her."

He reached for the door, but Sharkey grabbed his shoulder.

"Listen, we have to assume they're watching the house right now," he said softly. "Be ready for anything."

"I got it."

The cool, late night air washed over him as he opened the door and put on a light jacket from the duffel bag in the back seat. A few insects pulsated in the trees, a rhythmic and alien sound rippling through the night. A pair of moths pounded into the floodlight, spinning and twirling away into the darkness as they battled for the warmth of the light. Austin stretched again, reaching high into the air until his back popped.

Sharkey slipped out of the car, his gaze flickering around the yard. He turned around and glanced at the other houses.

"Let's go, Lieutenant."

"Yes, sir."

Austin walked toward the front door and knocked softly. After a minute of silence, he hit the door a little harder. From the front yard, Sharkey sighed and shifted his weight from one foot to the other. He hated to ring the doorbell so long after midnight, but he reluctantly pressed the dim oval next to the door. The bell rang bold and intrusive in the darkness.

He winced. "That's going to do it."

He thought of the Revelation Protocol Sharkey had explained in the car. Once the protocol had been initiated to citizens on a dark world, it was crucial to provide the remaining information quickly and efficiently. After getting the person or persons to a secure location, Sharkey said to stick to the "Ws" such as who, what, when, where, and why. He wondered how his mother would take all of this information. He balled his fists, thinking of the shadowy force that killed Ryan and wondered if they now hunted him.

Austin looked over at the garage door, the night he spoke with Josh on the phone about Star Runners coming to mind. His friend had just been suspended, and would soon dominate the servers which helped him earn his scholarship. After hanging up the phone, Austin had seen a shooting star before going inside. He remembered wondering if his life would ever change.

He grimaced. Everything had changed. He had looked forward to this moment, the homecoming, for so long. After all the studying and work he had put in, he had anticipated telling Mom about his degree, his scholarship, and his school experience even though he knew he had to leave out most of the details. Both of them had worked hard to get him into a school. None of this would truly be real until he told her.

The first homecoming had been delayed when he left Tizona for Tarton's Junction. That was bad enough. Nubern mentioned he might be able to eventually inform Mom about the Legion in order to possibly recruit her for a medical ship. While Austin couldn't wait to come home, see his old room on solid ground again, and visit with Mom, the possibility of giving her a life beyond this house of shattered dreams gave him hope.

And now when the homecoming had finally arrived, an explosion on the streets of San Francisco threatened to take everything from him as it had Ryan. Somehow, he knew Dax Rodon was behind these attacks even if others seemed hesitant to make such a connection. The reasons why were still unclear, but all that mattered was that his mother could be in danger. She wasn’t answering the door.

Was he too late?

He turned halfway around to look at Sharkey when the upstairs light finally switched on, followed by the hallway.

"She's coming," he said, almost like a prayer.

His mother stepped down to the foyer and paused. She moved a hand to her face.

Austin nodded. "It's okay, Mom. It's me."

The porch light came on, sending a blinding light into his face. Sharkey took a step back into the shadows in the yard.

The front door pulled back slowly. Mom stood in the doorway, her hair in tangles. She squinted as if trying to pry open her eyes, but they fought against it as she looked through the glass. She swallowed and rubbed her mouth while pushing back the storm door, revealing her yellow nightgown.

"Is that really you?" she asked, offering a weak smile.

He winced and focused on her pale skin, remembering when Dad had been coping with chemotherapy. Was she sick?

"It's me, Mom."

She lifted her arms and they embraced. She squeezed softly. Her body felt weak, frail like a paper doll.

"I, uh, I can't believe you are here," she said. "Uh, I thought you were coming tomorrow."

Austin studied her. She blinked repeatedly, placing her hand on the door. Grabbing her forehead, she swayed. Her skin turned the color of freshly washed sheets.

"My head is pounding," she murmured.

Leaping from the shadows, Sharkey shot past his mom without saying a word and stormed into the house.

Austin cradled her in his arms, and her head dropped onto his shoulder.

"Chief!" Austin yelled. "What is it? What's wrong with her?"

"Get her to the street!" he yelled from the doorway. He moved onto the porch. "Now!"

He grabbed her wrists. "Come on, Mom! *Move*!"

He moved her through the cold grass wet with dew. She moaned a protest. He pushed her quickly, heading for the street. Sharkey hurried to her other side, lowering his shoulder to dip under her arm. He stood up, draping her hand around his neck.

"Come on!" Sharkey yelled.

An explosion blasted through the silence, the shockwave ripping through tree tops and knocking them onto the grass. Leaves, bark, and wooden splinters showered the yard in a fiery rain. Austin rolled onto his back and stared at the fireball that, a moment before, was his childhood home. A black cloud of smoke mushroomed into the night sky. He gasped.

Dad loved that house.

"Lieutenant," Sharkey called, already getting to his feet. "We need to move. Help me get her up."

Austin stood, shaking his head. He stared into the inferno, the orange flames engulfing his home. The roof turned black, smoke flowing through the broken windows. Lights came on up and down the street.

"What the hell was that?" he asked, unable to turn away from the fire.

"Stone!" Sharkey barked. "We need to move! Get her up!"

Shaking sweat from his eyes, he helped Mom stand. He placed her arm over his shoulder. She mumbled as they marched her to the car. Mr. Henderson's garage light turned on, followed by Mr. Weaver's on the other side of the street.

"Should we stay for the authorities?" Austin asked as they pushed her into the back seat.

"Absolutely not." Sharkey glanced at his watch. "It's already started."

SHARKEY DROVE through the streets like a demon pursued them, screeching around turns with the skill of a Formula One driver. Mom tumbled across the back seat, her sense of balance non-existent. Austin grabbed the door handle, using his other hand to brace himself against the dashboard. Even with the seat belt pulled across his lap, Sharkey's movements sent him sliding across the seat.

"I need you to give me directions to Kadyn's house," Sharkey said, his tone icy.

"She's not far," Austin said through his teeth and told Sharkey to take a left out of the neighborhood. He glanced back at his mother. "She going to be okay?"

Sharkey watched the streets, the lights playing across his face. "I don't know. She'll have quite a headache for a while. Carbon monoxide poisoning will do that. Try not to worry. If we get her to some help after this, she should be okay."

"You mean like a hospital? How is *that* going to work?"

"We have resources all over this planet. We'll get there. We have to get to your friend first."

He looked back at his mother. Her eyes closed tightly, and her body folded into the fetal position on the seat. Her skin was pale and her lips trembled. He wanted to climb back and hold her, tell her everything would be fine. Despite the need to rescue Kadyn, his mind kept repeating the same, unescapable fact: If they had been a few minutes later, his mother would be dead.

"I'm taking it that wasn't an accident."

"No," Sharkey said. "It was not."

"These attackers caused a gas leak in my house?"

"Apparently. You know what I know."

"What does that mean?" Austin slammed his hand on the door handle. "They almost killed my mom! What are we going to do?"

"You're going to calm down." Sharkey nodded forward. "I'm going to concentrate on getting us to your friend's house."

Sharkey jerked the wheel, cutting a turn so close he hopped a curb exiting the subdivision. The car tires squealed, and the back end of the vehicle fishtailed into the other lane. The tires kicked up water from the wet streets. The headlights beamed into the haze lifting from the pavement. Sharkey maintained an intense glare, his hands never leaving the steering wheel.

"I need you to open the glove box," Sharkey said, his voice low.

"What? Why?"

"Open the box!"

Austin flipped it open. A pile of papers topped with a state map fell out onto the floor of the car. "What am I looking for?"

"There should be a button to the left, directly under the jack for the MP3."

"I see it."

"Press it."

When Austin pressed the button, a shimmering light shot across the car. The air wavered like they passed under a waterfall. The hood glowed for a moment before it disappeared, revealing the street below. The lighting effect looked familiar.

"You have a shroud on this car?" He spun around, gaping at the road behind them. Water kicked high into the air by the tires now hidden by the shroud.

Sharkey nodded. "Of course." He accelerated, the engine straining at the effort. "The gas leak would have killed your mother and the authorities would have thought it was an accident. Our arrival forced these agents to expedite their efforts, hence the explosion. Your mother's home was under surveillance, but there's no way to tell if they were there or if it was done remotely."

Austin sank into his seat. "They were watching us?"

"Yes. They might be trailing us now. My guess is they were watching with a drone. If we had time, I would've searched the skies and shot it down. Whoever these agents are, they are definitely targeting you and your contacts. Once they have eliminated them, they will move on to the next Star Runner or Legion target. This is not theoretical anymore."

"Oh, my God."

Sharkey glanced at him. "Tell me where your friend is."

6

Sunlight warmed his face. He listened as the surf rustled against the sand only to retreat back into the depths. Another wave, larger this time, crashed into the beach and sent hundreds of little rivers into small canyons between the towels. The cold water tickled his shriveled toes. A child laughed, running from the waves before being scooped up by his mommy. Warmth enveloped him like a blanket fresh out of the dryer, as if he had found the eternal source of joy and would be able to keep it for himself. His thoughts drifted.

Someone was with him. To his right. They were close, projecting security. They radiated, pulsating toward him.

He couldn't turn. His hands wouldn't move. He reached out with his fingers, but felt nothing. Out of the corner of his eye, the person moved. It was a woman with dark hair. The wind tussled the curls, sending them onto her bare shoulders.

"You have to wake up."

Kadyn's voice.

"How did we get here?" he whispered. "Where are we?"

"It doesn't matter, sweet one. You must wake up now."

"Kadyn!"

The beach pulled away, ripped from his mind. He reached for it, but only touched air.

"Josh." *A different voice.* "Wake up."

He pried open his eyes. The rocky cave ceiling spread out above him. A nauseating feeling invaded his gut at the smell of human waste. Cool air drifted into the area. A man coughed nearby. To his right, a familiar face, cracked and weathered, stared down at him.

"Delmar," Josh breathed, his throat dry. "I was dreaming."

"I know. About Kadyn, no doubt."

He leaned forward, sipping water from a pouch. "Yes."

"Who is Kadyn?"

He took another drink, longer this time. The image from his dream, while fiction, burned into his mind. It should have been a true memory, something from his past, but it wasn't. As he had countless times since Rodon and his men captured him to rot on this asteroid, he wished he had told Kadyn the truth.

"A friend," he said, wiping his mouth.

"Must be some friend with a dream like that." Delmar smiled. "Is she beautiful?"

He thought of her chocolate curls, her dark eyes. "Yes."

"Hmm."

He laughed. "Easy. She's my friend." He studied Delmar's dark, creased skin, trying to imagine the man's life as a smuggler before the Tyral Pirates took him. "How long have you been with these pirates?"

Delmar gazed away, his face expressionless. "Too long."

Josh started to press; he wanted to know more about his companion, but the questions died on his lips. The Tyral Pirates had moved them to this cave yesterday, the third in as many days. They had unloaded six freighters in that time, stripped eight total Legion vessels including two Tridents, and seen dozens of prisoners released into the vacuum of space. Every day he woke in this place, he believed this would be the day he, too, would receive what Rodon called "leave" and be released into space. Some of the workforce disappeared with the released prisoners, declared unfit for more labor. The guards shot others for refusing to work or simply looking in the wrong direction.

Josh had taken his blows, too. The second day, a guard smacked him across the side of the head with the butt of a rifle. He hadn't seen it coming. Apparently, the guard simply walked by and hit him, or at least that's the story Josh was told much later when he woke in another cave. Delmar had saved him, offering to carry him from the site after work detail. The tender lump growing above his ear reminded him of the guard's action, and of Delmar's kindness.

When they weren't stripping spacecraft or escorting prisoners to their deaths, the pirates dropped them in caverns deep into the asteroid to mine for minerals and precious metals. The work days stretched so long he wondered if he had ended up in hell itself. Delmar, his worn hands covered in callouses hard as the rocks they carried, was always there to offer assistance. Josh would be dead by now if not for Delmar. He would tell his friend as much, if it seemed like such things mattered to him. No, Josh thought, Delmar worked as if he would punch a clock at the end of the day. It was like he had a magical cloak to shield him from the horrors of this place.

"How do you do it?" he asked.

Delmar blinked, a quizzical look on his face. "How do you mean?"

"Day in and day out. You keep trying, keep moving ahead and concentrating on the task at hand. How?"

His friend's face warmed. "It is easy. I know we will be delivered. Some day. You will see."

Josh snorted. "I don't even know where we are. Even if I could—"

Suddenly aware he spoke loudly, he glanced over his shoulder at the cave entrance. Leaning forward and lowering his voice, he continued, "Even if I could get to a ship, I don't even know where we are."

Delmar grinned. "We are in the Amade Cluster, Quadrant Eight. This is the secondary base of the pirates, although I do not know the name of this specific planetary body."

Josh blinked, confused by the knowledge of this man. "How do you know that?"

A horn sounded and footsteps stormed down the hall. The other prisoners rustled. When the guards came every other day, it meant more work, food, or new additions to the workforce. Since Josh couldn't stomach the thought of eating more soupy snot, he hoped for more workers, but felt a tinge of guilt for wishing such a thing on any newcomers.

The gate opened and one Tyral Pirate stood at the entrance, his muscular arms crossed over his leather armored chest. "Get in there!"

The guard forced six new spacers inside the room and closed the gate. The men, dressed in an assortment of ragged flight suits, collapsed in an undignified heap of flesh in the center of the cell. Their tattered clothes clung to their bodies by threads. Fresh cuts and bruises covered their faces and bodies. These men had been in a fight.

Although their flight suits were torn and ripped, the similarities in the newcomers' attire seemed as if they belonged together. However, Josh knew they were not Legion types. He looked closer, saw no insignias or ranks. Still, the men seemed to be more than just a random selection of six spacers. They glanced around the cave, and their skin glistened with sweat. They cowered, except for one man in the center.

Josh studied him. With his bulky broad shoulders, the bold newcomer glared with ice-blue eyes at each prisoner in the cell. A thick, bushy red beard grew out like a fire frozen in time. He locked eyes with Josh, held the stare for a heartbeat, and moved on as if he silently challenged each man to make a move.

None did.

The man saw to the other newcomers, kneeling to provide a kind word or offer a pouch of water. After the ferocity in his face a moment before, the leader showed compassion toward his men. He checked their wounds, touched their shoulders as he spoke.

"Who are they?" Josh whispered.

"*Barracudas*, probably," Delmar said with a shrug, "but if they are, they've been the property of our hosts for quite some time."

"*Barracudas*?"

"A smuggling group. They operate throughout Quadrant Eight.

Have done so for years. They work on Legion planets and anywhere else they can operate."

He frowned. "So they're like the Tyral Pirates?"

"Not exactly." Delmar leaned against the rock wall. "These *Barracudas* operate in materials and objects, never in the slave trade. And they do it well."

He rested on his elbows. "Interesting."

THREE HOURS into the second day of pounding rocks, Josh's shoulders burned. He wiped his brow with his tattered shirt, the same garment he'd worn on his doomed return flight to Earth. He risked a glance around the cavern. Men focused downward on mining the boulders, covering the rocky surface like a busy bee hive. Delmar worked near Josh as always. Although older, the man never wavered. He lifted the pulverized stone fragments onto the hovering flat that moved away when filled.

The *Barracudas* adapted quickly to the extreme working conditions, filing into the work detail like experienced laborers. At the beginning of their second work day, the Tyral Pirate guards removed one Barracuda from the mining crew along with several others. Josh wondered where they had moved the new group, but Delmar advised against asking. He hoped the guards took them to strip another freighter, but thought it was a false hope.

The massive leader of the *Barracudas* often worked near Josh. With his bulging muscles and wild red beard, the bald man looked feral as he tore into the stone each day. It was as if the boulders themselves had wronged him. The man worked in silence except for the occasional grunt.

But today the man worked so close to Josh he could smell the man's sweat. They spent the first hours in grim silence. The Barracuda lifted the pick ax over his head and smashed it down. He used the ax to move around the rubble he had created before lifting the tool again. The force of his work shook the ground. Josh glanced at his arms, comparing them to the beast of a man near him. Having played football, he always thought his arms were toned, something that made him proud. Working next to this man made him feel small, weak.

As he gazed into the dense asteroid field surrounding their prison, the reality of his situation pressed on him. With the amount of guards constantly on watch, there would be no escape in his future. There would be no stealing a vessel. If he did, Rodon would pursue and hunt him down before he could plot a curve to take him to Legion space. Or they would just destroy him. He would never get out of here alive, and now he had to work next to an pungent body builder.

He sighed and lifted his pick ax. He plunged it into the rocks, trying to ignore the fact he did not make the ground shake like the leader of the smugglers.

A force pushed him from behind, thrusting his head backward.

"What the hell?" Josh cried out, spinning around.

The hulking man squared off with him, biceps swelling as if they would rip through the skin. His eyes blazed like blue fire.

"Watch where you swing that thing, little man," he said with a booming voice. Even with the translator working in his ear, the man's growl lifted above the chaotic noise of the workers.

Others turned in their direction.

"I didn't mean to do anything," Josh said, gripping the handle on his ax.

The man shoved Josh hard in the chest, pushing him backward. His heel caught a boulder, and he tumbled into a pile of rocks. The back of his head hit a stone. His vision wavered and darkened. Dimly, the outline of his attacker loomed over him like a gothic statue, the ax cocked like a weapon. At least, he thought, his days as a prisoner would soon be over.

Delmar burst into his line of sight, the smaller man grabbing the back of the ax poised to smash into his skull.

"They will kill us all if you do this!" Delmar shouted, his voice gruff.

The smuggler lowered the ax, shrugged off Delmar, and slowly turned back to his work.

Delmar knelt on one knee and offered to help Josh rise. He felt like he was on a carousel when he stood, the world spinning. His legs wobbled and he pressed a hand to the back of his head. A throbbing pain flashed. Delmar glanced around and led Josh back to his mining site.

"Come now," Delmar said. "No guards have noticed. Try to get back to work."

"I didn't do anything," Josh said, wincing as Delmar thrust the ax back in his aching hand. "I didn't even touch that guy."

"Quiet," Delmar said. "He is their leader, trying to exert his influence. You are fine now. Finish the day."

With his arms sapped of strength and his head still spinning from the collision, he spent the rest of the day attempting to look as busy as possible. The guards usually targeted the resting prisoners, so he focused on keeping his head low.

The hours dragged, the endless labor blurring one site with another until the entire universe seemed comprised of these peculiar black and gray rocks. He would obliterate a stone, load it on the drone cart, watch it fly away, and continue the process again. His lungs burned and his mouth dried up. Just when he thought the work day would end, the guards moved them to another site to begin the process over again. With artificial florescent lights illuminating the cave like a highway construction site, he had no sense of how long they had been working.

After what could have been two days or more, the guards halted the labor. Several prisoners collapsed on the rocks they targeted, some in mid-swing. Josh glanced around the room, his mouth hanging open like a caught fish as he gasped. Workers who remained standing gazed into space, their minds wrecked and any sense of humanity sapped away. The guards marched the prisoners who could still walk back to the common cell. Laborers still on the ground reached for them as they passed. A younger worker in front of Josh reached down to help an old man. A guard smacked the youth in the back of the head and he tumbled next to the gray-haired prisoner. He glanced at the man as he passed, saw the bloodshot eyes surrounded by wrinkled skin.

Two laser blasts echoed throughout the hall. No other workers tried to help the exhausted men who remained on the floor. More shots flashed. Josh struggled to put one foot in front of the other.

No one spoke, not even the guards.

When they entered the common cave, Josh collapsed next to Delmar. His friend tapped him on the shoulder as Josh rolled over on his back.

"Rest, my friend," Delmar said.

"Don't worry." Josh took in a long, slow breath. "Thank you."

"For what?"

"For being there." Josh closed his eyes. "Nice to have a friend."

Delmar murmured an affirmative as others collapsed around them. The workers fell in a heap. Snores rumbled in seconds. Josh drifted into a dreamless sleep.

When a hand the size of a baseball glove wrapped around his ankle, Josh thought he was dreaming. A strong force dragged him across the cave floor, slamming his head against the jagged stones. His teeth buried into his tongue and blood filled his mouth. When he stopped moving, he tried to stand, but his muscles refused. The massive hands clasped his shoulders and thrust him into the air like a doll. He fought for breath, but a hand pressed against his mouth.

"Stay quiet or I will snap your neck."

Despite the darkness, Josh knew it was the smuggler's leader. The man's monstrous silhouette loomed over him. He nodded and the giant removed his hand, placing him back down. The rest of the workers slept undisturbed. A pirate guard at the cave's entrance faced the other way, his attention on lighting some kind of cigarette.

"What do you want?" Josh breathed.

The man leaned in, close enough to feel the heat and smell the stench of his breath. "They say you are a pilot?"

"Who says that?"

"The other prisoners."

He thought for a moment. "Aren't you a smuggler?"

"I'm captain of the vessel *Sparkling Light*. I'm not a pilot." He gripped Josh's shoulder hard. "I ask you one last time; are you a pilot?"

He winced, his muscles sore as the man burrowed his fingers into his skin. "Yes. I'm a pilot. What of it? It's not going to do us any good."

The hands gripped harder on Josh's shoulders and pushed him into the wall. He clamped his lips shut, doing his best to keep quiet.

"What do you fly?" the man asked.

"Fighters."

The smuggler leaned in close. "You are military? You are a Zahl pilot?"

"No."

He shook Josh. "Legion, then?"

"I am a prisoner like you!" Josh snapped. "What the hell does it matter what I did before? You wanna talk the night away or did you wake me for some purpose?"

The man smiled, keeping his vice-like grip on Josh's shoulder. "Getting angry, little man?"

Josh grabbed for the man's wrist, but his strength could not move the massive arm. He sighed. "Yeah, I'm pissed off I have to be in here with you when I could be sleeping. Tell me what you want before I have to start a fight I'll lose."

The grip lightened and the man snorted as he steadied Josh against the rock. "You have balls, little man."

"I've got nothing to lose. What does it matter? I've been here longer than you and I don't have the strength to work another day, much less fight you all night." He looked into the man's eyes. "If you're going to do something, do it."

The man released his grip and gestured to the rock floor. "Sit."

Josh fell to the ground and leaned against the stone wall. His body went limp. He gazed into the darkness. The man sat next to him and grunted.

"I don't want to go out like this," the man hissed. "My crew expected better."

Josh shook his head. "This wasn't on my list of future plans either."

The man grunted, burying his hand inside his bushy red beard. "My name is Waylon Neary."

"I'm Josh." He rested his head in his hands for a moment, hoping the pounding headache would eventually subside. "So did you really wake me up to find a pilot or did you just want to fight?"

Waylon exhaled. "I don't know. Maybe both."

"Well, if you have a plan to get out of here, I'd like to hear it."

He folded his arms over his chest. "Needed a full crew before I could have a plan. Now that I know you're interested, I'll work on a plan."

For the first time in a long while, Josh felt a sense of hope. His heart raced as he thought of escaping this asteroid. "And what would this plan entail? It's not like there are a lot of choices."

Waylon paused. "When they brought us in, a line of freighters had just unloaded an assortment of supplies. It seemed regular, like it was scheduled."

"A scheduled delivery? Did the freighters leave?"

He nodded. "Seemed like they were prepping for takeoff."

Among other less than savory practices, the Tyral Pirates were known throughout Quadrant Eight for stealing ships of all kinds, stripping them, and selling off the pieces to the highest bidder. As for their supplies, Josh's CO on Tarton's Junction said Rodon stole all the resources he used to create his sad little empire. However, Josh had never heard of them doing any business that would result in a scheduled delivery.

"What was in the freighter?" he asked.

"Crates of some kind, looked official. Some kind of military equipment. I didn't get a chance to linger, you know?"

"The guards never go away, so how in the world do you expect to get off this rock."

"I'm working on it. We'll have to keep an eye on the next prize the pirates bring in here. Do they move us often?"

"I've been here for a while—I don't know how long. We work long hours and I've lost track of the time, but ships are constantly coming and going. They bring in freighters for us to strip. When we're not doing that, they put us in these caves to mine this mineral."

"It's Lutimite."

"How do you know?"

"It's what powers ships in the Zahl Empire. Pretty common in those space lanes, but we don't see a lot of it in Quadrant Eight. Powers Lutimite Reactors. Zahlians pay a pretty penny for it."

"Why would Rodon be using us to mine something for the Zahl?"

"I just got here, but I'd say for the money. Why else would they be doing it?"

Josh chewed on his bottom lip. "So we have to steal a ship?"

"I'd recommend that over escaping through an airlock on your own. I think you'd get farther."

"Right." He nodded. "Okay, I can help you but Delmar is coming with us."

"Who?"

"My friend. He's the man that was next to me today in the pits. The one you almost killed."

"The old man?"

"Yes," Josh said, looking at him. "Either he comes with us, or I'm out."

Waylon nodded. "You promise you can fly whatever we decide to steal coming through that hangar, and you can bring anyone you want."

7

Their shrouded vehicle shot across the grass at the entrance of Kadyn's neighborhood, invisible tires shredding through the greenery and shattering a sprinkler. Austin turned back, saw two trenches splitting the lawn front of the subdivision sign. Mud and grass clippings littered the roadway.

"Watch it!" he yelled.

"No time." Sharkey pressed down on the gas and Austin gripped the door handle. "Where?"

"Second left," he said. "Then about a mile down the road." He thought of his friend who was home for Fall Break and probably relaxing with her parents.

"You don't think anything has happened to her?" he asked.

"We'll find out soon enough."

The car eased into the left-hand lane, going around a winding curve. The tires screeched. Sharkey eased off the gas and let the momentum carry them through the turn. He accelerated through a stop sign without slowing and slammed on the brakes to prepare to turn onto the second street.

"Hang on."

Austin clutched his seat and door handle, preparing for the worst. Sharkey yanked the wheel left, the car fish-tailing into the corner.

"Number?"

"It's 318 on the right."

Sharkey nodded. "When I slow, I want you to hop out and run the rest of the way. Her house is probably under surveillance, so I wouldn't use the front door. I'll give you ten minutes to get her out."

“How am I supposed to do that?”

“Knock on her window, Romeo.”

“Her room’s on the second floor.”

“You’ll figure it out.”

“What about her parents?”

“Just get her out.” He slowed the car. “You got your sidearm?"

“They took it at Base Prime.”

Sharkey yanked a pistol with a silencer attached from inside his jacket and handed it to Austin. "All right, get ready."

The gun felt heavy in his hands. “This a real gun?”

“You think I handed you a toy?”

“No, I mean a *gun* that fires bullets? What about the laser pistol I trained on?”

“Same principle, just louder with some smoke. It’s prohibited. Off-world tech. You ever shot a man?”

He swallowed. “No, sir.”

“Whoever these guys are, they are hardened mercs, hired guns. They will kill you. You have to kill them first. Take the extra clips, too.”

“Yes, sir.”

Sharkey eased off the gas, allowing the car to coast toward the house. “Stay ready.”

Austin controlled his breathing as he watched the familiar houses pass. A hundred times before, he’d visited this neighborhood. He remembered children playing in the yards, jumping through sprinklers and shooting each other with water pistols. The houses appeared different in the darkness, looming on each side of the street. Nothing moved.

His fingers rested on the pistol in his jacket. He felt perspiration icing down his back. He hadn't seen Kadyn since before college. What would she say? He glanced at Sharkey, wanted to ask him what would happen next, but decided it had to wait. Would they take her to a secure location? Where would that be?

"Ready?" Sharkey asked.

He wanted to say he wasn't. He wished he were somewhere else. His mother moaned in the backseat, still suffering the effects of the gas. Whoever had done this to Mom, now targeted Kadyn.

Concentrate.

"Go!" Sharkey barked.

Austin cracked open the door and hesitated.

"Go! Now!"

He jumped out and tumbled into a flower bed in front of Kadyn's neighbor's house. He raised his head from the black dirt, saw the car's tire tracks splitting the damp streets, but couldn't see the vehicle. The sound of the engine faded, then disappeared. A soft breeze touched the leaves. Searching nearby houses for any sign of disturbance, he found nothing. His heart thudded as he slowly moved to a crouching position.

Ignoring a stray thought of a sniper zeroing in on his face, Austin sprinted across the lawn. He slowed at the side of Kadyn's house and leaned against the brick, felt the coolness on his back. He held his breath and listened. The neighbor's sprinkler system hissed to life, watering the yard and the flowers he had just destroyed.

With his hand on the gun resting in his jacket pocket, Austin stepped toward the backyard as if a mine would explode beneath his feet. He eased to the edge of the house, bypassed the idle air conditioning units, and risked a glance into the backyard.

A sole light illuminated the porch, sending far-reaching shadows like dark fingers stretching across the grass. He squinted, surveying the trees behind Kadyn's house.

Turning back to the house, he craned his neck for a view of her bedroom window. Dark, of course.

He bent down, searching for a pebble to toss. Instead, he found a heavy pinecone. He hesitated. A pinecone thrown hard enough could break through a window, and that wasn't exactly the result he was shooting for in this situation. A pine tree's bark a dozen feet away looked promising. Perhaps that could work.

He eased over and stripped off a piece of loose bark. Looking up at Kadyn's window, he tossed it. It hit brick and shattered without much sound. After trying unsuccessfully three more times, he looked back to the pinecone. If he didn't do something soon, Sharkey would assume the worst and come after him. He gripped it and looked at the window.

Please don't break, he thought.

Stepping back, he hurled the pinecone and hurried back to cover. The pinecone bounced below the window and rolled up the side of the house, skipping across the glass. *Man, that was loud.*

He pressed himself against the brick, focusing on the window. The bedroom light came on and a shadow loomed. Kadyn must be awake; the pinecone had done its job. Another noise would attract her to the window. Austin bent down, grabbed another piece of bark, and threw it at the glass. The lock slid back on the window and the pane slid up.

A bearded face poked against the screen.

Mr. Joyce.

Austin fell into the grass, not really knowing why. He pressed into the damp ground at the base of the house in hopes Kadyn's father wouldn't see him.

"Hello?" Mr. Joyce's deep voice called.

Austin flinched. Had the man seen him? Did he throw the pinecone at the wrong window?

"Listen, my daughter is asleep," Mr. Joyce said with a sigh. "If you don't leave, I'll have to call the cops."

The window closed and the light went off. Austin exhaled and leaned against the house. What now?

He looked back at the window and sighed. So Kadyn was home, but her father was guarding her every move. Nothing new there. He remembered prom when Kadyn had been chased by Jason Pruitt, the dorky defensive lineman on the football team. Austin had thought about asking Kadyn to go as friends, but that was right about the time Jason had been lurking beside Kadyn's locker after every class. He followed her around, asking her to prom after school every day. Kadyn finally relented, and Austin went to prom with his cousin Holly.

But he'd heard the story about gathering for photos before they left. Kadyn said Mr. Joyce hovered around her like a helicopter parent, watching Jason's hands as they posed for the photos. That same Mr. Joyce had just threatened to call the cops. Austin knew Sharkey was waiting in the car. What could he do?

As he looked around for inspiration, he heard the window open again. *Great*, he thought. Mr. Joyce was coming out with his hunting rifle.

"Jeremy?" Kadyn whispered. "Is that you?"

He stepped back from the house. "Kadyn!"

"I told you not to come here!"

"It's me, Austin!"

She paused. "*Austin*? Are you serious?"

"I need to talk to you," he said. The pistol in his jacket felt heavier. "Can you?"

It was too dark for Austin to see her face, but her head leaned out of the cracked-open window. If there were agents watching the house, they definitely saw that. He needed to get her out of here.

"Dad's going to kill me! I'll be right down," she said with a sigh. "This had better be good."

He looked around the backyard as he waited. He hadn't written Kadyn in weeks. Now, he'd woken her up in the middle of the night. He had no idea what he would say to her. The forest seemed to have eyes.

A minute passed.

Austin gripped the pistol, his fingers resting lightly on the side. The gun felt bulkier than his laser pistol. The grass rustled from the other side of the house. Somebody was coming. He knelt down, sliding the gun out of his pocket.

"Hey!"

He spun around. "What the—I'm sorry," he said, holding his hands up. "Quiet."

Kadyn, dressed in pink pajamas and tennis shoes, ran the last few steps and threw her arms around him. Her hair band fell out, releasing her brown hair from the pony tail. She smelled of honey and flowers.

"Oh, my God," she breathed in his ear. "I've missed you! What are you doing here?"

"Be quiet," he said, pulling her into the bushes. He placed a finger over her lips and listened. The insects still hummed.

"Aren't we past the days of rolling houses?" she asked.

He pulled her down to the ground and put his free hand on her shoulder. "You need to listen to me. I don't have time to explain this, but I've got to take you away from here right now, okay?"

Her face grew rigid in the moonlight. "What are you talking about?"

"I can't explain it right now." He gripped her hand. "We have to leave."

"Leave for where?" Her face, once filled with excitement, faded to terror. "You're scaring me."

He lifted his head over the bushes. "You need to trust me. Okay?"

Now that he'd made contact, Sharkey would be waiting at the street. If the enemy was not currently watching the house, they would be able to simply walk up to the shrouded vehicle and leave.

He froze. Kadyn wouldn't know about the shrouded vehicle. He looked back at her. "Grab my hand and everything will be all right. I promise. No matter what else happens, just trust me and I'll get you out of here."

She reached out her hand before recoiling back. "Oh, my God! Is that a *gun*?"

He thrust the gun into his jacket. "We have to go!"

"Oh, Austin. You're not going to rob a store or something, are you? I know you need money, but this isn't the way."

His face contorted. "What? No. You need to come now. It'll be okay."

She took his hand carefully as if he would tear it off. He squeezed it, but she didn't return the gesture. With Kadyn falling in behind him, they made their way along the side of the house to the front yard. Two houses down, the wet pavement split as Sharkey's shrouded car crept down the street. He paused at the corner of the house.

"We need to cut across the neighbor's yard and head for the street. If anything happens, I need you to keep running. You got it?"

She nodded, her chin trembling. "Austin, are you a drug dealer?"

He closed his eyes, his pulse pounding in his ears. His throat constricted, his muscles tightening. "Right now, I wish I was. You ready?"

"Okay," she said, squeezing his hand for the first time. "I trust you."

He nodded, trying to fake a smile. When he turned back, he lowered his gaze. The light shifted in the street in front of the house, just beneath the neighbor's tree. Although it was difficult to make out any details, it looked to be the shape of the Tizona sedan.

"Now!"

They broke for the neighbor's yard, their feet slipping in the wet grass. Kadyn clutched his hand hard enough to make the skin numb. She gasped as they sprinted. If they could make it to the shrouded car, the terror of the night could end.

A faint light flashed from across the street. Sparks exploded from the largest tree in Kadyn's front yard, showering speckles of burning embers into the grass. Austin ducked, his heart pounding in his ears. He didn't see the bolt, but knew from the sparks a laser gun targeted them. That meant off-world technology, which meant the mercenary force had found them.

"What was that?" Kadyn yelled.

Another shot blasted into the tree, the lasers still invisible. Small fires sparkled into the bark. He thrust Kadyn to the ground, gently pressing his knee into her back as he searched the woods. Staying low to the ground, he gripped the pistol and scanned the dense forest across the street. He saw nothing. Suddenly, he had the creeping feeling that something targeted him.

An engine rumbled close. Tire tracks appeared on the nearby damp pavement.

"Come on," he said, gripping Kadyn's shoulder, "we have to crawl."

"Crawl to where?" she asked, her face wet with dew from the grass. Behind her, small flames flickered from the burning bark that littered the front yard.

Lights flickered on from the houses lining the street. If they were going to leave unnoticed, they had better do it soon.

The air in front of them split open and produced Sharkey carrying an assault rifle trained on the other side of the street. He kept the car between him and the trees for cover as he turned around.

"Come on, Lieutenant!"

Austin heard two more invisible shots sizzle overhead, smashing into Kadyn's house. Sharkey returned fire, his silenced machine gun thumping through the early morning suburban world of hissing sprinklers. The spent shells hit the ground.

An invisible laser bolt smashed into Sharkey's shoulder. A torrent of sparks showered down as he grunted. He raised over the shrouded car and fired.

Austin gripped Kadyn's hand. "Can you run?"

"What the hell is going on?" she asked.

"You have to trust me!" he yelled. "Come on!"

She looked at him, her eyes wide and brimming with tears as she nodded. He gripped her hand and yanked her up.

The trees across the street erupted in faint flashes of light as if even the trees opened fire. Sparks flashed like lightning. Most of the invisible bolts went crashing into the front of Kadyn's house, breaking glass and igniting the roof. Sharkey fired until the gun ran out. He ducked behind the car, reloaded, and raised in one fluid motion.

Austin reached Sharkey and felt for the rear door. His fingers fell around the handle and he pulled back. A bolt buzzed by his ear. With his ears ringing, he blindly fired his pistol twice in the direction of his attacker. The bullets hit a tree, bark flying off the trunk.

"What is this?" Kadyn shrieked.

"It's just a car. Quickly—get in!"

He grabbed her shoulder and guided her into the shrouded vehicle. As she climbed inside, a shadow in the shape of a man appeared behind a tree across the street. He emptied the clip. Bullets smashed into the tree. It was too dark to see if he'd hit anything. He knelt down.

"I'm out. You okay?" Austin asked Sharkey, keeping low behind the car.

"Just a scratch. Get in!"

Austin slipped into the backseat with Kadyn and his mother. Sharkey, clutching his blackened and burned shoulder, crouched over the steering wheel, closed the door, and accelerated.

With his pistol still in hand, Austin turned around to look out the back window. The front of Kadyn's house burned in the darkness, illuminating the other houses in an orange light. Neighbors opened their doors and stood in the grass, all of them looking at Kadyn's burning house.

No one followed the car. Well, no one he could see.

"Can they track a shroud?" Austin asked, still focused on their rear.

"It's possible," Sharkey grumbled. "We need to get as far away from here as we can."

"What was that?" he asked. "I've never seen a gun like that before."

"A masker," Sharkey gritted out. "It's like a silencer for a projectile weapon, but it fires the laser without the tracer. Very professional."

He leaned into his seat. "Oh, that's just great."

Kadyn shivered, her pink pajamas wet from the crawl through the grass. She folded her arms over her chest.

"Here." He pulled off the Tizona jacket and draped it around her. "This should help. You're in shock."

She glared at him. "You *think*?"

"Ma'am," Sharkey said with a nod. "The authorities are on their way. We made such a scene back there that our attackers won't bother your family any more tonight."

"Attackers?" she breathed before turning to Austin. "Please, I'm begging you, tell me what's going on."

"It's a long story."

"Please."

He paused. After countless hours in classrooms being told to never speak about his life on Tarton's Junction or the Galactic Legion, they'd never briefed him on how to actually inform people of the truth. The lessons only covered how to deceive, how to cover it up.

"I would like to know, too," Mom said from the other side of the car.

Austin looked her. "Are you feeling better? Thank God."

"I have a pounding migraine, but it's getting better." She nodded toward Sharkey. "Your friend's driving certainly didn't help."

"I'm sorry, ma'am," Sharkey said, whipping the car around a corner.

Mom's jaw dropped. "Wait a minute. I know you. You're from Austin's school, aren't you?"

"Lieutenant," Sharkey said, his voice grim, "it's time to invoke Revelation Protocol."

"Yes, sir." He took a deep breath. "Don't know how to say this to you both, but my school, well, uh, this is harder than I thought it would be."

"Say what, honey?" Mom leaned forward. "Please, tell us what's going on. Are you in danger?"

"Yes," he said, nodding. "We all are."

"What did I do?" Kadyn asked, her face crumpling. She put her hands in front of her trembling mouth.

Mom draped her arm around her shoulder. "It's okay, honey."

Austin watched his friend, saw her pain. She shouldn't have had to go through this tonight. She shouldn't have had to see her house burning or worry about her parents. He thought back to Nubern in the swamp shack before they took the tube transport to California.

Nubern had said nothing would ever be the same once they passed through the doors. Even though Austin had understood what his mentor was saying, the statement had fallen hollow on his ears. After tonight, Mom and Kadyn could never go back.

A shiver shot down his back.

"Okay, look." He pursed his lips. "This is not going to be easy to hear. My school is actually an academy for the Galactic Legion. I was recruited to pilot fighters for the Legion. I went through training and I'm now a Star Runner with the Legion Navy. Earth is a part of Legion territory, but it is known as a dark world because we haven't started exploring beyond our solar system and—"

Kadyn slapped her hands on her knees. "Oh, come *on*! Is this part of that stupid game you and Josh used to play?"

"No, well, sort of. I—"

"Stop it!" She wiped tears from her cheeks. "My house is on fire, Austin! My parents might be dead! This is not a game!"

He held up his hand. "I know this is not a game, but you need to trust me. What I'm telling you is true."

"So you fly spaceships now?" Kadyn shook her head. "Am I really supposed to believe this? And you're saying this to your mom? Why am I involved, huh? Who attacked my house?"

"We don't know. We found out both of you were in danger, so here we are. If this hadn't happened, you would never have found out about any of this."

She shook her head and glared out the window. "I can't believe you've done this to me."

Austin opened his mouth to speak. He wanted to console her, make everything okay, but Mom shook her head.

They sat in silence. Minutes passed. Streetlights flickered across the backseat. Austin glanced behind them several times, but nobody was following them.

He gripped his mother's hand and looked at both of them. "I'm so glad you both are okay."

His mother placed her hand over his and nodded. "My head's still pounding."

"Carbon monoxide poisoning. You could have died."

She smiled. "But you saved me."

The car squealed around a corner and sped down an on-ramp leading to an empty four-lane highway.

"Where are we going?" he asked, leaning forward.

"We have a meeting in three hours," Sharkey said, his eyes focused on the road. "We'll report to the EIF agent at the outlet mall and get our orders. I think the worst is behind us."

"I hate when people say that." Austin rested his arm on the back of the passenger seat and studied the burn marks on Sharkey's shoulder. "You going to be okay, Chief?"

"Yeah. Whoever that was out there wasn't a very good shot."

"What makes you say that?"

"Because I should be dead."

"I'm glad that's not the case." Austin thought about Sharkey being killed in front of Kadyn's house. "What would I have done?"

"If I didn't make it?" Sharkey shrugged. "Contact Base Prime. They would have sent a unit to evacuate you all, if you were still around to be evacuated that is. I wouldn't think too much about it. We made it out."

A FEW HOURS LATER, the rolling hills of North Georgia stretched across the horizon. The bright sunlight burned down through a bright blue sky. Hundreds of people filled into the outlet mall just off the highway. Shoppers carried plastic bags of different colors as they laughed and walked together. As Sharkey took his second lap around the collection of stores, Austin wished he were one of the shoppers, walking around without a care in the world.

Kadyn and Mom sat in silence. He hoped Kadyn had finally fallen asleep. Instead, he saw she stared at the ceiling. Mom tilted her head back and closed her eyes, probably trying to fight the headache.

Austin battled a wave of fatigue. He needed coffee. After hearing laser bolts whiz by his head for the first time, the rush of adrenaline had faded in the boring drive north of Atlanta.

"I'm going to stop here in front of this nature store," Sharkey said, his voice rattling as he winced. "You need to get out and go buy a bag of bird seed."

"What?"

"Just do it," he said with a grimace. "Then walk to the food court and sit in front of the carousel."

"And do what, feed the pigeons? I thought we would get Mom and Kadyn to a safe house and away from danger."

"That's why we're here. Just do as I say, Lieutenant. These are the orders Commander Pierce gave me before you arrived at Tizona." Sharkey looked at him through the rearview mirror and held up a roll of money. "You'll need this money. Leave the gun."

Austin grabbed the cash. "What if they are here tracking us?"

"Doesn't matter. Stay public. Stay in the open. You'll be fine. We have people here."

"What people?"

Sharkey sighed. "Just do as I say. You'll be fine."

Glancing at Sharkey's cauterized wound, Austin nodded. "Sorry, Chief. I'll hurry."

He needed to remember his training. *Stay frosty,* he thought.

He glanced at Mom. "Guess I'll be right back."

She smiled, her eyes watering. "Be careful."

Sharkey stopped the car in front of the nature store and Austin stepped out. He strolled as casually as possible toward the store. A teenage girl wearing a bright yellow backpack smiled at him as he walked by. He glanced over his shoulder as she passed and saw Sharkey drive the sedan back into the sea of vehicles as if he searched for a parking place.

Austin pulled back the glass door and heard the bell jingle against the metal frame. Inside the store, a middle-aged woman smiled from behind the counter.

"Welcome," she said. "Let me know if I can help."

Austin nodded and pretended to look around. Bird houses and

wind chimes filled the aisles. A strong smell of incense hovered over the store. He glanced at the yard games, wondering if he would ever get to play badminton again. It was one of Dad's favorite games, but he hadn't played since the cancer diagnosis.

He wandered back to the stacks of bird seed in massive bags that had to be twenty or thirty pounds. He frowned.

"That's some of the best we have," the woman said.

He turned back to her. "Got anything smaller? I don't think I have that many birds."

"That's all we have," she said with a smile. "It's really good. It'll keep the birds coming back to your house all winter long."

"Is it? Well, I guess this will have to do."

Swinging the large sack over his shoulder, he strolled up to the counter.

The woman eyed him. "Do I know you?"

Austin placed the bag on the table and froze. "Me?"

"Have we met before?"

His pulse raced. Was this one of the "people" Sharkey had mentioned? What if this was one of the contacts he was supposed to talk with?

"I don't know. Have we met before?"

"I can't remember. Maybe you just look like somebody I know."

He leaned closer, ready to get past the code words and make contact. "Do you *really* think I need this much bird seed?"

She smiled. "I don't know. I just work here."

"So you think I need the bird seed? That's what I need? Or can I just get what I came for?"

"What?" She laughed. "You're kinda weirded out, aren't you? You have a rough night or something?"

Blood rushed to his face. "Just here for the bird seed. I'm sorry, ma'am. Have a nice day."

He hurried into the crowd, doing his best not to turn back and look at the lady who chuckled as he left the store. He should have never tried to play secret agent in the nature store. What was he thinking?

He hurled the massive sack of bird seed onto his shoulder and marched to the food court, which smelled of hot dogs and funnel cakes. Children laughed and ran toward the carousel, fragments of cotton candy hanging from their mouths. He chose a bench near a trash can and set the bird seed on the ground. He watched parents stand in line with strollers before boarding the carousel. Mothers gossiped about the latest celebrities and movies Austin had never heard of before. A lot had changed since he went to Tizona and Tarton's Junction, he thought.

A mother sat next to him for a few minutes, watching her child ride the carousel. She stood and left, arguing with a man Austin assumed was her husband.

He folded his arms across his chest. Sharkey had told him to just sit here, but he didn't say for how long. Was Sharkey going to drive around the parking lot until he came out there? He kicked the sack of bird seed. Would he have to bring this stupid sack of seed?

A man in a bright yellow shirt with black flowers sat next to him. He wore a white baseball cap and large, round sunglasses. He waved at a child on the carousel, who didn't wave back. Burying his hand into a bag of popcorn, he stuffed an entire handful into his mouth. "Don't look now," the man said with a mouth full of popcorn, "but it is good to see you again."

Austin's eyes widened. *That voice...*

He cleared his throat and forced himself not to look at the man. "I see."

Stuffing another handful of popcorn into his mouth, the man yanked out a cell phone from his shirt. "I'm your contact," he said into the phone. "Just act natural."

Austin couldn't place the voice. He twiddled his thumbs. "Have we met?"

"I'm disappointed in you, Austin." He made a clicking sound with his tongue. "After all, we did live together."

His head jerked to the side. "Stetson?"

"Easy," Stetson Levine said softly. "You'll blow my cover."

His jaw dropped. "How?"

Stetson snorted and pretended to work on his cell phone. "Not everyone who left Tizona Campus was sent home or expelled. We all aren't meant to be pilots. Some of us were recognized for other talents."

"You work in Intelligence now?"

He nodded. "Bottom of the totem pole, but moving up. I volunteered for this assignment though. I wanted to see you again. Nice job with the bird seed lady."

He shoved his hands into his pockets. "She's not with you?"

"Her name's Krista. She lives a few miles from here and has worked in that store since her friend Sherry opened it twelve years ago."

Austin rolled his eyes. "That's just great."

They watched the children play for a moment while Stetson typed into his phone. Austin thought back to the days on Tizona Campus. Stetson had been a helpless soul, cast adrift in a sea of angry, pushy students. Austin had wanted to help him when the other guys in the dorm threatened Stetson to cheat on an exam, but he didn't. Soon after, Stetson had been removed from the school.

"I'm sorry," Austin whispered.

"I'm not. You did the best you could. I'll never forget it. You're the only friend I've ever had." Stetson placed the popcorn bag on the bench between them. "Inside this bag you'll find your instructions."

Austin pulled the bag closer to his leg.

Stetson placed the phone to his ear again. "Tell Sharkey Star Runners are being targeted by Phantoms."

"Phantoms? What are they?"

"He'll know," he said in a deep, confident tone he never had when they were roommates. "I don't have time to explain, but let's just say they're mercenaries. The kind you don't want to mess with."

"What do they want?"

"It seems they want to disrupt our operations here on Earth. We don't know why, yet. I can tell you these guys are professional, well-equipped, and expensive. Whoever hired them means business."

He grimaced. "We got away. Are we safe now?"

"You won't be safe until you get to a government location. Your instructions will explain everything."

"Is Dax Rodon doing this?"

For the first time, Stetson looked at him. Austin saw his own reflection in the sunglasses.

"Follow your instructions and everything will be fine." Stetson nodded. "It was good to see you again, my friend."

"Wait," he said, "there's so much I still want to know."

"I know," Stetson said calmly, "but there isn't time. Sit here for another two minutes and then go to your car. Goodbye, Austin."

Stetson stood and strolled over to a hotdog stand, his sandals flopping. He bought an early lunch and disappeared into the crowd.

Austin waited as instructed, thinking about his former roommate and wondering what the past year and a half had been like for him.

Swinging the bird seed over his shoulder, Austin hurried to the parking lot.

"Where is this place?" Austin asked, pulling the visor down to shield his eyes from the sunlight beaming through the front windshield. He looked down at the information Stetson—now Agent Levine—had put in the popcorn bag. The crumpled paper, with numbers stretched out like a bar code, meant nothing to Austin.

However, Sharkey had nodded when he glanced at the paper. He drove away from the outlet mall, heading north on the two-lane highway winding through the forests and mountains of North Georgia. Mom and Kadyn passed out in the back seat. Kadyn leaned back, her mouth hanging open. Mom crumpled against the door, her arm folded up like a pillow against the glass.

"Not far off this highway," Sharkey said. "We should be there soon. If we're not being followed."

Tingles prickled on his neck. Austin glanced at the side mirror, seeing nothing but empty road. "Followed? You don't think this is over?"

Sharkey looked at him, his dark eyes hard. "You really believe that was it?"

He looked out the front window. "No."

"Neither do I." Sharkey shifted in his seat, his gaze lowering as he gripped the steering wheel. "Whoever launched that attack back there means business. Once we're stationary, I'll check in with Command. Something tells me all the Earth-bound Star Runners are having a hell of a night."

Austin sighed. He thought of Ryan Bean. After only a short time chatting on the plane and over one cup of coffee, Ryan had become a brother-in-arms. It was a camaraderie among the Star Runners he had seen on Tarton's Junction when they marched down corridors. They moved as one, even when they were not in the ships. And now Austin was one of them.

A sick twist penetrated his gut.

An unseen force attacked his family and friends, both on Earth and beyond. They must be stopped.

"Do you have any idea who hired these Phantoms?" Austin asked, rubbing his chin as he watched the landscape pass.

Sharkey's gaze darted to Austin. "Who said anything about Phantoms?"

"Agent Levine did. Said the attackers were Phantoms."

Sharkey slowed the car. "Be very clear. Are you sure he said that? Was he very certain the attackers were Phantoms?"

Austin looked at the road, replaying Stetson's conversation from earlier that morning. "He seemed pretty sure, sir."

Sharkey sighed, turning back to the road. He accelerated faster than before, the engine straining up a hill. "Then this most definitely is not over.

"What are Phantoms?" Austin asked, not sure he wanted to hear the answer.

"Mercs. Bounty hunters, sometimes, but there's not much difference in the two. They are hired guns, killers. Very professional, most of them ex-military who couldn't deal with peace time when their tour was up or simply saw the money and went for it."

"You don't think they're Zahl agents, do you?"

"I don't think even Zahl agents would use off-world tech like those masked rifles. Not because they have morals or anything like that, but they wouldn't risk a dark Legion world getting their hands on technology that could give them a jump. Most in the Zahl Empire believe our policy toward dark worlds makes us weak."

"You don't?"

"When a world comes willingly into the Legion's embrace, they're part of a family. They come to love the Legion and gladly do their part."

Austin remembered his conversation with Bean. "Then why do we recruit from dark worlds? If we are so benevolent and good, why do the recruiting?"

"Because the galaxy cannot wait. We need personnel—*especially* Star Runners."

"What does the Zahl Empire do that's so different?"

Sharkey hesitated. "When they see a dark world they need or want, they take it. Sure, they'll make contact with the natives of the planet, give them terms to join the empire. If they agree, good for them. If not, well, it's not pretty."

"Guess I should be glad Earth is in Legion territory."

"Be very glad," said without delay. "Be a much different life for you if the Zahl Empire came knocking on Earth's doorstep."

Austin turned to Sharkey. "You have a strong opinion about this, Chief."

Sharkey grimaced. "I grew up on a dark world."

Austin blinked. "You did?"

"Yes. In what is now Zahlian space. A planet called Codara." He paused, clenching his jaw. "My mother, father, and little brother were killed in the initial attack when my people refused to bow to the invaders. They were at first heralded as a new era for Codara. That didn't last long."

"What happened?"

"The war was devastating, but short. The Zahlian Regional Governor leading the conquest, a man named Tulin, had no mercy.

He seemed to love the blood, the carnage carried out on my people. Our technology simply couldn't compete. My uncle led a resistance force for a short time. I joined him. I was only a teenager." He tensed, his face contorting. "After his execution, the younger guerrilla troops were sold into slavery. I was being transported by a slave ship near the border when a Legion patrol intercepted it and rescued us."

"I had no idea, Chief. I'm sorry."

Sharkey looked at him, a lopsided grin forming on his face. "I'm not. I'd be dead if a Legion flyboy like you hadn't decided to investigate the slavers' ship."

Movement from the back seat caught his eye. Austin turned back to Kadyn, who pressed against the passenger door with her face obscured from view.

"Hey," he said, touching her shoulder as he leaned between the front seats. "You okay?"

She turned around, her face damp with tears. "I'm sorry. I don't know what to do. I'm scared."

"I know. Can you sleep?"

She shook her head. "I can't. I can't believe this is real."

"That sounds familiar."

"Really?"

He nodded. "Sure. It took me a while, too. I've come to accept the strange and unbelievable over the past year. The world is not what I thought it was." He watched the rural land pass the window for a moment. "But I never thought my past would crash into my present the way it has today. I though these two parts of my life would stay separate, you know?"

He looked at his mother, who had pulled away from the window, her eyes drowsy.

"I didn't want to have to tell either of you," he said. "Not like this. I wanted to protect you from this because...I'll admit sometimes I wish I didn't know what I know. There has been a little part of me lately that has been wishing everything was just normal. I guess this proves you can't always get what you want."

"I'm proud of you," Mom said. "I don't pretend to understand all of this, but I am still proud of you."

"You *should* be proud," Sharkey cut in. "Your son saved the life of two veteran pilots while putting his own at risk. It's the reason he was able to come home early. He earned his wings and has become quite the story in the Legion Navy."

He pulled his knees together and sat up. "I think that's enough, Chief."

"That is wonderful news," his mother said, her voice straining.

"What's wrong?" he asked.

She paused. "I always knew you'd grow up to find success, but this...this is a little tough for a mom."

"Why?"

"I don't want anything bad to happen to you."

Austin reached back and squeezed her hand. "I know exactly how you feel."

8

"Zaka tawa!"

The voice rumbled down the cavern, bouncing off the walls like a thunderclap.

The group of prisoners rose from the cave floor, grumbling to anyone who would listen. The new guard, a bulging mass of humanity with a scarred left eye and bushy black beard like a fungus, had been riding the prisoners for the past day. Josh had recognized the voice and the damaged eye as the pirate who had incapacitated him on the day he had been captured.

Josh wondered where Rodon found these specimens of lowly humans. Did he have a cesspool to choose from? How did the Tyral pirates fill their ranks?

The other prisoners called the man "Cyclops," but wouldn't dare say it loud enough for the overseer to hear. After seeing Cyclops beat a man to death for falling down in the rock pits, it wasn't worth it.

After handing out tiny, rusted translators to the ragtag group, Cyclops led the men down the same corridor they had been walking every day for at least the past month. However, they did not stop in the Lutimite pits this time. The day before, they'd worked once again in the rocks until their muscles ached and their mouths went dry.

During their grueling shift, six pirate fighters flew over their heads and left the hangar. They returned hours later, their hulls battered and bruised with laser burns. A Legion merchant ship limped into the hangar near their pit. Two gaping holes in the hull signified the ship had been boarded and captured. Rather than take prisoners, however, it seemed the pirates had vented the passengers and crew directly into space.

They must have enough of a workforce.

Pirates off-loaded supply crates from the merchant ship. Josh overheard their discussions about stockpiling supplies, but heard no details. Why would the pirates be hoarding reserves? Captain Braddock always said the pirates stole enough for the short term, but rarely took surplus in fear of other gangs stealing it. This resulted in the repeated raids. If they were amassing supplies and other goods, what had changed?

One thing they were not taking in was slaves. Guess they had all the labor they needed, he thought. Now, they were going to make them work even harder in the Lutimite pits until there was nothing left. Delmar had said he worried they were nearly finished with the work in the asteroid. If there wasn't work to do, Rodon might decide it was their turn to take a walk in space.

Instead, Cyclops led them to a transport in the main hangar. Dozens of crates as large as a car neatly lined the deck. Josh glanced at the containers, saw a stenciled script burned into the sides. He couldn't read the language, but the crates looked far too official to be something the Tyral Pirates created.

"It's time to eat, you worthless sacks," Cyclops grumbled. "Get on board."

The landing ramp lowered.

"Hey!"

Josh turned to see Rodon strolling toward the group.

"Wait here," Cyclops said to the prisoners.

Rodon leaned in close to his subordinate, but Josh could hear some of the words.

"Our benefactor...more should be arriving today," Rodon whispered.

"Yes, sir," Cyclops said. "I will be back by then."

Josh frowned. Benefactor? Who would be supporting a pirate gang leader? He thought back to the latest news regarding Rodon and his pirates, their mysterious successes and their uncanny ability to have more technology and weapons of war than the Legion ever planned to combat in Quadrant Eight. Yes, he thought, a benefactor would make sense and explain the great deal of troubles now facing the Legion in this area of their territory. In fact, it might be the missing puzzle piece.

Of course, this led him back to the original question: Who would support the Tyral Pirates?

Rodon focused on the prisoners. "Been a pleasure having you here, gentlemen. Enjoy the rest of your days, however long that will last." He laughed and walked back to his control room at the hangar's edge.

As they filed into the transport ship with seats lining both walls and facing one another, Josh sat down, wondering what Cyclops meant by saying it was time to eat. Maybe he didn't want to know.

Waylon nestled his large frame into the seat across from Josh. He nodded when their eyes met. He returned the gesture, glad such a monstrous man no longer wanted to kill him. They had not spoken since their exchange, but Josh knew Waylon spent his time planning the means of their escape. For the first time since arriving on the asteroid base, it seemed the Tyral Pirates needed their slave workforce elsewhere.

Or they planned to jettison the entire group into space.

Either way, Josh's spirits lifted the moment the transport's engines rumbled to life. He didn't care where they ended up as long as it was away from that rock.

"Glad we're leaving," he said under his breath.

Delmar glanced at him. "Tired of being on that asteroid?"

"Aren't you?"

"I suppose, but I don't know what awaits us."

"True." He allowed the sound of the engines to relax him. "Why do the men call our new guard Cyclops?"

"The myth of the one-eyed monster."

"You have that myth, too?"

"I think everyone does. It's very old."

"I know, but I thought it was based on Earth mythology. You know, from Greece."

Delmar bit on his dirty fingernails. "Not all stories originate on Earth."

"I guess not."

"My people believe there was once a planet of giants who had only one eye, so it's not that unusual for me."

Josh looked at him. "Your people? And who are your people?"

Delmar gazed up at the ceiling, a pleasant expression forming on his relaxed face. "I am Shoborian."

"What does that mean?"

He smiled. "Oh, Josh, you should see my planet. My people have explored more of the galaxy than any other faction. We believe in peace and exploration, documenting everything so we can expand our knowledge of the universe. Somewhere along the line, my people must have found evidence of a one-eyed giant."

Josh snorted. "We were told in flight school there was no such thing as aliens."

"Of course they would say such things."

"Why?"

Wrinkles deepened on Delmar's cheeks. "To keep you focused."

As the transport rocked, Josh fought back a wave of nausea. "Are they going to kill us?" he asked softly.

"We'll find out soon enough."

"How did you get caught?" Josh asked.

Delmar appeared to consider the question. "I was traveling on the edge of Legion space, conducting long-range scans of the space beyond the Fringe when they got me."

"I'm sorry."

"So am I." He closed his eyes. "Get some rest, son. We don't know when we'll get another chance."

As Delmar tried to sleep, Josh thought of flight school and the history of the galaxy. Never did any of the instructors speak of aliens or even a faction known as the Shoborians, but perhaps Delmar was correct in his belief the Legion wanted their Star Runners focused? Or perhaps Delmar had a few screws loose himself?

Josh fell asleep as he contemplated.

The flight felt like it took a few hours. Josh wasn't sure because his nap turned into a deep sleep once the transport left the asteroid field. The ship passed through no curves on the way, so wherever their destination, it was close enough for normal propulsion. After a rough trip when the ship must have passed through the atmosphere, the transport settled down. The interior lights flickered on and, for just a moment, it seemed just like any other flight Josh had taken in his life.

"Get moving you stinking lyker pellets!" Cyclops yelled. "Now!"

The transport door opened with a groan and slowly lowered, illuminating the vessel's interior with the brightest light Josh had seen in months. He squinted, reveling in the warmth touching his face. Air rushed into the transport, *real* air. It surrounded him, filled his lungs and rustled his matted hair. He hadn't thought about it before, but he hadn't inhaled true, atmospheric air since he left Earth.

Tingles rippled across his skin. He shuddered.

"Come on, son," Delmar said. "It's time to move."

The prisoners marched side-by-side into the open air. Brown grasslands stretched into infinity like a carpet. Low mountains covered in morning blue mist rolled on the horizon. Josh wanted to sprint across the fields, disappear into the hills, and jump into a frigid stream. He could build a cabin by a pond and live there forever. Forget about the Tyral Pirates, Rodon, the Legion, his parents—all of it.

Let it slip away.

Cyclops slapped the lead prisoner, directing him to a rickety, brown barn surrounded by a wooden fence. Goats, chickens, and cows dotted the area beside one side of the transport. On the other, rows of crops lined the land.

"Beautiful," Delmar said.

"Move it!" Cyclops shouted. "Fall into lines inside the fence! It's time you all started working for your food."

If Cyclops referred to the active snot soup they'd been eating, Josh didn't want to waste time creating it. The thought of it wiggling down his throat still made his stomach turn.

As they marched forward, Waylon moved in close. "This isn't good," he whispered.

"What do you mean?" he asked. "This is the greatest thing I've seen since we were taken—and we don't have to wear those steel cages over our heads anymore."

Waylon looked around. "You see any other ships? The idea was to steal a ship and escape. I don't think we'll go far on a cow."

"Give it time," he said, almost to convince himself. "We'll have our opening."

THE HOE PLUNGED deep into the soil. The movement made a squishy sound. Two dozen other prisoners did the same, again and again. The sun's orange light baked everything on the land, which stretched as flat as a hardwood floor to distant mountains.

The transport remained where it had landed earlier, a few hundred yards from the collection of barns and the fenced area for livestock. Cyclops had moved the prisoners to the fields shortly after they arrived and forced them into hard labor. The sun invigorated Josh and the other prisoners, and they all moved faster and more energetically than before, hopping from one area to the next. He didn't seem to be alone in enjoying a breath of fresh air.

Thunder echoed, the sound bouncing off the land.

"Back to work!" Cyclops screamed for the tenth time in as many minutes. "Anyone looking to the sky will spend some time with the lash!"

Josh kept his eyes on the soil. He turned the dirt as another boom cut through the air. Waylon worked next to him, grumbling.

"Something's coming through atmo."

Delmar cleared his throat in acknowledgement. "Sounds like a smaller craft, fighters maybe."

"Fighters?" Josh asked. "Hang on."

He pulled on the hoe twice as if the soil wouldn't release the tool. Crouching to his knees, he scooped the dirt around. Waylon and Delmar stepped closer to him, shielding him from view. Josh shot a glance to the heavens, using his hand to block the sunlight.

When he stood, the other men glared at him.

"Well?" Waylon barked, his voice rattling like he had something stuck in his throat.

Josh kept his gaze toward the ground. "Four fighters descending, looks like a mismatch of craft. Tridents and some others I don't recognize. Standard for the Tyral Pirates."

"Four?" Waylon looked at Delmar. "What do you think?"

Delmar remained silent as he worked. "This could work. We'll have to see how long they stay."

Four fighters coming to this backwater planet. Either it was Rodon coming by for an inspection of one piece of his little empire, or it was a Tyral raiding party coming for a respite from all the pillaging.

Minutes later, the fighters formed into a semi-circle two hundred feet above the farming compound. The craft lowered in unison, sending a tornado of dust and pebbles around the area.

When they landed, Josh watched the best he could while pretending to continue working the soil.

Four pilots exited the craft. Other workers emerged from the structures to greet them. One pilot stood out from the rest, his clothing bright red even from this distance. The brightly colored pilot pointed as if giving orders, and the workers ran in the ordered direction.

Josh rubbed sweat from his eyes. Using his hands to cover his mouth, he said, "Might be Rodon."

"Here?" Waylon asked. "Are you sure?"

"Not at this distance, but it could be him."

"It doesn't matter who it is," Delmar said. He locked eyes with Waylon, then Josh. "They brought spacecraft. That's all that matters."

JOSH'S MUSCLES burned and ached. His shoulders throbbed whenever he lifted his arms above his head. His lower back flashed with a stabbing pain as if bones rubbed together beneath the skin. The others had ceased all conversation long after the sun reached its zenith, and they toiled in silence in the intense heat. The hot temperatures pulsated in waves like they worked in a furnace. The energy provided by being in the actual outside air dissipated by late afternoon when the sun dipped low on the flat horizon. The blue sky, flawless like a turquoise stone, faded to black in a gorgeous transition. Stars flickered into view like sparkling flecks of ice on a black highway.

His mind had wandered during the grueling work. He thought of Austin. His thoughts drifted to another place, another time, when he'd played football, hit on girls, and logged in to play Star Runners every night with his best friend. He thought of Kadyn, the one love who would never be, and the afternoons he'd stolen a glance at her while the three of them drank coffee. Austin accused him once of staring at Marilyn Monroe, but Josh had really been looking at Kadyn. When he nearly got caught staring, he always turned to Marilyn. He'd stressed out about life then, worrying about games and girls, classes and scholarships.

"Stop!" Cyclops boomed, his good eye wide. "Drop your tools and fall into line where you stand. We're heading back to the barn. Once there, you will sleep. We didn't finish our goals today, you lousy sacks of dung. No dinner for you. Perhaps this will teach you to work instead of spending the day lazing in the sun. Let's move it!"

Josh's stomach turned with the mention of dinner, but the pains throughout the rest of his body took over. He tossed the rusted tool into the field, knowing he would return at first light, and shuffled his feet into line. Waylon bumped shoulders with him, his large frame gasping for breath.

The two lines of prisoners marched forward. Cyclops and his minions barked orders from both sides. One guard smacked two men near the front of the line. Josh flinched at the sound of skin smashing into skin. War was brutal, he knew that much. But fighting in spacecraft at least shielded you from the horrors of death and suffering. In fact, he struggled to remind himself shooting down a fighter also ended a life. Destroying a bandit in a dogfight meant more than a kill marking on the side of a Trident.

But what did it matter? *He might never fly a Trident again...*

"You two," Cyclops pointed at Josh and Waylon. "Step out of line and come over here."

His breath froze like ice water in his lungs. "Me?"

"Yeah, you!"

Josh stepped out of the line with Waylon next to him. Cyclops raised his hand and waited for the rest of the prisoners to trudge by. What did he want? Did he somehow know they planned an escape? Had he seen something to doubt that they were just beaten prisoners?

"I saw you two lovebirds talking earlier today," Cyclops said in a remarkably calm tone, his good eye separately taking in both of them. "Don't even bother denying it."

He spit on Josh's leg, a brown slushy liquid sliding down his skin like a slimy snake. He closed his eyes for a moment, trying to hide his disdain for the man.

He shifted his weight. "It didn't affect our work, sir."

"So, you admit you were talking? What was the big topic for today? You braiding each other's hair later? Hmm?" He slapped Waylon across the face and turned to Josh. "Or will this one hold you when the sun goes down and it gets cold?"

Josh opened his mouth to speak, but Cyclops hit him hard enough to see stars.

"You just lost your dinner privileges tomorrow as well," he grumbled. "Tonight, I want both of you refueling those ships and waxing the hulls until I can see my face. I want it done before daylight. If the boss complains about his fighter, I will be the least of your worries. Got it?"

Josh nodded. *So Dax Rodon was here,* he thought. "Yes, sir."

He glanced at Delmar, who nodded.

Guards led Waylon and Josh to the fighters. The hulls appeared to be stitched together with chewing gum and dirt. He counted three colors of metal wielded together in the first vessel. As he walked closer, he noticed the fighter's long narrow nose and the wing bristling with an assortment of weapons like the pilot couldn't choose his favorite. Actually, this was probably the truth. Pirates were not known for their failure to shoot back, and with wings holding this amount of weaponry, Josh believed it.

"You are to wash and clean these fighters till they shine!" Cyclops shouted. "When you're done, you'll refuel 'em and, if there is still time before daylight, you can catch some sleep before you go back to the fields. Your choice. Get to work."

Waylon and Josh began with a modified Trident. Using a ladder, they washed the entire ship. The pirates grilled an animal of some kind a dozen yards away. Josh shivered at the sizzling aroma of cooking meat. It smelled of barbecues and afternoon baseball games in the lush grass of a summer backyard under a sky blue enough to make you squint. Mom and Dad used to marvel at those afternoons. Austin would come over when they were young, and they would play until the sun set behind the trees. Even then, they would continue whatever game they played in the dark unless they were called into the house. Mom might order a pizza or let them rent a movie, and they would spend the night seeing who could stay up the latest.

He shook his head, focusing on the task at hand. If he ever wanted the chance to have any life again, he had to survive this first.

The guards finished eating and sat around a fire under the starry sky. Some dozed where they finished eating while others talked quietly, the weapons never far from their reach.

The black sky lightened in the distance. How short were the

nights on this planet? Better yet, how long had they been working on this project?

"I don't know what's going on, but something has changed," a guard grumbled, breaking through the quiet. "Rodon's up to something."

"'Bout time if you ask me," another responded. "We've been raiding freighters for so long, we need to hit something big to get our share. I'm getting tired of doing this without any scratch to show for it."

Josh tried to keep up his work and listen at the same time. The two guards talking must have been the only still awake, but he didn't want to draw attention to himself.

"Scratch is coming, for sure."

"Why do you say that?"

"Word has it we've been hoarding our goods for a surprise raid on a Legion planet."

"Legion? That's suicide."

"No, not this one. Heard the other guys saying this one's dark. Should be a cakewalk if we have the supplies. Have you seen all the stuff coming across the border for us? Never seen so much merchandise coming into camp. It's like a holiday. More supposedly on the way, too."

"When?"

"I don't know. Soon."

Josh's eyes widened. He finished cleaning his second fighter and looked over at Waylon who was fueling the second vessel. Had he heard the guards as well? If he understood, the Tyral Pirates planned to attack a Legion dark world soon. He glanced back to the guards by the fire and noticed their gaze focused on the smoldering embers.

Josh swallowed and strolled toward Waylon. Waylon leaned against the fighter, his eyes closed tight.

"Waylon, did you hear that?" Josh asked.

"Every word," he said, his eyes still shut. "I have a plan."

"What is it?" he asked, kneeling down as if he worked on the fuel pumper.

"We need to act beaten, defeated."

He snorted. "That won't be hard.

Waylon didn't smile. "When they think they have their perfect, obedient slave force, we take these fighters and escape."

He nodded. "We need to do it fast. I should warn my people."

"Not my business. Besides, there's no sense talking about that, yet," he said, disconnecting the fuel line as he topped off the ship. "Gotta get out of here first."

9

The winding Georgia mountain roads stretched for miles. When Sharkey advised they were close, Austin thought he meant it. After sliding back and forth across the seat for what seemed like forever, he wondered if "close" meant something different where Sharkey came from.

As the day wore on, Austin's head pounded. He hadn't slept since he'd arrived in Atlantis yesterday.

Was it only yesterday?

His last true sleep had been on Tarton's Junction the night before he left. Skylar had come to say goodbye to him. She seemed sad. He couldn't believe after all the time they'd spent at the Tizona School they were now on their own. She would soon finish her training, and he wouldn't be there to see it happen. He needed to get a message to her and Bear, let them know he was all right. Of course, he didn't know if he believed it himself.

Ryker would be in the midst of rehab by now, on a world known as Oma on the other side of the galaxy. Austin wondered if he would ever see Oma. Maybe someday. He gazed out the window, thinking of the last time they'd spoken. She had seemed so weak, so fragile on the infirmary bed. She no longer had the emotional wall in front of her, protecting her from the evils of the world. She had gripped his hand softly. He closed his eyes, picturing her face.

"You awake, Lieutenant?" Sharkey asked.

"Yes, sir. Of course."

"Activate the shroud again, will you?"

Austin opened the glove box and did as instructed. "Trouble?"

"Hope not."

Activating the shrouding technology, Austin knew the it could not remain on for hours at a time without a source of power greater than a car battery. Even in the Trident, the shroud took up most of the ship's power capacity. A shrouded craft could not maintain a laser or shield charge for long, and engines would not operate at peak efficiency. He figured the car had the same principle, minus the lasers and shields.

Sharkey eased into a long, winding turn. Boulders loomed at the side of the road, casting dark shadows on the pavement. A red reflector glistened on a tree. He applied the brakes and turned right, the tires bouncing onto a two-path dirt road. Long weeds brushed against the bottom of the car and nearly concealed the view beyond.

"Shroud off," Sharkey said.

"Got it." Austin pressed the button, the light around the car growing brighter. "It's off."

The thick forest canopy blocked most of the faint sunlight. Sunbeams shot down through the leaves in spots, illuminating the rotting wood, moss, and mushrooms of the forest floor. The car bounced, the tires bouncing into a deep hole in the dirt road.

"Sorry," Sharkey said, glancing back to the passengers in the back seat. "We obviously haven't had to use this place in quite some time."

"And what is this 'place'?" Austin asked as he grabbed the door handle in preparation for the next bounce.

"A safe house."

"I gathered that, but what is it? We need to contact Command."

"I know," he grumbled, negotiating a sharp turn in the small path. "Part of Revelation Protocol prohibits open communication anywhere but a safe house. These places were set up by the government decades ago and utilize landlines to avoid, or at least limit, the chances of interception."

"Landlines? You mean actual cables going to Base Prime?"

"Exactly. When most of the world transitioned to cellular networks, miles and miles of analog lines were left dormant and sold cheap. The Legion government has been scooping these up for a day like this."

"Oh." Austin turned back. "You guys okay?"

Mom and Kadyn nodded. Black circles puffed under his mother's eyes, and Kadyn's burned red. He sighed. While he had been under stress, they had experienced a long, bizarre night. He remembered his first introduction to the "real world" after he was transported to California. Although it happened fast, he'd had Nubern to ease the transition. His mother and Kadyn had been forced to adjust to this reality while running from unknown attackers. He tried to show strength for both of them, but fatigue started to weigh on him. His hands shook as the image of masked laser bolts sizzling over his head flashed repeatedly in his mind. What if they had hit Kadyn? Or Mom?

He shuddered.

After more than ten minutes of traveling through dense vegetation, the path opened to a clearing large enough for a wooden cabin with an outbuilding behind it sealed with a silver padlock. The grass reached as high as the car doors. Tree branches stretched overhead, concealing the cabin from the air. Sharkey turned off the car and the four of them sat in silence until Austin's ears hummed with a ringing sound.

Sharkey exhaled. "We made it. Looks like we're in the clear for now." He turned to Austin. "You think you could patch up my shoulder? It's burning."

His lips parted. "Uh, okay. Let's go."

"I could help if you need it, sweetie," Mom said.

He smiled, cocking his head toward his mother. "She's a nurse."

"I know," Sharkey said. "Let's move."

With thoughts of his basic first aid course on Tarton's Junction running through his mind, Austin opened the door. The quiet of the forest surprised him. No air conditioners or the constant drone of traffic ruined the tranquil landscape. A bird called from far away to break the peace. He took in a breath of the musty, damp air.

He opened the back door and helped Kadyn to her feet. Her face was pale and she grimaced as she stood in her dirt-stained pink pajamas. Her eyes were barely open as she hugged herself, and strands of curly hair covered her right eye.

"Maybe there's something inside for you to wear," Austin said, gripping her trembling hand.

Mom slid across the backseat and stood without assistance.

"My head's feeling better," she said. "If it really was carbon monoxide, you two found me at the right time."

Austin touched her shoulder. "I think so."

Gripping his blackened shoulder, Sharkey walked across the thigh-high grass still wet with morning dew. Water droplets splattered his uniform and darkened the Tizona blue. He produced a key card from his pocket and waved it in front of what looked like a doorbell. The button came to life with a yellow light and transitioned to green. An ancient wooden door opened to reveal darkness. One-by-one, lights inside the cabin popped on and buzzed to life.

"Let me guess, Chief," Austin said, forcing a smile, "there's an underground room with sim pods just waiting for us."

He snorted. "Hardly."

The cabin's antiquated exterior disguised the modern technology inside. Against the wall, a black radio with a headset and a microphone sat on a workbench covered with cobwebs in the corner. Two couches faced one another in the center of the room with a fireplace at one end and a table at the other. A green freezer with a row of cabinets lined the back wall near a secondary rear door. The room's sole window faced the clearing with the Tizona car.

"Cozy," Austin said.

"I'll say," Mom said.

Sharkey shuffled over to the couch and collapsed. He grunted and winced. Austin moved over to the chief and cut off his blackened uniform sleeve. The skin beneath had been torn apart, twisted and burnt. He winced.

"I know it looks bad," Sharkey said, his eyes still closed. "It could have been worse."

"Mom, please check the cabinet for a first aid kit and bring some cold water."

"I got it," she said, her tone shifting into her nurse mode.

"Kadyn, sit down and try to rest," Austin said, picking out pieces of fabric melted on Sharkey's wound. "We may not get another chance for a while."

"What does that mean?" Kadyn asked, grunting as she stretched her legs on the couch. "Am I stuck here?"

He frowned. "Well, you're not stuck."

"Then can I call my parents?"

"It's not safe, yet, to use any devices. I'm sure your parents are fine."

Mom returned with a first aid kit and popped open the silver box. "I've never seen anything like this," she said.

Austin remembered his first aid training and grabbed the steel cylinder. "I have. This reforms tissue."

Her jaw dropped. "You can't do that."

"I know I can't." He held up the cylinder. "But *this* can."

Mom watched as he worked, applying the knowledge he had learned from his training to patch up Sharkey. She smiled.

"I'm so proud of you, Austin."

"Thanks, Mom." He looked at her. "You don't know how many times I wanted to tell you about all this."

"I know you would have if you could."

"I didn't tell you at first because it was against the rules, but later I wanted to keep you safe," he said, his attention on Sharkey's treatment. "But Nubern made an offer when I left I had hoped you would consider. That was, of course, before all of this happened."

She blinked, shifting her head to the side. "What offer? For me?"

"Yeah. He had said you might be able to join a Legion Medical Frigate or something like it."

She gazed over his head into nothingness. "On a ship? In space? I don't know."

"I know how you feel," he said, nodding. "I didn't know, either."

Austin focused his attention on Sharkey's wound. It took less than an hour for Sharkey's arm to transition from blackened and burnt to hairless and light pink. He wiped sweat from his brow.

"Nice job, Lieutenant," Sharkey said, his voice weak. "If nobody minds, I'd like to take a few minutes."

"Not at all, Chief."

"Remember, no phone calls. Lieutenant, I did my job and got you and your contacts to safety. You need to contact Command and see what the next step will be." He pointed at the radio behind him. "Go ahead and use that."

"Got it. Get some rest, sir."

Sharkey drifted to sleep within seconds, his nose whistling softly as the sunlight filtered in through the cracked window. Austin nodded to his mother and they moved to the table. He glanced at Kadyn, who sat in silence on the second couch as she stared out the window with a blanket pulled around her shoulders.

"She'll be okay," Mom said as she slid into the wooden table. "She's in shock. I know how she feels."

He sighed and leaned on the table, resting his head on his hands. "I'm so sorry, Mom. This isn't how I imagined my homecoming."

"Oh, I'm not talking about just this." She looked at her hands. "I remember when your father told me he had cancer. Hit me like nothing else." She shook her head and held his hand. "I missed you. So, give me the whole story. I leave you at the gate and drive back to Atlanta. What happens then? When did you know your school was what it was?"

Austin laughed, but realized she meant what she said. "Well, part of me knew you were right when Nubern first came to visit. Remember you thought it was a military school? I feel kind of stupid now not knowing this from the beginning, but I was too excited to be in college—I didn't care what they called me!"

He told her everything. Describing the early days of Tizona and the time he'd actually thought it was an eccentric private school brought back more memories than he expected. He told of meeting Skylar and struggling to make their physical requirements. He explained the difficult classes and how the "rec room" was actually a simulation room. Discussing the Gauntlet was something he would have rather forgotten. But he enjoyed reliving the night they left Tizona on the tube transport to California and, of course, he could hardly wait to tell her about the first time he saw Atlantis and the glowing creatures floating above them in the depths of the Pacific Ocean.

Through it all, she gazed at him in silence. "My goodness, Austin."

"Yeah, when I was transported to Atlantis, which is a base on the floor of the Pacific Ocean, I think I was in shock for a week after that. It's the busiest Legion port on Earth. You wouldn't believe it. There's a bubble in the main room where you can see the sea life and, well, you're going to see it if you take Nubern up on his offer."

She leaned over the table. "And then what?"

"I was transported to Tarton's Junction, the primary space station in Quadrant Eight. That's where Earth is."

She nodded. "I see. What was that Sharkey said about you saving lives? Can you tell me about that?"

He swallowed. "It was the end of my training. I didn't save..."

He paused. He heard Ryker's screams on the radio, the smack of Nubern's helmet on the canopy as the Trident spun out of control, and the fire...the explosion taking two of his comrades.

"There was a girl," he said, his voice wavering. He closed his eyes.

She rubbed his hand. "It's okay, honey, you don't have to tell me about it."

"No, it's all right." He cleared his throat. "There was...a little Star Runner named Etti Mar." He paused for a long moment. He opened his mouth several times, but the words wouldn't come. "She had red hair."

He wiped his face and looked away. He tried to continue the story, but his voice cracked. He didn't realize how hard it would be to talk about all of this, to relive it.

"Maybe another time." She squeezed his hand, her eyes brimming. "I can only imagine what you've seen."

She stood and stepped over to the kitchen area. "Let me check this fridge and see if there is anything I can make us."

He cleared his throat. "I need to contact Command."

Glad for the distraction, Austin fired up the electronics. The equipment seemed archaic compared to what he worked with on Tarton's Junction, but the simple interface made it easy. The radio's computer rumbled to life, emerald letters flashing across the screen. Brushing away the spider webs, he pulled the microphone with the large black wind guard closer to his mouth. He slipped on the massive headphones, heard crackling static.

"Post Nine-One-Nine, this is Base Prime," a female voice said into his headset. "We have received your activation. What is your SIT-REP, over?"

He leaned forward into the microphone. "Yes, this is Lieutenant Stone, call sign Rock."

"Reading you loud and clear, Rock."

"We have two officers and two civilians in need of transport."

"Civilians? Have they been briefed?"

He glanced at his mom, who searched through cabinets. "They're longer in the dark, Base Prime."

The operator paused. "Understood. Stand by."

He rapped his fingers on the workbench. Sharkey said they would get evacuated from this cabin, but he hadn't said how exactly this would happen. Perhaps the outbuilding had a tube transport?

"Rock? Do you copy?" the woman said, returning to the radio.

"I copy."

"Is your position secure?"

"For the moment."

"You will be evacuated under cover of darkness. ETA: Twelve hours."

Austin glanced at his watch. "I copy. Where is the extraction point?"

"Point A will be the cabin. If the need arrises, Point B will be the body of water one-point-five marks northwest of your position."

"I got it. Anything else we need to know?"

"Keep transmitting in the event we need to update your transport. Otherwise, stay low and stay quiet, Rock. We are coming."

His insides warmed. "I copy, Base Prime. Good to hear. Over and out."

He took off the headset.

"Here you go," Mom said, offering a hot cup of coffee. "You must be hurting if you need this half as much as I need mine."

Austin took the mug, allowing the steam to rush into his face. "You have no idea."

"There's some crackers, cans of beans, stuff like that." She shrugged. "No eggs, bacon, or pancakes today. Sorry."

"Oh, man, wouldn't that be great?" He smiled. "I'm very disappointed."

"I bet you are. Been a while since we had a breakfast like that together." She leaned against the counter. "I've been thinking about what you said about a medical spaceship. You know, I don't really have anything here. Since your father died...I've struggled to find my way. Does that make sense?"

"Yeah." Austin thought about what his life in high school might have been like had Dad survived. The world changed when he was diagnosed with cancer, turned upside down when he died. School and life didn't matter so much afterward. "Me, too."

She nodded. "I guess I never hid it very well."

"Mom." He waited until she looked at him. "You did great."

She sipped her coffee and turned to the window.

He took a drink and let the warmth run down his throat.

Kadyn dozed on one couch, her head tilted back. She must have passed out, he thought. Poor thing was overwhelmed. As soon as he was able, he would have to check into her parents or at least have the Legion do so. They owed her that much after ripping her from her house in the middle of the night, and then leaving her to wonder if her parents had been killed by these mysterious agents, these Phantoms.

Austin's brow lowered. At least two hostile agents had fired on Kadyn's house the night before, possibly more. Nubern said all Star Runners had been targeted by an unknown force. He didn't elaborate, but Austin wondered who funded the launch of a massive covert assassination mission to disrupt activities on Earth and other dark worlds in Quadrant Eight. It seemed too highbrow and too expensive for an organization like the Tyral Pirates, even though Rodon and his motley crew had been active in the quadrant since Austin joined the Legion Navy.

He finished the coffee and decided to walk around the area. Slipping his gun into the jacket, he left through the cabin's back door into the refreshing morning, careful not to wake Kadyn and Sharkey on the way out. He kicked through the wet grass toward the shack behind the cabin. Using Sharkey's key card, he unlocked the padlock and went inside, where he found three ATVs and an assortment of tools. He tinkered with the tool box, wishing he could be as talented as the mechanics on Tarton's Junction. He searched through tools he didn't quite understand. The still air and silence of the storage shack surrounded him. He straddled an ATV and took a deep breath. He closed his eyes and relished the moment of peace, milking it for all it was worth.

He strolled back to the cabin. The sun stretched into the sky and burned away the fog, the final white wisps twisting and curling between the thick weeds. He paused at the door and stared into the forest. He heard nothing, not even the traffic from the highway.

Sharkey still slept on the couch, but Kadyn smiled weakly as he entered. The blanket was around her shoulders and her knees were folded under her arms. Mom sat at the end of Sharkey's couch, just out of reach of his feet.

"Where ya been?" Mom asked.

"I checked out the storage building," Austin said softly. "We have ATVs back there."

"Oh," she said with a grin, "maybe we need to go for a ride."

"Maybe." Austin looked at Kadyn. "What do you think?"

Her face softened, but the grin faded the same as the morning fog outside. "I just want to go home."

He nodded and sat down on the couch next to her. "I know. I'm so sorry about all this."

"I know you couldn't help it," she said, sounding almost like the positive Kadyn from high school, but only for a moment. "I don't understand all of it. I keep thinking it's a dream."

"I understand. We'll get you back home as soon as we are able. We'll at least get you to your parents if your house is not okay."

"The house is okay," she said quickly. "The fire department got the fire out and saved it. The fire was just in the front. My parents are fine—I just want go home now."

Austin blinked, unsure if he understood what she had just said. "You sound so certain of that. That's good. Think positive."

"I am certain," she said, tilting her head to the side. "I checked it on my phone. I barely had any service, but I went to the Atlanta paper's site."

His stomach twisted. "You did that? You used your phone?"

She frowned. "Yeah. Why? Is something wrong with that? You said no calls."

Austin rubbed his face with both hands as he fought the urge to vomit on the floor. He glanced at Sharkey still asleep on the couch. He stood and hurried to the window facing the two-path road.

"When did you do that?" he asked.

"I don't understand—"

"*When*, Kadyn? I need to know."

She glanced at the front door. "While you and your mom were sitting at the table drinking coffee earlier this morning."

He rushed across the floor to stare out the back door.

"Austin, did I do something wrong?"

"No communication meant no cell phone use of any kind," he said, biting his lip. "Checking a website on your phone can be traced."

He pulled his gun out of his jacket. "I'm checking the perimeter. Wake Sharkey and get to the back of the cabin."

"But I—"

"Now!"

Leaving through the rear door, Austin stepped back into the daylight, but this time the forest did not seem so peaceful. Every tree concealed a potential attacker. The wind touched the leaves, rustling the plants. Blood rushed into his ears, pounding with each rapid heartbeat. He glanced at the pistol, thinking he should have brought something more substantial. Perhaps there was something in the storage building, he thought.

He sprinted. The padlock dropped open with Sharkey's card. He checked the ATVs, the tool boxes, and other containers lining the floor. He didn't know what he searched for, but suddenly, something didn't feel right. A tingle crawled down his back like a spider.

He moved outside, searching the forest again. The two-path road continued farther behind the cabin. It must lead to the lake Command was talking about, otherwise known as Point B.

Something clicked in the forest. Not a sound of nature, but a metal-on-metal *pop*.

He tensed, gun facing the ground. He lowered to rest on one knee. Was somebody watching? Or was his mind playing tricks on him?

Time passed. He didn't hear the sound again.

"Stupid," he said under his breath, sliding the pistol back into his jacket.

And you're supposed to be a Star Runner of the Legion Navy.

He cursed himself once more before shuffling back to the cabin.

An explosion rippled through the forest. A shockwave sent trees toppling. Burning leaves twirled and fell in fiery embers. An energy wave slapped him to the ground like a doll in a dog's mouth. He spun backward into the weeds and smashed into the storage structure. Pain flashed on his back and legs. He heard nothing but blood pumping in his ears. He focused to keep his eyes open.

Fighting back the darkness threatening to overtake him, he touched his ears, saw blood on his fingertips, and stood on wobbly legs. Smoldering flames burned on his jacket arms. He tore it off, throwing it to the ground.

The front of the cabin had disintegrated into a burning crater.

Mom.

He yanked his pistol from under his jacket. Keeping his head low, he sprinted to the rear of the cabin as laser bolts splattered into the Tizona car and the burning front door. Whoever had targeted the building was about to finish the job.

He burst through the back door. Black smoke poured into his face. He lowered to one knee and saw Sharkey, Kadyn, and Mom crawling on the floor toward him.

"Come on! Get out!" he yelled. "We need to fire up the ATVs!"

They coughed and convulsed on their way out. Austin remained at the back door, his gun focused through the raging fire. Through the flames, a wavering image of a man materialized near their car and peered into the back seat. His body shimmered and flashed like he wore a wet suit able to shift him in and out of visibility.

A shroud.

Turning away from the car, the shrouded man aimed his laser rifle into the cabin as he scanned the area. Austin squinted and watched in disbelief as two more men in similar suits appeared from the forest.

Austin shook his head. *The attackers wore personal shrouds.*

The attackers appearance normalized, a few remaining fingers of electricity dissipating from their arms, and Austin got his first clear look. They wore sleek black battle suits hugging their lean bodies and carried enhanced rifles across their chests. Exposed skin painted black and dark green concealed a good view of their faces. Without speaking, they dispersed to flank the cabin. He had to do something.

The lead man waved his arm, apparently ordering the other mercenaries around the building. Austin tensed.

He raised his pistol, his hands shaking as he aimed through the burning front half of the cabin. He exhaled, placed his finger on the trigger, and fired.

The bullet struck the attacker in the throat. With his eyes bulging, the mercenary fell back, writhing in pain. Austin spun around and leaned against the rear of the cabin. He had done it; he shot a man.

Without being able to see it, he knew the man's life bled out into the weed-filled ground.

Keeping low, Sharkey led the women to the storage building and slipped into the door.

Two more attackers hurried toward the storage building around the far side of the cabin and into Austin's field of fire. He emptied his clip. He fired wildly but struck another attacker who spun around like a top, disappearing into the weeds. He dropped down as a laser repeater counterattacked, spitting red bolts. The mercenaries no longer worried about using maskers. They were here to kill.

Austin pressed himself to the ground. The mercenaries did not know his location. Laser fire covered the area, striking the cabin, storage building, and trees. The world caught fire. Energy bolts sizzled the air from all directions. He stuck his face into the dirt beside the burning cabin. After ten seconds, the fire ceased.

He lifted his head, his ears still ringing from the explosion. Sweat rolled into his eyes. They would find him first, force him to be a pawn to lure the others into the clearing. Whoever they were, they would kill them all and leave their bodies in the woods.

A sudden rush of energy filled his veins. Grabbing the final clip from his pocket, he slapped it into the gun and waited for the attackers to claim their prize.

Footsteps pressed into the ground near him.

This is it.

More laser fire erupted, filling the air with the distinctive burning sound of laser bolts igniting the oxygen it passed through. This time, however, an engine crackled to life as the lasers fired. Rising to his elbows, Austin surveyed the scene.

Blazing fires completely engulfed the cabin, the heat surging across the clearing and burning his skin. Two ATVs burst through the storage building's wooden door, Sharkey at the lead with a rifle in hand. Ash coated his damp face. Kadyn wrapped her arms around Sharkey's waist, her face buried in his back. Sharkey blanketed the area with his own laser fire, the bolts dropping shocked mercenaries too slow to dive for cover.

Behind Sharkey was Austin's mother, driving like a bull rider unsure if they could hang onto the wild animal. Austin rose to one knee, his gun still trained on the yard now free of the attackers. Sharkey's fire had swept the mercenaries into cover for now.

The ATVs screeched to a halt.

"Get on!" Sharkey yelled.

With her skin covered in black soot, Mom shifted back on the ATV, allowing Austin room to drive.

"Where are we going?" he asked.

"Follow me," Sharkey said, his voice cool.

He accelerated away from the scene, the forest catching fire and thrusting plumes of smoke into the sky. Two stray laser bolts exploded into the trees as they fled, sending a shower of sparks falling in their path. Pulling back his wrist to accelerate, Austin followed Sharkey closely, his vision still blurred from the explosion. His eyes burned, but he pressed on. Hanging branches scratched at his face and arms as they sped through the forest. Mom gripped his shoulders tightly, her hands squeezing each time the ATV bounced over a dip in the road.

"Hang on!" he yelled.

"Yeah!" Mom screamed in his ear. "Thanks for the idea!"

At the crest of a hill, Sharkey turned off the road and stopped his ATV. He slipped off the vehicle, swinging the repeating laser rifle around in front of him as he slapped in a fresh energy pack, and took aim back down the path.

Austin stopped next to Sharkey and tapped his mother's hand. He looked at Sharkey's weapon. "Thought you couldn't use that on dark worlds."

"Seemed like the thing to do at the time," he said with a wry smile. "Report me later." He leaned against a tree and surveyed the trail behind them.

"What are you doing, Chief?"

"Making sure you aren't followed." He dropped to one knee. "Kadyn, ma'am, you need to get on the back of Stone's ride."

Austin's face went slack. "You're staying here," he said. "That's crazy."

"Needs to be done." He gestured forward. "This trail leads to the lake. Your ride is coming tonight. With any luck, they've picked up on that attack and are on their way now. We need to hold out until they get here."

"But you don't know how many of them are back there!"

"Lieutenant, please," Sharkey said. "You'll frighten the women."

Sharkey pulled another laser rifle from his ATV and offered.

"I've never fired anything like this in my life," Austin admitted.

"No time like the present." He leaned close, his face softening. "Just remember, shoot and move. Don't let them get your exact position if you can help it. Take this knife, too."

"I don't think this is a knife fight, sir."

"If fate is good," he said, passing over a large hunting knife, "it won't become one."

Taking both weapons, Austin slipped the rifle's strap around his back and secured the knife at his belt. He studied the trail continuing down the mountain. The sun had reached the midpoint in the sky, meaning dusk was still a long way off.

He looked at Sharkey. "Phantoms for sure?"

"With that tech? Absolutely." Sharkey wiped his face. "I need to make myself less visible. Get to that lake, Lieutenant."

"I think we should stay together, Chief."

"I appreciate that, Lieutenant." He nodded toward the smoke from the destroyed cabin towering high into the sky. "Anyone with eyes is going to see that smoke from our altercation. I doubt these mercs will want to hunt us *and* dodge local authorities. We probably bought ourselves a few hours."

"You think they're still coming?"

"I know they are. I don't know who hired them, but it doesn't matter. With the tech they're carrying and the force they're willing to use, these guys are playing for keeps." He cracked open a silver container the size of a tuna fish can, revealing a black, tar-like substance. Using two fingers, he dipped into the sticky goo and smeared it across his face. "I'll stay concealed here until darkness. Once I'm notified you're clear, I'll find my own exit."

"We really should stay together."

"So you said." Sharkey gestured down the path toward the lake. "Lieutenant, go."

Mom squeezed his shoulder. "Come on, honey," she said, her voice wavering. "Let's go."

Kadyn shuffled over to the ATV and slipped onto the vehicle in slow motion. Her soiled pink pajamas were torn at the edges, the corners blackened and burnt. She trembled as she settled in between Mom and Austin on the ATV. Austin started the engine, staring at Sharkey covering his skin with black.

"I won't forget this, Chief."

"I'll see you soon." He jerked his head toward the trail. "*Go.*"

Austin nodded. He accelerated down the trail, ducking under a branch. Rotting logs covered the path. The tires obliterated former trees, turning wood into a powder. The trail flattened. The trees spread out, the land between the towering hardwoods covered in lush green grass. The two-path road smoothed, the ride becoming easier. Kadyn's grip on his hips lessened, through fatigue or relaxation, Austin couldn't tell.

The path wound around a clump of trees and led to a small mountain lake with a surface smooth as glass. A wooden dock stretched out into the water, spiders scurrying around the planks. Austin pulled the ATV off the path and into the trees, careful to hide the vehicle behind plant life.

He killed the engine and exhaled. With the exception of a distant bird call and wind rustling through the treetops, silence surrounded them. He slipped off the ATV and pulled the rifle out. Walking back to the path, he saw the black smoke rising from the other side of the mountain.

"Mom, come over here," he said.

Mom tapped Kadyn on the shoulder and stepped up behind him. He surveyed his mother's torn and tattered clothing. Several spots of blood had seeped into her dirty blue robe. The skin under her eyes was mixed with black and blue, and her brunette hair reached out in different directions like a squirrel's nest.

"What is it?" she asked.

He handed her the pistol. "I want you to have this."

"I don't shoot, Austin."

"These men do." He clenched his jaw. "You might need to return the favor. If something should happen to me, I want you and Kadyn to hide in the woods and move when you think it's safe."

"Nothing'll happen to you."

"If it does." He pressed the gun into her shaking hands and closed her fingers around it.

He looked at the water. "Why don't you and Kadyn clean up? I'll keep an eye on the trail and come get you if we have any visitors. As soon as we get where we're going, I'll make sure you both get a change of clothes."

Mom glanced at the water and then back at Kadyn, who hunched over the ATV. "I don't know how much longer she's going to be able to keep going."

"We just need to make it to night. Then everything will be okay."

"Why are they doing this to you?"

Austin braced himself, thinking of Phantom's relentless pursuit and how he nearly shot down Rodon's fighter. "I'm not sure," he lied.

"Are you okay?" she asked.

"I have to be." He paused, staring down at the ground before adding, "I killed people today."

"You didn't have a choice."

He blinked hard, his gut rumbling as he recalled the mercenary spinning to the ground as his hands clutched his throat. "I know."

Walking away, Austin made his way down the path. Mom gently led Kadyn to the water, speaking in soft, assuring tones. Austin found a toppled tree and slipped in behind it, making sure he could cover the path with the rifle. He leaned the weapon against the log and sat in silence. He closed his eyes, listening to the forest.

When he opened them, the sunlight seemed brighter. The clouds dissipated and made the sky a brighter blue. He took in a deep breath of the cool, mountain air. The sun continued on its descent and he wished he could push it farther. Somewhere in the forest, the Phantoms hunted them. Sharkey, the first line of defense, stood on guard about a mile from their position. But if the mercenaries came in force, if they called in more reinforcements, Sharkey wouldn't be able to hold them by himself

He remembered Flin Six. The hours he'd spent avoiding the Tyral Pirates as they searched for Ryker. How had he done that? It seemed like a different person had achieved that escape, almost as if he had accomplished the rescue without thinking about it. He thought it made him nervous then, but now his stomach twisted and turned as he thought of the mercenaries storming this position. He wasn't an infantry soldier–he had never been forced to defend a position with a laser rifle. He hadn't even done it in video games, always preferring to spend his time in the Trident cockpit.

He wished he had his fighter now, wondering idly who flew his Trident while he was on leave.

The black smoke in the sky transitioned to gray, fading the higher it stretched into the atmosphere. Either the fires had died, or something had put them out.

He looked back to the sun. The transport would arrive soon. The tension in his chest eased. Maybe, just maybe, they would make it.

A laser shot crackled through the forest, echoing like a thunder clap. Austin gripped the rifle, his aim trained on the trail. More shots followed, the sounds sizzling like a dozen sparklers on Independence Day. A man cried out in terror, other voices barking. The wails cut off sharply. More laser fire ripped through the silence. He tried to calm his breathing, keeping his rifle aimed toward the incline. The firefight continued, disrupting the quiet.

Sharkey had engaged the enemy.

10

The laser shot echoed over the flat land, the body slumping to the ground. Cyclops snorted and holstered his massive pistol, kicking the dead man into the garbage pit. He swung around to face the rest of the prisoners, his large hands resting on his hips. His broad bare chest swelled and he glared with his good eye.

"This is what happens when you steal," he grumbled. "This man said he was hungry, so we now have one less mouth to feed. As the wind changes and sends the smell of his rotting corpse into your nose while you work, I want you to remember your actions have consequences."

Josh glanced at Delmar, who looked on in grim silence. Waylon stood near his men, all of them carrying tools.

Cyclops slapped his hands together, the sound like someone smacked two raw steaks. "Back to work!"

Josh and Delmar moved back to their plow line. Shielding his eyes from the sun with his hand, he peered at the end of the field several hundred yards away.

"You'd think they'd bring some horses in here," he mumbled. "This is going to take all day."

"If we're lucky," Delmar said, beginning to work in the dirt.

He glanced at him. "You like working in the field?"

"Better than being part of it," he said, nodding to the garbage pit now holding one of their former coworkers.

"I suppose so."

The sun raised and beat down on their backs. Sweat poured from his face, drenching the tattered work clothes he had been given back on the asteroid. He once thought he must smell like a locker room floor after two-a-days, but now couldn't care less. His arms, shriveled in the past months of hard labor and little food, were now transformed into wired muscles over bones and nothing else. He moved like a machine over the field, working in silence by Delmar. Waylon and his crew labored on the other side of the field. He looked in their direction occasionally, but most of the time kept his eyes on his work. It was safer that way.

Waylon hadn't mentioned his plan in a few days. Of course, there hadn't been time for talking. From sun up to sun down, the only rest came in the short nights. And no one felt like discussing escape by the time the darkness came. There were times he allowed fatigue to take him before he bothered to eat whatever gruel the pirate cooks had left for them.

At midday, a sonic boom echoed. Josh searched the sky, wondering at first if he had been wrong and a storm would soon mercifully bring in the first rain he had seen since they arrived. A rectangular ship flanked by two Tyral fighters descended from the sky, ending his hope of rainfall. Out of the corner of his eye, he watched the plain transport ship settle next to the fighters. A pilot exited the rectangular ship and he realized there were actually two ships.

"It's a tug," Delmar said without looking.

"A tug?" Josh blinked. "Hauling what?"

"That's the question, isn't it?"

Josh thought about the tug and the contents of the container it transported. Could it have something to do with the operation he heard the pirates discussing? Had the mysterious benefactor sent more equipment to aide in the pirate campaign?

"We have to check it out," Josh said.

"You probably won't be able to get near it."

"I'll have to try. It might be the answer to our escape."

"I thought your friend Waylon was supposed to help you with this escape?"

Josh looked at Waylon across the field. "It won't hurt if I look, too."

Delmar stared at the tug and its cargo container for a long moment. He bit down on his lip, then nodded as if he'd made a decision.

"I can do this," he said.

Josh frowned. "Do what?"

"I will get us closer."

"How?"

"Quiet," he snapped. "Let's get back to work."

Delmar worked in silence the remainder of the afternoon. He focused on the row until they reached the end of the field. He and Josh finished their row first, and the sun had yet to pass beneath the horizon. Cyclops strolled in their direction, his fingers playing with a whip resting in his hands.

"Someone is showing initiative today! If this old man can finish, the rest of you are slacking off!" he yelled at the others. He leaned in close to Delmar and cackled. "You looking for a raise, old man?"

"No, sir."

Josh's mouth dropped open. Delmar had never spoken to Cyclops, had barely even looked at the giant.

"You two, come here," Cyclops said, his voice grim. "You finished your row first today. I want you both at the ship unloading the cargo over there. Got it?"

Delmar looked at the tug. "That ship?"

Cyclops slapped him in the back of the head. "Of course that ship, you ignorant fool. Get over there before I change my mind."

Rubbing the back of his head, Delmar shuffled out of the field. Josh followed him, aiding the man as they hurried past the other workers. He met Waylon's eyes for an instant, nodded and kept going.

The guards remained at the edge of the landing pad. Ever since Waylon had decided to act like a beaten worker, the Tyral Pirates' attention on the prisoners had lessened. Sure, their captors drank and drinking led to intoxication. The situation differed very little from the high school parties full of alcohol, jocks, and hot girls. He knew a bored drunk was a dangerous thing. The workers kept their heads low and their attitudes lower. As a result, the pirates kept to themselves for the most part. They seemed to be waiting for a signal, an order telling them what to do next. After Rodon left late yesterday, Cyclops ruled the camp.

Scary thought, Josh thought.

The two guards at the landing pad watched Delmar board the cargo container, but shifted their attention to the beer and cards atop a weapons locker. Josh stepped in behind his friend.

"Are you okay?"

Delmar rubbed his head. "Acting." He stared at the fuel cells, laser power charges, and scrap metal. "You wanted to get in here?"

"I did." He held his arms out wide. "There's plenty of room in here for a lot of us."

Delmar swung around to look at him. "You want to escape in this? That's a bad idea, my friend."

"We load all who can't fly into this container. Those who can fly, pilot a fighter on the way out. Trick'll be coordinating a curve before the pirates can get any reinforcements down on us."

Delmar gazed into the stale blue sky. "Who knows what they have in orbit?"

"Perhaps nothing."

"Maybe, but would you bet your life on it?"

He sighed. "No."

"Good. We shall be ready for anything."

They unloaded the cargo, stacking the crates in two large piles at the edge of the dirt landing pad. Josh and Delmar emptied half the container by the time the field workers finished for the day and hobbled back to camp. The largest and last item tucked in at the back of the container shocked Josh. Unlike the wooden containers, the final object was placed in a smooth silver case shaped like a bullet.

"What is this?"

Delmar stepped closer, his fingers sliding across the shining box. "It can't be."

"Can't be what?" Josh glanced over his shoulder. "We can't stay back here long. The guards are probably lit by now."

"I need to see this."

His heart sped like a jackhammer. He searched found one last wooden crate. "I'll take this one out and give you enough time to do what you have to do. Hurry."

With a grunt, Josh lifted the crate and carried it out into the darkness. The guards still sat around a crackling fire, playing cards and laughing deeply. The tug pilot had joined them, a spark plug of a man with a wide gut and stumpy legs. He glanced up as Josh set the crate down next to the others.

As he turned back toward the container, Josh knelt down to rub his ankle, trying to act as if he had hurt himself. He listened to the three pirates hurl insults toward one another.

"The hell with it!" the tug pilot barked. "I'm leaving tomorrow anyway, so take all my damned money."

"When are you coming back?" a guard asked, laughing hard enough for tears to roll down his cheeks. "I could use the money."

"I'll be back the day after next," the pilot said, his voice lowering. "You better be here. I plan on winning the money back."

"Like hell!"

"What's that supposed to mean? Are you cheating me, Mise?"

When the two men squared off, Josh stood and hurried across the pad. So they had another day to rest up and plan their escape. Perhaps it would work, perhaps they could all leave.

Josh stepped into the container, the musty odor stifling the air. During his absence, Delmar had opened the silver container.

"What is it?" Josh asked, keeping his voice low. Inside the crate, a six-foot-long cylindrical object glistened in the faint light. It looked like a water heater with more gauges and displays. "We don't have much time. The guards are getting wild out there."

"I haven't seen one of these since the last war," Delmar breathed. "It's a power relay."

"A power relay? Who cares?"

Delmar waved his hand. "You're too young. It's a curvature amplifier. We Shoborians played with this idea for a while, especially for use as a peace weapon. They could expel enemies from our sector. They're best used when placed as navigation beacons. You know, for plotting distance curves."

Josh tapped his foot. "So?"

"So the curvature drive uses up more power the farther you travel. During the last war, the factions carried out campaigns across entire quadrants. The magnificent war galleons of those days were quite a sight, son, but they couldn't navigate the stars worth a damn."

He shifted his weight. "What's the point? They'll be back."

"These relays were set up along waypoints by smaller scout ships to allow the fleets to navigate safely across tremendous distances without draining their power supplies."

He stood still. "So Rodon is planning on going somewhere, huh?"

Delmar nodded. "And wherever it is, it's a long way from home."

"Who could afford something like this?"

He smacked the crate shut. "Rodon can't. Two years ago he wasn't powerful enough to lick a warlord's boot. He's getting support from somewhere or someone in order to launch an attack on a backwater system."

Josh thought of the past months and the growing aggressiveness of the Tyral Pirates. Delmar's hypothesis made sense.

"Another faction?"

"Either political or corporate."

"So what do we do?"

Delmar smiled. "When we leave, we try to take this with us. Otherwise, the gate'll be wide open for whatever unsuspecting star system Rodon's benefactor wants him to attack."

11

Austin pressed against the tree, listening to the battle sounds echo. Men shouted orders. The carnage made his blood boil. He wanted to sprint screaming to help Sharkey fight off the Phantoms, but he had orders to wait by the lake for his extraction.

He glanced back at Mom and Kadyn hunched behind a huge log on the banks of the mountain lake. Mom had her arm placed around Kadyn's neck. The two women, battered and bruised, looked ready to collapse into the soft clay of the shore.

At that moment, Sharkey fought to protect them. Austin should be there, should rush through the forest to aid his comrade. He had known Sharkey since he first arrived at the school. He knew the man would die in the line of duty if it was needed.

And right now, Sharkey's sense of duty the only thing protecting them.

The laser fire slowed, then stopped. Three rounds of a standard shot, probably a pistol, fired. The distinct sound of a bullet blast sounded harsh when followed by the laser bolts, and it echoed through the treetops.

Silence.

Austin gripped his rifle tighter. *They were coming.*

He glanced back to Mom and nodded. She covered Kadyn and they pressed down behind the log in the late afternoon light.

Austin turned back and faced the forest. Should he move? Perhaps take the fight away from Mom and Kadyn?

He studied the two-path road. No, he thought, the mercenaries would have to come this way. This was the place.

He switched off the rifle's safety. An uneasiness filled his body, and he wondered if he would be able to remain still. He wanted to run away with Mom and Kadyn, but at the same time, he wanted the Phantoms to show their faces. He wanted the fight to begin. Come on, he thought, let's get this over with.

As the minutes dragged, he wondered if he had done the right thing in leaving Tizona during the night with Bear and Skylar. After all, staying meant he would have gone home for Christmas and he wouldn't be here in the forest at this moment, fighting for his life against intergalactic mercenaries who wanted him dead.

Shaking away the thought, Austin maintained his watch. He knew a shroud could be spotted if you looked close enough. The leaves moved with the wind, and he wondered if the mercenaries had more of the personal shrouds.

The sun cast long shadows over the path, stretching darkness through the forest.

He froze.

A tree branch moved.

Something metallic glimmered. A silhouette of a man moved quietly near a batch of trees on the far side of the road. Austin held his breath, waiting to see if more revealed themselves.

They'd killed Sharkey. They must have. And now they had come to do the same to them.

Two more figures moved in behind the first, their shapes distorting the trees behind them as the shroud technology hid them from view. Another figure stepped down on his side of the road, followed by a second man.

Five total attackers were moving on his position, closing at twenty yards. He shifted his aim, bringing the rifle to bear on the mercenary on his side of the road.

Shoot and move. Shoot and move.

His finger rested on the trigger. The Phantom moved without making a sound, pushing a leaf out of the way.

Austin fired.

The laser blast sizzled through the quiet. Several more blasts followed. Repeaters spit death through the trees as his first three bolts struck the lead Phantom on his side of the road. Sparks rained down from the trees.

"Down!" a voice yelled.

Austin kept his finger pressed on the trigger. Bolts seared through flesh and wood, sending flashes and splinters spinning. Two Phantoms dropped before the mercenaries returned fire. He rolled away from his cover, staying low in the vegetation.

Laser bolts incinerated the log he had used for cover. Fire raged in the spot where he had spent the afternoon. He knew he had cleared his side of the road, leaving three other Phantoms on the far side.

He hoped there would be no more in the trees moving toward him.

Austin remained on his back, listening to his enemy firing into dead wood. He breathed for the first time since the engagement. He rolled onto his stomach without making a sound and scanned the trees.

Nothing.

He heard a whimper, a sniffle.

What was that?

It came from the lake. A consoling voice, softer.

Kadyn.

His friend cried and his mother tried to stop it.

He had to move in and keep them quiet.

Waiting only a moment longer, Austin brought himself to one knee and held the rifle in front of him. A bolt burned past his head and crashed into the tree behind him. Without thinking, he sprinted through the trees, knocking back clinging branches and leaves. He ran toward Mom and Kadyn. A thorn ripped the flesh on his cheek as he ran, the skin splitting and sending a flash of pain through his body. Laser bolts zipped around him like demonic fairies. One clipped his shirt, slicing the fabric. He dove into a bed of pine straw and spun around on his stomach.

He fired in the general direction of his attackers, the bolts flashing as they burned through the trees. Sparks flew from bark, and the forest caught fire in the fading light of day.

If these Phantoms try to get closer to Mom and Kadyn, he thought, *they're going to have to kill me.*

He wiped blood from his face and searched for a target. His cheek burned from the scratch. Flames twisted and swirled, reaching higher into the treetops. Leaves shriveled, ignited, and dropped to the ground like crackling pieces of burnt tissue paper. The falling, flaming leaves fell like rain. Heat seared in waves, the wind tussling the embers into a hellish tornado.

Austin fired twice, thinking he had a shot. The rising temperature made the trees and flames shimmer, everything looking like one of the shrouds. More bolts crashed into a burning tree in front of him, sending more sparks into the fray. He ducked in time, a bolt soaring over his head. He had to keep the attackers away from the lake.

He moved toward the water, trying to keep a safe distance from his mother and Kadyn. A pistol fired. He froze.

Mom.

He ran toward their position, screaming until his throat burned. He fired blindly into the trees, hoping to draw attention to him and away from Mom.

It worked.

His upper chest flashed with pain, a bolt burning into his collar bone. He spun around like a top and fell into blackened pine straw. The energy weapon worked its way into his skin, hissing as it ate away at his flesh. He buried his face into the hot ground and howled. Tears mixed with sweat and dirt on his face.

He sat up. Why was this happening? Would his life end here in the mountains next to an isolated body of water? What about Mom?

And Kadyn? Was this the end of their stories, too? Resolved in a way he hadn't felt since Flin Six, he stood in the center of the fire, flames twirling around him. This would not be the end, not for them.

He tore off his ravaged shirt, felt the heat from the burning forest on his bare chest. Ignoring his better judgment, he glanced down at his wound. A charred hole had burned through his skin, exposing his blackened collar bone.

"*Mom*!" he yelled. "I'm coming!"

Austin ran through flames, jumping over a burning log. To his right, a Phantom materialized in the fire, his shroud running out of power. He fired the rifle from his hip, shouting as he unleashed the full repeating power into the mercenary's chest. The man toppled into the inferno.

A bolt seared through the air, striking Austin's calf. He spun around to the ground and fired in the direction of the shot. Two attackers shot at him from behind two trees, the bolts kicking up pebbles and pine straw. He returned fire as he crawled, hoping to make it behind a tree.

Another shot exploded on his thigh. He rolled over on his back. His skin felt like it had caught fire, the pain running through his body like battery acid. He fired again without looking.

Footsteps pounded the dirt from behind him. They had surrounded him. It was all over.

The Phantom knelt beside him. "Can you walk?"

Austin blinked, unsure if what he heard was a dream. "Mom?"

She fired the pistol twice into the woods. Her eyes flickered to his wounds. "We need to move."

A bolt flashed by her head. Austin rolled over on his side, firing the remaining charge toward the mercenaries. Mom pulled his arm over her shoulder, firing the pistol till it clicked.

She tossed the weapon into the trees. "Come on! Head for the lake!"

They hobbled. Mom yelped, sparks flying from her back. They toppled to the ground.

"Mom! *No!*" Austin ignored his throbbing wounds and rolled her over. "Where are you hit?"

She smiled at him, gripping his hand. Her eyes rolled back and closed.

"Mom!" he yelled, his head shaking.

He stood between the laser fire and faced his attackers with an empty rifle. He glanced down at his mother, her sweet face turning to one side.

Not like this, he thought. *Oh, Mom, I'm so sorry.*

With a smooth movement, Austin slipped the hunting knife from his belt. One way or another, he would finish this day. Taking a deep breath, he charged, screaming with everything his voice had left. The mercenaries fired, laser bolts filling the air.

And then the world went straight to hell.

An explosion sent him flying into the forest, his back crashing into a tree. Concussions of heavy laser fire tore through the ground. Debris crashed onto him. Branches, pine straw, and dirt showered him.

A fog covered his mind as he stood in the flames, wobbling as if the Earth shook beneath him. He shuffled through the burning debris, grabbed a blackened branch, and held it like a baseball bat as he prepared to fight.

"Lieutenant!" a voice called from behind him.

Austin didn't turn, assuming he hallucinated. He walked toward the last position of the Phantoms. They deserved to die. They'd killed his friends and the only family he had left. And they had done it for money.

"*Austin*!"

He blinked. His body shook. His vision blurred. A silhouette of a man beckoned toward him through the smoke, his hand outstretched. Darkness surrounded him, his world tipped, and he crashed to the ground.

12

"We have a problem."

Cyclops strolled before the prisoners who knelt in three lines of ten. He clasped his hands tight behind his back. His muscular chest swelled as he spoke. Josh swallowed. He had heard this tone before. Back on the asteroid, Cyclops would start a speech like this and end it by forcing prisoners out of the airlock.

"Someone has opened a most important box," Cyclops said, nodding at two of his men. "This is disturbing."

The two guards dressed in dirty black rags moved forward in the morning light. They each held a long wooden stake about as tall as a man. Marching in front of the prisoners, they split and went to opposite sides. When they reached the edge of the group, the two men in unison slammed the stakes into the ground. They bowed and backed away.

"I am going to give the violator a chance for redemption," Cyclops said. "Come forward now, and there will be less punishment. Reveal yourself now, and we won't have to tell Rodon about this when he returns."

Josh knew Waylon knelt on the opposite side of the group. He didn't risk a glance to his comrade. Delmar remained at Josh's side, his shoulders tense and back rigid.

"No one to volunteer their sins?" Cyclops made a clicking sound with his tongue and shook his head in melodramatic fashion. "This is not good."

A guard forced Delmar to his feet and pulled him forward. A green, rope beam erupted from the pinnacle of both stakes. Using thick gloves like something Josh had seen in a restaurant kitchen, the guards took the pulsating lasers and wrapped them around Delmar's wrists. The lasers burned into his flesh, filing the air with the smell of frying meat.

"This man was on duty last night," Cyclops said. "His job was to empty the cargo ship. One of the boxes had been forced open. This man is a traitor and deserves a traitor's punishment. Since no one has come forward to admit their guilt, this old man will die."

Delmar's face formed into stone. He looked at Josh, allowed a slight smile.

The lasers yanked Delmar's arms, lifting him into the air. His feet pulled off the ground until his toes just touched the dirt. A breeze moved across the plains. Then, the air stood still.

Cyclops pulled a thick bullwhip from a satchel and rolled it in his hands. He stood behind Delmar and lifted the bullwhip high about his head.

"Stop!" Josh yelled.

He stood. The other prisoners stared at him. Some gasped, while others gazed in silence.

Cyclops grinned, revealing his battered and blackened teeth. "Good, a brave soul. I knew this man did not work alone. It is disappointing, pigs. After all we have done for you, taking you to this beautiful planet and allowing you the chance to work outside. And you repay us with this vile treachery. Cowards."

Two pirates lunged forward and marched Josh to the front. When they forced him to the ground, Delmar shook his head.

"This man will still die," Cyclops announced. "He is old and not valuable to our efforts."

Josh glared at Cyclops. "You said I would share his punishment and he wouldn't have to die."

"I said no such thing. I said he would be punished alone. Now, you have decided to take your punishment and join him. You might wish you were dead, but I have no plans to kill you." He gestured to the fields. "For now, you still have value."

Josh swallowed, staring at Delmar. Then he closed his eyes.

Cyclops turned to address the other prisoners.

"Gentlemen, this is what happens when you use your brain and disobey us," he said. He swung the whip into Delmar's back. It cracked into the old man's weathered skin with each sentence.

"We are your lords!"

Crack.

"You are nothing!"

Crack.

"You work for us!"

Crack.

Delmar cried out.

"This is your life!"

Crack.

Josh's friend wailed as blood fell into the powdery ground.

"This is all you will ever know!"

Crack.

He stopped listening. He only heard the crack of the whip punctuating each sentence. Grinding his teeth, he tried to take his mind into another place.

The whip would turn on him next.

FLAMES IGNITED the flesh on his back long into the night. The guards had dumped Josh on his face into the dirt. His wounds burned as if he had never felt pain before. When he thought his skin had grown numb, a breeze would move across his back, like rubbing a cheese grater across a third degree burn. The guards must have left them for dead. During the whipping, he passed out several times only to have Cyclops rip him back to consciousness. Sweat mixed with the blood and sand coating his body.

As best as he could comprehend, the guards had forced the other prisoners into the field following what Cyclops called "the show." The pirates left Josh where the prisoners had slept. The breeze increased in intensity, smacking into his ripped skin like a razor. He wondered if anything remained on his exposed back but tissue and bone.

He cried. He sobbed. Nothing mattered. *Please, Lord,* he thought, *let me die.*

He tried to swallow, but his throat filled with sand. He coughed, the movement hurting his back. Pain throbbed, burning through his veins.

The stench of human waste and rotting garbage drifted from the nearby trash pit and surrounded him like a fog. He usually ignored it, but thought of Delmar. Through the labor on the asteroid to this forsaken planet, his friend had always been there for him. Even though Josh had passed out during his whipping, he knew the guards would have dumped his friend in the pit.

Insects buzzed around his face, squirming and fluttering into his nose. As he struggled to focus, he knew he would die. His vision darkened. When he opened his eyes, the sun had nearly finished its trek across the sky.

He faded in and out of consciousness. He fought the weight of his head but finally surrendered, allowing his face remain in the sand.

He blinked and looked up, wondering how much time had passed. Stars covered the black sky. A fire popped somewhere, sending flickering orange embers into the blackness. He closed his eyes.

Moments or hours later, he raised his head to look around, but he had no strength left. He fell back onto the dirt again. He drifted through time and space, transitioning from Earth to Tarton's Junction and back again. The space station wavered before him. His Trident glimmered under the station's florescent lights. Kadyn stood before him, her eyes peering over large sunglasses.

"Why didn't you tell me?" she asked.

"I'm sorry," he said. "I should have...I should have told you."

She disappeared. Cyclops's whips cracked. He jolted at the sound. Was he here? Had he come to punish him again?

Darkness.

The morning sun beat down on him, burning away sleep.

"Josh?"

He turned. Waylon knelt beside him.

"Where is Delmar?" Josh asked, although he knew the answer.

Waylon looked past his sand-caked beard to the ground. "They took him."

He nodded, closing his eyes. He thought of the crate in the cargo container holding the curvature power relay. Delmar hadn't wanted to go in, but he did anyway.

"I'm sorry." Josh convulsed. "He was right. We shouldn't have gone."

Cool air scraped his back. He winced and clenched his teeth.

Night.

He must have passed out again. Waylon slept near him in the dirt. Prisoners snored around him.

He sat up, the skin on his back splitting. He cried out, his throat sore as if it had been scorched by a blow torch.

Burying his face in his hands, Josh sat in silence. What had happened?

He opened his eyes again and tried to swallow. A large, sandpaper-covered softball clogged his throat. The ditch was filled with new garbage and rotten food, sending the smell drifting over the lines of prisoners. Waylon, his rags ripped on his back and the bloodstains turned a blackish brown, remained next to him. Josh touched his shoulder, but his friend didn't move.

"Waylon?"

He nudged his shoulder, but the man didn't move. Better to let him sleep, he thought.

Thinking about Delmar and his role in the kind man's death, Josh wept, the sobbing only intensifying his wounds.

Footsteps stumbled through the dirt a short distance from their camp. Josh fell on his side and remained still. He squinted, watching as a guard urinated at the edge of the ditch. The pirate gazed into the sky, took a long drink from a bottle and tossed it in with the rest of the garbage.

By daylight, the hunger pains faded and the dryness in his throat had subsided. He leaned back, but his stomach turned and he vomited. His throat burned. Tears, snot, and sweat covered his face. His dry lips cracked.

"So you're not dead," Waylon grumbled, sitting forward.

"Wish I was," Josh said in a raspy voice.

Coping with the pain flaring on his back, he turned around to stare at the landing pad. The fighters and the tug remained near the barn. Pirate guards sat around the crates listening as Cyclops spoke. They turned and walked in their direction to begin the day.

His cracked lips parted.

"I don't know if I can do this," he said.

"What, work?" Waylon asked.

"Yes."

He nodded. "I'll cover for you. We'll get through this."

HOURS BLURRED INTO DAYS.

The guards rushed them, driving them to finish planting the field, never explaining the need for the rush. Josh struggled to keep up, but Waylon did twice the work to cover for him. Impressed, Cyclops provided Josh with medicine. At first, Josh wondered if the pills would end up being poison. But then, he figured the man would have killed him by now if he wanted him dead. Cyclops drove the workers hard, filled with a new ferocity. Something pushed him, and Josh figured it had to be Rodon. A deadline must be approaching, and the prisoners had to finish this field for some reason.

Captives received punishment for not performing up to the standards of the Tyral Pirates. Guards beat several workers each day, whipped others. They dumped three dead workers into the ditch at the beginning of the third day since Delmar's death. Two had wounds from Cyclops' bullwhip and the other man, one from Waylon's group, had no visible wounds. Josh assumed he had been worked to death.

On the third night, Josh killed a desert rat with his bare hands, breaking its neck when it tried to gnaw on his toe. In his survival training, the Lobera instructors in California had gone over the details of eating a fresh animal and living off the land. Of course, he had assumed they meant deer and not this tiny rodent. Still, meat was meat.

Gathering together a shovel from the edge of the field and some grass, he built a small fire and cooked the animal for him and Waylon to share. While small, the rat provided them with the first fresh meat they'd eaten in months.

"Better than milky green snot," Waylon said with a smile, his teeth crunching bones.

"Yes." Josh surveyed the landing pad and the barn. "Something's up."

"Up?"

"At the landing pad."

Pirates swarmed over the tug, attaching the container. Two men working on the ship's engine closed a metal plate. The thrusters fired and the guards cheered. The container carrying the curvature power relay lifted into the air behind the tug. Three pirate fighters flanked the tug as they powered for deep atmo, the boom signifying they'd surpassed the sound barrier.

Josh sighed as he watched the vessels twinkle and disappear.

The power relay Delmar died for had escaped. Whatever planet Rodon and the Tyral Pirates planned to attack would have to defend itself.

He shook away the thought. *Focus on getting yourself out of here.*

By the fourth day, the searing pain from his wounds had dulled, although he knew it would never totally go away. Despite the situation, he felt stronger today. Whatever medicine Cyclops had provided must have prevented an infection.

Earlier in the day, his shovel hit something hard. When more guards worked the fields, he would have yanked out whatever caused the disruption and tossed it away. However, he was not under the same amount of surveillance.

He knelt down, finding a hardened root about two feet long and several inches thick. Breaking off a piece with his shovel, he stuffed the root into his worn clothing.

As they finished their work, he studied the field. They would soon be done plowing and planting. With no additional fields in sight, Josh wondered what the Tyral Pirates would do when they finished.

Turning back to the landing pad, he saw only three pirate fighters remained. Also, there were no cargo containers. Wherever Rodon gathered his forces, he must have all the supplies he needed.

He watched Cyclops meeting with the guards near the fighters. After several minutes of talking over the gusting wind, the pirates broke off and loaded equipment into the fighters. Dread filled Josh's chest.

They were leaving.

No more cargo containers and no more fields to work meant the pirates would leave the prisoners on the planet. They would die in the fields. Either the pirates would fly overhead and execute them from the air, or Cyclops and his men would leave them to rot. The fields would be there when the pirates returned to find a harvest waiting for fresh prisoners to do the picking.

Josh sat in the dirt. Rodon had probably done it this way for months, maybe years.

He looked at the three fighters. One way or the other, he would die here if the pirates fled.

He had to make a move tonight.

AFTER SETTLING INTO THE PRISONERS' sleeping area, Josh watched the guards. Four relaxed near the fire. Their boxes had been loaded into the fighters' cargo bays.

Most prisoners collapsed where they stopped, too exhausted to walk any further. Their resting bodies filled in the land between the field and the landing pad. The guards didn't force all captives to their sleeping area this night.

Josh's muscles ached, his back flaring up as the wind brushed against it like it ripped off a crusty scab. He winced.

Night fell across the plains.

One of the pirate fighters took off just after sunset, blasting the silence and disappearing into the distance. Josh glanced back to the landing pad and didn't see Cyclops. He must have left.

Without their commander around, the guards passed around a bottle, all four keeping their guns within close reach. Josh figured they must be waiting to leave in the morning for some reason. Studying the scene and noticing the lack of transport, he realized the guards would either kill the prisoners from the air or leave them to starve. This meant Rodon planned to move, and he planned to do it soon.

Josh tied a rag around his forehead and looked out across the space between the camp's dump and their landing pad.

Time to go.

Waylon had gone to sleep. Without disturbing him, Josh moved back to the field to find a rock. He searched in the darkness and found a small stone. Using his fingernails and the stone, he worked on sharpening the root as fast as he could manage. He pulled back strips of the root until it came to a point. Pushing it against his palm, he decided it was as sharp as he could make it. He should have paid more attention in his survival training and Boy Scouts.

He kept low to the ground, trying to avoid the flickering firelight playing across the dead grass. Two guards leaned far back in their metal chairs, their mouths hanging open. Their breath formed clouds of mist like ghostly halos in the crisp night air. The remaining guards gazed into the fire, their eyes nearly closed. One guard sat on a stump, his head leaning towards the fire, an empty bottle against his boot. The other pirate leaned on his palms and stared into the sky.

Wind brushed the taller grasses. Prisoners groaned and snored, too tired to contemplate escape, too sick to fight off weariness.

Josh moved from row to row, making his way back to Waylon. The men smelled almost as bad as the filth of the garbage pit. Flies buzzed around them, some crawling into festering wounds while others hovered over excrement from men too tired to move to the latrine.

In the darkness, he nearly gave up finding Waylon until he saw his large frame at the edge of the camp. Waylon stared into the darkness, his elbows resting on his knees as Josh slipped up behind him.

"What do you want?" Waylon asked without turning, his voice weak.

"I want to leave," he said. "And now is the time."

Waylon turned. "Where did you go?"

"Quiet now."

"You were gone. I thought you were dead, friend."

Josh studied his surroundings. "Where is the rest of your crew?"

Waylon gazed into the darkness. "Acks'll probably not make the night."

He made a silent count. "You're all that's left? How?"

"We've been out here too long living off too little and asked to do too much. It was only a matter of time."

Josh remembered what he had seen earlier on the landing pad. "We don't have time for this. The pirates are leaving. My guess is they'll be gone by morning and either kill us, or leave us here."

"Either way, I'd thank them. I've had enough of this life."

Josh thought of the *Barracudas*. Delmar had acted somewhat impressed with their credentials, and he wondered if the reputation of the smuggling group had merit.

"There are others, right?" Josh asked.

"What do you mean?"

"Others in your group, you know, back from where you came from. The *Barracudas*?"

Waylon thought for a long moment. Perhaps he considered if he could trust Josh, or maybe he wondered if acknowledging the question would violate a sacred trust among smugglers. Whatever the reason, Waylon's face softened.

"Yes, there are others," he said, his tone neutral. "We have a base of operations in Quadrant Eight. They're my family."

Josh leaned toward him. "Then escape with me. Take me to your people and we can avenge our time here. Do it for your men. Do it for Delmar. Do it for yourself. When we first met, I told you I would be able to fly us out of here. Well, now it's just us. Help me."

He pointed to the landing pad. "I think Cyclops left earlier on a fighter. Those two fighters are our only route off this planet. It's now or never."

Waylon sighed. After a moment, he balled his fists and his mouth hardened. "What's the worst that could happen? We're gonna die here anyway. What's your plan?"

Josh froze. "I'm not sure, yet. I think there are only four guards left."

He looked at the light in the distant sky, the black night beginning to transition to dawn.

"Whatever we do," Josh said, "we have to move fast."

13

His consciousness came in like the tide and washed out the same way, lulling him into a dreamless darkness. Voices called to him. Light flashed, followed by searing pain. The darkness always returned.

Austin heard the soft drone of computers, possibly an air conditioning unit rumbling to life.

"Keep resting," a familiar voice said.

He tried to pry open his eyes, ignoring the flash of pain in his face, but gave up the fight. He couldn't feel the rest of his body anymore. No pain, no comfort, nothing but the sting of a cut on his cheek. His head fell to the side and the darkness returned.

When he opened his eyes this time, an unfocused white light surrounded him.

You died.

The thought shocked him.

He sat for a moment, contemplating the reality he might have died. He felt a blanket brushing up against his chin. No, he thought, he wasn't dead. But where was he?

The last thing he remembered—

He jolted, his eyes clamping shut.

He remembered the fire, the flames circling him like a fiery nightmare. Laser bolts striking his body. The Phantoms closing in on his position after murdering Sharkey. Mom on the forest ground, her body damaged and broken. Kadyn gone. Flaming embers twirling from the treetops.

What had happened?

His arms refused to move. After a struggle, he opened his eyes. To his left, two chairs lined the wall of a white sterile room. A bright light pulsated above. With an effort, he turned his head to the right. A kind face moved closer, staring down at him.

"Nubern," he whispered, his throat parched.

"Easy, son. I came here as quickly as I could." Nubern touched the side of his face, running his hand across a fresh scar on Austin's cheek. "You've had a time."

Austin blinked, scanning his surroundings.

"It's just us for now," Nubern said. "You've been transported to Base Prime in California. You've been here for two days. The transport provided air support during the attack in the mountains. I called to you at the time, but you collapsed. We brought you on board and here we are."

Austin shook his head, not remembering any of what Nubern said.

Nubern touched his shoulder. "With the exception of your head, your muscles have been incapacitated while your skin regrows and heals itself. Don't worry. You had half a dozen direct laser burns. The doctors are allowing your body time to repair."

He glanced at the monitors behind Austin. "Given your condition at the time, we decided it best to wait until we tube transported to Atlantis. You were...fragile."

Austin nodded. "Mom? Kadyn?"

Nubern's face grew icy. "Your mother's wounds were severe just like yours. She is in isolation at the moment under observation by our best doctors. It looks like she's going to pull through. Both of you were shot to hell." He sighed. "Your friend on the other hand is suffering from PTSD and two laser burns. Her mental state is crumbling but physically she's recovering. This happens when people experience trauma. Also, some can't take the realization their planet is just one of thousands in the known galaxy. She was also under constant fire since learning this new information, so that didn't help. It'll take time. Of course, Revelation Protocol is usually carried out with less excitement. She is currently being given sedatives to help her sleep."

Austin winced, knowing the next information would be difficult to hear. "Sharkey?"

Nubern broke eye contact and looked at the bed. "He didn't make it, son. We found him in the middle of four dead mercenaries. He didn't go without a fight."

Austin's throat swelled. "He saved us."

"That he did," Nubern said, his voice cracking.

"Who hired them? Do we know for certain?" he asked, thinking of the mercenaries.

Nubern gazed over his bed. "EIF is sure they are Phantoms. A highly trained outfit comprised of ex-military from all across the galaxy. They are deadly. They are expensive. Even if Rodon is behind this, I find it hard to believe he could afford such a...luxury."

He blinked and looked back at Austin. "Now we have to get you rested. We're not out of this, yet. I came here because the situation for Quadrant Eight is worse than we first realized."

"How could it be worse?"

Nubern took in a slow, deep breath. "Our surveillance satellites picked up Tyral Pirate activity in the Amade Cluster. Lots of it. Fighters and tugs pulling a large amount of containers. They didn't stay long. We launched a recon mission, but the tugs and containers bugged out before our ships arrived."

"What's in that system?"

"Nothing much. Only habitable planet is grasslands full of a whole bunch of nothing." He crossed his arms over his chest. "Smugglers have been known to use it in the past. We're in the process of sending a scout to the surface to do a little recon planet-side."

Austin frowned. "What does this have to do with Quadrant Eight?"

"Well, mix the intelligence with what's happening in the Amade Cluster with the fact our system disruptor was recently hacked."

He shook his head. "Disruptor?"

Nubern smiled. "It's a piece of technology utilized in dark world systems like this one. What it does is simulate flares from the local star in the event something needs to be hidden. While you were out, people on Earth thought they were battered by a series of solar flares. It was actually our disruptor that had been hacked. Also, we lost contact with four more Star Runners here on Earth. The rest are safe and accounted for."

Austin chewed on his bottom lip. The attack on Lieutenant Bean in San Francisco seemed to kick off the recent series of attacks against Legion forces on Earth. The Phantoms targeted him, his family, and killed Sharkey. Now, they hacked a disruptor to simulate solar flares smacking into Earth. Why?

"We still don't who hired them?" Austin asked.

"No, but they've targeted only Star Runners and their families. The rest of their plan is unknown. We don't know if the Phantoms had anything to do with the disruptor."

"They had to," he said. "Why would anyone want to simulate solar flares?"

"Lots of reasons, actually, but none of them make any sense."

A shiver tickled the back of his neck. "Like what?"

"It could be used to disguise troop movements, mask communications. Perhaps to hide landing large ships if you didn't have a shroud capable of masking them."

"You're talking about an invasion."

Nubern nodded. "Yes."

"Of Earth."

"That's why this doesn't make any sense. A mercenary outfit wouldn't have the means to carry out a full scale invasion. Besides, why would they? Even with superior technology, they couldn't hope to hold the entire planet against Earth's response."

Austin looked at the white wall. "What if it's not an invasion but the early moves to prepare the way for one? You know, for a force more powerful?"

Nubern reached over and squeezed his arm. "Listen, we are working on this. Right now you need to sit back and rest. You've been through quite an ordeal." He glanced at a tablet and frowned. "I'll be back to check on you later this afternoon."

"Captain?"

Nubern hesitated. "Yes, son?"

He paused. "Thanks for coming for me, sir. I am sorry about... how I acted during our last conversation."

"We all have doubts at times. Get some rest."

"Can you tell me what you meant?"

Nubern cocked at eyebrow. "Meant?"

"You said there were things going on in Quadrant Eight you wanted to tell me about. I think I deserve to know."

He sighed. "There is no simple answer and this is a controversy that has nearly torn the Legion in half. We're usually not permitted to talk about it, but given our background, I have to admit you mean more to me than a typical recruit. You deserve to know the truth." He sat at the end of the bed, his eyes on the wall. "Things are going much worse for the Legion than is generally known. Decades ago, it was recognized that the Zahl Empire had expanded much faster than the Legion and we started to search for advantages. It was quickly evident we would be in danger should the Zahl ever decide to start a war again."

"Why did they expand so fast?"

"You've touched on the basic argument. Since the Zahl Empire doesn't believe in a planet's sovereign right to develop at its own pace, they take all inhabitable worlds they come across. They believe it is the creator's destiny that they bring their light across the universe. Some try to resist, but it doesn't last long. They have several factions in power in the Zahl government; some are war mongers and have a strong desire to swiftly carry out their expansionist policy. With the

Legion's policy of allowing dark worlds to naturally expand, we grow at a much slower pace."

Austin thought of the secretive recruiting measure of monitoring an online game. "Has the Legion considered more direct measures?"

"That's the argument. Or, rather, it was." Nubern cleared his throat. "See, there was a movement within the Legion government to reverse our hands-off policy. With tensions growing each year and the Zahl Empire building their defenses along the border, as well as the relentless pirate activity, we needed recruits and we needed them as soon as possible. The Legion needs manpower in order to protect its space. The 'game' was our best recruitment tool in years."

"Why not just come out and say it at Tizona?"

"Because that would break our government desire to allow Earth to naturally develop."

Austin eyed him. "And what about the enlistment terms?"

"You've heard about that?" Nubern asked. When Austin nodded, Nubern pursed his lips. "I see. Yes, you will be given your assignment and expected to sign a five-year enlistment. The offer was supposed to come at the end of your leave."

So it was true, Austin thought. "And what happens then?"

"You will receive your assignment."

"And where will it be?"

Nubern's brow wrinkled. "Difficult to say. I wouldn't presume to guess. Most likely, it will be a carrier task force on the border or perhaps along the Fringe. I beg you, son, to please consider this carefully before you agree to the terms."

"Why?"

"Because you will not be back here on Earth for a long time, perhaps the entire five years."

"Oh." Austin frowned.

Nubern looked at him. "I would like to point out, though, that the Legion protects Earth. Without it and Star Runners like you, the worst in space would be in Earth's orbit."

"That's happening anyway," Austin snorted.

"I can't argue with you there," he said. "It's why we need to take care of this situation." He stood. "I'll let you rest. I'll be back soon. Think about what we talked about. You won't have to make a decision until you get your leave...whenever that is."

Nubern left.

Austin took a deep breath. He couldn't shake the sight of the burning forest. He shuddered and tried to think of happier times, of Mom and Dad at home. No matter how hard he tried, he couldn't ignore the thought someone had targeted him and his family. But it was more than that; despite Nubern seeming unconvinced, something lingered at the edge of Austin's mind.

Someone targeted Earth.

BRUISES SPOTTED her face and arms, mixing with red scrapes and burn marks. Her chest lifted and fell in deep, calming breaths, much different than when she'd gasped in pain on the burning forest floor. Austin leaned forward in the wheelchair, pressing his face against the glass to stare at his mother. He wanted to go in there, but the Legion doctors said she needed another day in hibernation for her body to recover.

"She's going to be okay, Lieutenant."

Austin smiled at Nubern, who hurried toward him with a tablet in hand. He nodded at the nurses he passed, seemingly in control despite the current events.

"I know, sir. I'm looking forward to speaking with her tomorrow." He gestured at the wheelchair. "Speaking of recovery, I'm ready to get out of this thing, too."

"I'm told that'll be tomorrow after the last bout of tests." He tapped Austin's shoulder. "Laser burns are nothing to take lightly. They eat away at the flesh, and it takes time for the tissue to rebuild itself."

With Earth's current technology, it would have taken months of skin grafts and who knew what else for the burns to heal.

"I'm feeling much better," he said, "like I could get out of the chair right now."

"You probably could," Nubern admitted, "but I would wait till tomorrow."

Austin nodded and looked back to his mother. He wanted to have a moment to hear her voice, tell her everything would be fine.

He thought again of his arrival on Earth and the conversation with Lieutenant Bean. "Captain? May I ask you something?"

"Of course."

He glanced down at his hands. "Why did you recruit me?"

"What?" Nubern blinked. "Why did I recruit you? You had the necessary skills to become a great Star Runner, which is exactly what you've become. Why?"

He rubbed his chin. "The other pilot I sat next to on the way in was coming home to decide if he wanted to re-enlist or not. He told me some things."

"Ah. And what were these *things*?"

"He said the Legion recruited pilots who were dreamers or who had nothing to lose."

"And this bothered you?"

"A little."

Nubern sighed. "It is true we search for an 'X' factor, something that would be right for a Legion Star Runner."

"Why?"

"Life as a Star Runner isn't easy. I never wanted you to think it was, but I warned you at the shack in the swamp that nothing would ever, ever be the same. Didn't I?"

Austin thought back to the night before he came to Atlantis. "You did. Bean seemed sad about what he had missed on Earth. Guess I never really thought of it."

Nubern reached out, squeezed his shoulder. "You're meant to serve, Austin. It takes the sacrifice of your normal life, sure. That's why it's not for everyone. You're different, son."

"Is it true I'll get my assignment when my leave is over?"

He laughed. "After what you've been through, I don't think your leave ever began. However, you will get your assignment soon."

Austin nodded. "Any idea what it will be?"

"No."

"Will you be there?"

"I'm a recruiter and a trainer." Nubern gazed down the hall. "My days of serving on carriers are long done. You will be assigned far from here, probably far away from Quadrant Eight. You are too good to be hidden back here."

"Thank you, sir."

The tablet in Nubern's arms beeped and he snapped to attention.

"I need you to come with me right now, though."

"Now? Where?"

"You have been summoned to a meeting with Command."

His throat constricted. "Command? *Me*?"

Nubern moved behind Austin's wheel chair. "Yes. It is important. They want to hear a report directly from you. You are the only officer to survive an up close and personal encounter with this force of Phantoms on Earth."

Austin's stomach turned. "You mean no others have made it?"

"They're in hiding or trying to get to an evacuation point. Some are lying low awaiting extraction. You're not the last Star Runner on Earth that's actually from here, but you are the first to make it back to Base Prime. Some had a lot farther to go." He pushed the wheelchair down the hall. "Ready?"

"You weren't kidding, Captain." He sighed. "I'm ready as I'll ever be."

As Nubern pushed him through the busy infirmary halls, his wounds burned and his stomach twisted into knots. He didn't know if the pain killers had worn off or if he was dreading a conversation with Command.

"I've never liked public speaking," Austin said as they rounded a corner. "Not one of my skills."

"Wasn't mine, either, but it gets easier. Part of being an officer, son."

Circular white doors, looming at the end of the hall like a giant's eyeballs, dilated to reveal the bustling grand junction of Base Prime.

Businesspeople and military personnel swarmed like a disturbed ant hill. Austin remembered his first time in the busy port when he'd seen a cart hovering without wheels.

He smiled. It felt like another lifetime.

"When we reach the briefing room, I will take you to the podium when they call for you," Nubern said, speaking loudly over the noise of the hall. "I'll hand you a microphone and then sit behind you if you need anything at all."

"A microphone?" A cold chill rippled down his face. "How many people are going to be at this thing?"

"A dozen staff and senior officials." Nubern weaved around a slow-moving group of officers. "The microphone is for the recording that will be sent back to Fleet."

"Fleet?"

"Yes, sir. Most of the Legion has heard about the troubles of Quadrant Eight. Command wants officers across the quadrants to hear what has happened because it could happen anywhere. Also, it's not every day Revelation Protocol is announced."

"Right." Austin didn't know he would be speaking to the entire Legion. This day just kept getting better and better.

Nubern pushed him through the crowd and three security gates. Guards nodded at Austin. Civilians nearly bowed when he passed. Conversations ceased when they saw him. He shifted uncomfortably in the wheelchair.

"Your story has been shared through the Legion channels," Nubern said, reading his mind. "People have heard about your struggles, and what you did to save your mother. Hell of a story. Probably be a medal in your future once this is all over."

The pressure on Austin's chest eased. *A medal.* He hadn't done anything to deserve a medal, except nearly get himself killed. He didn't want the attention. He had done nothing but get burned by several laser bolts. He just wanted to get back in his Trident where he belonged.

They entered a room full of screens and holograms. Security personnel hovered at their stations, observed by officers strolling behind them. One screen caught his eye. A news feed from a television station displayed the bombing in San Francisco, the bombing that killed Lieutenant Bean. Text flashed across the screen: **TERROR ATTACK IN AMERICA?**

"Looks like the news is still all over the bombing," Austin murmured.

"You don't know the half of it," Nubern said. "Since you left San Francisco to retrieve your mother and Kadyn, the news cycle on this planet has been relentless. All these idiots talking non-stop about the threat to America. How it's terrorists or homegrown radicals. They have no idea."

Austin watched as a reporter looked into the camera, her eyes wide and her golden hair perfectly straightened. He couldn't hear her, but saw the roped-off street where Bean had died in the explosion. A team of officers circled the taxi's wreckage. Beneath the image, a scrolling text moved. The first story acknowledged the solar flares and the effect it had on cell phones.

They entered a small auditorium. Faces turned to look at him as Nubern pushed him to the front. Austin stared at his hands, feeling every eyeball on him at once. Nubern rested one hand on his shoulder.

The wheelchair came to a stop next to the podium facing four seats on stage. Nubern handed him a microphone as promised and sat behind him.

And then they waited.

Austin sighed. *Let's get this over with.*

Several minutes passed. The crowd, completely silent at first, stirred and spoke quietly. Austin studied his reflection in the podium. His cheeks were more prominent, the dark circles under his eyes more apparent. Small scrapes covered his face, but the scar on his cheek had nearly healed. Tiny hairs poked through the skin on his skull like sandpaper. Someone would make him shave his head again before he'd be allowed back in a Trident.

The lighting over the audience dimmed. A white beam centered on the four seats on stage. A door dilated at the rear, and five officers marched through, taking their seats on stage in unison like automations. Austin recognized Admiral Tolan Gist from Tarton's Junction, but not the others. He shifted in his seat, feeling both the eyes on his back and the new gazes from the officers.

Gist nodded. "It's good to see you again, Lieutenant." He turned to his companions. "This is Admiral Downs, Admiral Haberland, Admiral Denmark, and Commander Hobson. For those of you who are unaware, these very fine officers make up the command of Quadrant Eight. Hobson commands the Earth Guard Squadron, charged with defending this planet if need be. We are looking forward to your report, Lieutenant."

Austin propped his elbows on the podium and leaned into the microphone. "Thank you, sir."

"I am sure you've already been notified why we have called this meeting. We want to hear from you exactly what happened since you arrived on Earth for your leave."

"From Atlantis?"

"That's correct."

Austin sighed. He recounted his conversation with Lieutenant Bean followed by the explosion in San Francisco. His voice wavered when he spoke of Sharkey and their trip to Atlanta to save his mother and Kadyn. He paused when he reached the part about North Georgia and the mercenaries.

"Proceed, Lieutenant," Gist said.

"Yes, sir." He took a deep breath. "Shortly after our arrival at the safe house, we came under attack."

"By whom?" Admiral Downs asked.

"I don't know, sir. Security Chief Sharkey seemed to be confident these were Phantoms."

"Describe them," Hobson said, his voice quick and loud.

"Professional. They wore jump suits—no—that's not right. More like wet suits." Austin looked away, remembering the recent attack as if it happened years ago. "They had personal shrouding tech and—"

"Shroud?" Hobson asked. "You are sure about this?"

"Absolutely, sir. They could only use it for short bursts it seemed, so I only saw it once at the beginning of the attack. I think it was when they thought they had us."

"But they didn't," Gist said. "Chief Sharkey made sure of that."

"Yes," Austin said, realizing Gist aimed to help him through this questioning. "Sharkey stayed and covered us while we made it toward our extraction point."

The officers glanced at one another. Gist turned to Austin. "Thank you for your time, Lieutenant."

Nubern stepped behind him and pulled the wheelchair back. Austin closed his eyes briefly and exhaled.

"You did well, son," Nubern said. "Better than I could have."

Austin whispered, "I *hated* it.".

Gist stood. "The rest of you have been brought here so we could provide a briefing of the current situation on Earth and throughout Quadrant Eight."

He turned and activated a hologram of the quadrant. The expansion map zoomed in on Earth. A dozen red circles flickered across the globe, pulsating like a bad case of chicken pox.

"There have been a dozen events on Earth in relation to the twelve Star Runners currently on leave on this planet," Gist said. "Lieutenant Stone is the only Star Runner under attack we have safely brought back to Base Prime here in San Francisco. Since there was an attack right here on our doorstep, we believe the next move by this force will be to take out Base Prime itself to eliminate our ability to communicate in the event of an invasion."

"But who is planning an invasion?" an officer called from the back of the auditorium.

"We are unsure at this point if that is even a possibility, but we do believe Base Prime *could* be the target. These efforts could be the work of Phantoms, but their technology reveals they have support from a greater power. When the disruptor was hacked and activated, it was long enough for vessels to enter Earth's atmosphere undetected. We have to assume the worst. Enemy vessels could have landed on Earth."

"Admiral," a woman asked from the auditorium, "how exactly are these vessels curving into the solar system?"

"We are unsure at this point. One potential theory is that the enemy is using a power relay to focus long distance curves into this system." Gist gestured to the front row. "In accordance with Revelation Protocol, we have consulted our liaison with the United States. Admiral Barrow?"

An officer in a crisp white uniform stood from the front row and marched to the stage. Austin's jaw dropped. He leaned close to Nubern.

"The United States? For *real*?" he asked. "Did you know about this?"

Nubern frowned. "No one of my rank knew about this."

Admiral Barrow took to the stage. He squinted in the light, tiny wrinkles around his eyes deepening. The man inhaled, his shoulder growing broader. The bright florescent lights glimmered off his closely cropped dark hair peppered with gray. Austin marveled at the officer's chest decorated with medals and ribbons on the flawless uniform. The U.S. Naval officer faced the Legion Command.

"Good day to you all," Barrow said, his voice echoing across the auditorium. "We know you are on high alert at the moment, so I will keep this short. It is the desire of our government to keep this situation out of the public eye if at all possible. Our media is being fed the normal possibilities of a terror attack or homegrown militias being responsible for the bombing in San Francisco. These seem to be working for now as we leak leads to send the stories in different directions. This has the American public focused on the bombing and not the solar flares."

Barrow sighed. "With San Francisco already experiencing a significantly violent event, we know it is possibly a target given your operations here in the city. My people would like to avoid an evacuation if at all possible and keep this entire situation in the dark, but plans are secretly underway to manage an evacuation if needed."

Barrow snapped to the right and nodded. The hologram shifted to the Pacific Ocean off the coast of California. He used a laser pointer to highlight a blue collection of circles west of San Francisco.

"Here we have a carrier task force on standby to assist the situation," Barrow continued. "We have four VFA squadrons comprising forty F-18s and five growlers, as well as surface ships. The *Amberjack* and *Corvina* are deploying to provide missile defense if required. We are ready to support. Our people have been notified that this is just a training exercise. Our best pilots are on alert status and will be sworn to secrecy if they need to be called into action. The U.S. Navy will be ready, gentlemen. Admiral?"

"Thank you, sir," Gist said. He turned to face the audience as Barrow took his seat. "All our forces are on the highest alert since the disruptor was hacked. We were blind for approximately three Earth hours and I want the word spread across the planet to report any unusual activity. We are still unsure of what we missed during that time. However, we have the disruptor back in our control and it is operational."

The hologram shifted to show the coast of California. A crimson square pulsated around San Francisco. Gist gestured to the west and focused far into the Pacific Ocean.

"As for our current defenses, all efforts of counter-espionage are underway. Our ground units are staged at Base Prime and Base Beta on the other side of the world and will be moved into action where required. In the event the attack comes from the orbit, we are currently redeploying available craft from Quadrant Eight to Atlantis. I have been informed Atlantis will have a total of sixty-three Tridents prepped and ready to fly."

"Excuse me, Admiral Gist," Hobson said. "We currently only have twenty-two Tridents on alert status stationed at Atlantis and not enough seasoned Star Runners to fly them. What if this expected attack on San Francisco happens sooner than you think?"

"We cannot risk moving more forces to Earth in the event this is a ruse. Pray any attack doesn't happen sooner."

14

Josh pressed against the sand, watching as the pirates woke before dawn. The sky grew brighter in the distance. Two pirates stretched and strolled over to work on the fighters. The other two sat at a crate serving as a table near the spacecraft. They studied a battered display and held a discussion in hushed tones.

"Those two must be the pilots," Josh whispered, pointing toward the crate. "If this is going to work, I'll have to take out one of them first."

Waylon grumbled. "I don't know if I like this plan."

"It's the best we've got and only two hours until sunrise."

"All right." He thrust a massive finger in Josh's direction. "You just make sure this works. Got it?"

"If I can't, I won't be around for you to harass."

"True enough. Fate be good."

Waylon crawled away to work on his part of the plan. Josh waited, his head spinning. Hunger twisted his gut. His mind wandered and his eyes threatened to close. He smacked his cheek and tried to sharpen, tried to...*stay frosty.*

He smiled.

Stay frosty.

They used to say it whenever they went into combat on the servers back on Earth. "Combat" seemed too grand a description for what they did back then, even if the game served as an early simulation. Austin probably had his wings by now, might even be serving somewhere else in the galaxy and flying Tridents, instead of these scrappy, make-shift pirate fighters on the landing pad.

The Tyral modified fighters could pack a punch, he knew that firsthand, but he had never flown one. Even if some of the pirate fighters had been born as Tridents, the heavy modifications and customized features made each Tyral spacecraft unique. He had once asked about it in class, but was told the modifications could be as varied as the pilot. He knew it might take him a moment to learn how to fly again.

But Waylon was counting on him to remember. Fast.

The horizon flickered beyond the landing pad, oranges and yellows rising from the direction Waylon had run. Sparkling embers twinkled into the sky. A moment later, the ground ignited, dry grasses roaring into a cloud of fire. Waylon's inferno lit the heavens.

Josh watched the pirate group point toward the fire. Two of them ran toward the flames while the other duo remained on the landing pad.

He tensed, watching the two pilots discussing something. The men spoke and pointed, nodding as they did so. The pilots parted. One headed toward the fighters. The other, the one wearing the red sash, hurried to the tent as he studied a tablet.

Now!

Josh sprinted from the sands, rushing for the pilot at the tent. His legs wobbled, his knees buckling as he ran. His feet kicked sand high into the air. He gripped the sharpened root in his right hand. His starved muscles burned. He kicked his legs high, remembering to keep his weight on the front of his feet like springs.

The pilot wearing the red sash fell into darkness away from the light of the flames. Josh reached the landing pad, but still found twenty yards to go until he reached the tent. He pressed on, the light of the flames washing over him. The red sash exited the tent and halted, staring at him.

For a moment, the two men locked eyes. Josh hesitated. He gripped the root. The pilot stared with bloodshot eyes, his hand hovering over the holster strapped to his left leg.

A heartbeat passed.

Then, the pilot yanked his pistol from its holster. Josh lunged forward. A bolt sizzled past Josh's wiry frame. A second shot blasted through his ear. He screamed but never slowed.

The two collided, the impact sending them tumbling back into the tent. Sand soared into the air. Grit burned his eyes. They rolled, Josh ending up on top of the pirate. Thick fingers pressed into his throat. He couldn't breathe.

Using what strength he could muster, Josh thrust the root forward as hard as he could. The sharpened edge pierced flesh. Hot blood squirted down his hand.

But the pilot hurled Josh away. He rolled through the canvas. His vision blurred. He found his feet as the pilot ran for the fighter.

When Josh stood, he heard the engines from the other remaining fighter rumbling to life. The thrust sent howling gusts twirling. Tents tumbled off into the dusk sky, the engines creating a sandstorm as the fighter lifted off. In the center of the howling sands, the remaining pilot clutched his stomach and stumbled toward the only remaining fighter.

Josh pursued him.

He ran until his body threatened to stop. Darkness surrounded his vision and his head wobbled.

"Hey!" he yelled, grabbing a crate for balance.

The enemy fired without looking back, his attention still on the fighter. Josh dropped to one knee, the laser bolt passing over him. He shook away dizziness and continued forward. He closed the distance.

The pilot reached the ladder leading to the cockpit just as Josh ripped him from his craft. The pirate fell to the ground, the pistol falling into the sand. Josh loomed over him, the sharpened root ready to strike.

"Please, no. Please, just take it." The pilot held up his hands. "I beg you."

With the root above his head, Josh hesitated. He looked back at the idle fighter.

It was all the time his foe needed.

Whipping a weapon from his tunic and rising to one knee, the pirate pulled back, his arm cocked, ready to hurl a sharp curved knife.

Two massive hands engulfed the pilot's head and snapped his neck. The pirate, a shocked expression still on his face, collapsed into the dirt.

Josh recoiled to see Waylon's hulking frame towering over the pilot's twitching body, his sweaty skin gleaming in the firelight.

"Go!" Waylon pointed to the sky. "*Go*!"

Josh followed his gaze. The fleeing fighter screamed hard for the horizon, but swept in a long, slow arc to change course back toward the landing pad. The pilot planned to eliminate their prisoners.

He searched the dead pirate's clothing and found what had to be the keycard for the fighter craft. It did not seem much different than the security on a Trident. When he passed the card in front of the canopy, the cockpit's electronics whined to life. He climbed the ladder and jumped into the cockpit. A cool emerald green pulsated off the control board as he shot through the checklist, exhaling when he saw the pirate's flight tablet was already inserted into the console dock.

He ran out of time. The *pom-pom-pom* of laser guns told him the clock was ticking. Crimson bolts spit death, igniting entire rows of prisoners. Men incinerated to ash in an instant. One man running for the barn was vaporized. The pirate fighter shot overhead. Somehow, Josh knew the next pass would be aiming for him.

"Hurry up!" Waylon yelled.

"I'm trying! This ain't like starting a scooter!"

"A *what*?"

The engines came to life a second later. Josh prayed these pirate morons had done all the prep work the night before. He lifted ten feet off the ground, the exhaust shooting sand in all directions. He glanced down, saw Waylon, offered a salute, and hit the throttle. As the engine rumbled with power, he smiled and exhaled.

The fighter accelerated toward the aqua-blue dawn sky. His head rocked as the ship accelerated, bumping against the cockpit, sending a flash of pain where the pilot's blast had burned his ear. The horizon rapidly transitioned to orange. He hugged the ground, trying to keep his fighter low. He focused on the sensors and tried to ignore the fact he hadn't been in the cockpit since the Rockshot competition.

The enemy closed, his targeting computer hunting Josh's signature and beeping inside his cockpit. He eased more power into his engines while he checked the topography: flat grasslands until the ground split into a dozen canyons like capillaries. If he could make it to the canyons, he might have a shot.

Lasers fired over his head.

This was it.

Josh eased everything into the throttle, the engine's whine growing higher in pitch. He banked, rolled, carried out every evasive maneuver he'd learned in training and even improvised. The pirate stayed with him, laser bolts blasting the ground in front of him. The stray bolts ignited the grasslands with a shower of sparks and golden embers.

The grasslands gave way to deep canyons. Josh dove into the crevices at his first chance, dodging sharp rocks stretching out like teeth. The laser fire ceased. He checked the sensors.

The bandit still trailed him, close.

Josh's knuckles turned white on the stick as he pressed near the fissure's floor. He whipped across a raging river close enough for mist to dot his windshield. He couldn't risk a glance, but knew his exhaust had to be sending up a spray into his attacker's face.

A laser bolt sizzled into the water in front of him. He looked up but already knew his error. The pirate had gone for altitude, and now shot at him from high above the canyon.

Josh clenched his teeth and yanked back on the stick, bringing the fighter to a ninety degree angle. Gravity pressed him into his seat.

He fired in the pirate's direction but only had enough power for one shot. The bolt passed underneath the bandit.

The pirate's counterattack lit up the sky with streaks of red. Josh rolled but kept his direction trained on his enemy. A bolt smashed into Josh's wing, the shields flickering. Another charred his tail before he passed directly underneath his opponent in the opposite direction.

Josh pulled back, bringing his fighter to bear down on the bandit as he shot for higher orbit. He transferred power from the shields to lasers. He rolled his head around and cracked his knuckles as he bore down on his target. It was now the pirate's turn to evade.

"Let's see what you got," he said.

The chase hugged the atmosphere, both ships skipping across the planet's protective barrier. The primitive shields buckled but held. The modified fighter didn't have the same power resources as his Trident. With his engines powered at maximum, the computer diverted the remaining energy into the emergency shielding battling the atmosphere, causing the lasers to charge slowly. The laser energy banks flashed green once on his HUD, signaling he had enough to provide one shot.

Josh fired. The laser bolts shot forward and dissipated off the pirate's shields. He pulled up, his shields nearly gone from the planet's atmosphere.

Time to make him drink his own medicine.

Josh flew away from the atmospheric effects. He banked right and peered over the edge. The pirate fighter left a long, orange streak across the atmosphere of this cursed planet. He hovered over him, like a hawk waiting for the right moment. Apparently this guy didn't realize how to defend against his own tactics. Or, Josh thought, he figured the atmospheric disturbance would save him from laser fire. Whatever his plan, Josh wasn't going to give him the chance to realize his error.

And then it hit him.

The pirate stalled for time, and hiding at the edge of the

atmosphere was a good place to get it. His enemy had either sent a signal for reinforcements or he plotted a curve to get out of here.

This needed to end. Now.

The laser's energy banks read full.

Finally.

Josh pushed forward on the stick. His fighter zipped forward like a missile. He leaned forward, his shoulders tensing. The crosshairs bounced just ahead of his target. The HUD blinked once, turning yellow to signify he was in laser range.

Wait.

The fighter bounced, hitting the upper edge of the atmosphere. The crosshairs transitioned to green.

Wait.

Josh held his finger gently on the trigger. He waited until his fighter came closer, so close he read the blackened numbers on the enemy's tail.

He pulled the trigger. The lasers erupted in crimson. Bolts smashed into his enemy's twin engines. He spun down out of the atmospheric cover. He stayed on him, unleashing the full power of his guns. The shots pounded the enemy fighter. The bandit's shields buckled and fizzled out. Pieces of debris spun off like sparks off a welding torch. The engine exploded. A flash of fire and light illuminated the atmosphere. He pulled away.

Leveling off, Josh banked left to watch the fiery wreckage tumble through the sky. The debris sent sparkling lines across the atmosphere like fireworks. He lingered, breathing heavily. The last bits of the fighter disappeared in the clouds. He leaned back in the seat, gazing into the sky.

No ejection pod or parachute. The pirate he had seen at the fireside early was dead, gone forever. He had killed a man.

Josh touched his burnt ear, the skin flashing with pain. The pirates had tried to do the same to him and nearly succeeded.

Time to pick up Waylon and get off this rock before any reinforcements arrive.

He eased forward on the stick, tilting his trajectory toward the ground. Scanning the horizon, Josh searched for the blaze Waylon had set for both a diversion and a signal fire. Black smoke twirled into the sky to the east, looming like a spring tornado. He thought of his partner in the middle of the inferno.

I hope Waylon is still alive.

15

"This is crazy." Austin gripped the arms on the wheelchair hard. "I feel fine. I need to get back out there."

"Give it one more night," the nurse said. "You'll be able to walk freely first thing in the morning."

The nurse helped Austin to his bed. She shut off the lights and left, leaving him staring at the ceiling. He sighed, trying to chill. He imagined being in a hammock, relaxing with a glass of lemonade as a breeze caused him to sway.

But his mind wouldn't let him relax.

A fight neared, he felt it in his bones. Something wasn't right. Even though he was now in the center of Base Prime, perhaps the most secure Legion compound in the whole of Quadrant Eight, he saw the shadow-like Phantoms every time he closed his eyes. He saw the men materialize from nothingness, clad in clothing black as night. They hunted him. They'd chased his mother. They'd hunted Kadyn. They'd killed Sharkey.

"Lieutenant."

"No need to whisper, Captain," Austin said. "I can't sleep."

Nubern chuckled as he moved into the room. He sat down in the bedside chair. "Feeling that great, eh?"

"I don't think my problems are physical, sir." He swallowed. "I can't stop thinking about it."

"I know," he said. "I wish I could say it gets better."

Austin grimaced. "It felt different destroying a spacecraft. I saw the explosion and marked another kill. It wasn't a person. This killing up close—and trying not to be killed—is...difficult."

"I know."

They sat in silence. Austin enjoyed the quiet and listened to the heart monitor.

"Your treatments are almost done," Nubern said. "You should be back at one hundred percent by morning."

"That's what they say. How's Mom?"

"Better," he said with a nod. "Improving every hour. Kadyn's in recovery and has been talking with our people. She is going to be okay, but it'll take time."

"I know how that feels."

"Unfortunately, you don't have that luxury, Lieutenant."

Austin heard the change in his tone, a shift reflecting the chain of command. "Yes, sir."

"You heard the briefing. Command is trying to shuffle resources around the quadrant. Earth only has so many fighters as it is. More are coming, but it's going to take time. You know what we have to do. We have more ready fighters than we do Star Runners. I know you're tired and you don't have much combat experience. If San Francisco is about to be hit, we will need you up there."

He nodded. "I'll be ready."

"Good." Nubern tapped the side of the bed. "First thing tomorrow, you'll be transported to Atlantis. Once you have your Trident prepped, we have been authorized to carry out shrouded patrols just off the coast of California."

"Sounds good, sir." He smiled, welcoming the idea of getting back into the cockpit. Of course, he had never flown in Earth's atmosphere, never dreamed he would have the chance. "Any idea what we're looking for, sir?"

"Anything that seems out of place. Any ships coming into the atmosphere. We don't know more other than the fact Earth is in the crosshairs."

Austin nodded and slid his fingertips over his laser wounds, felt the smooth skin.

"Your skin has regenerated and created new flesh," Nubern said. "You won't be able to tell the difference."

He shivered, thinking of the intense burning when the laser hit him and smelling the frying flesh. "It doesn't matter," he said, still gazing at the wall. "I won't be forgetting this soon."

Nubern touched his shoulder. "You won't ever forget it, son." He smiled. "I'll see you in Atlantis tomorrow. I'm heading out now."

"Ready to get down there, sir."

Nubern paused in the doorway. "Ah, Stone, one more thing." He nodded to someone in the hallway and a nurse appeared, carrying a tablet in her hands. "You received a recorded message during the night."

He blinked. "A message? For me?"

"Yes, Lieutenant. I will see you tomorrow."

As Nubern left, the nurse smiled and set the tablet in Austin's lap. A white screen glowed with a yellow arrow in the center.

"Press play when you are ready," she said, leaving the room.

Austin sat transfixed on the screen. He had no idea who would have sent him a message. He took a deep breath and pressed the arrow.

The screen flickered and white static flashed. The image stabilized, revealing a beautiful and familiar face.

"Hello, Rock," Ryker said with a grin. Her black hair was pulled back. She wore a Tizona blue sweatshirt with a silver sword emblazoned on her chest. Behind her stretched a gray mat like one would see in a gym. "I'm glad you are okay, Austin. Nubern sent me a message."

Austin cocked his head to the side, bringing the tablet closer to his face as she spoke.

"The docs say my leg has rebuilt itself. I have learned to walk again and I am getting stronger. I should be able to return to duty in a couple days." She looked at her hands. "You know, I wouldn't have been able...I wouldn't be, ah, I wouldn't be here at all if it weren't for you." She cleared her throat. "Anyway, I know your leave hasn't gone the way you had hoped, but I'm so glad you are safe."

She leaned closer to the camera and stared. "I wish we could have spoken live, but you know the distance between the Oma and Earth is too far. I wish it wasn't. I...wish a lot of things." She shook her head. "I'm stalling...I wanted to invite you...here. After my rehab is complete, I'll wait for you if you, well, want to come. I will wait. I miss you and hope you would like to come see me. If you want. If you can't and you want to stay there for leave, I understand. I, ah, hope we can be stationed together. Take care and I will be in touch, one way or the other." She touched the camera, gave her crooked smile, and killed the transmission.

Austin sighed, staring at the black tablet.

BASE PRIME's hallways seemed empty compared to yesterday. One nurse had passed by his room earlier in the morning, smiled, and continued on her rounds. A medical robot trolled by after her, its servos whining.

Austin sat up in his bed and stretched, reaching his hands high above his head. His new skin tingled, but there was no pain as he moved. He shifted his legs out from beneath the blanket and slowly stood as if he traveled on a ship in rough seas. Wobbling, he steadied his legs.

The familiar nurse stepped through the doorway. "Ready to get up and going, Lieutenant?"

"You have *no* idea," Austin grumbled. "My legs feel strange."

"You haven't used them in a couple of days," she said, descending upon him like a doting mother. She checked his body sensors, pulling electrodes from his skin. "It will feel odd at first, but you should be fine in a couple minutes. Just don't go play any Ember Ball tourneys today."

Austin looked at her pale skin and purple eyes. “Ember Ball? Never heard of it.”

Her eyes widened like plums. “You’ll have to try it. It’s raging at the capital worlds right now. Might even replace Jouncy as the main pastime.”

Austin chuckled. “I don’t know what you’re talking about.”

She stopped working. “Have you not been to the capital worlds?”

“No.”

“Where are you from?”

“Here.”

Her jaw dropped. “Really? You’re from Earth?”

“Born and bred.” He shrugged and slipped on his freshly pressed Tizona blues. “I’ve only had my wings for a few days.”

“You’ve had quite a ride then.” She shut off the final monitor at his bedside. “I hope to see you at a game in the future.”

“Yeah. Me, too.”

Austin strolled through the empty halls. He passed doctors and two officers focused on tablets. Mostly he paid attention to the tingling in his legs. He paused at a terminal station and checked for the location of his mother’s room.

When he found her, she was focused on a television in the corner of the room. The news played images of the San Francisco car bombing. Text along the bottom of the screen announced the solar flares had come to an end, but “hundreds of thousands” complained about the interruption in their cell phone coverage. Austin looked back to Mom.

The skin on her face seemed stretched, her cheeks more prominent. Puffy red welts mixed with black splotches under her eyes. He composed himself as he stepped in the door. When she looked to him, the tension in her face eased.

“Austin,” she said, her voice raspy. “Oh, honey. You look so handsome in your uniform.”

He clasped her hand. “How are you?”

“Oh, I’m okay. I *think* I’m okay.”

"I'm so glad. When they told me, I wanted to come see you. They said I couldn't move, something about my skin repairing itself."

"They told me you were okay, so I knew. I can't tell you how glad I am."

He sat on the edge of her bed near her feet. "You sure you're feeling all right?"

"Some of this technology is beyond me and I'm a nurse."

"You'll learn."

"I don't know. I'm old."

"Only when you think you are." He smiled. "Besides, you've always been the one to teach me everything. Guess it's my turn now. I want you to be out there with me, Mom. I know we'll be on different ships, but I hope you want to do this. I can't imagine leaving you here."

She rubbed his hand. "Are you okay?"

He hesitated. "Before all this happened, I was having trouble realizing I would have to leave Earth for years at a time. That meant I'd be leaving everything I've ever known." He looked at her. "I didn't want to lie to you. In a funny way, I'm relieved you know. I just wish you hadn't found out like this."

"I know, honey." She squeezed his hand. "When I saw you in the woods, the gunfire all around us and the forest catching fire, I thought I'd never see you again. Are the doctors sure you're going to be fine?"

He gestured to the most serious wound on his collar bone. "Yes. They healed the wounds and regenerated skin over the burns. I know we've only been here a couple days, but I'm feeling well enough to return to my duties."

Her brow wrinkled, her eyes flicking toward his holstered laser pistol. "Duties? What does *that* mean?"

"It means I'll be transferring to Atlantis soon. They need pilots, Mom, and that's what I do."

She closed her eyes and sighed. "I understand. You have to do what you have to do. I just can't get over, well, I just can't believe what you've been through."

Looking away from him and back at the television, she wiped tears from her cheek. "This isn't the college your father and I wished for, that's for sure. I wanted you to have fun, to enjoy yourself, find a little bit of happiness. I didn't want life to become so serious. You need to enjoy this, Austin. You worked hard and never took a moment in high school to enjoy yourself. You've always been focused like a missile, even ignoring friends. Sometimes I think you only played baseball because your daddy wanted you to or maybe you thought it would lead to a scholarship. I dreamed you would fall in love, have a job you would be proud of. I thought you were on the path of being happy, finding some joy. But you've changed. You grew up, fast, and have taken on this insane and tremendous responsibility."

"I've done what I had to do, Mom, just like you."

"Your father would have been so proud of you. He would have wanted to see this. I wish we had time to talk. Can you tell me more?"

He held her hand and kissed it. "No time today, I need to get going."

"Already?"

"I need to get there. I'll miss you, but you'll be so busy you won't have time to notice I'm gone."

"Why's that?"

"I've been told you start your transition classes today."

"What's that?"

"Because you live on Earth, you're already a Legion citizen by default. The transition classes are supposed to give you the history of the Galactic Legion of Planets and other things."

"Oh." Her eyes widened. "Fun."

He smiled. "After that, you'll begin basic training to serve on a Legion medical ship, if that's still something you'd want."

She grinned like a little girl. "Yes. It sounds fun."

Austin stood. "Once they let you start walking around, could you check in on Kadyn for me?"

"Sure, honey."

"I'm worried," Austin said, his gut twitching. "I can't believe this happened to her."

Her face grew rigid. "None of this was your fault, sweetie. None of it. You saved us. I've been sitting here replaying the past days in my head. The image of you standing in the flames...fighting off those men, protecting us. Kadyn knows, honey. Give her time."

He nodded. "I will, Mom. See you soon."

THE BRIGHT LIGHTS of the tube transport chamber glowed like a star. Austin blew a bubble with his chewing gum as the hatch opened.

"Welcome to Atlantis, Lieutenant," the crewman said.

"Thank you."

He reached up for a hand

"Get yourself up," the crewman grumbled and walked away.

"Thanks a lot," Austin said, climbing out of the tube. "What's that all about?"

"Just drop it." The crewman glared back at him, his face rigid and covered in stubble.

The regulations in Atlantis must be lighter than the rest of the navy. Austin had never seen a man on Tarton's Junction with such a beard.

Shaking his head, Austin hurried across the room and the exit door dilated. The bustling control room pulsated with activity. The dome stretched high above his head, a glowing green hologram of Earth floating in the air. Dozens of red circles signified alert areas across the planet.

Beyond, a pair of deep sea creatures glowed, swimming in three pairs. They shot in different directions as a spacecraft rumbled past. Bubbles danced around like living creatures. He stood with his mouth hanging open, watching the glowing blue fish. Hundreds of staff worked at stations throughout the dome, some staring at standard computer monitors while others worked on holograms.

Austin made his way down the steps. The staff hurried to different stations, the conversations frantic and rushed.

"I want those six Tridents moved away from the civilian hangar immediately!" an officer yelled, sending staff scurrying like scared birds.

Austin blinked. Commander Carv Wallace, the man who knew Lieutenant Ryan Bean.

"Commander Wallace?" he asked, walking toward the muscular man. "Commander?"

"What?" he barked, his eyes glaring. His expression softened. "I don't have a lot of time, Lieutenant. Sorry. What's on your mind?"

Wallace grabbed a tablet from the table and started walking. Austin shook his head and followed.

"We met the other day when I arrived with Lieutenant Bean."

"Bean?" he asked, his attention focused on the tablet. "Bean was a good man. Great Star Runner. The Legion will miss him."

"Yes." His legs still tingled like they had fallen asleep, and he hurried to keep up with Wallace. "I'm supposed to report to Captain Nubern. Has he been through here?"

"Look, it's Stone, right?" Wallace sighed, gesturing to the tablet. "I've got all manner of problems coming through here today. Half the planet's trying to leave and squadrons from all over the quadrant are scheduled to arrive over the next two days. Just managing the traffic of people trying to depart and fighters coming in has been crazy. I just had six Tridents diverted to the civilian hangar because the control tower fouled up the incoming traffic. Now you want me to page a captain for you?"

Austin looked at his feet. "I'll head to the military hangar. I've never been here for anything other than shuttle traffic to Tarton's Junction. I'm sorry I bothered you, Commander."

Wallace placed his hands on his hips. "Look, Lieutenant. Things here have been, well, crazy." He pointed to the far side of the dome. "You head that way and follow the glowing red rectangles on the wall. That'll lead you to the military hangar where almost every Star

Runner currently in Atlantis is staging to begin shrouded patrols. You should find your captain there."

"Thank you, sir."

Austin nearly ran away from Wallace. The man exuded an annoyance with the entire world. His nostrils flared when he looked back at the tablet. The fluid workings of Atlantis had broken away, only to be replaced by chaos and frenzy. It was like watching a tornado of humanity with Wallace at the center.

Austin weaved his way through the crowd. As instructed, he followed the glowing red rectangles to the military hangar, passed through a massive doorway and paused. Rather than seeing freighters and shuttles looming in the hangar as he had seen before, Trident fighters lined the expanse from wall to wall. Star Runners in different colored squadron uniforms mingled with the mechanics. The crew's faces were smeared with grease. The pilots studied tablets and conversed in excited tones. Sparks flew from welding torches.

"Watch it there," a gruff voice called.

"Ah, sure," Austin said, moving past a pair of fighters he didn't recognize. They looked related to the Tridents, but had canisters under the wings and dual tails instead of one. The craft's bulky nose looked like a bulldog's, with two cannons under the cockpit, much larger than the standard laser cannons onboard Tridents. Like the Trident, the wings curved above the fuselage in its landing position.

His feet scuffed the deck as he moved through the madness. He felt overwhelmed. The amount of weaponry in the hangar impressed him. This must be what it was like on a Legion carrier. He had never, until now, realized what it would truly be like to be standing in the center of a galactic power.

"Can I help you, Lieutenant?"

Austin turned to see a tall, muscular woman wearing familiar Tizona blue. She had her blonde hair tied back in a bun, tight enough to pull the skin back on her forehead.

"I have orders to report to Captain Nubern."

"Nubern?" She glanced up like she was thinking. "From Tarton's Junction, right?"

"That's right."

She nodded. "Nubern left with a couple other Runners to help transfer some Tridents from the freighter hangar. Got some geniuses up there running the tower, but that's nothing new. Am I right?"

"Yeah." He smiled, not really knowing why. "Did he leave recently?"

"Five minutes tops. If you hurry, you can catch him."

He gestured back the way he came. "That way?"

"You got it."

Austin hurried back to the dome. He focused on the Earth hologram above as he walked, careful not to crash into the work stations. Green and blue blips soared to and from the planet, signifying the busy traffic coming and going. The hologram flickered.

He paused a moment before he heard a shockwave rumble beneath his feet like an earthquake. The drone of workers stopped as everyone looked up from their station. Another vibration shook the ground, somewhere from behind him.

He turned around. Massive bubbles rushed up into the water above the dome. A light illuminated the air pockets in an orange light. The gleam in the command center dropped to a dull red.

"ATTENTION! ATTENTION!" a female voice boomed over the intercom. "HULL BREECH DETECTED IN HANGAR THREE. ALL COMPRESSION DOORS CLOSING. REPEAT: ALL COMPRESSION DOORS CLOSING."

In one unified movement, the crew turned toward the military hangar. Austin looked at the doors he had just passed through. Water exploded through like a dam had burst, howling like a wild animal. Water swept him off his feet and he crashed to the deck, the force throwing him toward the wall. He collided with a desk and ended up in the corner, frigid water rising to his neck. For a moment, he wondered if the entire dome had collapsed. Water rushed around him like an icy river, numbing his skin, taking his breath away.

He shook his head and tried to stand.

A compression door on the far side of the dome clamped shut, closing off any further water from entering the room. The crew stood from their stations. Binders and books floated in the standing water around him. Austin gasped for air.

"Everyone to their stations," Wallace said calmly over the intercom. "Red alert. I need a SITREP."

"Commander. OPS," another voice, less calm, said over the intercom. "Hangar Three has been destroyed."

"What?" Wallace barked, his voice rising. "*How*?"

"Unknown. All connection with the hangar has been lost. I am attempting to get confirmation from outside Atlantis."

"Do it!" Wallace yelled. "An entire hangar can't disappear!"

Austin stood, the chilly water at his thighs. Papers, tablets, and other debris swirled around the surface. He tasted the salt on his lips and wiped at his face. Reaching over, he helped a female officer to her feet. A bright red gash on her forehead bled down her face. He steadied her with his right hand, trying not to fall into the swirl of water.

"The inbound freighter, *Brazen Bryce,* just confirmed an explosion over Hangar Three," radio traffic buzzed.

"Tell all incoming planetary traffic they have to reroute to Base Beta," Wallace said. "Defense, I want the point weapons manned and ready. Get—"

An explosion ripped through the command center. Fire whipped into the air. A row of computers disintegrated. Staff members burned and writhed, falling into the water with a fizzle. Two men flanked the door to the tube transport chamber, laser rifles pointed into the room. Austin recognized the scruffy man on the right from his arrival, the one who did not fit in.

"There!" he yelled.

Too late.

The men fired into the crew, laser bolts burning through officers and control stations. Sparks shot up. Austin pushed the bleeding officer behind a control station for cover, his heart pounding.

He pulled his sidearm. When the laser fire paused, he peeked over the control station. Bolts sizzled over his head. He ducked back.

"INTRUDERS HAVE ENTERED THE BASE ON DECKS ONE,

THREE, AND FIVE," a female voice announced. "WE ARE UNDER ATTACK. I REPEAT; ATLANTIS IS UNDER ATTACK. ALL PERSONN—"

Static screeched over the speakers. Austin looked at the officer near him.

"Are you okay?" he asked

"Head's spinning." She pressed her hand against her forehead, blood seeping through her fingers. "We can't let them get control of this room."

He risked a glance. "There's two of them at the door."

"Do you see Wallace?"

"I can't see anyone."

She nodded. "You can't let them take this room. If they do, they have Atlantis."

"Right," he said through chattering teeth.

"Hey," she said, grabbing his shoulder, "don't get shot."

"Already done that. Don't plan on it happening again."

Austin knelt in the cold water and peered around the corner. The attackers fired into another area on the far side of the dome. Now was his chance.

He dove into the water and moved for the next row of control stations. Laser fire continued, the firefight intensifying. Men and women screamed. He glanced over the stations again, saw an attacker firing to his left. Raising his pistol, he emptied his charge. Bolts ignited the attacker's uniform. The man spun around and disappeared into the water.

The other attacker, now alone, backed up toward the tube transport chamber. He fired and disappeared out of sight.

"I think we're clear!" Austin yelled. He stood with caution. "Commander?"

"Wallace is out," a voice said. A woman stood from behind a control station in the center of the dome. "I'm in charge for now."

"Who are you?" Austin asked.

"Security Officer Brannen."

Austin kicked through the water, moving slowly like he was back in the swamp around the Tizona School of Excellence.

"Officer Brannen," he said. "What's going on?"

"Wait a minute." She gestured to two soldiers on the far side of the dome. "You two, silence our guest in the transport room. Be careful."

Brannen turned to face Austin, her skin covered in cuts and bruises. "What is it, Lieutenant?"

"What's going on?"

"We have reports of attackers on several decks. Hangar Three's gone. Our alert fighters have engaged an enemy vessel on the outer perimeter, but we're only getting fragments. Someone has fired a system-wide disruptor."

Austin shook his head. "I thought we had the only disruptor in the solar system."

"So did we, but another's been fired. Electronics across the planet have been going haywire for the past few minutes. Right now, we're blind."

Laser fire erupted from the transport room. A minute later, the two soldiers came through the door and gave a thumbs up.

"We got him, Brannen!" one shouted. "Found the normal transport staff tucked into four out-of-service tubes. No telling where these intruders tubed in from."

"Well done, Marines!" she yelled.

"What about Wallace?" Austin asked.

"He's over here," she said, moving behind the control station. "He got swept up in the water and hit his head. Concussion, I believe. He's out."

She glanced at her tablet, typing in orders as she spoke. "We just took out another team trying to get to the life support systems."

"Who are they?"

"Phantoms."

"*Here*? Are you sure?"

"Absolutely."

"How'd they get here?"

Brannen grimaced. "They must have had help from the inside. Must have taken tubes over the past couple days. They have targeted Atlantis, but for what, I have no idea."

Austin glanced down at the dark displays. "We have no clue what's going on out there?"

"No, but we know our alert fighters have engaged something moving across the ocean floor at the outer perimeter."

"Do we have any defense cannons?" another officer asked, wading through the water.

Brannen nodded toward the burning row of electronic wreckage. "That explosion took out the automated systems. I've ordered crews to the cannons, but I don't know if the message went through."

"I'll make sure of it," the officer said.

On his way to the door, the man grabbed four other crewmen. The five went through the hatch leading to other corridors, grabbing laser rifles as they made their way through the destruction. Distance explosions rattled the station, sending ripples across the standing water.

"Pozorski, Everitt," Brannen said, pointing at two crewmen, "I need power in here and I need it yesterday. Start with the sensors. Then get the pumps operating. We can't do our job if we're freezing."

Austin clenched his chattering teeth and holstered his weapon. He thought of Nubern in the civilian hangar moving the six Tridents back to Hangar Three.

"So much for the target being San Francisco. What about the civilian hangar?" he asked.

"You know what I do, Lieutenant."

"Other than what's on alert now, we lost all our fighters." He thought of the muscular blonde pilot he'd seen moments before the explosion. "And our Star Runners."

"I know." She handed him a headset. "This'll work anywhere in Atlantis. You run into resistance, I want to know about it."

Austin grabbed the headset and turned to leave. The power flickered like lightning. The hologram of Earth faded and disappeared.

Displays came to life, then died. After a moment, the power kicked back on full.

"The disruptor has ceased," Brannen said, her gaze fixed on the hologram. "Our sensors are coming back online."

The officers able to stand clapped. Austin slapped Brannen on the shoulder and smiled, until he looked closer at the displays.

Six large vessels surrounded Atlantis, skimming across the ocean floor from all sides and closing in fast. Torpedoes moved toward the other three hangars, including the civilian hangar. Defense cannons dispatched the torps, but alert fighters had disappeared, probably destroyed by the incoming vessels.

"If they wanted to destroy us, they could do that from a distance," Brannen said. "They mean to board and take Atlantis."

"Why?" Austin asked.

"This is the center of Legion activity for the entire system. If this falls, the system is wide open to invasion."

"Can we hold?"

"We're manning the cannons to deal with incoming submersibles," she said. "Inside, we'll set up defense stations at all access points to the main control room. If they board, they'll run into a fight."

Explosions rumbled in the distance, followed by sporadic laser fire and screams. Brannen's eyes darted around the room, staring at displays and holograms.

"The defenses have to hold," she said, capturing his gaze. "We will not allow Atlantis to fall. I may need you to help coordinate the defense on the northern corridor."

"I'll do what I can to help." Austin nodded.

He looked up at the flickering Earth hologram. A clump of red spots appeared in high orbit.

"Wait. Zoom in on that," he said.

Brannen ordered a crew member to enhance the area. The hologram illuminated the red grouping and zoomed.

"Oh, my," she said.

"What is it?"

"Looks like fifty small craft grouping in high orbit. They're descending in attack formation."

"Fighters?" Austin asked, thinking of Mom and Kadyn in San Francisco. "Whose?"

She leaned over a nearby display. "Unknown, they have no transponders, but the vessel type matches the hybrid vessels and modified Tridents used by the Tyral Pirates. They're entering the atmosphere now and are coming, fast."

He swallowed. "To where?"

"Here. They're coming here. San Francisco was never the target." She shook her head. "Atlantis is."

A wail resounded throughout the station.

"What is that?" Austin asked.

Brannen stared at her control board. "There's a transmission coming in."

"From where? Earth?"

She keyed for a gamma wave trace. "It's originating from orbit."

"From the incoming fighters?"

She nodded and pressed a button. An electronic screech filled the air, echoing throughout the water-filled command center.

"Atlantis."

The voice boomed. Austin winced, an icy chill rippling through the hairs on his neck. *Dax Rodon.*

"Atlantis," Rodon sneered, "I am thrilled to speak to you at last."

Brannen looked at Austin, her chin quivering.

"Atlantis is surrounded with my submersibles. We have fighters inbound ready to bomb you from the air. I am giving you this chance to surrender."

Brannen grabbed a headset. "You will never get away with this, Rodon. We have reinforcements—"

"Spare me," Rodon barked. "We both know there are no Legion reinforcements on the way. You are spread out across the quadrant in a vain effort to stop us. We will board and take Atlantis. And you will let us."

"Never," she said, strength fading from her voice.

"You will regret this," Rodon said. "Remember, as you lay dying, I gave you this chance."

The transmission ceased.

Brannen focused on her control station. When she looked at Austin, her bloodshot eyes filled with worry. She shook her head, her lips pressing together.

Austin touched her shoulder. "Don't worry," he said. "I'll get to the civilian hangar, see what I can do."

16

Flames soared hundreds of feet into the air. Fierce winds whipped the fiery inferno until it looked like a twister from hell. Josh adjusted course, the temperature bouncing the modified Trident fighter around like a toy. He tightened the harness over his shoulders and banked into a long, slow turn to circle the farm.

Waylon's blaze had reached the crops. Prisoners scurried. A horde of men sprinted in the direction of the hills, away from the encampment. Others moved toward the compound. Just outside the barn, standing like a statue in the midst of chaos, stood a large man brandishing a laser rifle. He fired twice at an angle. Warning shots sizzled into the air and dissipated in the distance. Prisoners who got too close to the compound ran away from the man's laser fire.

Waylon.

As Josh descended through the flames, he lowered the landing gear. He dropped the fighter near the barn, hoping the fires wouldn't hit his spacecraft. He dropped to twenty feet, twelve, then gently touched down. He opened the canopy and leaned over the side, staring at Waylon standing in the flames.

"Come on!" he yelled.

Screaming toward the mass of prisoners, Waylon fired twice more over the crowd and sprinted for the fighter. Three prisoners rushed through the field fires wielding farming tools over their heads, their faces wild with fury.

"Don't leave us here!" the closest one shrieked.

"Look out!" Josh screamed.

Waylon spun around. He dropped to one knee and fired. Two prisoners fell into the dirt. The survivor slowed. He tossed his shovel to the dirt, shaking his head.

"You'll just leave us here then," the man said.

"Here, you'll have a chance to live," Waylon said. "Take another step forward and I'll end you."

The prisoner fell to his knees, his arms falling limp at his side. "Do what you will."

Waylon held the rifle at his side, apparently ready for another surge of prisoners to rush the fighter. The fire's heat swirled into the cockpit. Josh checked his sensors. The hull's temperature climbed as if he was passing through the atmosphere. He couldn't activate the shields with his canopy open.

"Let's go! *Waylon*! We have to go!"

Walking backwards, Waylon kept his weapon trained on the fields. The prisoner on the landing pad remained kneeling. Waylon reached the fighter and Josh stood to allow him to climb into the back.

Waylon paused. "That's a small seat."

"It's a small fighter." He jerked his head. "Get in! We don't have much time."

Waylon folded his massive frame into the back seat designed for small personal items. After trying to jam the rifle inside, he tossed it into the dirt. Josh lifted off the ground before he shut the canopy. Heat waves pushed the fighter left, the landing gear bumping against the barn's roof. He looked down, saw the prisoner staring up at the fire surrounding him as winds howled in from the plains.

Josh righted the craft and settled into the seat. He activated the shields, effectively creating an atmosphere around the ship. Pulling back on the stick, he eased the throttle forward. Glancing back, he saw the inferno had reached the compound, engulfing the barn in a ball of flame. Prisoners rushed around in frantic panic. Rodon would have no food supply to return to now. When he returned, he would only find dirt and ash.

He grinned. Facing forward, he took a deep breath and pull all the Trident's power into the engines. The cockpit smelled of sweat and fire as Waylon gasped from the backseat.

"You okay, man?"

Waylon snorted. "Could use some water."

"Me, too."

A meaty palm slapped Josh's shoulder. "Glad you came back."

"You didn't think I'd leave you, did you?"

"You never know." He leaned back. "I might have left *you*."

Josh knew he was kidding. Or he hoped so, anyway. He pushed the throttle and pulled back on the stick, accelerating at a ninety-degree angle with the land. The blue morning sky transitioned slowly to the black of space. Stars poked through the atmosphere like sparkling beacons. Earth was among them, somewhere.

With everything he had experienced in recent years, he marveled at the fact Earth remained untouched by galactic events. *Pure luck*, he thought. Hundreds of dark worlds were still unscathed. The powers of the known universe moved around them like a river bypassing rocks.

But now, the Tyral Pirates had their power relay. They had the ability to strike at a dark world far from the capital worlds, and Josh had been unable to stop it.

"I need the coordinates to your base," he said, peering back at the land disappearing in the clouds.

"Right." Waylon leaned forward, pressing against Josh's back. "Where's navigation?"

He snorted. "You still don't trust me?"

"You get me home and we'll talk."

Shaking his head, he pointed at the navigation computer. Reaching over Josh's shoulder, Waylon punched the keys as if they had done him wrong. The keyboard shook with each stroke from his thick fingers. Josh held his breath, the man's wretched body odor hitting him in waves.

When Waylon sat back, Josh worked on prepping the ship's curvature drive. They had enough power for one curve. Waylon had better know his coordinates or they might have an interesting trip. Josh decided to keep his opinion to himself.

While he waited for the curvature drive to warm, he activated the air vents to circulate the stench. After all, he knew he didn't smell too good, either. He brought the fighter into a high orbit and enjoyed a moment of peace.

"Be about two minutes," Josh said, closing his eyes. "Drive's beginning with a cold start."

Waylon exhaled. "Take your time. Just glad to be off that stinking toilet bowl of a planet." He shivered. "Freezing though."

"Space is cold."

"Don't I know this," he murmured, rubbing his arms. "Spent more time in space than you have, boy."

"True."

"I grew up in space, you know. Got used to that planet. I feel more at home in the cold."

Josh leaned against the canopy, staring down at the brown and blue planet. The fighter didn't have updated star charts, so he couldn't even verify their location. He knew it was somewhere within the Amade Cluster, but the planet had no name on this chart.

"It wasn't so bad down there," Josh said quietly.

"No?" Waylon said, smacking his lips as if he had nearly fallen asleep. "You want to go back?"

"I didn't say *that*."

"By the way, you have my gratitude."

"Yeah? For what?"

"Coming back."

"So you said."

"I mean it," he said, his voice rising. "I saw your fighter disappear over the horizon with that pirate on your tail and I wondered for a moment if I would spend my last hours wandering an empty planet. Thanks for coming back."

Josh smiled and nodded. "We're a team."

He played with the navigation computer. If he could trust these outdated charts, the fighter's last location had been in the middle of an asteroid belt near the Zine System. It *had* to be the location of the main Tyral Base where they had been kept before, but having the enemy's coordinates was one thing and having a force to attack it was another.

The curvature drive beeped. The power cells had charged and were at full power.

"Okay, we're ready to roll," Josh said. "You ready?"

"I was ready last month. Just go."

He activated the curve. Space wavered. Colors surrounded the ship. He eased forward, his stomach dropping and twisting. Dizziness surrounded him like a whirlpool but faded. Space normalized around them.

Josh exhaled, relieved the curvature drive on this fighter had actually passed through a curve and not smeared them into particles across five systems.

"Okay, we're through." He pulled back on the throttle and checked the surrounding stars in the navigation computer. "Verifying our location. We're in the Tormada System. It's a binary star system with four planetary bodies. Tell me where to go."

"I know where we are." Waylon—and his smell—returned as he leaned forward. "Third moon of the fourth planet."

"Heading there now."

"Hand me that headset."

He passed it back. "Tell me what to do."

"Once we get into orbit, I'll contact my people." He laughed. "Of course, they might not be there."

Josh frowned. "Seriously?"

"You never know."

Josh brought the fighter into orbit with the third moon. The fourth planet loomed to his right, a fiery yellow giant gas.

"Okay, ease into orbit," Waylon said. "Change your frequency to four-zero-five and we'll see what happens."

"You sound worried."

"You're flying a Tyral Pirate fighter. You're damn right I'm worried."

Josh pulled back on the throttle. He hadn't thought of what it would look like to the other *Barracudas* at their base. Waylon had offered his services to help take out the Tyral Pirate base. Josh hadn't asked for many details back when they were prisoners in the farming compound, but he'd assumed Waylon's smuggling group had dealt with the pirates before. Otherwise, why would Waylon be certain the other smugglers would want to help?

"Waylon?"

"Yeah."

"Why are you called the 'Barracudas' anyway?"

"I don't know," he said, craning his neck over Josh's shoulder to gaze down at the moon. "Sounded scary, I guess."

Pausing, Josh chose his next words carefully. "We never decided how we're going to do this."

"Do what?"

"You said we needed to get off the planet before we decided how to counterattack. Well, we're off the planet."

Waylon grunted. "I see."

He waited. "Well?"

"Taking out the Tyral Base will help our operations, so I don't think we'll have much trouble convincing my people."

"I thought you were their commander?"

"I'm their boss, but I can't order them to launch an suicide attack. We're businessmen. Sure, we can take care of ourselves, but we're not soldiers."

"I see." Josh's stomach dropped. "Well, thanks in advance. I appreciate it."

"Sure. If it were up to me, I'd kill every one of the pirates. Would love to start with Rodon if I could."

The tension on his chest eased. He had to put his faith in Waylon. He owed him after the man had risked his life to set the grasslands on fire while Josh flew away in a fighter. Now it was his turn to place faith.

"Transmit," Waylon said.

He complied. "You are live."

"Dinner is cooking. It's going to be larba stew tonight. I repeat, larba stew with too much salt."

Static met the message. Waylon repeated it. Josh shook his head. *This is crazy*, he thought.

"We copy, Boss," a voice cut through the static. "We are hungry."

Waylon slapped his hands together. "All right! Welcome to Sanctum!" He grabbed Josh's shoulders with such ferocity the fighter drifted off course. "Let's land and grab some dinner—some *real* dinner! No more green snot!"

Josh's stomach growled at the mention of food. He'd been eating nothing but that rotten green slop for months. Dinner sounded good.

"Tell me where to land."

AMIDST A CAVERN of stalactites hanging thirty feet above artificial steel deck, Josh devoured his first taste of meat in months. The bowl of mystery meat stew disappeared in a matter of minutes. An older man with a white beard offered a second bowl, saying something in a language Josh couldn't understand. Since his translator needed charging, he accepted without saying a word. Hunger, it seemed, was universal.

Upon approach, the moon's gray surface looked like the edge of a volcano. Waylon had directed him to a canyon in the northern hemisphere. As they had passed over the landscape, Josh saw no plant life or water sources. When the chasm came to an end, they passed through a cavern opening. The subterranean Barracuda compound Waylon called Sanctum took up several caves, including one housing a hangar large enough for half a dozen Trident fighters. That is, of course, if this smuggling group could afford a spacecraft as extravagant as a Legion Trident. From what Josh had seen on the way in, most of the equipment seemed to be pieced together with bubble gum and scrap metal.

A team of sixteen men and four women had welcomed them before sitting to dine at a long table. The stew's aroma filled the room, saturating the rags he passed off for clothing. Waylon showed emotion Josh had never seen from him when he reunited with the crew. He embraced each and every crew member, holding them close for long moments. Tears fell freely as the group swept Josh aside. He didn't mind.

Josh was starting on the second bowl of stew by the time Waylon made his way to his table. His friend smiled, his yellowed teeth peeping through the bushy red beard. The grin softened as he looked at all of them. His gaze fell to the floor.

"Tabloo dar treka, eh? Oh." Waylon handed him a charged translator.

Josh popped it in his ear. "Don't tell them, yet," he said quietly. "They'll ask soon enough."

Waylon nodded, his gaze focusing on nothing.

"How did you find this place?" Josh asked.

"My wife's father started the Barracudas and found it on a scouting mission long before I met Tyra," he said, his voice monotone. "We don't know who built this. They were gone long before we got here. They've never come back, so we've made it home."

"It's impressive," he said, staring at the rocky ceiling.

"I love it here."

A spoon tapped on one piece of glass at the head of the table. The older man who had served the meat stew stood and grinned.

"Waylon," he said, his voice soft and gentle like a grandfather, "I think I speak for all of us when I say we're glad to have you back. You have been missed."

"Thank you, Pa. Thank you."

Josh held his breath, knowing what would come next.

"What happened, Waylon? Where are the others? Drexel? Gate? Acks?" Pa held his hands outward. "Are they on another ship? Should we go get them?"

Waylon held up his hand. He suddenly looked much older, as if gravity pressed on his shoulders. After a long exhale, he launched into the story. He recounted their capture by Rodon and the Tyral Pirates. Skipping over the gruesome aspects of their captivity, he told of their hours of hard labor, from mining, to stripping freighters, to tilling the ground on the unnamed planet. When he came to the part about the farm, his speech became labored and shaky. He mentioned the abuse, Cyclops' "management," and, finally, he told them of his men's deaths. The group stopped eating, then they stopped moving.

And they cried.

Men comforted sobbing women and children. Josh stared at the bowl, his appetite disappearing like a lit match in a breeze. He listened as families consoled one another. He stayed quiet in the corner, watching these people deal with the worst possible news.

A well-built man sat across the table from Josh. He showed none of the emotion of the other *Barracudas*. A foot-long knife hung at his belt on one side and a pistol rested in a worn leather holster at the other.

"I should have been there," the man grumbled, rubbing his black beard.

"You wouldn't have wanted to be there."

"How do you know what I want?"

Josh frowned. "You're alive. Being a captive of the Tyral Pirates is no way to live."

The man leaned over the table. "Name's Tocol."

"I'm Josh."

"Where you from Josh?"

"Earth."

"Been there once," Tocol said, sipping on a drink from a metal container. "Didn't take."

"Maybe you didn't visit the right part."

"Picked up a package in the snow on one of the poles. I can't even remember what it was." He slid his thumb over his jagged fingernails. "Just a job in a lifetime of jobs."

"I've never been to the poles."

"So what did you do?"

"I'm a Legion Star Runner."

"I know that much." Tocol took a drink. "I meant before your days with the Legion."

"I'll try to think that far back." He nodded, staring into the bowl. "I was a student. I played football."

Tocol laughed. "Football? Putting my foot on a ball doesn't sound like any game I'd want to play."

For the first time since his arrival, Josh laughed. "When you put it that way, I don't want to play either."

A small woman carrying a metal lunchbox walked up to him. She placed the box on the table and opened it. Pulling out a bandage and a spray can, she stepped over to Josh.

"For your ear," she said in a high-pitched voice.

"Oh, okay," he said. "Do you want me to, ah, lean forward or something?"

"Just going to clean it up." She sprayed his ear, filling the air with the scent of alcohol.

"Yow." Josh gritted his teeth.

"Oh, come on," Tocol said. "Be a man."

"Almost done," the woman said. "I'm Matta."

"Oh." He winced and gave his name through his clenched mouth.

"I know." She placed the spray can on the table and attached the bandage on his ear. Pressing with the tender touch of an experience nurse, she smiled. "Who did this to you?"

Josh closed his eyes, ignoring the pain flashing through his body. "Pirate."

"Did you get him?" Tocol sneered.

"We got him."

A radio squawked through the cavern.

"Ah, everybody," a voice crackled over an intercom system embedded in the rock, "the *Sparkling Light* has landed. We need some help with unloading."

Waylon wiped his face and stood. He took two steps toward the end of cavern and stopped. Josh followed his gaze.

"You're back," Waylon said.

A woman in a gray mechanic's coverall stood at the entrance. Her hair was folded like strips of dried brown rope under a small cap. Grease was smeared across her smiling face. Her eyes filled with tears as she gazed at Waylon.

Josh leaned close to Tocol. "Who is that?"

"His wife."

"I thought you were dead," the woman said.

Waylon rushed to her. "Tyra."

A young boy stood at her thigh. "Daddy!"

Waylon embraced his family as the rest of the *Barracudas* chattered. Josh watched the man he'd spent months around, the man he didn't really know. He kissed Tyra on the forehead and rubbed the boy's hair.

"I'd like you to meet someone," Waylon said, pointing at Josh. "This is my friend. He helped me escape."

"We helped each other," Josh said.

Tyra smiled. She walked toward him slowly, taking off her hat. Her hair tumbled around her shoulders and her chin quivered.

"And your name?" she asked.

"I'm Josh, ma'am."

"Ma'am?" She turned back to Waylon, a playful smile on her face. "It's just plain Tyra around here. And you are most welcome to join us."

Waylon held the boy high, wrapping him around his shoulders. The boy giggled. "This here is my son Cornic, but we call him Scrappy."

The group sat back at the table. Pa offered Josh another bowl of soup. By the end of this one, his stomach rumbled and turned over. He leaned back into his seat and burped as the *Barracudas* discussed business and events around Quadrant Eight.

Tyra had returned from a delivery of livestock, apparently for a significant profit. Others spoke of Tyral Pirate attacks, new Legion trade regulations, and the Zahl-Legion cold war. The discussion lingered on the politics and events, but dipped into personal topics as the group brought Waylon up to speed on the happenings of their team.

For a long moment, Josh felt like he sat around the family dinner table. A calmness fell over him. Of course, it might have been the effect of the first full stomach he had enjoyed in months. He felt lightheaded and happy. It was like a moment from his past, a moment he knew couldn't last.

An hour passed. Tyra cleared the plates with her son. The conversation slackened, replaced by grunts and sighs of full stomachs.

Waylon stood, taking a slow drink from a thermos. "Okay, Josh, I need to make some introductions."

He stood behind three of the largest men in the room. "This is Tocol, who I think you've met. These are his brothers Moda and Drad."

They nodded.

"And what do they do?" Josh asked.

Waylon glanced at them. "Besides eat a lot, they help convince other businessmen to, well, accept our deals." He pointed to the petite nurse at the end of the table with two men on either side of her. "That's Matta, a great pilot. Her brother, Lark, also a pilot. And Rist, who *claims* to be a pilot."

"Funny," Rist said, rubbing the stubble on his face.

"Nice to meet you all," Josh said with a smile.

"I wish we could say the same," Rist said, glaring at him.

Waylon slapped the table. "This is a friendly place, Rist. Josh is our guest."

"I know that!" Rist snapped. "I also know a Star Runner wouldn't be here unless he was desperate." He looked at Josh.

"When are you going to get to the point? Why are you here and what do you want?"

"We were captured and we escaped together!" Waylon shouted. "You will stop with this questioning."

"It's okay, Waylon. I understand." Josh cleared his throat and stood on shaky legs. "I'd like to say something, if you wouldn't mind."

Waylon waved him forward. "You are welcome to say whatever you want." He eyed Rist. "You are one of us now."

Josh's face warmed. "Thank you. That means a lot. I want to ask for your help."

"How so?" Pa asked.

"I need to attack the main Tyral base."

Laughter echoed around the hall.

"And I'd like a golden chamber pot!" Tocol yelled.

Waylon held his hand high. "Let him finish."

"We know Rodon plans to attack a dark world," Josh said, "so most of his forces are probably massed somewhere else. We found a power relay on the planet where we were held captive. This would allow the pirates to strike deep into the rear of the Legion territory."

"Yeah," Rist muttered, "what's that got to do with us?"

"I know you've been dealing with the pirates the same as the Legion," Josh said, feeling as if he treaded water. "If they expand their base of operations, if they continue to utilize this support from wherever they are getting it and take an entire world for their use, they'll be unstoppable and you'll be out of business. We have the location of their main base on the navigational computer of the stolen fighter. We know where they are. We just have to get to them."

Silence hung over the table like smog. Some people looked at one another. Others stared at their hands.

"He's right," Waylon said, his eyes locking with Josh's. "And what about our men they killed? My men...are we just going to let them die in vain? Are we going to let Rodon think he can prey on this quadrant forever?"

"But we could lose everything if we attack," Rist said.

"And we could lose everything if we do nothing." Waylon towered over the table. "I for one don't want to sit around and let Rodon rule over our destiny any longer."

Slowly, nods spread around the room. Waylon grinned and placed his fists on the table.

"Yes," Tocol said, glancing at the others. "Yes!"

Waylon looked at the rest of the group and nodded. "We're with you, Star Runner," he said, his voice deep. "When do we leave?"

17

The corridor shook. Lights flickered as a second shockwave rocked Austin's feet. He kicked through icy water, thinking of the thousands of feet between Atlantis and the ocean's surface. *These walls better hold.*

Explosions rumbled, this time closer than before. He grabbed the handrail for balance. Sparks showered onto him, fizzling out when they hit the water. He kept making his way toward the civilian hangar, his legs growing numb from the cold. He hoped Nubern—and the Tridents—would still be there.

Water fell from the ceiling, streams striking his face like ice chips. The Tyral Pirates had destroyed the main hangar in their first move and tried to take out Command. If the recent explosions had come from the civilian hangar, Austin could be rushing to his death.

He pressed the headset to his mouth as he ran. "Officer Brannen, do you copy? This is Lieutenant Stone."

"Copy Stone. Go ahead."

"More explosions on this side of the base. Should I proceed?"

"Affirmative. We destroyed an inbound bogey."

Shutting the headset off, he turned the corner, saw the hangar door, and exhaled.

As he reached the hangar door, he stopped. Dirty blackish water covered the floor, washing debris in all directions. A freighter burned to his left. A steel beam from the ceiling had fallen onto the hull. Most of the spacecraft from the previous time he'd come through the hangar had departed. The six Tridents remained parked at the far side. Crew hurried under the fighters, helping to finish the start-up sequence and get into the fight raging around the station.

"Stone! Get over here!"

Austin saw a man, hands on his hips, standing on a Trident's nose. He couldn't make out the face at this distance but knew it had to be Nubern. He ran through the water and across the hangar.

"Captain," he said, breathing heavy, "ready to assist, sir."

A red gash split Nubern's cheek. His dark blue flight suit dripped water. "Any idea on the recent explosions?"

"The cannons and alert fighters have taken out an inbound attacker."

"All right, Stone," Nubern said as if he had not heard Austin speak, "you're just in time. We're prepping the six Tridents we have in reserve for Atlantis defense and we have four pilots—now five."

"Five against fifty?"

Nubern blinked. "Who said anything about fifty? Before our sensors were knocked out we saw six vessels bearing down on the station from the ocean floor. Where did *fifty* come from?"

"Six under water and fifty in orbit."

"My God," Nubern breathed. He straightened his flight suit. "Where are they headed? Base Prime?"

"No. Here."

He jerked his head back. "*Here*? Atlantis?"

Austin nodded. "Fifty fighters are coming in. We're all that's left to put up a defense."

"If that's the way it has to be then." Nubern dropped down into the cockpit. "Take number three, Stone. It's time to go."

"But I don't have a flight suit!"

"Have Tyce fix you up!" he shouted, closing the canopy as his fighter's engines whined.

Austin sprinted to the third Trident in line. A crewman handed him a Lobera green helmet. He frowned, glancing at the other four Star Runners boarding their Tridents. Two red flight suits from Excalibur squadron, a green Lobera recruit, and Nubern in his Tizona blue.

"Where's the pilot?" Austin asked, turning back to the crewman.

He glanced over at a fallen beam and sparkling debris. "He's not flying today."

He paused. "You Tyce?"

"Yes, sir."

"I'm Rock. I need a flight suit."

"Take Jaber's," Tyce said, pulling a Lobera flight suit from a cart. "It's a little big."

"It'll do," he said, getting dressed. When he finished, he climbed the ladder and sat in the cockpit. "Let's start preflight and do it fast."

The Tridents' engines roared and filled the hangar in minutes. Tyce slapped Austin on the helmet and climbed down to the deck. He gave a thumbs up and closed the canopy. Electronics hummed, replacing the engines' roar. Austin finished his start-up sequence and locked the helmet in place.

"Rock, this is Talon. You ready?"

Austin slapped down his visor. "Yes, sir."

"Attention all of you," Nubern transmitted. "I'm Captain Nubern and I'm in charge of this flight. I just spoke with Command. We've been ordered to engage the incoming fighters."

"What about the ocean floor attack?" another pilot, sounding much younger, asked.

"Our job is to concentrate on the incoming fighters. They're entering the atmosphere as we speak, heading directly for our location. Let Atlantis defend itself down here or there won't be anywhere to land. We're better than they are. These are pirates. We're Legion Star Runners. Let's get up there and show them what that means."

"I count fifty-three," the same pilot said. "What good are we going to be against that?"

"Then we better see how many we can drop on the first pass. Let's go!"

The Tridents lifted off simultaneously, flying toward the hangar's airlock. One by one, the fighters locked into position in the smaller airlock created for interplanetary shuttle traffic rather than the freighters. Austin cracked his knuckles as the hatch closed behind them. His heart raced, thumping through the oversized flight suit. He took a deep breath.

"Telmi, Dart," Nubern said, "check your sensors. See those bandits drifting off the pack and trying to attack from the west?"

"Copy," the two Excalibur pilots answered in unison.

"I want you two to head in that direction and drop what you can. Those are Tridents. They have the only shields capable of withstanding the depths of Atlantis. They could dive and attack from below. They must be taken out. The others will bomb from the air."

Austin looked at the sensors. Six bandits moved away from the pack, heading on a direct course toward the ocean.

"Rock, you take the bandits to the east. The rookie, Dizzy, will stay with me and take'em head on." Nubern paused. "Once this airlock hatch opens, I want you screaming hard for the surface, top speed you can manage."

"Yes, sir," Austin said, his throat swelling up.

"Do what you can. I know it looks grim, but we're all that's left. Do this for your comrades in the hangar. Do this for the officers still fighting onboard Atlantis. Do this for yourselves. Without us, the Legion loses Atlantis *and* Earth today. That's not going to happen."

"No, sir!" the other pilots yelled, screeching static into the headset.

"It's been a pleasure, sir," Austin said softly without transmitting.

His fingers rested lightly on the stick. He fingered the throttle with his right hand. Water bubbled over the canopy. *Not long now.*

The blue lights transitioned to yellow. The hatch rumbled open.

"For the Legion," Nubern said.

The lights went green. Austin slammed his throttle forward. Bubbles and white water swirled around the canopy as his Trident shot into the darkness. He focused on his sensors and navigated the dark, cold depths of the Pacific Ocean. It felt similar to flying through space. The Excalibur pilots scrambled toward the west as instructed, their blips on the radar pulling away from the pack. Nubern and Dizzy stayed in the center. Austin altered course, bringing his nose to bear on the fighters moving in from the east.

Daylight transitioned the water from black to a dull blue. The Trident burst into the sunlight, free from the water's resistance. He spun, maintaining his nose on his assigned targets. Beads of water vanished from his canopy. Fifty-three tiny dots appeared in the sky like black stars.

This is suicide.

He gripped the stick tighter, transferring his auxiliary power to lasers. With this amount of potential incoming fire, shields wouldn't make much of a difference. He would just make himself impossible to hit.

He smiled.

Having mercenaries and pirates shoot at you on the ground is one thing, but this was different. This was almost unfair.

For them.

I know I can take all of these bandits myself. I just have to stay frosty. Hit'em and move. Hit'em and move. Don't stay on one target. Move, and move fast.

"One minute to engage," Nubern said. "Good hunting!"

"Why aren't they firing missiles?" Dizzy asked.

"We're not waiting to find out," Nubern said.

Thirty seconds.

"This is it!" Nubern barked.

To the west, the sky ignited in laser fire. The Excalibur Star Runners engaged the pirate Tridents. Fighters swarmed together like gnats. Austin chose his target, clicking on the distant outline of a Tyral Pirate fighter with his thumb on the stick. A red bolt shot past his canopy.

Here we go.

Austin dropped in within range, laser bolts surrounding him, but he waited for missile lock. He rolled, trying to become a more difficult target while maintaining his lock. The bandit maintained his course for Austin. The range dropped. Closer. *Closer*.

The bandit pulled up, ending the game of chicken. Austin squeezed the trigger, unleashing a lethal missile shot into the fighter's belly. The craft vaporized in a ball of fire. Fragments shot across the sky.

"They're too fast!" yelled the rookie, Dizzy.

"Stay with me!" Nubern barked.

"I'm hit! I—"

Dizzy's transponder disappeared from the sensors.

"Heading your way, Talon," Austin said.

He pulled back on the stick, finding another target. He steadied his course, centering his crosshairs on the enemy. He fired his lasers. The fighter exploded the same as the last. He fired again and again, his lasers and missiles finding targets wherever he turned. He rolled. He dropped. He looped. Targets filled the sky. His limited shields crackled and burned as the bolts surrounded him like a meteor shower.

But he danced between the sizzling laser bolts and blindly fired missiles.

Telmi disappeared from the sensors. Austin growled and closed in on a damaged foe. He pounded his target with laser fire, following him to the ocean surface. He pulled up. The pirate craft smashed into the water, sending debris flickering across the ocean's surface.

As he pulled up and shot into the sky at a ninety-degree angle, he allowed his laser energy banks to recharge. He zipped through the chaos. An orange ring flashed across the sky, transitioning to a black cloud.

"Talon, Dart," the gamma wave crackled. "I'm hit. We let a Trident slip through. It's heading for the surface."

"We're on it," Nubern said. "Pull out. Get to safety."

Dart vanished from the sensors.

"Dart?" Nubern asked. "*Dart*?"

"He's gone!" Austin yelled.

"Rock, can you get that last Trident?"

"I'm on it." The G-forces pushed Austin back into his seat, his helmet rocking.

He pulled away from the fighters he had engaged, locking his targeting computer on the enemy Trident descending toward the ocean.

The pirate flew directly into the water, disappearing under the surface.

"He's gone deep," Austin said, transferring power into his shields. "I'm after him."

"Hurry," Nubern said, his voice straining. "That's the last fighter they have that can withstand the pressure. If he gets in close, he'll be able to attack Atlantis."

"Roger."

Austin dropped his crosshairs on the position where the enemy had submerged. He braced himself, resisting every urge to pull up. With his shields at maximum, his Trident blasted into the ocean. The impact slowed his descent, but shields pushed the water away. His head moved forward. He sat up straight and focused on the targeting computer.

Directly ahead, the enemy bore down on the Atlantis civilian hangar. Looking up from his sensors and peering into the ocean's darkness, he couldn't see anything. He had to rely on his instruments. The crosshairs blinked yellow as it searched for a lock.

"Come on, come on," Austin said. He keyed for transmission. "Atlantis, Rock. You have an incoming bandit. Looks like he's headed for the civilian hangar."

"Roger, Rock. We've got the defense cannons prepped."

"I hope you don't need them." Austin adjusted his course.

The enemy Trident continued, unaffected by Austin's search for missile lock. The pirate must not know how to detect an attempted missile lock.

The crosshairs turned blood red. "Got you."

He pulled the trigger. The launching missile rocked the fighter as it shot away from his Trident. He pulled up, heading back for the surface. Glancing back at his targeting computer, he watched as his missile crashed into his enemy. The dark ocean water lit up, a shockwave rippling out from the remains of the pirate Trident. He smiled.

"Atlantis, Rock. Forget about that incoming bandit. He's gone."

"We see it, Rock," Brannen said, her voice cracking. "You need to get back to the surface. They may be dropping blind shots into the ocean, but these fighters are dropping too many missiles for us to get them all. We don't have much time."

"I understand. Are you picking up any more Tridents?"

"Negative."

"So there are no more fighters capable of entering the ocean?"

"Correct."

With no more fighters able to descend into the water and attack Atlantis, the remaining Tyral Pirates would have to fire from the air.

"I'm going back," he said. "We'll take them out."

Sensors showed the Tyral Pirates firing dozens of projectiles into the water. Nubern's transponder moved between the cloud of pirates.

He's still alive, he thought.

"Talon, let's link up," Austin said, his Trident bursting through the ocean's surface and flying hard for altitude.

"Roger," Nubern snapped. "Turn to four-oh-six. Be there in a bit."

Austin glanced back at the mass of enemy fighters. The majority flew for the ocean's surface. Missiles shot into the water, sending white plumes skyward.

"I took out the last Trident," Austin said. "They're hitting Atlantis from the air."

The two Legion Tridents soared side-by-side for a moment, the sun beaming behind them, the fighters heading away from the primary engagement. Austin took in a deep breath and stared at the burning wreckage from the fight falling into the ocean. At least forty pirate craft remained in the skies over the Pacific Ocean, most of them firing missiles in the direction of Atlantis. He knew they had to continue the fight, knew they couldn't sit idle and allow this to happen.

But two versus forty?

He glanced at Nubern.

"Ready for another pass, Talon?"

"After you, Rock."

Austin cracked his knuckles and gripped the stick. "Here we go."

He pushed down on the stick, his stomach lurching like he passed over the first hill in a roller coaster. The pirates massed together as they tried to form up for another assault.

"I'll take the grouping to the west," Austin said, his voice straining as the force of the engines pressed him into his seat.

"Roger, I got the east."

Austin locked a bandit, fired a missile. Without waiting on the result, he moved his crosshairs to lock another pirate. Nubern did the same, firing two missiles. Austin maintained another lock and fired his final missile. White trails shot forward ahead of their fighters. Explosions lit up the sky like fireworks. No time for celebration. He switched to lasers.

Nubern and Austin blew through the mass of fighters, shattering the enemy formation. Fighters filled the sky in chaos. Laser fire flashed. Two bolts fired his rear shields. He grunted, yanking the stick to barrel roll away from the engagement.

"I'm hit!" he grunted.

He balanced power to the shields with his left hand. The world spun around his cockpit. Bolts flashed like lethal strobes.

"Lost shields," Nubern said in an odd, quiet voice. "I'm heading for the deck."

His vision blurred, but he could just make out Nubern's Trident screaming hard for the ocean's surface. Six pirate craft trailed him, igniting the air with relentless fire.

Afraid he might pass out from his evasive maneuvers, Austin straightened his flight path and turned back. Nubern pulled up and flew parallel to the surface close enough to send water shooting into the air.

"Bank east," Austin said. "I can cover you from above."

"Don't bother. My computer's fried. Down to one engine. Take out as many as you can, Rock. You hear me?"

He shook his head. "No."

He pulled back on the stick, forcing the Trident into a sharp loop. Leveling out, he brought his crosshairs to bear on the pirates pursuing Nubern. The rest of the pirates fired missiles into the ocean while Austin zeroed in on Nubern's attackers. *Sure would be nice to have a missile right now.*

"Hang on, sir. I'm on my way."

Three pirates broke off from the main group and moved in behind Austin, but he stayed on Nubern's attackers. *Almost there.*

Laser fire blasted away his rear shields. Austin flinched but stayed trained on his target. He wouldn't last much longer out here. Glancing at his sensors, he did a quick calculation. The fighters on his six were too fast and his Trident was too low on energy to reach Nubern. It was only a matter of time. Still, Austin pressed on. His mentor was in trouble. He rolled to make himself a tougher target but stayed focused on Nubern's attackers, still waiting on his laser banks to charge.

A bolt crashed into his tail. Sparks shot from his dash board. *This is it. They've got me.*

"Attention, Legion craft," a voice crackled on the gamma wave. "This is Grumbler of the United States Navy. Do you need assistance?"

Austin looked at the controls. *What?*

"Roger, Grumbler," Nubern said, his voice rising in Austin's ear. "This is Talon. Your help is most appreciated."

The pirates broke off their attack on the wounded Tridents. From the east, flying in tight formation, soared thirty-two F-18 Hornets. Austin pulled back on the stick and watched the Tyral Pirates scream hard toward their new enemy.

The U.S. Navy pilots launched a series of missiles toward the Tyral Pirates, but the advanced scrambling equipment blocked any radar lock. White missile trails crossed the blue sky.

"Grumbler, this is Rock. Your missiles won't lock. You'll have to engage with guns."

"Roger, Rock. We live for this."

The assortment of pirate fighters, apparently saving any remaining missiles for Atlantis, unleashed their lasers into the Hornets. An interplanetary dogfight erupted while Austin and Nubern caught their breath. The Hornets squared off against the pirate craft. Fireballs filled the sky with smoke and burning debris. The F-18s exploded too quickly, the more advanced pirate craft cutting through them like a hot knife through cake. He glanced up from his dashboard to see a Hornet blasting away at a modified Trident fighter on its way to the ocean.

"Trying to link up with you at ten thousand feet," Nubern said. "This baby only has so much more it can give me."

"Be ready in a second, Talon," Austin said, coaxing energy back into his shields after the direct hit on his tail. "We have to get back in there. Those guys aren't going to last long."

"They're buying time for Atlantis."

18

The ship sailed between the asteroids, moving only by utilizing maneuvering thrusters. Waylon had cut the main drive before they even entered the main asteroid field. He wanted to sail silent, hoping to draw no attention to their movement. According to their stolen Tyral fighter, the main pirate base lurked somewhere in this field of floating rocks in the center of the Zine System.

Of course, they could be under surveillance.

"Still nothing on the sensors," Josh whispered as if the pirates could hear him. "Where to now?

Waylon grumbled, his fingers disappearing into his beard. He stood in the cramped bridge of the *Barracudas*' smuggling transport, *Sparkling Light,* and moved to study the local charts. "I don't want to break radio silence yet."

After spending his training in the comforts and technology of the Legion Navy, Josh shook his head at Waylon leaning over a flickering monochrome screen to monitor the surrounding space. Four of their fighters had slipped through a curve on the dark side of a nearby moon and awaited orders to attack. Four fighters didn't seem like much, so surprise would be crucial if they were to find any success today. After serving as a scout ship, the *Sparkling Light* would coordinate the attack and provide long-range missile support.

"Hmm." Waylon pointed at three large clusters. "These seem to be the only rocks large enough to hold the size base we were held in. Don't you think?"

Josh stood from the helm and stepped back to review the charts. Three massive asteroids, larger than some moons, floated in the same field.

"That's our best shot." He did a mental calculation. "These two would take hours to reach using thrusters."

"We don't want to risk detection." Waylon glanced at him, propping his knee on the edge of the control board. "What if the entire pirate force is home?"

"We would be in trouble." He thought of the ships he had seen during their time on the asteroid base, recalling the number of vessels and fighters. "Okay, you're right. Let's head for the closest rock?"

"Go."

Josh sat back at the helm and eased forward on the thrusters. After a moment, he pulled back, allowing the inertia to take him through. Rocks spun around the ship, bouncing off the hull without incident. It sounded like a light hail on a tin roof. The ship moved forward at a crawl. He kept an eye on the sensors, seeing nothing but more asteroids.

"I went a little faster the last time I was in an asteroid field," he said.

Waylon sighed. "Really? How's that?"

He gazed into nothing. "My best friend was with me. It was Rockshot."

"Rockshot? Huh?"

"It's training," he said, staring at the largest rock in the distance. "It's a timed race through an asteroid field."

He snorted. "And this is what you call work?"

"Yes, it's work. It was one of the best days, the last good days. I went on leave right after that."

When Josh did not continue, Waylon remained silent.

"So," Josh said, wanting to change the subject, "why don't the Tyral Pirates ever use warships?"

Waylon shrugged. "Too valuable, I expect. You can strip apart a warship and sell it. Your people could live off that payday for months. Warships also need personnel and personnel costs money."

He leaned back, watching the space around the ship. Twenty minutes passed before he flashed the thrusters lightly to correct course. Their destination loomed ahead behind another cluster of rocks.

"I want to thank you again for doing this," Josh said. "You're risking a lot, and you didn't have to."

"My family has been operating Quadrant Eight for two generations." Waylon's jaw muscles clenched. "We've always had competition. That's the smuggling business. Lately, though, it's been different. Something's changed."

He eyed him. "Legion pressure?"

"Nah, nothing like that," he said. "You guys cause your own problems for us. Trade regulations and such, but these Tyral Pirates...they were small at first, nothing more than pesky insects. Recently, around the time Scrappy was born, they had weaponry most of us could only dream of. At first, we thought they'd scored a big raid on a military convoy and enjoyed the ride. But it didn't stop."

His eyes met Josh's. "We couldn't stop them. They had advanced weapons we'd never seen 'cept with the Legion, and we run or submit when you guys show up. These pirates, they were relentless. They pursued without mercy, killed without care." He paused, gazing into space. "They killed my brother."

"I'm so sorry.

"It doesn't matter. I only tell you now to let you know your gratitude is unnecessary." A hint of a smile crept across his face. "I would have done this job for free."

Josh turned back to the controls. "Where do you think the pirates got this technology?"

"Someone with money and resources. Either government or

something beyond me." Waylon crossed his arms. "Does it really matter?"

"I suppose not."

The tracking sensor squealed. The lights burned red.

"All stop," Waylon said. "Shut her down, make like the void."

Josh killed the sensors, shutting down all power but the life support. Something had been triggered. He peered through the floating rubble.

Far in the distance, starlight reflecting off something metallic.

"There," he said. "See it?"

Waylon grunted, studying his monitor. "I do."

Turning around, Josh peered over his shoulder. The flickering monochrome seemed designed to induce nausea. He turned back to space and looked at the largest asteroid directly ahead. Perhaps Rodon hadn't yet gathered his forces for the attack on the unsuspecting dark world. Perhaps Josh and Waylon had arrived fast enough. If they could launch the attack on the pirate base before they prepared, they might be able to take down the nest before it even stirred.

He scanned the asteroids.

Still no patrols.

Arrogant, he thought. *Very arrogant.*

"It's a fighter alright," Waylon said after a moment. "Heading below our destination. I can't get a reading."

"Jamming?"

"I don't know," he said, shaking his head. "Transponder's just blank like there's nothing there."

"Do you have a ship type?"

"From this distance, it looks like a Trident."

Josh squinted. "A Trident?"

"Looks like it."

What would a Trident be doing out here? A lone scout mission?

He shook his head. Command would never had allowed something like that. But why then? Perhaps the Legion intelligence had finally found the location of the pirate base. Maybe the Tyral Pirate threat would soon be over.

"Oh, wait!" Waylon said. "Ah! I lost the signal."

"What did it say?"

"For a moment, I saw the transponder flicker a Legion signal. I froze the image, but only had it for a second. It's very blurred."

Josh stood up and moved behind Waylon. "Let me see."

Waylon nodded and turned to allow him to lean over. He peered into the old screen. The transponder code certainly matched a Legion fighter. He scrolled through the secret code and paused.

"I know this ship," Josh said.

"What?" Waylon asked.

Josh glared back at their destination. "This ship was stationed on Tarton's Junction. It belonged to Captain Rolling."

"Friend of yours?"

"Comrade." Josh remembered Austin speaking highly of Captain Rolling; an Earth pilot also recruited by the Legion. "They must have taken him like they took me, but they got his ship."

"This is it," Waylon inhaled, slapping Josh on the shoulder. "We're in the right place."

Josh sat back at the controls, his face flushed red. He gripped the stick, his fist tightening.

"You okay?" Waylon asked, typing into the comm station.

"What?" he asked. "I'm prepping for engine start-up."

"That's not what I mean."

Josh thought of another Legion pilot being killed by these pirates. "Let's just make things right today, huh?"

"You got it." Waylon continued punching keys. "I've signaled our friends to move in slowly. If anything shows its face out there, we'll lock a missile and take it out. These guys have *got* to have a patrol."

"I agree. If they don't, they're even dumber than I thought."

Four Barracuda fighters, older models Josh had only read about in his studies, emerged from the dark side of the nearby moon, four thousand micro units away. They swept into the asteroid field, dodging the rocks with the skill of veteran pilots. Power levels remained so low they would avoid most sensor sweeps unless the pirates searched the exact point.

Josh warmed the engines. "We're ready if needed."

"Scanning the larger rock," Waylon whispered. "Our stolen Trident is still headed straight for it. I'm ready to get a lock if needed."

The Barracuda fighters soared in two pairs. One pair made their way above the rock while the other made straight for the lone fighter.

"Three thousand MUs away," Josh said, keeping his eyes on his HUD. "Two thousand."

"Is this guy blind?"

"Let's hope so." He verified the range between the *Barracudas* and the Trident fighter. "One thousand."

Light flashed from the Trident, the fighter spinning around to face the incoming *Barracudas*.

"This is it!" Waylon yelled so loud Josh jumped. "I've got a missile lock."

"Firing!"

Josh squeezed the trigger. The thrust of the outgoing missile sent their ship spinning on its axis. Using the thrusters, he brought the nose back on the stolen Trident. The missile soared. To the prey, the missile must have come out of nowhere.

Without waiting to see the missile strike, Josh fired up the engines.

"Moving into support position."

"Got it," Waylon said, pulling a lever at his station. "Loading another missile."

Something from the rock caught his eye. Josh sighed. "Two more fighters coming from the main asteroid. Here we go."

"Missile loaded," Waylon said. "Searching for a lock."

The engines roared, rumbling Josh's chair. He watched the *Barracudas* fire on the stolen Trident. According to his sensors, his missile had fried the Trident's shields. A moment later, the Trident exploded from a Barracuda laser shot.

"Nice job," Josh said under his breath. "What else we got?"

"Two more coming out of the nest," Waylon said, "but that's it."

"Can't be. Run it again."

"Checking." He grumbled. "Just did. We outnumber them."

His gut twisted. "There has to be more. That's not right."

"What's not right about it? Attack!"

The *Sparkling Light* shot forward at top speed. The Barracuda fighters clashed with the two Tyral Pirate fighters, their lasers illuminating the dark asteroid field. They battled amidst the rocks, dodging lasers and asteroids.

"Rist, Matta, break hard for point two-five-seven," Waylon said. "Make like you're breaking for it. Tima, Geo, sweep in and take them out."

Two Barracuda craft broke off from the furball and headed away from the asteroid. Josh watched their position lights blinking in the darkness. His eyes flicked back to the main rock, wondering when the rest of the pirate force would launch. Laser bolts tracked the fleeing *Barracudas*, vaporizing asteroids. The pirates pursued as planned. Tima and Geo stayed on their tails, lasers spitting across the black.

"Head for the base," Waylon said. "If this is all the response they got, I'm not giving them time to realize their mistake."

"Got it."

Josh pressed for the base as the dogfight raged in the distance. He focused on their destination, ignoring the battle as best as he could. One Barracuda, Geo, took a direct laser hit, spinning away from the battle and bouncing off the asteroids like a sparkling pinball. The other three locked into combat with the pirates, continuing the deadly dance. A moment later, lethal Barracuda assault ensured the two pirate crafts twirled and burned like embers over a fire. One pirate fighter, a plume of gas erupting from his engine, limped back toward the rock. It disappeared into a crater, leaving the *Barracudas* in possession of the space around the massive asteroid.

"That's it!" Waylon clapped his hands together.

"For now."

"Land and make sure they don't get the chance to launch a counterattack," he said. "Let's find out if this is really the base where they held us."

"Heading in now." Josh adjusted course, following the gas trail of the damaged fighter. "Might want the guys ready downstairs in case of a welcome party."

"Heading down now." Waylon turned, but hesitated. "You got this?"

Josh waved him off. "Go."

Waylon grinned, his teeth shining in the midst of the red beard, and marched off the bridge. In the cargo bay of the *Sparkling Light,* four beefy *Barracudas* sat waiting with the best weapons the smuggling group could afford. Josh snorted at the thought. Or rather, the best weapons they could pick off derelict spacecraft located throughout Quadrant Eight. This boarding party had been Waylon's idea in the event the Tyral Pirates left a welcoming crew of their own. Having less experience with the pirates and with Quadrant Eight in general, Josh deferred to Waylon's expertise.

"Flanking your position now," Rist said as the fighters surrounding the transport.

"Copy," Josh said.

Even over the gamma wave, Rist's disgust for this mission—and for Josh in particular—came through loud and clear. Josh knew Rist's attitude came from years of dealings with the Legion, and he tried his best to let it go. Still, the man's voice bothered Josh like nails on a chalk board. But if Waylon trusted him, he had no choice.

The transport lined up with the asteroid's slow rotation, providing Josh's first glimpse of their destination as the faint starlight cast long shadows across the rocks. The light revealed a hangar bay large enough to house the burning wreck of the fighter they just shot down and a freighter stripped of half its hull. Another smaller secondary entrance revealed stars and the asteroid field a few hundred yards away from their current entrance. Nothing moved in the bay except for flickering flames of the crashed fighter. As the *Sparkling Light* passed through the energy shield protecting the interior from the void beyond, Josh scanned the area for anything familiar. Was this the same place they had been held for so long? After all, a rock is a rock.

His eyes fell upon the back of the hangar just to the right of the secondary entrance, and he jolted back.

An airlock door.

He buckled over, wincing. The families...the families the pirates had sent through the airlock. The families who died because Rodon had decided to steal their freighter and strip it for scrap. Josh remembered their eyes, wide with terror, pleading with him to help just before the airlock door closed. Delmar had prevented Josh from doing anything to get himself killed.

Looking away from the airlock, he saw the control room where Rodon had disappeared after torturing the prisoners. He remembered the man, his arrogance, his complete disregard for the passengers released through the airlock. Rodon never seemed to pay attention to the comings and goings of the freighters brought in for scrap, the innocents killed. He always marched away, his attention on other matters.

"Waylon," Josh said into the ship's intercom, his voice rough, "we're at the right place."

"Are you sure?" he asked after a pause.

"Believe me, I know." Josh shook his head, the image of the families staring at him flashing in his mind. "Where do you want the ship?"

Waylon thought in silence for a moment. "Any sign of resistance?"

"Just the wrecked fighter and a stripped freighter." Josh brought the freighter to hover over the hangar deck. He rotated the ship in a slow turn to survey the entire room. "I don't see anything."

"Then land wherever you want."

"Copy."

Josh lowered the landing gears, ignoring the voice in his mind, disbelieving the pirates would simply abandon their base. The transport settled onto the deck, gasses hissing while the engine whined. He flipped a dozen switches, shutting down the systems and placing the ship on standby. Grabbing the ancient gas-powered projectile rifle Pa had given him back at Sanctum, Josh hurried to the cargo bay.

The five men checked their weapons, some slapping fresh energy packs into their repeating rifles while others checked the latches on their makeshift armor. The largest of the four, Tocol, a man who rivaled Waylon in terms of his size, slid a curved sword into a sheath hanging at his belt and put on a steel helmet. None of the others—Lark, Moda, or Drad—looked up as he entered. With torn rags hanging off his body, Josh did not have much in terms of defense.

"Still nobody out there?" Waylon asked as he looked down the front sight of a wicked black laser rifle.

"Not yet," Josh said just above a whisper. "You're heavily armed for businessmen."

Waylon produced a crooked grin. "All business can get hostile."

"We gonna sit here and sing a song or can we get going," Tocol muttered, holding a rifle across his broad chest.

"Hold on." Waylon stepped over to the gamma wave transmitter. "Tima, you copy?"

"Copy, Waylon."

"I want you outside flying cover. Any of these pirates come back, I want you to let us know and cover our escape."

"Got it. Moving out now."

Waylon nodded at Tocol. "Let's do this."

The landing ramp servos squealed as the walkway lowered. Josh sucked in the repugnant air, thinking of the countless days he and Delmar had spent toiling in these conditions to fill Tyral Pirates' pockets.

Waylon coughed. "Definitely the right place."

They descended onto the hangar bay spotted with black puddles and discarded engine parts. The smugglers swept through the room like a trained SWAT team, moving with purpose and covering all angles with their weapons. His head still spinning from the physical ordeal of the past few days, Josh brought up the rear as they'd agreed. He aimed his rifle toward the glass windows of the room he assumed served as air traffic control for the base.

Two Barracuda fighters, their triangular craft hovering behind the *Sparkling Light,* descended to the hangar floor. The engines whined to a halt. Brandishing a flashy laser pistol, Rist ran toward the center of the deck, followed closely by the small woman named Matta. Rist slowed, flashing a disgusted look in Josh's direction, before coming to a stop at the transport's nose.

From the other side of the hangar, Tocol kicked back the burnt metal covering the Tyral fighter; a modified Trident fighter. Josh's stomach soured at the sight. *Another stolen Legion craft.*

"No pilot!" Tocol yelled, adjusting the rifle to sweep the hangar. "What about the holding pens you mentioned? Caves down the tunnels?"

"Right," Waylon said, hurrying over to the fighter. "Secure the hangar and we'll move that direction."

Waylon glanced at Rist. "Okay, let's do this." He pointed toward the room encased in glass. "Josh, Tocol, and I will check out the room over there. With any luck, it'll provide some answers as to why we've found this base emptied."

Josh nodded and glanced at the glass room. Perhaps the mystery of the power relay would be solved inside. Then they would know exactly what dark world had been targeted by the pirates—if it wasn't too late.

"Rist," Waylon said, turning to face the tunnels leading to the prisoner holding pens, "I want you to take—"

A laser bolt flashed through the hangar. The energy burned into Rist's chest, sending sparks showering around his body. He fell to the floor like a sack of sizzling meat, a fire crackling on his chest. For a heartbeat, the group stared at their fallen comrade.

"Cover!" Waylon yelled.

They scattered as a torrent of pirate fire blasted from a tunnel. Josh tumbled behind a discarded metal crate. Matta scrambled next to him. She fell to the hangar deck with a loud grunt. Blue bolts seared the air over their heads. Fire exploded into their cover. Golden sparks showered onto his head. He stretched his neck to peer over the crate.

The ruthless attack from the tunnel continued. A bolt spit into Tocol's shoulder. He stumbled behind the burning fighter, grabbing Waylon to the deck with him. Lark dropped with a shot to the gut. He writhed in pain until another bolt hit the back of his head.

Moda and Drad stood in the open, returning fire. Their repeating laser rifles fired until the muzzles glowed orange. A bolt smacked Moda's face. The man spun like a toy, falling still next to Rist's body. Drad sprinted out of the line of fire, finding cover next to Waylon and Tocol.

"Stay down!" Waylon yelled as Tocol fired over the crashed Trident.

Josh nodded. He raised the ancient rifle over the crate and fired blindly. The projectile weapon crackled like a thunderclap.

"Here!" Matta handed him a laser pistol. "Get more shots this way!"

"Thanks!"

Josh hesitated before raising over the crate. He fired till the charge ran dry. The bolts hit near the tunnel opening. Tiny, candle-like fires formed in the rock. Two fallen pirates, their bodies contorted into unnatural positions, littered the tunnel entrance.

At least some of our fire found its mark.

Return laser fire filled the air with blue bolts. Fires erupted across the hangar. He ducked behind the crate. Matta tossed him a charge pack. He reloaded as she fired.

"They're dug in there like lykers!" she yelled, coming back to one knee. Return fire blasted the crate. "One of them's gots one eye."

"We can't stay behind this crate for long!" He stared at her. "Wait, what did you say?"

"One of those men tryin' to kill us," she said, her steel eyes wide. "He's got one eye and a big beard."

His stomach turned. "Stay down."

He leaned to the side of the container. Waylon reloaded as Tocol fired like a madman over the burning Trident's tail. Drad aimed and fired slower than Tocol, his method precise and methodical.

"Waylon!" Josh screamed over the firefight's chaos. Waylon ducked behind the fighter and looked in his direction. "Cyclops!"

Waylon nodded, smacking Tocol on the back and saying something Josh couldn't hear.

"What is a Cyclops?" Matta asked.

"Bad news, that's what," Josh snapped.

19

"I'm hit!" Nubern's voice strained, crackling over the gamma wave. "I'm going down!"

"Pull up!" Moving away from his burning target, Austin searched the sky for Nubern's Trident. "On my way!"

"Too late! I'm—"

The gamma wave screeched.

Banking left, Austin brought his fighter to an ascending angle and viewed the Pacific Ocean littered with burning scrap. Through the deadly furball of mismatched Tyral fighters and F-18 Hornets, he watched Nubern's flaming fighter skip across the ocean's blue surface. He flinched.

Nubern.

"Talon, this is Rock. Do you copy?" He paused before whispering, "Talon, come in."

A warning bell blared in his earpiece. Enemy fire dissipated his rear shields. He yanked the stick, forcing the fighter into a stomach-churning downward corkscrew. The G-force pressed him into his seat. With his free hand, he diverted the engine power he could spare into his guns.

Ignoring the thought of Nubern sinking to the bottom of the

Pacific, Austin steadied his descent and checked the sensors. He blinked through his eyes blurred with tears, seething as he deciphered the situation. The Hornets dropped fast; the pirates' modified fighters were simply too well-equipped. A dozen bandits broke off from the dogfight and headed west, firing missiles into the water.

Not good.

"Atlantis, Rock. If you are still receiving, I'm alone except for our local friends." He thought of the pirates' missiles. "Prepare for some chop."

"Copy, Rock," Brannen said after a short delay. "Activating outer defense measures. Do not approach Atlantis. Repeat, do not approach."

The sky filled with Tyral Pirates battling the Hornets. He didn't want to look at the sensors for a count. He knew they were outnumbered.

I won't be returning.

"Grumbler, Rock. Do you copy?"

"Still here," the F-18 pilot responded.

Austin rolled, laser bolts passing beneath him. An unlucky pirate fighter soared in front of his crosshairs. He squeezed the trigger hard, his bolts exploding into the enemy's cockpit. The nose ripped apart in flames.

"If you can, Grumbler," Austin said, grunting as the gravity pressed him into the seat, "you and your men break off the attack. Head for those bandits to the west. Bombers. See them?"

"Copy. Where's your wingman?"

"Gone." Austin swallowed. "Go in guns blazing. I'll cover you."

"Copy, Rock. I hope you know what you're doing."

Austin watched the remaining Hornets break away from the scrap with the pirate fighters. A laser bolt clipped one Hornet's wing, sending the fighter into a twirl toward the ocean's surface. The lead Hornets fired their guns, igniting the sky with tracer rounds.

"Hurry, Grumbler," Austin said.

Bearing east as if he retreated back toward Base Prime and San Francisco, Austin watched his scope to see his plan come together.

The Hornets attacked the pirates firing on Atlantis and attracted pursuers, the remaining bandits closing in behind the F-18s. Austin braced himself, hoping his laser banks would charge quickly enough for this to work. The remaining Hornets formed up and soared toward the bombing Tyral Pirates with nine enemy fighters in pursuit.

Austin rattled his fingers on the stick as the pirates closed in behind the Hornets. The lead pirates fired, too ignorant to know their lasers couldn't hit at that range. He watched his gauges as the laser banks topped seventy-six percent. *That'll be enough.*

He looped, the world turning end-over-end. Rolling, he brought the horizon around until the ocean stretched out beneath him. He centered his crosshairs on the unsuspecting Tyral fighters as they formed up in a vulnerable line as they pursued the Hornets. They may have somehow acquired state-of-the-art equipment, but this filth had no training.

Let me show them what Legion training can do.

His Trident swept over them, dropping three on the first pass with well-placed shots. The remaining pirates broke formation, apparently unsure what had hit them, and scattered. He rolled, looped, and charged forward like a rabid beast. His Trident fired until the banks ran dry, but he remained in the chaos, providing a target for the pursuing fighters. He eluded them until his energy banks allowed two more shots. Another Tyral pirate exploded.

"Splash four bombers," Grumbler said.

As if from a great distance, Austin heard the gamma wave sizzle. His vision clouded. The Trident's engines whined. A darkness formed at the edge of his sight. His fingers tingled. Straightening out his course, he soared away from the fight. His experience flying in gravity had taken its toll, the forces from his maneuvers pressing on his head. The Trident could do things in Earth's gravity his body couldn't handle.

He continued in a straight line, blinking several times.

The Trident shook. A laser bolt disintegrated his rear shields. The fighter rattled as another bolt crashed into his wing.

I can't do anymore.

Fatigue washed over him. The gravity pressed against him. His head pounded. For the first time in the cockpit, he wanted to vomit. He felt another hit on his fighter. Weakly, he pressed forward on the stick, attempting evasive maneuvers. Gravity threatened to knock him out. He eased on the stick, closing his eyes. Without his maneuvers, he flew across the sky like a drone target.

This is it. I'm going down.

"Boys, this is Grumbler," the gamma wave hissed. "See how many you can drop on the next pass. Stay together."

The gamma wave came to life. Grumbler barked orders as his Hornets clashed with the bombers. Maybe they could save Atlantis, maybe.

Austin leaned over the stick and took in a deep breath, awaiting the inevitable kill shot.

"Rock, do you copy?"

Austin's neck tingled. *I know that voice.*

"Rock, this is Tiger inbound with reinforcements. Where do you need us?"

Braddock.

He looked up. Twelve Legion Tridents descended into the atmosphere, flying in tight formation with Captain Ty Braddock at the lead. White contour lines trailed off the wings of the gorgeous Tridents. He grinned, energy once again surging through his veins.

"Welcome, Tiger. Anywhere you can help!"

"We'll drop what we can," Braddock snapped. "Tizona, give'em the sword!"

The Tridents unleashed a flurry of missiles. Explosions erupted across the heavens. Tyral craft tried to dodge the incoming fire. Hornets intermingled with the Tridents and pirates.

"The Hornets are friendly," Austin said, blinking and still dealing with the effects of nearly passing out.

"Got it," Braddock said.

Two pirates broke formation, heading toward Austin's position.

"You've got some friends. Mind if we get rid of them?"

Austin inhaled at the sound of Skylar's voice. "Cheetah! They're all over me. My ship's about spent."

"We got you covered, buddy," Bear's voice hissed through radio. "Head for the surface. Open up our shot."

He leaned on the stick, the ocean filling his forward view. He didn't know how they had done it, but Tarton's Junction managed to send reinforcements to defend Atlantis before the rest of Quadrant Eight could respond. Twelve fighters might be enough to turn the tide.

He slowed his descent and allowed his Trident to dip beneath the waves. Skylar and Bear dispatched his pursuers with well-placed missile shots.

Out of the enemy's sight, Austin redirected his power to the laser banks and shields. As the energy recharged, he allowed the Trident to float down until the blue waters of the Pacific darkened. He caught his breath. Sweat filled his oversized flight suit, his skin slippery.

Using his sensors, he surveyed the situation. Braddock and his squadron of recruits joined the F-18 Hornets. He listened to the radio chatter, Skylar and Bear calling out kills like veteran pilots. The pirate missiles descending on Atlantis slowed, then stopped completely. He checked below and gasped.

Atlantis must have fought off the submersibles or they had gone out of sensor range, but still, the damage had been done. The entire main hangar had been completely destroyed. Several of the outer perimeter defenses no longer appeared operational. Long trails of bubbles rose from the entire port, heading for the surface. Only the primary civilian hangar still existed. The friendly fighters above barely had a place to land.

He took a deep breath as his energy banks reached full charge. Balancing his power distribution across the lasers, shields, and engines, he pulled back on the stick and launched full throttle.

"Tiger, Rock," Austin said. "Heading back into the fight."

"Copy, Rock."

He growled, "Let's finish this."

20

Two bolts shot over his head. Ducking behind the burning crate, Josh gestured back to the *Sparking Light.* "What about the turrets on that thing? You think you could get back to the ship?"

Matta's face contorted, his upper lip rising. "You serious?"

"Yeah."

"Those weapons could blow up dis entire rock!"

Josh cursed himself. Of course, Matta was right. The transport's turrets would destroy their enemy, but could also weaken the foundation and bring the asteroid down on top of them. Besides, there could be more prisoners back there.

The firefight between the *Barracudas* and the Tyral garrison had reached a stalemate. If it continued, Josh knew they would soon run out of charges. Even the ancient projectile weapon only had so many shots left.

"Josh!" When he looked, Waylon remained crouched behind the fighter. "I need cover fire!"

Josh nodded and swept back behind the crate. "Get ready to fire."

"What's going on?" Matta asked.

"Just get ready."

Josh peered at Waylon who provided instructions to Drad and

Tocol. Waylon's face shimmered with sweat in the low light. A fresh laser burn slashed through the flesh on his cheek as he grinned at Tocol, smacked him on the shoulder, and moved to the far side of the Trident. Tocol glanced over at Josh with a lopsided grin.

"Here we go."

Tocol raised over the fighter, his laser rifle unleashing blue bolts. Drad followed, adding to the fire.

"Now!" Josh yelled.

He rose to one knee, pulling the trigger at the tunnel's entrance. Matta screamed as she fired next to him. The hangar filled with pulsating light and the smell of burnt hair. The rock around the tunnel's entrance ignited in a sea of sparks. Boulders glowed a collage of reds and oranges from the onslaught.

Taking advantage of the cover fire, Waylon sprinted toward the tunnel. He moved with the agility of a running back. He jumped over discarded crates, sliding from cover to cover, keeping a small object tucked under his arm. Josh fired into the opening in the rocks, unsure if anyone remained to fire back. He squeezed the trigger until nothing happened.

He crouched. "Need another!"

Matta threw her hands up. "I'm out."

Josh leaned to look at Tocol and Drad still firing away. He yelled for them, but they must not have been able to hear him. Glancing down at the ancient rifle, he sighed and rested the weapon over the crate. He aimed at the tunnel, waiting for a clear shot of Cyclops. He thought of the torturous days under this man, relished the thought of a bullet ending it all and providing justice.

He calmed his breathing, his finger resting on the trigger.

"Come on," he whispered. "Show yourself."

Waylon sprinted from a line of crates close to the prisoner tunnel. He dove and slid up against the rock to the right of the entrance, holding his hand high. Tocol and Drad ceased fire. Matta crouched on one knee and lifted her pistol toward the ceiling. Josh kept the rifle pointed at the smoke-filled tunnel. An odd quiet fell over the hangar.

Smoke hung over the area. The fires popped, sounding loud without the raging firefight. Josh squinted.

Waylon leaned against the rock. He lifted the black object, pressed a button on its surface, and hurled it into the tunnel. Spinning around, he dove to the ground.

A blinding white light flashed from the tunnel. A wave of gray smoke rolled out, filling the area with clouds. Two figures stumbled into the open, both wearing the dark tunics of the Tyral Pirates. Tocol and Drad fired, dropping both of them. Josh hesitated. Had Cyclops been one of them?

Waylon stood with caution as if the nearby pirates would reanimate and charge. He pulled a handgun, keeping it trained on them as he strode toward the tunnel entrance. A milky white smoke hissed out.

"What was that?" Josh asked.

"Gas," Matta said. "Anyone left in there won't stay long now."

Seconds passed, Waylon aiming his weapon into the tunnel. An engine cranked, and a beam of light shot through the smoke. A clump of figures all wearing the dark rags of the Tyral Pirates, garments covering their faces, rushed out of the tunnel like screaming furies.

Backing away, Waylon fired into the mass of humanity pouring into the hangar. In the midst of the cloud of rushing bodies, the four-wheeler the pirates had used to carry equipment burst out of the tunnel with Cyclops on board.

The vehicle crashed into Waylon, but the man held on. Tocol and Drad fired into the group of pirates. With their weapons empty, Josh and Matta could only watch.

The vehicle sped across the hangar, the wheels bouncing on the uneven surface. Waylon grasped onto the handlebars while Cyclops pounded his face. Josh stared wide-eyed as the four-wheeler crashed into the airlock. Waylon and Cyclops tumbled to the floor, locked in hand-to-hand combat. The men grappled, rolling as they fought.

Tocol and Drad jumped over the burning fighter, rushing the remaining pirates. Tocol brandished the curved sword as he ran.

Drad pulled out two daggers. They crashed into the charging pirate garrison, slashing and pounding through the havoc. A violent struggle raged across the hangar.

"Come on!" Matta yelled, sprinting away from the burning crate.

Without thinking, Josh rushed into the fray, his weakened legs carrying him as fast as he could make them. Blood splattered across the floor. Men battled. Screams and grunts surrounded him. Entering the fight, he hoisted the rifle over his head like a club, swinging and connecting with a pirate's shoulder. The man turned, but Tocol's sword sliced into the pirate's shoulder.

A blunt object struck his head from behind. Josh grunted, the back of his head searing. He tumbled to the ground. The pirate Tocol had slashed fell next to him and remained still. As his head throbbed, he remained on his face as the world spun around him. The sounds of fighting ceased.

Josh raised his head. Tocol's boot stepped on the fallen pirate's shoulder.

He rolled over on his back. "Thank you."

"You aren't much for fighting are you, little man?" Tocol offered a hand and lifted Josh to his feet.

Josh put his arm around Tocol's shoulder and surveyed his surroundings. Six pirate bodies were sprawled across the bloody hangar floor. Drad, his daggers sheathed, stood in the middle of the carnage, helping Matta stand. The tiny woman's body was drenched in sweat. Her gray, oil-stained pilot coveralls ripped across her knees and tore at the sleeves. A trickle of blood moved down from the crack in her lip.

"You guys know what you're doing," Josh said, gasping. "I'm a pilot, not a warrior."

Tocol snorted, wiping his brow. "No, you're not a warrior." He slapped Josh's shoulder. "But you have the heart of one."

A laser shot fired from the airlock. Josh stared. *Waylon!*

Waylon stood at the airlock door, his back toward them. He aimed a laser pistol in front of him. Drad and Matta ran toward him while Tocol helped Josh across the hangar to the airlock.

When Josh arrived, he saw the crumbled wreck of the four-wheeler at the back of the airlock. Cyclops, the man who had tortured them for months, leaned up against the wreckage. A fresh laser burn sizzled on his shoulder, a wisp of smoke drifting up from the wound. His good eye bled, already swelling shut from Waylon's wrath. Cyclops breathed slowly, his gaze on the floor.

"Just do it," Cyclops hissed. "End it."

Waylon looked down at the man as the other *Barracudas* stood near him.

Allowing Josh to balance at the airlock door, Tocol raised his sword.

"I'll do it," he said, taking one step into the airlock.

"No, no." Waylon sighed, as if coming to a difficult decision. "I think this should end the way it ended for all of those families."

He took a step backward and nodded as his hand rested on the button for the airlock's outer door. Josh and Tocol moved back as he pressed the button.

The airlock door hissed and lumbered forward. The *Barracudas* watched as the door slid across. The yellow warning lights blinked.

"Cowards!" Cyclops yelled. "You're all cowards! You can't even face me like men!"

Seething, Cyclops glared at Josh, their gazes fused together.

The door shut. Josh couldn't stand anymore, and fell to his knees. His eyes remained on the airlock. With one whooshing sound, it was over.

"Let's get you to a place you can rest," Waylon said, placing his hands under Josh's armpits and pulling him to his feet.

21

"They're right on me!" Skylar screamed, her voice creating static in Austin's earpiece.

He squeezed the trigger, discharging a volley into the rear of a pirate craft. It collided with the ocean's surface, fragments skipping across the water as a plume of white mist erupted high into the air. He banked, barely avoiding the spire of water.

"I'm coming, Cheetah," he said, bringing the Trident around. "Where are you, Bear?"

"Busy," he said, his voice straining. "Be there when I can—they're all over!"

Austin risked a glance as he made for higher altitude. The situation had evened out; the pirates no longer outnumbered the combined forces of the U.S. Navy and the Legion. Skylar scrapped with a pair of pirates far from the main battle. Two pirate craft stuck close to her tail, firing a trail of fire.

Forcing shield power into his engines, Austin made up the distance in a fraction of the time it would have taken otherwise.

"Keep evading, Cheetah."

"Ya think?" she shot back. "Just get over here!"

Austin adjusted course, bringing his crosshairs on the closest bandit painted black with bright yellow bars on the tail.

"Bank left!" he yelled.

Skylar's fighter did as instructed. When the Tyral fighter changed course to pursue, he flashed his engines directly into Austin's crosshairs.

"Gotcha," Austin said under his breath without transmitting.

He fired, the first shots striking the engines. The pirate sputtered, tilted forward, and exploded.

"Splash one!" he yelled.

The other bandit broke off from Skylar's tail, pulling back into a sharp loop. Austin yanked on the throttle, trying hard to keep the pirate in front of him. The bandit shot upward faster than he could adjust and made it behind him. He cursed himself for getting cocky.

"Need some help, Bear. Got a trailer."

"Be there in ten seconds."

"Make it five," he said as the pirate corrected course and closed in, laser fire lighting up the sky around him. "He's right on me! I'm breaking for the surface!"

He pushed forward on the stick, the ocean surface replacing the sky outside his canopy. G-forces pressed him in his seat, twisting his stomach around with the maneuver. The harness's shoulder straps dug into his skin like a bird's talons. Red bolts shot past the canopy, one sizzling his starboard tail. More fire vaporized waves on the ocean's surface.

"I got a tingle, Bear," Austin said, his voice straining. "You coming?"

"Getting a lock," he grumbled. "Skim across the surface and I'll nail him."

"Copy."

Austin brought the Trident within five hundred feet of the ocean and pulled up. The pirate's laser fire sent clouds of superheated salt water splashing across his canopy. He put the ship's energy into the shields and engines. The Trident bolted forward like a spurred horse, pressing him into his seat. His helmet rattled. The waves zipped past the canopy as he pushed hard for the battle's edge.

"He's locked," Bear said. "Got him."

The pursuing fighter broke off the pursuit as the missile closed. Austin twisted his neck around, watching the bandit pull up and break for altitude. The pilot had waited too long and the missile was too fast. The explosion lit the late afternoon sky.

"Thanks, Bear," Austin said, the tightness leaving his chest. "Good shooting."

"Tizona squadron, Tiger," Braddock said. "Bandits bugging out. Form up at point three-oh-seven for pursuit."

"Copy," Austin said, checking his sensor. "Grumbler, do you read?"

"I copy, Rock," the pilot responded.

"Thank you for your help today." He watched the bandits flying into the upper atmosphere. "The battle's going where you can't follow."

Grumbler snorted. "Too bad. Maybe someday. Take one out for me, Rock. Good hunting."

The Hornets broke off and headed east toward the coast. The U.S. Navy had certainly done its job defending Earth today. Austin wondered what the pilots had been told, what they *would* be told during their debriefings. He frowned. Compared to when they arrived, far fewer Hornets flew away from the battle...

Austin brought his Trident to bear on the rally point. The sensors showed four remaining Tyral craft headed for deep orbit. Within twenty seconds, they would be in space.

"Tower, Tiger," Braddock said, his tone laced with concern. "Do you copy?"

"Copy, Tiger."

Austin recognized the voice of Commander Carv Wallace, littered with static. At least that meant Atlantis had survived the bombardment.

"SIT-REP," Braddock said.

"What's left of us is safe for now," Wallace said. "The defense cannons did their job. The final surviving submersible fled across the ocean floor and disappeared."

Braddock hissed. "We'll worry about that later. Can Atlantis hold?"

"Damage control teams are doing what they can." Wallace paused. "We'll hold."

"Copy. I need the disruptor fired. The enemy is trying to leave the party. We don't need anyone else to know."

"You got it," Wallace said. "Solar disruptor fired. You've got thirty minutes."

"We won't need that long." Braddock clicked over to the squadron frequency. "Tizona, all Star Runners report in."

Six recruits announced their call signs, including Skylar, Bear, and Gan. The other five must have been destroyed in the battle. When the reports ceased, Austin keyed for transmission.

"Rock, reporting in."

"Rock, Tiger," Braddock said. "You have *got* to be bingo fuel. Report back to Atlantis for resupply."

Austin frowned. "With all due respect, sir, there aren't many of us here." He looked at his fuel display. "Permission to stay."

Braddock paused. "Granted. Form up and prepare for pursuit."

The eight Tridents fell into formation in high orbit. Austin balanced his power levels and tapped the dashboard.

"You've done good, girl," he whispered. "Real good."

The controls felt more sensitive, more responsive. As the glowing blue of the atmosphere dissipated behind them, the Tridents left Earth's gravity. The Trident had arrived back in its home environment. Austin smiled. Perhaps it was where he belonged, too.

Something metallic glistened. Sunlight flickered off an object in deep space. He did a sensor sweep.

Four Tyral pirates flew in tight formation heading for Earth's moon: Austin saw three fighters and some kind of modified fighter-bomber.

"Four bogeys at six-three-oh," Skylar announced, pulling closer in formation to Austin's left.

"Copy, Cheetah," Braddock said. "Tighten it up, Toad."

Austin grinned.

Gan Patro had a lower point total than Bear when Austin had left Tarton's Junction, leaving him the furthest from graduation. Braddock must have scraped the bottom of the barrel to bring newbies in on this mission. Command probably didn't like the idea of sending Tarton's Junction's alert fighters away to Earth, having to risk all of Quadrant Eight for the possible threat against a dark world. By the time word got out Earth was truly threatened and under attack, the Legion couldn't react fast enough. *The Legion really got caught with its pants.*

But Braddock knew.

His reputation as a true Star Runner had been more fact than myth. Austin smiled as he glanced over at Braddock's Trident in the lead position of their formation. If not for Braddock, the Tyral surprise attack would have taken out not only Atlantis, but could have signaled the end of Earth as a dark world in Legion space. If Rodon had taken over, the entire planet could have eventually been enslaved.

"I need a missile check," Braddock ordered. "I'm out."

Most of the young pilots called out empty, their missiles used up in the defense of Atlantis. Austin glanced at his readouts. A complete lack of missiles didn't worry him as much as his fuel levels dropping below ten percent.

"I have two," Gan said, his voice quiet.

"Stunners?" Braddock asked.

"Negative."

"Copy, Toad," Braddock said. "I need you to form up next to me. We're under three-hundred MUs out and closing. I want you to get a lock and take out two of these guys when we're in range."

"Copy, sir."

The formation shifted, allowing Gan to fly on Braddock's wing.

"Listen, Toad," Braddock said, his voice low. "When we're in range, this scum is going to wiggle out like a crushed insect under a boot. I want you to stay on them. I want two of them down before they have a chance to fire back. You got it?"

"Yes, sir," Gan said, his voice cracking.

"That's good, Recruit," Braddock said. "The rest of you, get your guns hot and be ready to scrap. The pirates are going to curve out on the dark side of the moon."

"How is that possible, Captain?" Bear asked.

"They've stashed a power relay on the moon," Braddock said without delay.

"A power relay?" Skylar asked.

"Boosts a curve," Braddock said. "Cut the chatter. We're two-hundred MUs out. Everybody get ready. I don't want this scum escaping again today. Toad, get your lock."

Austin cracked his knuckles. Ignoring his weary eyelids, he sat up straight in the cockpit. The Trident had given him everything she had today. Now, with Rodon fleeing, he needed a little more from his battered fighter.

Rodon.

He thought of their last encounter in the space around Flin Six. He'd nearly had him. The dogfight had been fast, too quick to lead to a resolution. Rodon fled, vowing to fight at another place and time.

Well, Austin thought, grinning, *the other place and time had arrived.*

"One-hundred MUs," Braddock announced. "Get that lock!"

"Copy, Tiger," Gan said.

Despite willing his fighter to move faster, Austin stayed in formation while his comrade searched for a lock. The sensors of Gan's targeting computer hit one of the Tyral fighters. The modified stolen Trident broke off from Rodon's foursome and launched into evasive maneuvers.

"Stay limber, Tizona," Braddock said.

The formation loosened but remained focused on the pirates.

Come on, Gan, Austin thought. *Take them out.*

A second later, Gan launched a missile. The weapon drifted in space before it activated. The missile shot off into space like a unleashed predator hunting its prey.

"I've got him," Gan said, his voice shaking.

Austin wasn't sure what had happened since he left Tarton's Junction, but he knew this had to be Gan's first kill. The seconds ticked by as the missile hunted the Tyral fighter. Eight seconds later, the weapon found its mark. The explosion flashed, but disappeared in the void of space. The enemy transponder faded out.

"Good shot, Toad," Braddock said. "Lock another one. Fast."

The recruit Star Runner found a lock quicker the second time. The Tridents were at a distance of seventy MUs. Gan fired his final missile and another Tyral craft exploded. Only two pirates now showed on the sensors, both driving hard for the moon which was still a glowing speck in the distance.

The final pirate craft split up, one flying hard for the moon while the other looped around to face the Tridents.

The distance dropped.

"All right Tizona," Braddock said quickly, "this is it. Keep your cool. This pirate must have balls the size of asteroids to come straight at us."

The eight Tridents clashed into the lone Tyral pirate as both sides reached laser range. They collided into a jumble of laser fire.

"Rock!" Braddock yelled. "Take Bear, Cheetah, and—"

Space flashed a white searing light. Austin winced, the burst burning his retinas. When he opened his eyes, the Trident's dashboard had gone dark. He blinked.

The hum of his engines had vanished. The constant hiss of his life support and the drone of onboard electronics ceased. The Trident drifted, its nose pitching forward. He pulled back on the stick.

No response. The Trident had died. A frigid tingling crept up his back. His speed dropped. Looking around, Austin saw the other Tridents floating lifelessly in space.

Far in the distance, the only remaining Tyral craft grew smaller. Rodon *had* to be piloting the modified fighter-bomber.

Austin punched the dashboard. Nothing responded. His ship had lost all power. Without the engine running the onboard systems, he would either freeze to death or die of asphyxiation.

He swiveled his head around, searching the other Tridents around him. All the other position lights had darkened. The pirate craft floated in the midst of them like a piece of burnt charcoal. Its blackened hull looked like a sheet of fried metal.

The dashboard flickered.

"Come on baby," Austin said, pressing the console. "Wake up."

The electronics warmed as the system rebooted.

"Tiz...addock...mayday...day..."

Austin tapped his helmet. The gamma wave popped in his earpiece, but he couldn't make out the words.

He keyed for an engine restart. The engine whimpered. He tried again. This time, it rumbled to life.

"...addock, do you copy? Tizona squadron, restart your engines. Do you copy?"

"Tiger, Rock. What happened?"

"Rock! That inbound bandit was on a suicide run."

"What?"

"They rigged that fighter to be a manned stunner missile," he said. "Must have been flying as Rodon's personal escort. The guy fired off a stunner the size of a fighter and sent the shockwave through all of us!"

Austin glanced toward the moon. "Can you fly?"

"My ship's banged up, but I'll make it," Braddock said. "You?"

He ignored his fuel readings. "I can make it."

"All right," Braddock said. "Tizona, any other Star Runners copy?"

"I copy," Skylar said, her voice straining like she just woke from a restless nap. "What *was* that?"

"I'll tell you later," Braddock said. "Form up on my wing, we're pursuing Rodon."

"But we'll never catch him now," Skylar said.

"We're going to try."

The three Tridents left the other floating Legion fighters. Braddock soared in front with Skylar and Austin on his wings.

Rodon can't get away again. It must not happen.

The distance to Rodon's ship dropped. The moon loomed in the distance, the shape becoming more than a distant speck of light. Minutes passed as they closed in.

"Where would he get a stunner the size of a ship?" Austin asked. "I've never even read about that technology."

Braddock murmured something inaudible. "We'll chew that food when it's on the table. Wish I had a missile."

"Copy."

As Rodon's craft shot inside into lunar orbit, Austin dropped all power to his shields. He shot ahead of Braddock and Skylar.

"We can't let him get away!" he yelled.

"Rock, pull back," Braddock said. "Dropping power to your shields is suicide."

"He's entered the moon's orbit, Captain. If he gets away, he'll regroup and try to ravage another dark world."

Braddock remained silent.

A moment later, Braddock and Skylar closed in behind him. He managed a weary smile at the sensors before glancing back at his crosshairs. Rodon's modified fighter-bomber banked left as it circled the moon.

Soon he would escape.

Austin gripped the stick. He slapped the side of the cockpit. Rodon was going to escape. He transmitted onto an open gamma wave.

"Rodon, this is Rock," he said. "You wanted another time and place. Does *this* work for you?"

Static met his taunt.

"Rodon, I'm amused by your fierce reputation."

The modified craft looped into another direction. Austin smiled, lining his crosshairs with his fighter.

"Be careful what you wish for, Rock," Rodon sneered.

A flurry of missiles released from the pirate's craft.

"Evade!" Braddock said.

Austin veered left. Skylar pulled up. Braddock shot to the right. The missiles fired hot, seeking their targets. The missile's targeting computer pinged, the sound hitting his earpiece. He rolled and spun, two of the missiles zeroing in on his sensors' signature. He dropped countermeasures, hoping the decoy would divert the incoming missiles. Straightening his course, he headed for the lunar surface at full throttle.

"Cheetah, report," he said.

"I've got this," she said, her voice confident.

Austin flew away from his comrades, the two missiles still on his tail. One diverted to the countermeasures and lost its track. A moment later, it sailed off toward deep space and away from the Tridents. The other, however, reacquired a lock on Skylar's Trident.

He looped around. "Cheetah, make for point oh-two-four."

"Copy!"

Her Trident swung around and flew for deep space. The missile adjusted course, providing a larger target for Austin's trajectory. He checked his energy banks; he'd have a few shots at most. The missile closed to within thirty MUs. Austin fired, the bolts soaring off toward infinity.

"Hurry up, Rock," Skylar said.

Eighteen MUs until the missile would strike her.

Austin changed course, the crosshairs bouncing on top of the missile. He fired again, the bolts sizzling past.

Missed!

Gripping the stick, he rested his index finger on the trigger. One more shot—that's all his energy banks would give him before he'd have to divert from the engines.

And he didn't have time.

"Hang on, Cheetah," he breathed.

Seven MUs.

The missile lined up behind Skylar's fighter. It stopped rotating, the onboard sensors locking onto her signature.

Three MUs.

Austin led the missile, the crosshairs just above the projectile. He thought of Skylar at the stick, fearing for her life and wondering if the missile would be the end of her.

Please, let this shot be true.

He fired.

Two bolts left his laser cannons, the red illuminating the darkness of space. His energy banks flashed empty. The shots crashed into the missile. It spun and exploded.

Austin gasped, slamming back into his seat. "You're clear, Cheetah."

"Thanks, Rock. I owe you for that."

"That one's free."

Austin turned his Trident around and formed up behind Braddock. "You okay, Tiger?"

"Missile hit my countermeasures too close to the fighter." He sighed. "Took some flak in the engine, but she's flying."

"Where's Rodon?" Austin asked.

"Check four-six-oh."

Austin looked at his sensors. Rodon's ship had turned back immediately after firing his missile volley. A curve opened on the dark side of the moon. The ship shuddered forward and disappeared from the scope.

Despite their best efforts, Rodon had escaped again.

22

"Take this." With his oversized hands, Waylon passed a cold rag to Josh. "And this."

He accepted the rag and the cup of coffee. "Thank you."

"Word of warning; there's a little extra something in the coffee. Should help with the pain."

He smiled. "Whatever works."

The lump on the back of his head had swelled in the hours since the fight for the asteroid base. He'd passed out for a few minutes on a pile of blankets Waylon had offered, dreaming of torture and laser fire. When he woke, the back of his head felt soft and tender like thawed meat, the pain flashing through his body with each heartbeat. He sat as still as possible, taking short, shallow breaths as the *Barracudas* cleaned the hangar bay and doused the fires. They tossed the bodies of the Tyral Pirates into the airlock with the rest of the trash, ending their reign of the secluded rock in the middle of the Zine System. The Barracuda vessels had refueled using pirate supplies and had started filling storage tanks for transfer.

As he watched his crew salvage the hangar like vultures on road kill, Waylon sipped on coffee and sat next to Josh.

"We spent too much time working down there," Waylon said,

nodding to the hangar bay where they had spent countless hours stripping vessels stolen by Rodon and his men.

"Rather not think about it," Josh said, closing his eyes as he fingered the tender lump on his head.

Waylon took a drink, his eyes on Josh. "Who is Kadyn?"

Josh blinked, the cup of coffee steaming in his face. "What?"

Waylon grinned, his beard moving with the gesture. "When you were out earlier, you kept saying that name."

He winced. "That's a long story."

"We have plenty of time," Waylon snorted.

"I didn't know you cared."

"You're one of us now," Waylon said, staring into his coffee. "With what we've been through, you are *definitely* one of us. I'd like to know anything you feel like sharing."

Josh sighed and raised his eyebrows, his stomach tightening at the thought of Kadyn's brown hair as she sipped on a massive beverage from the coffee shop. "She's a friend, a good friend from long before any of this happened."

"You are joined with her?"

"You mean married?" He shook her head. "No. I don't think she even knows I feel this way."

"Strange world."

"How's that?"

"Where I'm from, life is short and hard." He gestured to the *Barracudas* cleaning the hangar. "This is my family. They know I would die for them. I say this because it could happen any day at any time. There is not always tomorrow."

He bit his lip, thinking of Rist falling to the hangar floor and Geo's fighter exploding in the asteroid field. "I know. I'm sorry about your losses today."

Shaking his head, Waylon reached out and squeezed Josh's shoulder. "You are my family, too."

Josh thought of the first time he'd seen Waylon in this asteroid. "First time I met you, I thought you were going to kill me."

"All great friendships start that way, yes?" He slapped Josh on the shoulder.

"Not on Earth."

Waylon cocked his head to the side. "Tell me of Earth."

Josh exhaled. "I honestly don't remember. Is that weird Seems like a different lifetime." He gazed at the field of stars visible through the asteroids. "It's a good place. A safe place. There is law and order... for the most part."

"I've heard it's a warlike planet," Waylon said, stretching his legs out in front of him.

"Sometimes, I guess that's true. Used to be much worse I would imagine."

They sipped on the coffee, enjoying the peace.

"What's next for you, Waylon?"

He considered the question. "We could move here and start over. The base is well hidden, more room than we could ever dream of using. More than we have on Sanctum. It's a good location for shipping, too."

"You don't think Rodon will come back?"

"Perhaps. I suppose it's always possible. Wherever they have gone, I hope they decide to stay." He eyed Josh. "We could use a good pilot to help get us running. I know it's not as fancy as being a Legion Star Runner, but it could be a good life."

Josh looked away. Working for the *Barracudas* would not be his dream job, but serving in the Legion Navy had brought him nothing but...

He sighed. Whenever he closed his eyes, he saw the blood and toil sacrificed as a slave of the Tyral Pirates. The past few days had been a blur. His body ached, and he sometimes wondered if he could even walk to the bathroom when the time came. Becoming a Barracuda and working for Waylon might provide him a break since the Tyral Pirates no longer had a base to terrorize Quadrant Eight. Of course, they would come back whenever they—

Josh's heart thumped and seemed to skip a beat. What was he thinking? He couldn't sit around and drink coffee. The Tyral Pirates had left this base, bound for a dark world somewhere. He needed to find out where and warn the Legion.

"Waylon, I would love to stay," he said. "You have a family here, a group that loves and respects you. I have that, too, back with the Legion. I have to find out where that power relay was going. The entire Quadrant Eight could be in danger."

Waylon nodded as Josh spoke. He buried his hand inside his beard and rubbed his chin. "How can I help?"

He glanced over at the control room. "Before we had our welcoming party with the pirates, I wanted to check out that control room."

"Sounds like a good idea."

Waylon carefully draped Josh's arm around his neck and lifted him. He winced, keeping the cold rag on the back of his head. The floor shifted, darkness closing at the edge of his vision. He paused, fighting the feeling of passing out.

"Easy," Josh said, "I feel like the room's spinning."

"You took a knock on the head," Waylon said, grunting as he took on more of Josh's weight. "That's normal."

They shuffled across the hangar to the control room, the other *Barracudas* glancing at them as they moved. Matta smiled, pushing a floating dolly through as Tocol ignited a welding torch. Waylon reached out and opened the door with his free hand. The chamber smelled of burnt circuit boards. Computers hummed on standby. He led Josh to a chair with wheels in front of what must have been the main control desk.

"What did they use all this for?" Waylon asked as he looked around.

"I think it was air traffic control," Josh said, switching on the computer terminal. "I really don't know. They probably ran their entire operation in here. Our operatives would have a field day with his stuff."

Waylon scoffed. "I'll bet."

While the computer warmed up, the green screen flickered through a series of diagnostics. The software included a language option, a feature common on all Legion space vessels. Pushing away any thoughts of how the Tyral Pirates had gained such software, he keyed for the translator, selected "Earth" and found English. Waylon activated the rest of the room while Josh sat in the chair, the cold rag still pressed to the back of his head.

The diagnostics revealed the base had a missile defense system, military grade communications, and long-range sensors displaying a hyper-accurate readout of the entire asteroid field. A hologram projector loomed overhead, allowing the control room to double as a planetarium. If any ship decided to head into this system, the Tyral Pirates would know about it. Other information poured into the computer including updated activity in several nearby star systems. One particular system caught his eye. He keyed to magnify the information on Flin Six.

"What's that?" Waylon asked, placing his hand on the back of Josh's seat.

"Not sure."

The system information popped up on the screen. Flin Six itself had nothing special enough to include in the file. No minerals or precious metals showed up on the survey. However, this information suggested the Tyral Pirates had salvaged several Legion Tridents from the area. What had the Legion been doing there?

"Friends of yours?" Waylon asked.

"I hope not," Josh said, sliding his hand across his mouth, "but Rodon gained a few of our fighters here for sure."

He minimized the screen and looked back to the asteroid readout. "I'm going to warm up this missile defense system while we're here. If Rodon returns with his fleet, we'll have plenty of notice. You need to decide if you guys are really moving in."

"I understand." Waylon pointed at the defense system. "How could pirates afford such technology?"

"I have no idea." Josh surveyed the room full of a mismatch of technology. "One thing's for certain, they have quite the benefactor."

For the next several minutes, Josh pored through the files searching for anything on the curvature power relay. Apparently growing tired of watching Josh search through files, Waylon left, giving orders to his crew.

Josh watched them through the window for a moment and sighed. Staying with the *Barracudas* would certainly be easier than trying to find a way back to a Legion base. Gaining transportation to Tarton's Junction or any other Legion station was a topic Waylon might not be too keen on discussing anytime soon. For one, he wouldn't want to get so close to the law. For another, he probably wouldn't want to loan out a spacecraft, either. Perhaps Josh could send out a distress signal? With any luck, a Legion vessel or even a civilian cruiser would detect his signal and come pick him up.

Josh shook his head. Once again, this idea would make using the asteroid base impossible for Waylon and the *Barracudas*.

After finishing his review of another file, Josh stood and stretched. He limped over to a different terminal. Several encrypted files prevented him from searching the details. Perhaps this was a waste of time.

"Josh," Waylon said, bursting into the room. "I think you'll want to see this."

Moving as fast as he could manage, Josh scuffed his feet to the hangar bay. The crew had started stripping the crashed Tyral Trident fighter for worthy parts and dragging the trash to the airlock. Tocol stood on the Trident's nose like a champion hunter and hurled a piece of scrap metal to the hangar deck.

Matta ran up with a tablet in her hand. "This is the navigation tablet from dat fighter."

"Yeah?" Josh said, his eyes darting between Matta and Waylon. So?"

She looked at Waylon and back at Josh. "We think it's the fighter that one-eyed man was flying. Anyway, there's a series of coordinates locked into the drive. Waylon said you'd want to see it."

"Let's go back to the control room."

When they made it back, Josh hooked up the tablet into the terminal's input and downloaded the information. His head pounded. He sat back in the chair and asked Matta to finish downloading the information. Resting his head in his hands, he waited for the files to transfer. Tocol and Waylon watched them work.

"Everyone step back," Josh said, wincing as his head continued throbbing.. "I'll activate the star chart hologram."

When everyone moved away from the center of the room, a black lens with a circular base descended from the ceiling. It glowed a dull aqua blue. The room filled with an electronic purr. A holographic projection of the surrounding field glimmered, and images of asteroids tumbled through the control room. Tocol flinched, backing into the wall with a thud.

"You're scared?" Waylon laughed.

"Shut up," the large man grumbled, ducking as a holographic asteroid floated past his head. "What is this?"

"It's a map," Josh said, his voice filling with strength, the internal officer returning. "We're trying to figure out where Rodon and the rest of his rabble went."

Tocol nodded, crossing his arms and leaning against the wall. Matta sat on the floor, crossing her legs and staring up at the asteroids as if she were a child in the grass on a summer evening. Waylon stroked his beard as he took in the hologram.

"This is us," Josh said, pointing to a large asteroid in the center of the image. "If I zoom out a bit, like this, you can see the rest of the system."

The view pulled away to reveal the entire Zine system. Two uninhabitable planetary bodies circled the star. The large asteroid field loomed, taking up the majority of the room. Absolutely nothing called attention to the system, probably the reason Rodon had chosen it.

"There are several coordinates keyed into the stolen Trident's navigation," Josh said, feeling like an instructor. "I'm going to cycle through the previous locations now."

He punched in the first coordinates. The holographic map pulled back farther, flying through space to another backwater system of Quadrant Eight.

"This is the Amade Cluster," Josh said, glancing at Waylon. "We know this system way too well."

Waylon scowled. "That we do."

"That confirms this was Cyclops' ship. He'd been to the Amade Cluster." Josh punched in the next location. "These coordinates I'm punching in now were keyed in when the Trident crashed. It's safe to say these are the coordinates Cyclops planned to travel to next."

The holographic chart pulled back again. The stars swirled as if the control room tumbled through the cosmos. Matta clapped, her face lighting up. Tocol leaned against the wall as if the stars would smack him in the face. The images slowed and settled on a gray moon covered in craters.

"Okay, then," Josh said, shifting his head to the side as he studied the planetary body. "This small moon was his next destination. The power relay is buried here and...wait."

"What is it?" Waylon asked, stepping forward.

Josh pulled the star chart back. The image shifted, moving away from the moon to see the planet it orbited. The blue and white marble of a world glimmered over their heads.

"Where is dat?" Matta asked from the floor.

Josh zoomed out a bit more to see the nearest planetary body after the moon. A dull red planet also orbited the yellow star. Pressure built in his chest.

Waylon placed his hand on his shoulder. "You know this place?"

"I do." He stared at the display. "It's Earth."

"Earth?" Matta asked. "Where's dat?"

Waylon held up his hand, silencing her. "What do you mean? That's your home?"

"Yes."

"Rodon wouldn't dare attack a Legion dark world."

He winced. "It appears he would." He thought of Kadyn, of his parents. He scrubbed his hands across his face as the holographic colors swept over them.

Waylon shook his head. "He doesn't have the resources to pull off such an attack."

"Apparently, he does."

Quiet fell over the room. Even Matta remained silent. Waylon squeezed Josh's shoulder.

Turning away from the star charts, Josh rested his elbows on terminal. The Legion had to be warned. A surprise attack on a backwater planet like Earth could provide a beachhead to open up the entire Quadrant Eight for invasion. A power relay with enough energy could provide the beacon for an entire task force to waltz into the rear of Legion space.

"I need to go back," Josh said.

"To Earth? That would be suicide, brother."

"I need a ship." He turned to face Waylon, his fatigue forgotten. "I need a ship now."

Waylon's jaw dropped. "I—"

The map burned red, washing the room in a bloody hue. An alarm blasted like a bull horn.

"What?" Matta blurted out, leaping to her feet.

"It's not good." Waylon pointed at Tocol. "Get everyone ready to leave. Now!"

Tocol scooped Matta up with one hand, grabbing her shoulder. "Got it."

"Let's see what we have." Josh shifted the map back to the local star system. A lone vessel entered at the edge of the asteroid field, a curve closing behind it. "Here's our newcomer."

"Who is it?" Waylon asked, taking a step back to view the entire hologram.

Josh zoomed in on the vessel. "It's a modified fighter-bomber. Whoever it is, it's alone."

"Who would come way out here?" Waylon glared at the screen. "Has to be one of Rodon's men."

Josh focused on the sensors. "There's no identification."

The vessel flew through the asteroids like a professional, heading directly for their position.

"I don't like this," Waylon said. "I don't like this at all."

A new alarm sounded.

"What now?" Waylon asked, his voice rising.

"There's another ship coming in."

"What? Where?"

He zoomed out. "Here—at the edge of the field."

The holograph shimmered at the edge of the asteroids. A capital ship passed into the space just outside of the asteroid field. With the massive cannon under the ship's bow and the four torpedo tubes, he did not recognize the vessel from his studies.

"What is that?" Josh breathed, turning to Waylon. "Have you ever seen anything like that before?"

"No. It's not Legion."

Josh keyed for identification. "It's squawking a Zahl transponder."

"Zahl? Here?"

Josh re-verified the identification. The information pinged back. The vessel was large enough to carry hundreds of personnel. A hangar bay opened at the base of the vessel. The transponder popped up on the screen, providing ship information.

"It's called the *Dauntless*," he said. "This computer doesn't have the class in its memory banks."

"A new ship?" Waylon smacked the back of the chair. "Are you sure?"

"I've never seen anything like this before."

The *Dauntless* slowed. The fighter bomber turned around, changing course from traveling toward the asteroid base and facing the *Dauntless*.

"Quiet," Josh said as he slipped on the headset, searching the gamma waves for any transmissions. "I think I've got it."

He patched the signal through to the interior speakers. Outside the window, the *Barracudas* rushed around the hangar. Some carried crates while others detached fuel hoses from their ships.

"We are growing impatient with your lack of progress," a voice hissed over the speakers.

"I wasn't supplied well enough."

"Rodon, please. You have been given more than enough supplies over the years to dominate the competition. You promised to wreak havoc on the Legion backwater planets. You chose Earth. You have failed."

"I need more time. Tell Tulin I need more time."

"Your time has run out."

"I underestimated the defenses on Earth. I just need—"

"Unfortunately for you, your time has come to an end. And I'm afraid Tulin has decided there are to be no witnesses. You and your base will be destroyed."

"But I—"

"Goodbye, Rodon."

Static screeched throughout the control room. Josh killed the transmission and stared at the holographic map. Waylon crossed his arms over his chest and stood in silence. A flurry of missiles launched from the *Dauntless* toward Rodon's ship. Rodon looped around, heading quickly into the asteroid field. The missiles exploded into the rocks, sending fragments twirling into space.. High-powered laser cannons erupted destruction, shattering larger rocks into tiny particles. Rodon's ship spun, rolling through the rocks before disappearing into a collection of sharp asteroids. His transponder disappeared from the sensors.

For a moment, Josh thought the *Dauntless* would turn around and leave the system. As if to prove him wrong, Interceptors launched. Twelve horseshoe-shaped fighters soared in perfect formation into the path cleared by the capital ship's heavy weaponry. The *Dauntless* followed, the colossal cannon under its bow obliterating larger asteroids floating close to the ship. He predicted their trajectory back toward the asteroid base.

He yanked his attention from the disturbing scene playing out on the hovering holographic map. "What do you think?"

Waylon strode toward the door. "I'll start the evacuation."

23

"I'm way low on fuel, Captain." Austin tightened his eyelids and opened them again. Fatigue pressed on him. He took a deep breath and gripped the stick with both hands.

He descended into Earth's atmosphere, his Trident rocking as he pulled back on the throttle. A cloud hovered over his heart. Rodon, the man who had killed Josh and countless other Legion pilots, had escaped once again. Worse yet, Nubern had crashed into the Pacific Ocean.

"You take the lead," Braddock called back. "Once you hit the water, activate your shields and use the maneuvering thrusters to land. You'll conserve fuel."

"Copy."

After pursuing the pirates halfway to the moon, the other Tridents incapacitated by the Tyral suicide attack had rebooted their systems and returned to Earth in formation. Austin tried to stay awake on the descent.

Debris littered the ocean's surface. Burning pieces of metal peppered the blue waters. Long streaks of fire trails stretched across the ocean. Many pilots had lost their lives today, and for what?

He scanned this sector and found no surface contacts.

"Atlantis Tower, Rock."

The gamma wave hissed. "Copy, Rock."

"Eight Tridents coming in for a landing. Can you direct?"

"Copy, Rock. Follow the landing beacons to the civilian hangar."

Austin closed his eyes. *The civilian hangar.*

He had hoped his previous sensor reading of Atlantis had been faulty and the damage had not been as grim as it seemed. Now, the matter wasn't up for a debate.

The Tyral Pirates had destroyed three hangars in one afternoon. He eased the Trident into the water, following the green brackets on his HUD toward what was left of Atlantis.

WATER FELL from the hangar's ceiling as if it rained, rivers running off the fighter canopy. Austin landed, the landing gears submerging into three feet of water. He switched off its systems, and the fighter powered down as he opened his canopy. He slipped off his helmet, his sweaty hair pressing against his head like plastic wrap. Salty water dripped on his head and into his mouth. He wiped his gloves over his face and sat up to get out of reach of the water, wincing. His muscles ached.

Crewman Tyce, dried blood covering the right side of his face, brought the ladder to the Trident's side and smiled. Austin lifted his feet over the canopy and stepped down the ladder, plunging his feet into the frigid water.

"You all right, Lieutenant?" Tyce asked.

"I'm okay, Tyce," Austin said in a raspy voice. "Thank you."

"Water?" he asked, holding out a bottle.

"Sure." He took a long drink. "How are things here?"

Tyce's smile disappeared. "Bombs fell from above. They wouldn't stop. I thought we were going to die. They destroyed most of the station. The attackers boarded on the third corridor when our defense fighters were destroyed. I heard the cannons are gone, too. They used some kind of transport to penetrate the hull." He looked at the water that surrounded his feet; it was mixed with blood and oil. "Lost a lot of buddies."

Austin tapped his shoulder.

"Austin!"

He looked up. Skylar trudged through the water as quickly as she could, her helmet in hand. Her blonde hair was pressed against her skull. A small cut on her cheek spilt blood onto her otherwise perfect skin.

Austin moved toward her and fell into her arms. She nearly collapsed under his weight.

"Oh, my God," she breathed. "Are you okay?"

"Tired," he whispered.

Skylar turned to Tyce. "How long was he up there?"

"Hours, ma'am."

She pulled Austin around so she could look him in the eye. "Can you stand?"

He pulled it together. "I feel weak, but I'm okay."

"Infirmary?" she asked, looking at Tyce.

"Destroyed, but we've commandeered a disabled freighter for the wounded." He pointed. "It's over there. We're using the storage bays."

"Got it."

Skylar supported Austin through the filthy waters. Debris continued to fall from the ceiling. Small fires burned across the hangar. They passed Braddock, Gan, and Bear, who stood near their ships. The Star Runners sipped on water bottles, their eyes gazing across the standing water. Austin nodded to each of them, trying to manage a smile.

When they reached the freighter Tyce had indicated, they found dozens of cots lining the storage bay inside the vessel. It felt good to climb the ramp and leave the freezing water behind. Wounded bled onto the white sheets as staff tried to provide water and care the best they could. Skylar pointed toward an empty bed.

Austin squeezed her shoulder. "I'm not wounded. These people are truly hurt. I'm just tired."

"Then rest." She pushed him to the cot and knelt in front of him.

"My God, Austin. Are you all right? You look terrible. It's like you've lost fifty pounds."

He released a weak laugh. "It's not mine."

"What?"

Gesturing to the flight suit he'd received from Tyce, he said, "It's not mine. Belonged to a bigger Star Runner."

Pausing for a heartbeat, she said, "Whatever. You still look like crap."

She grabbed a wet rag and pressed it to his forehead, then dabbed at his face. He leaned against the wall and closed his eyes as he shifted his legs onto the cot.

"What happened to you?" she asked, washing the rag in a bowl. "We were doing training on the Junction and suddenly got called into action by Braddock. He explained the mission en route to Earth. Next thing I know we're dogfighting pirates over the Pacific Ocean."

Austin swallowed, his throat dry. "It's good to see you."

Her expression softened for a second before she said, "I'm serious, Austin. You were supposed to be on leave. What happened?"

"Earth was being attacked."

"I know that much. What do you mean? What happened?"

"Not attacked directly," he said, shaking his head. "Phantoms."

"Phantoms?" She shook her head. "What does that mean?"

"Some kind of mercenaries. They targeted my mother and my friend Kadyn."

She placed her hand on his knee. "Are they okay?"

He nodded slowly. "I'm tired, Sky. Exhausted, really."

Skylar squeezed his knee. Moans and screams of the wounded surrounded him. He looked into her face, watched her cheeks crinkle when she smiled.

"Come a long way, you and me," he said, touching her shoulder, looking at her worn Tizona blue flight suit. "I've missed you."

"You always say that. You always look at me and say...these sweet things. But, well, never mind." She eyed him. "Been weird on the station since you left. Nothing's been the same. I've been trying to get through my classes and the training. Just sick of Tarton's Junction, ready to get moving."

Austin winced when she pressed the rag on his forehead. "What was it like flying for Braddock?"

She chuckled. "When we heard our destination was Earth, I think we would have flown for anyone. I was so glad to get off that station, but I never would have imagined all this was happening." She looked him in the eye as she pressed the cool rag on his head. "Might have even flown for Pavolsky."

"Oh, man," he laughed, thinking of the cocky Lobera pilot he'd nearly destroyed in the Tarton's Junction mess hall, and the punishment he'd received afterward. "Just thinking of that guy makes me think of latrines. You must have really wanted to come here if you'd fly for him."

She stood. "I did."

Austin studied her, wishing he had something to say. The image of Ryker in her bed, recovering from her shattered leg, appeared in his mind. The incident on Flin Six had broken her. She probably waited for him to come to her side. Her voice echoed in his thoughts, saying "thank you" in English. He pressed his fingers together, no words coming to mind.

Across the room, he watched someone enter the storage bay. He squinted as a woman marched toward his position. Her uniform was torn and ragged, a freshly bandaged cut on her neck. She stepped up to Austin's cot and snapped to attention.

He smiled. "Security Officer Brannen."

Despite her hair matted with oil, Brannen managed to return the grin. "I had to come down when I heard you landed."

"Thank you, Brannen."

She beamed. "I don't know how you did it, but you kept the missile attack off us long enough so we could provide adequate defense from the offensive down here." She shook her head. "You might not know it, but you nearly didn't have a port to return to."

Austin gestured at the standing water outside the ship. "I gathered that."

"We fought off the intruders, managed to battle off the submersibles with our defense cannons before they were destroyed. Fighting on the ocean floor isn't easy, required us to rely on our sensors only. They fought like crazed lunatics, those who boarded. I called everyone into action; cooks, mechanics...we fought them back, saved Atlantis." Her expression glazed over; she was clearly exhausted.

"Anyway..." She offered a salute, bringing her attention back to the present. "Well done, Lieutenant. I'll make sure Command doesn't forget this."

Austin returned the salute. Brannen spun on her heel and marched out of the storage bay.

His helmet tucked under his arm, Braddock passed Brannen and strolled into the makeshift infirmary. He stepped next to Austin's bed and nodded.

"Well done, Lieutenant," Braddock said, his voice low as he glanced around at the wounded.

"A full-on captain leading Tizona recruits," Austin said, gesturing to Braddock's rank. "You must have been desperate."

"You have no idea. Had to leave my squadron to guard the station in case this was all some elaborate ruse."

Austin sat forward and started to stand.

"Please," Braddock held up his free hand, "stay seated. You've had quite a time, Stone."

"Another day in the service."

Braddock allowed a crooked smile. "I know you're exhausted, but we need to talk."

His stomach fluttered. "Nubern?"

"Search and rescue teams have found seven wounded pilots in the waters above." Braddock nodded. "Nubern was one of them. He's banged up, but he's tough. I know he'll be fine. Two of the U.S. pilots were also rescued. I'm told we're making arrangements for their return at this very moment."

He pressed his palms to his eyes. "That's good news, sir."

"There's more that's...not so good."

Lowering his hands, he grimaced. "Yes, sir?"

"Our teams are surveying the wreckage from the downed submersibles used to attack Atlantis. The sensors here are shot to hell. It'll be weeks before the station is up and running. It appears Rodon's filth tried to destroy all the outer structures and take the primary dome. During the attack, Atlantis thought they had destroyed all of the subs."

"So I'm told." Austin looked at him. "And?"

Braddock's face was still as a statue. "There's one missing."

He glanced at Skylar. "So? What does that mean?"

"I've kept this quiet." Braddock pursed his lips, glancing over his shoulder. "We don't need to cause a panic. Most of the soldiers are dead or wounded, and we don't need these people under any more stress than they're already experiencing. But with one submersible escaping, it means they could be heading anywhere on this planet. Our sensors won't be able to pick them up if they skim slowly across the ocean floor."

"Wait a minute," Austin said, "what would they want to do? What's their endgame?"

"We intercepted a transmission from Rodon to his forces on Earth. It said, 'Mission abort. Destroy all facilities possible.' We've already seen firsthand his supporters are fanatical and willing to die for their leader. With this order, they've given up on Atlantis."

Austin looked at his hands, the scenarios running through his mind. A submersible with otherworldly technology unleashed on the people of Earth could be devastating, apocalyptic even. A sour feeling whirled in his stomach.

"What does Command want us to do?" he asked, and then made a wide sweeping gesture with his hand towards the disorder of the hangar. "It's not like we can mount a hunt in the state we're in."

"Command knows the situation. They know I brought a bunch of students down here to help defend Atlantis. The reinforcements we expected from the rest of Quadrant Eight should be arriving over the next twelve hours. We have eight operational Tridents at our disposal. They want us to head off and conduct a systematic search of the surrounding waters."

"When, sir?"

"As soon as our fighters are fueled and restocked."

Skylar shook her head. "He needs to rest, Captain. Look at him."

"Thanks, Sky," Austin said, "but if this is what we need to do, let's do it. How do we search the ocean's depths?"

"Every fighter will get his or her coordinates to search for the next eight hours," Braddock said. "We'll use energy sensor bursts that send a wave fifty MUs out. This is technology that was created during the last war to prevent the enemy from trying to mask a task force in a nebulae, or something similar that scrambles standard reconnaissance. Our laser cannons are being reconfigured for underwater use, and we are bringing over ordinance to the civilian hangar for use."

Braddock studied Austin. "I understand, Lieutenant, if you cannot make it. I've heard the past week has been quite an ordeal. On top of that, you've been in the cockpit all day defending this base. For you, this is not an order."

Skylar looked at him, shaking her head.

"Captain," Austin asked, "does command have any idea what happens if you and the recruits do not find this escaped sub?"

Braddock squared his shoulders. "The closest possible target is Base Prime."

A shiver shot down his neck. "San Francisco?"

"It's possible. We really don't know."

Austin thought of Kadyn recovering in rehab in San Francisco, trying to make sense of her world being turned inside out and upside down in a matter of hours. His final friend from his old life. Hundreds of thousands of innocent civilians who would die in whatever attack this rogue vessel had in mind.

He stood on quivering legs. "I'm with you, Captain. Lead the way."

24

Another concussion rocked the asteroid. Josh stumbled, falling into the mix of oil and circuit boards on the floor of the control room. He stood, brushing the liquid off his ragged clothing. Red lights flashed across the hangar, washing the area in crimson. The Zahl missile strike pounded the former pirate base, explosions growing closer by the second. The holographic map showed the Interceptors coming within eighty MUs and unleashing a fresh missile volley. Fires the *Barracudas* had worked to extinguish were reignited with a fresh fury, transforming the hangar into a fiery inferno. The glass cracked as Josh peered through, watching the *Barracudas* working hard to start their cold vessels.

They needed time.

Josh searched the controls, trying to find the activation sequence for the Tyral missile defense system. A drop of sweat burned into his eye. Green screens flickered as another explosion rattled the control room. He cyphered through the commands organized in no apparent order. Finding the missile defense routine, he activated the system.

The holographic map shifted in the control room. Small yellow crosshairs automatically swept out into the asteroids, searching for a lock on the incoming bandits. A moment later, a dozen of the crosshairs switched to red. With a soft concussion, the Tyral missile defense system launched a volley of missiles into the field.

That'll keep them busy.

Josh took one last look around the control room, knowing this entire base would be destroyed in a few minutes. Seeing nothing of value, he sprinted toward the door leading to the hangar. He stopped.

The coordinates.

He ran back to the holographic map and opened the file for the coordinates of the power relay. He found a shred of paper and a pen. He copied the numbers down hard enough to nearly rip the paper.

When he finished, he ran back to the hangar. Gusts from the starting engines swirled debris and burning embers. The four fighters warmed up, sending their thrust into the tornado forming inside the installation.

Waylon stood with Tocol under the *Sparkling Light,* unlocking the fuel hoses from the hull. Josh ran toward them, waving his hands.

"Launched missiles," he said, gasping. He pointed at the hangar doors. "A couple more direct hits and the base won't be able to power those energy shields. We're dead if that happens."

Waylon looked at Tocol. "Get the tank to port! Help me here, Josh!"

"I need a ship, Waylon!"

"No time! Get on board!"

Unlocking a nozzle to help Waylon, Josh dropped the hose just as another concussion rocked the asteroid. "I need to warn Earth!" He glanced back at the fighters. "Let me have Matta's ship! I promise I'll return!"

"No time!" He looked back at Tocol, who gave a thumbs up. "Get on board!"

"Waylon! I'm begging you!"

He stopped and stared at Josh. Sparks from the blaze shot around them, one sizzling into Waylon's beard. The man pressed his lips together and grabbed Tocol's shoulder as he ran past.

"Tocol! Get Matta off her ship!"

"But that's hers! She's not going—"

"Just do it! No time to argue!" Waylon glared at Josh. "I have assurances the fighter will be returned."

Josh clasped Waylon's hand. "Thank you!"

"I'll see you soon, brother!"

Josh ran behind Tocol. They waved, trying to get Matta's attention. Her compact, triangular fighter had lifted two feet off the ground when they reached it.

Tocol slapped his large hands down on the angular wing. Matta glanced to the side, her tan leather helmet swaying. Josh couldn't hear her, but could tell she wasn't happy.

The canopy lifted. "I can't carry another, you stupid oaf!" she yelled.

Tocol shook his head. "Get out! Boss said this one's for Josh!"

"What?" Matta stared at Josh in horror. "He can't take *my* ride!"

"He just did!" Tocol unhooked her harness and lifted her from the cockpit, her little legs kicking in the air. He dropped her on the hangar deck. She landed on her feet and tumbled to the ground.

Josh reached down to help her. She slapped his hands away.

"You better bring her back!" she screamed. "You hear me?"

He grabbed her hands, staring into her brown eyes. "I'm sorry, Matta!"

She waved him off and sprinted toward the *Sparkling Light.*

Tocol hopped down from the ship and grabbed Josh by the shoulders. He pressed close until their noses nearly touched. Fire and engine gusts swirled around Tocol, making him look like the devil.

"I've grown to trust you, Josh," he sneered. "*Don't* make me regret it."

He didn't wait for an answer. Instead, the hulking man ran for the *Sparkling Light.*

Josh turned around and boarded the small fighter. He stepped across the wings and plopped into the cockpit. Slipping on the headset, he got his bearings for the controls. The cockpit seemed simple enough, more so than the Trident. The canopy shut, filling the cockpit with the sterile smell of recycled air. The basic control board flickered to life, a short-range sensor displaying fifty MUs around the asteroid base. Boulders tumbled to the hangar deck, the impact shaking the base.

Time to go, he thought.

The other *Barracudas* lifted off, flying for the exit on the far side of the asteroid. Josh wanted to check his sensors, find out the location of the incoming Interceptors, but the rudimentary sensors on this tiny vessel did not stretch far enough. He had no idea where the Zahl Interceptors were, but he knew they closed in. Besides, the magnetic composition of the asteroid caused all interior sensors to waver.

Josh eased back on the stick, the Barracuda fighter lifting off the deck. He looked through the main hangar entrance. A pair of Interceptors fired at missiles shot by the defense system. Laser bolts flashed throughout the asteroid field. He smiled, swinging his fighter around to head out the rear hangar entrance.

"*Sparkling Light*, this is...Razor," he said, realizing the transmission could be monitored. "Right on your six, boss."

"Copy, Razor," Waylon's voice came back. "Any trailers?"

"Not yet," he said, re-checking his crude sensors. "I think they're still dealing with the presents I sent them."

Waylon breathed into the microphone. "Good job, there."

The *Barracudas* hit the asteroid field first, soaring away from the base on the opposite side of the Zahl vessel. Josh surveyed their surroundings as he exited the base, half expecting another Zahlian capital ship to be shadowing them like a predator.

But nothing greeted them but more asteroids.

"We're plotting our course," Waylon said. "You good, Razor?"

"Copy," he said, veering back toward the asteroid and bringing his vessel to a stop. "I'm covering your exit."

"You're a good man, Razor," he said after a pause. "See you soon."

Josh spun his fighter around halfway to keep an eye on the asteroid and watch the *Barracudas* exit. Space rippled in front of the *Sparkling Light*. He thought of the crew on board he had briefly been a part of, wondered if he would ever see any of them again. But he had comrades and an entire planet he had to warn—if he wasn't already too late.

A lump formed in his throat as the *Sparkling Light* moved forward, shuddered, and disappeared. The *Barracudas'* three fighters followed suit, vanishing into space.

Josh floated in space alone.

He pulled the scrap of paper from his pocket, hoping he could read his handwriting. He keyed for the coordinates to Earth, piggybacking off the power relay placed by the Tyral Pirates.

Movement fluttered from the asteroid and two Interceptors emerged from the hidden hangar door. Josh pinged their distance with the simple sensors: seventy MUs. His stomach turned. *Close enough for missiles.*

He slammed down on the throttle, keeping one eye on his rear sensors and the other on his navigation computer. Considering he would have to distribute power to the two onboard laser guns, he checked the power levels and decided against it. These lasers would be like popguns against an Interceptor. Making matters worse, the calculations for the curvature drive were taking much longer than they would in a Trident. He should have been keying in the coordinates long before now. His fighter would be no match for Zahlian Interceptors.

Pulling back on the stick, he maneuvered into a cluster of rocks in hopes it would buy him time. The beeping of a missile lock attempt filled his ears. *Try to find me in here.*

He prayed he had enough skill left to dodge these professional pilots. Checking his sensors, he grimaced. Fifty MUs—close enough for lasers.

As if they heard his thoughts, the asteroids shattered from laser bolts. The surrounding space flashed and lit up like fireworks, the red bolts engulfing the asteroids. A shot blasted his aft tail, sending the tiny fighter spinning. His head smacked the canopy.

This was like cutting-edge fighter jets taking on a crop duster, he thought dimly.

He launched into evasive maneuvers, trying to make his tiny fighter a small target.

The navigation computer pinged. Finally. He yanked back on the curvature drive. The small vessel shuddered as the space before him shimmered.

"Come on! *Move*!" he screamed.

Laser bolts burst around him. The missile lock warning wailed, and a projectile appeared on his sensors.

"Oh, please no!"

He throttled forward, leaning into it as if he could will the fighter through the curve. The green wave shot over the canopy, encapsulating the vessel in its emerald embrace. His stomach dropped, the familiar shifting a welcome shock.

The missile lock screech ceased, the translucent clouds dissipating around the fighter. Before him drifted the gray surface illuminating the night sky for mankind since the beginning of time. Slowly pulling back on the throttle, he took in a slow, deep breath and released it as he watched the crater-filled lunar surface drift in front of him. As the petite fighter dropped to a stop, Josh knew home was just beyond the moon.

The silence surrounded him like a blanket.

He turned around, but nothing trailed him except the black void of space.

He pressed his hand to his forehead, resting on his palm.

"Thank you, God," he breathed. "Thank you."

25

"I know you're all tired," Braddock said, moving to the front of the briefing room, "but I need you all with me right now. I've asked our doc to supply you with stimulants if you need them."

The six Star Runners collapsed into their seats and let out a collective sigh. Austin stretched his legs. His muscles ached from the hours inside the Trident's cockpit. A brief hot shower had washed off some of the stink from the day's battle, but nothing erased the fact Rodon had escaped. Again.

Braddock activated the wall screen. A layout of the ocean floor surrounding Atlantis spread behind him, rising twelve feet over his head.

"Okay," he said, "here we are. I know you Star Runners are still wet behind the ears, but this planet needs you now. Atlantis lost its alert fighters earlier today, and our reinforcements are still hours out. There's still the possibility this is all a setup for a larger attack, perhaps even an invasion of Earth. Somewhere out there, the last pirate vessel is lying low under the ocean. We have every reason to believe they are up to no good and plan to attack."

Skylar glanced at Austin. He tried to smile, blinked hard, and stared at Braddock's map.

"We have to do this old school," Braddock said, using a laser pointer to highlight sectors surrounding Atlantis. "Since we believe the vessel is currently on the ocean floor and running dark, we cannot detect them up on sensors. Each of you is responsible for searching a sector. You'll proceed on your designated route, dropping these sensor bursts along the way. A ping will search about fifty MUs. You then move off to the next sector and do it again."

Braddock pointed the laser to the western sectors. "Bear, Toad, PowPow, you take these three sectors to the west of Atlantis. Thrasher, Spark, take the south. Rock, I want you and Cheetah taking the sector to the east. I'll take the north." He hardened his gaze. "This final pirate planet-side has nothing to lose at this point, a fact that makes him very dangerous. We must assume he is planning a suicide attack to cause as much damage as possible."

Bear raised his hand. "Sir, we'll have no visual this deep. It'll be like flying blind."

"That's correct," Braddock said with a nod. "Your training with sensor flying will be put to the test today."

"What do we do if we make contact with the vessel?" Skylar asked.

"Report in for orders. Your cannons are being reconfigured as we speak, and most of you will be resupplied with at least a partial load of missiles. Do not engage unless ordered to do so. I don't want anyone of you taking on this pirate without assistance. Copy?"

The Star Runners nodded and sat forward.

"Questions? No?" Braddock slapped his hands together. "Let's not waste any more time, then. This planet's waiting on us to save it. Dismissed."

Austin stood and stretched, wishing he had accepted pain medicine with the stimulants he'd taken before the briefing. He held his trembling hands out before balling them into fists.

Zipping up her flight suit, Skylar walked in front of him. "How ya feeling?"

"Good as can be," he said, grinning. "Too bad we don't have time for a run."

Nodding, she bit her bottom lip. "Maybe after?"

His mind wandered to the days of running on the Tizona campus in heat of the South Georgia swamp. "Maybe so."

"Stone!" Braddock snapped. "Nubern asked to see you. The rest of you, get down to the hangar for preflight."

Skylar looked at him. "I'll see you down there."

———

MORE WOUNDED HAD BEEN BROUGHT to the storage bay infirmary since Austin left. He found Nubern and rushed to his side. Nubern had the cot inclined, his head wrapped in bandages.

Austin stood over his mentor, unsure if he was awake or not.

Nubern's eyes opened. "Hello, Lieutenant."

"It's good to see you, sir," Austin said, pulling up a stool and sitting beside the cot. "Glad to see you awake."

"I have quite a hangover."

"What are they saying?"

"Concussion. I need to be observed for a day. The ocean's not soft."

He laughed. "No, it's not."

He tried not to stare at the bandages wrapped around Nubern's forehead. Turning away, he looked at the rows of wounded. A woman slept on the adjacent cot, burn marks covering her shoulders.

"We really got hit yesterday, didn't we, sir?"

"Worst I've seen in a while," Nubern said, cringing. "They really got hit hard here. I've heard the ground battle turned hand-to-hand at the end." He sighed. "I really need to stop ending up like this when we work together, Lieutenant. I'm starting to think you're bad luck."

"Nice, sir." Austin frowned. "Why did this happen?"

"Rodon wanted to disrupt our operations. Who knows why? I don't think he hoped to take the entire planet, but I really have no idea. He did this for a reason. I know it. I feel it in my bones. There has to be more to this." He motioned for Austin to come closer. "You need to end this, son. That final sub must not be allowed to carry out any attack."

He nodded. "We'll do what we can, sir."

"No," Nubern said, shaking his head. "There's no one else. The surprise was complete. If this final sub is allowed to carry out an attack, Earth will never be the same."

Austin's brow furrowed. "What do you mean?"

"I've seen dark worlds on the border attacked by warlords, pirates, and other scum of the galaxy," he said, coughing. "Society as you know it will collapse. The people will turn on their governments when they realize they cannot be protected by what lies beyond their own atmosphere. It'll be pure anarchy if this attack happens."

Austin's stomach twisted. If Earth was attacked by an otherworldly technology, the people would first search for some terrestrial explanation. When word reached the general population the attack came from beyond Earth, he could imagine the planet descending into disorder.

"I understand, sir."

Nubern placed his hand on Austin's flight suit, pulling him close. "You need to end this. Today."

"But Rodon got away."

"How do you know?"

He wiped his hand over his face. "We pursued him to the moon. I tried, sir, we all did. But he got away." He looked at his hands. "He slipped right through my fingers."

"You mustn't do this to yourself," Nubern said. "You are still a rookie Star Runner, and you can't save the world, Austin. You're good, but don't beat yourself up." He waved his hand in front of his face. "He's lost his power. It'll take him years to recover. If ever." His face stiffened. "Your enemy is out there, somewhere in your ocean. Find him. End this."

"I will, sir." He squeezed Nubern's hand. "Get some rest."

Nubern nodded and closed his eyes.

Taking one last look at his battered captain, Austin surveyed the rest of the storage bay. Men and women cried out as nurses and staff did what they could to help. A tangible feeling of dread fell over the room.

Austin hurried out into the hangar.

Crews clustered around loud pumps which they had used to remove water from the hangar deck. The deck was still wet, but they were mostly down to large puddles. Welding torches flared along the hangar's ceiling, sending sparks falling down like fiery waterfalls. The water had ceased falling like rain, reduced now to sporadic droplets. Atlantis had started to mend. He knew it would take years for the base to reach its former glory, but at least it had survived.

Austin jogged through the coordinated jumble of activity, nodding at crews as they carried tools and scrap metal into piles. The battered remnants of the Trident squadron charged with defending Atlantis was lined up between the various types of star freighters. Gan stood on the wing of the closest Trident, a grim look on his face. Austin nodded at him, but Gan's attention appeared elsewhere.

"Lieutenant!"

Austin turned to see Tyce emerging from beneath a Trident. Even through the grease covering his face, Tyce had dark circles under his bloodshot eyes.

"I've done the best I can with your fighter's tail," he said, his expression darkening. "She really went through it yesterday."

"That she did. Can she fly?"

"Refueled and rearmed. She should be ready. The rear thrusters might be a bit sluggish."

"I understand. I can handle it." Tyce turned to leave. "And Tyce? Good job."

He nodded. "Thank you, sir."

Austin climbed the ladder to his cockpit. For the first time in his short career as a Star Runner, he felt too tired to get behind the stick of a Trident. He shook it off. Going through preflight, his fingers flew across the controls. His hands trembled. Must be the stimulants. The engine hummed, the dashboard coming to life.

He thought of Nubern's words, the warning his captain had probably learned from a dozen other worlds hit by an otherworldly force. Earth must *not* meet the same fate.

The fatigue faded, his adrenaline pumping as the stimulants rushed through his body. He locked his helmet into place, looking to his right at Gan as he dropped into the cockpit of his fighter. Austin offered a thumbs up. His eyes weary, Gan returned the gesture as his canopy closed.

Austin activated his gamma wave. "Tower, Rock. Are we cleared for takeoff?"

"Whenever you're ready, Rock."

"Copy. Leaving in sixty seconds."

Braddock's Trident lifted off, the thrust sending swirls of water shooting across the deck. Crew scampered around, most gazing at the fighter as it hovered above them. They waved.

"Good hunting, Tizona," Braddock said. "Mission clock starts now. Take your sectors and report any contact. Send your data back to Atlantis when you have it. Use the Whisper. Otherwise, maintain radio silence."

The Star Runners acknowledged and the Tridents lifted off one at a time. When Austin's turn came, he lifted off and peered over the canopy, watching the crew wave. He saluted their gesture and eased forward to the exit airlock, tucking his Trident next to Skylar's. She offered a small smile as the airlock closed and filled with water.

"Let's go get this guy," Braddock said.

A minute later, the outer door opened. Bubbles fluttered around the canopy. The Tridents left the airlock and entered the complete darkness of the ocean depths. Each fighter shot off toward its designated direction.

Focusing on his sensors, Austin used his navigation computer to move toward his sector. The sound of water rushing around his shields made moving the Trident underwater louder than flying through space. He stared at his sensors, maneuvering around a series of mountains stretching out from the ocean floor. They loomed on the sensors like invisible giants.

He reached his designated point, dropped a sensor burst and

watched the result. An energy wave pulsed from his location, providing a detailed digital view of the landscape as it moved away from his position.

Debris littered the area. Some of it looked like pieces of crashed spacecraft. Most likely the result of today's battle. He passed a destroyed submersible, the bow buried into the slush.

He scanned for movement.

He scanned for an electronic pulse.

He scanned for gamma waves, for running engines, for any sign of the missing sub.

Nothing.

Transmitting his data back to Atlantis via the Whisper, he continued forward. Fighting the urge to look through the canopy and into the darkness, he focused on his sensor display.

An hour passed as he flew from one spot to the next, dropping sensor bursts at each stop. He searched a deep trench and maneuvered through another mountain range, seeing nothing with his own eyes but a few creatures glowing in the darkness. The farther he moved away from Atlantis, the less debris he found. Soon, the ocean's currents would erase any existence of the battle. He reached his sixth marker and dropped another sensor burst.

The pulse shot, mapping the terrain. Shifting in his seat, his back aching, he sighed and watched the data return. Perhaps the other fighters were having better luck.

The sensor flickered.

Wait a minute.

Austin rolled his head around, felt his neck pop. An indentation in the topography popped up on the scan. Strange. He pinned the location in his navigation computer and veered right, bearing down on the location. Stopping above the position, he checked his global coordinates.

Eight hundred miles southwest of California.

He licked his lips and thought for a moment. The indentation in the muck formed a dip in the ocean floor about two hundred yards long. Whatever had stopped here was large enough to be one of the submersibles. Deciding it was worth the risk, he hit the lights.

The landscape stretched out in rolling hills until his beams of light ended. He tilted the fighter forward, his lights hitting rocks and casting long shadows over the floor which was devoid of life. The indentation came to a point, angles forming together like a large triangle. Nothing in nature could have made this shape. The enemy submersible had definitely stopped here.

He checked the topography for the next fifty MUs. Nothing but sweeping flats with no trenches or mountains. If the enemy vessel had headed this direction, there would be no obstacles.

He swiped at his face, felt a cold chill pass through the cockpit. He wondered what the temperature of the water was just outside his shield.

Checking the Whisper, he saw Atlantis had transmitted nothing in the time since he'd left. Neither had Braddock or the other pirates. This had to mean they had found nothing, either. The dip in the ocean floor had to be the best evidence so far.

Powering forward into the darkness, he skipped his next sonar burst marker and dropped one late. The pulse shot away from his Trident in all directions. At thirty MUs, the pulse smacked into something metallic, something two hundred yards in length. He jolted forward at the sight, his eyes wide.

The submersible!

The missile detection alarm squealed in his ears. An incoming projectile appeared on his scope.

He yanked back on the stick. Pressing forward on the throttle, he dropped countermeasures, the sound of water rushing around his shields as the Trident shot through the depths.

"Tiger, Rock. Do you copy?"

Nothing.

"If anyone is reading me," he said, his voice straining as the thrust mixed with gravity and pressed him into the seat, "I'm under attack. Track this transmission to my location. I repeat: I've located the pirate vessel and I'm under attack."

The pirate missile hit the countermeasure behind him and exploded. A bubble illuminated the darkness of the depths. The Trident tumbled, its nose spinning end-over-end. Austin's helmet smacked the dashboard. Recovering from the blast, he corrected his course.

"Rock, Tiger," his gamma wave hissed. "Do you copy?"

"Copy, Tiger."

"SIT-REP. We detected a blast and are en route."

Austin looked at the dashboard, saw the submersible was driving hard to escape the sensor burst's reach. "The enemy vessel is heading for Base Prime, for San Francisco, sir."

"Maintain your track," Braddock said. "On our way. Tizona, break off your search and head for Rock's point. I'm just to the north of your position and on my way."

The submersible's sensor image flickered. A projectile emerged from the enemy's signal, breaking away and blasting toward the surface.

"Tiger!" Austin yelled, leaning forward. "The bandit has launched a missile! I repeat: A missile has been fired and is heading toward Base Prime!"

"Rock, you have to take down that missile," Braddock said, his voice calm. "The rest of us will target the submersible." He paused. "You *must* take out that missile."

Austin clenched his jaw, adjusting his power configuration. "I copy."

Diverting all his power to the engines, he buried the throttle. The Trident lurched forward. He adjusted his course to a forty-five degree angle, driving hard for the surface. The sensors showed the missile screaming away from the submersible. As he passed high over the enemy vessel, he dropped one more sensor burst, painting the pirate for the other Star Runners.

"You have your target, Tiger," Austin said.

"Copy," Braddock said.

The missile shot away from him, the distance growing. Austin tensed, willing his Trident forward. He pursued but his speed was greatly reduced by the drag of the ocean. The missile broke through the water's surface and adjusted course, flying parallel with the ocean. After a moment, the missile disappeared from his sensors.

Austin's Trident broke through the ocean's surface and into the dusk sky. He rolled twice, the water flying off his shields. The fighter increased speed, free in the open air. Leaving enough power in his lasers for a volley, he dropped his shields to nothing and watched the energy banks drop, effectively turning his craft into a flying missile.

He gripped the stick. *A missile to catch a missile.*

Activating his targeting computer, he searched the area for any contact. Behind him, the sky glowed orange as the sun set. Even after seeing the wonders of the nebula near Tarton's Junction, the sunset of the Pacific Ocean rivaled its beauty. His sensors picked up two commercial flights off the coast of California, but nothing else within one hundred MUs. He leveled off at five hundred feet over the surface.

"In open air and in pursuit," Austin said.

"Roger. Engaging the bandit," Braddock announced.

"Copy."

Austin listened to the other Tizona Star Runners battling the pirate vessel in the depths, orders rattling across the gamma wave. He heard Skylar's voice, calling out a hit. They would make sure another missile wouldn't threaten Base Prime, but they counted on him to shoot down this missile screaming for San Francisco. Pulling his attention back to his task, he continued checking his sensors as the coast of California came closer. *Where was the missile?*

He pulled up, increasing his altitude to get a better vantage point on the missile and possibly catch a glimpse of the projectile's thrust in the fading light of day. As he closed in on Base Prime, he knew he wouldn't have much time to take out the missile before it descended on San Francisco. Mom, Kadyn, and the entire city would be destroyed in the blast.

Nubern's warning would come true if he missed. The dynamics of the world's perspective of Earth's place in the universe would shatter and fade away, like a sand castle in front of the incoming tide. It would all end.

An alarm sounded.

The missile broke through sensor range near a small fishing vessel, climbing hard away from sea level. Even in the darkening sky, he saw the water shoot up into the air like a geyser, the thrust close enough to the ocean's surface to send water spewing across the fishing ship. The missile moved fast. Thirty MUs ahead of him.

He lowered the Trident's nose, bringing the fighter down on a steep angle. His speed increased, faster than he had ever flown before. His helmet rocked, the canopy and the dashboard rattling. Risking a glance at his laser's energy banks, he estimated he could squeeze off four shots, maybe five, before the power would be dry.

He focused his gaze. The MUs ticked down on his targeting computer. Twenty-five. Twenty. Fifteen. The crosshairs fell just ahead of the missile.

He squeezed the trigger.

Two laser bolts passed over the missile, striking the water. Clouds of vapor shot into the air. He pulled back, fired again. A bolt passed under the missile. The pirate's weapon flashed, kicking into another speed and pulling away. The MUs increased. Eighteen MUs. Twenty-two.

The missile closed on the city, shifting into its final approach and soaring farther away from him.

He looked up. The city lights flickered in the dusk, sending colored reflections trickling out over the water like electric currents.

He had time for two shots. *Maybe.*

Twenty-five MUs away.

He fired. The bolt passing just under the missile's wing as it shot away from him.

Thirty MUs.

He braced himself. *Please.*

Holding his breath, a calmness fell over him. As the missile arched up, increasing altitude off the coast, he adjusted his course and aimed for what he hoped would be the downward angle of the missile. He rested his crosshairs below the missile.

Wait.

Thirty-five MUs.

Wait.

Forty MUs.

The missile dipped, aiming for the heart of the city and falling into Austin's crosshairs.

He pulled the trigger.

The sky exploded. A blast wave shot across the bluish light of early dusk. He leaned back, gasping. Changing course to fly parallel to the city, he watched the burning wreckage of the missile fall. It crashed into the ocean, sending plumes of water shooting into the air. He banked, circling his kill like a vulture and verifying the missile hadn't hit a civilian vessel.

He distributed the Trident's power, shifting as much power back into the shields as possible. Once the power transferred, he activated the shroud and looked at the city lights of San Francisco. He checked his sensors. Nothing flew over the city.

Smiling, he thought: *Why not?*

He soared over San Francisco, the city he had just saved. A warmth washed over him. Somewhere down there, Mom and Kadyn had no idea what had happened. The population, unaware an invisible "UFO" flew over the skyscrapers, would be safe.

He leveled off and watched the sun disappear into the ocean, the sky transitioning to darkness. He knew there was one last thing he had to do. He took a slow, deep breath and exhaled. He smiled.

He changed course. In the dying light of his long day, the traffic on the Golden Gate Bridge would never know a Trident of the Galactic Legion had flown underneath.

Austin flew in silence, taking in the moment.

Keying his navigation computer, he searched for the other Tridents under the ocean. Several signals popped up on his sensors. He pressed to transmit.

"Tiger, Rock. Do you copy?"

"Copy, Rock. We've taken care of our problem. SIT-REP."

He grinned. "Our projectile is no more."

"Very good, Rock." Braddock paused. "Toad took a direct hit and is headed back to the nest. Are you okay?"

"Fine." He frowned, recognizing the concern in Braddock's voice. He glanced at his sensor, noticing the Tridents linking up above the ocean. "What's the problem, sir?"

"We've another incoming vessel," Braddock grumbled. "Just curved in around the moon."

He sighed, punching the side of his canopy. "What now?"

"We're going to check it out," Braddock said, his voice fatigued. "Form up on our wing."

Austin smacked the side of his cockpit again. Rodon's lackies were back. "I'm on my way, sir."

26

The Tridents soared through the cloudy darkness like angels of the night, their position lights twinkling as they formed into a perfect seven-craft "V" formation.

Atlantis granted another solar disruptor to render Earth's detection technology useless. Artificial solar flares would prevent radar from detecting the Tridents as they rushed to meet this new threat.

The angle of their trajectory steepened until the Tridents soared into the upper atmosphere at ninety degrees. Austin yawned and knuckled his eyes, wishing again he had taken a few stimulants with him before he left Atlantis.

"Any sign you were seen back there?" Braddock asked.

"I don't know," Austin admitted. "Sorry, Tiger. Base Prime is safe, though."

"Well done, Lieutenant."

Wisps of clouds shot past the canopy as the stars poked through the atmosphere like beacons in the darkness. The Tridents pulled away from Earth's embrace, the presence of gravity leaving. Austin took a slow breath and looked to the side, watching as the curvature of Earth stretched out to the horizon. The sun dipped behind the planet as the terminator line swept over the Pacific Ocean, leaving darkness in its wake and the sparkling lights of night. The Tridents flew fast and true, heading toward the lone incoming spacecraft.

"Spread out," Braddock barked, shattering the silence. "I want plenty of space between us—ten MUs at least."

The Star Runners acknowledged without question. Austin understood the order. The incoming vessel could try a suicide stunner run, rendering the Tridents useless and opening the Earth up to whatever attack the pirates still had up their sleeves. He pushed away thoughts of a weapon of mass destruction, a last ditch effort to try and destroy a Legion backwater planet.

He shook his head. Rodon had wanted Atlantis intact. He wanted the port. The only question remaining was why?

Austin focusing on the incoming vessel flying from the moon. He ran a sensor check and glanced at the results. A triangular fighter he had never seen before. The vessel was small, about a quarter the size of the Trident. The tiny craft headed directly toward them, squawking a transponder his computer didn't recognize. No missiles bristled from the wings of the small fighter, just two small laser guns sticking from the angular wings. A weak power signal emitted from the incoming bogey.

"I don't have a reading, Tiger," Austin said.

"Neither do I," Braddock said. "Maintain your track."

He sent a sensor wave again, searching for identification. Nothing. "Sir, I can't tell if this is a friendly."

"Copy. We'll find out soon enough." Braddock paused. "It's my call. Given the events of today, we shoot first and ask questions later."

The bogey dropped to within one hundred MUs. Austin activated his targeting computer. The sensors searched for a signature to track the incoming craft.

"I'm not picking up any weapons other than those pop-pop laser guns," Austin said, shaking his head. "I don't even think this guy could hurt us."

"We're not taking that chance," Braddock said.

A moment later, the targeting computer achieved a lock. The

crosshairs turned red. The missile lock squealed. Whoever piloted the small fighter knew the Tridents had them locked.

"—copy?" the gamma wave came to life, hissing in Austin's ear. "I repeat: this is a Legion Star Runner requesting assistance."

Austin froze. *It couldn't be...*

"Please. This is a Legion Star Runner requesting assistance."

Josh.

Austin switched for a secure channel using the Whisper. "Tiger, I know this pilot."

"It's a trick," Braddock said. "Preparing to fire. Tizona squadron, I've got this."

A missile dropped from Braddock's wing. A second after it dropped, the missile engaged and propelled toward the triangular bogey.

"Bye, bye," Braddock sneered.

The bogey launched into evasive maneuvers. Austin watched, marveling at the pilot's skill. It looped and rolled, tricking the missile into thinking it had its prey, only to soar off into the void. The deadly dance continued until the missile ran out of fuel, tumbling harmlessly into the darkness.

"I'm a Star Runner! *Please!*" the bogey pilot screamed. "Call sign: Razor. Registration: Charlie-Hotel-Alpha-Delta-oh-nine-two-one! Hold your fire!"

Austin leaned over the stick. "Tiger! I know this man!"

His heart raced as he thought of his friend. Josh had died on board the *Saber*. Hadn't he? Could he really be returning to Earth after nearly a year? Was that even possible?

Braddock transmitted on Whisper. "Rock, voices can be altered. This could be a scheme. It's *not* real."

"Captain, we outnumber this bogey seven to one," Austin pleaded. "Can we give him a chance?"

Braddock paused, the range to target dropping. The triangular fighter piloted by someone claiming to be "Razor" leveled out after the impressive maneuvers and continued on a course parallel to Earth.

"Tizona," Braddock transmitted via Whisper, "form up behind the bogey. Maintain a missile lock. Rock, I'm giving you one minute. If this guy changes course one MU toward Earth, I want all fighters to fire. We'll see if he can dodge that."

He sighed. "Very well, sir."

Keying for primary transmission, Austin took a deep breath. "Unknown vessel claiming to be the Legion Star Runner known as Razor, this is Rock. You must maintain your current course parallel with Earth. We have your vessel locked and we are prepared to fire. If you change course to flee or make a move toward Earth, you will be destroyed. Please respond."

After a long pause, the weak voice responded, "Rock? Is it *really* you?"

Austin swallowed. "This is Rock. Please verify your identity."

"How?" the pilot breathed. "I've known you your whole life. What do you want me to say?"

He chewed on the inside of cheek. "We need verification of your identity."

No response came back from the fighter, but it maintained its parallel course with Earth.

"Rock, I understand," the pilot said after a long pause. "You were at my house when you found out your dad died. We were playing a board game."

Austin's eyes watered. He keyed for the Whisper. "Is *that* good enough, Tiger?"

"You need more. That information could have been in your file or gleamed from your Earth accounts."

"Yes, sir."

He maintained his missile lock on the peculiar fighter, the crosshairs burning blood-red. He transmitted on the gamma wave, "Okay. Keep going."

"What do you mean?" the pilot asked, frustration mounting in his tone. Finally, he continued. "I watched you play baseball. Not much, but I did watch you play."

He nodded. "Go on."

The Tridents maintained their track, ready to pounce on the bogey if it made a move. Austin leaned forward, waiting for the response.

"Austin," the pilot whispered, "I just want to go home. I want to go the coffee shop. I would like to see Kadyn, listen to her laugh while we pretend not to look at Marilyn." His voice cracked as if he choked. "I want to go home, Austin. I don't have anything left in me. Do what you will."

Austin blinked several times, thinking of the friend he had lost. No one else would have known about the coffee shop, about the black and white photo of Marilyn Monroe hanging on the wall. He closed his eyes, imagining they could return to the coffee shop after all of this as if they headed home after being away at college.

But those days were long gone, and they would never come again.

Opening his eyes, he transmitted in the open. "Tiger, Rock. This is definitely Razor. A Star Runner's trying to return home. I say we let him land."

27

"I'm getting too old for this." Nubern had his arm folded in a sling, his face bruised and puffy. A red splotch split his lip. Medical screens on tall, metal poles with wheels surrounded Nubern even though Austin had been assured his mentor would be fine. "These doctors descended on me like a swarm of lykers since I saw you last."

He smiled. "You sound like the movies."

"How?"

Shaking his head, Austin sat down at the edge of the bed near Nubern's feet. "In all the action movies, someone is always too old for what's about to happen." He added with wry grin, "You have to know Earth culture to understand."

"Earth culture? Ha!" he laughed, wincing. "I know *enough* of your culture."

The image of Nubern's fighter crashing into the ocean flashed across his mind. "I thought I had lost you, sir."

"Very nearly." He closed his eyes. "That's twice you bailed me out, son."

"Happy to do it, sir."

Nubern smiled, but the expression faded. "Maybe I should get behind a desk. I'm getting slow."

Austin tapped Nubern's hand. "Now's not the time to make such a decision. I, for one, would be crushed if you weren't flying."

Nubern studied him. "You have done so well, Austin. I don't know how you caught that missile. It's all the Atlantis staff has been able to talk about when they've come to see me. I've become quite the hero for recruiting you. Undeserved, of course."

"I would disagree with you, but I was told not to contradict my superiors."

He offered a wry smile. "That's right."

Austin looked out over the freighter's storage bay. It had been transformed to a regular infirmary since yesterday's attack. Nurses and doctors had been flown in from Base Prime to help with the wounded. More and better equipment had arrived, enhancing the efforts of the medics and staff trying to save lives. With the amount of laser burns and battle wounds he'd witnessed since he arrived yesterday, he knew better than to ask for any more details of the assault. The Phantoms had done quite a number on Atlantis, and Austin doubted the base would ever be the same. It already seemed more closed, guarded than the day he arrived.

"What about Razor?" Austin asked.

"He's still with EIF."

EIF agents had allowed little time for a reunion when Josh had landed yesterday. When he climbed out of the fighter, Austin gasped. Josh was emaciated and pale, peppered all over with purple bruises. He stumbled and collapsed, and the agents promptly pulled Josh's arms over their shoulders. His ragged clothing barely covered his body; the torn fabric frayed at the edges. Jagged cuts sprinkled across his body like red paperclips.

Austin didn't recognize the look in his best friend's eyes. He had been through something terrible Austin couldn't understand. Whatever it was, whatever Josh had been through, the life he had was ripped away. For a second, however, his friend's face brightened like a ray of sunshine on a dark day when he saw Austin. He had offered his best smile in return before Josh's expression faded like a cloud passing over the sun.

They'd prevented Austin from even shaking Josh's hand. The agents swept him away. When he asked, an agent informed him Josh would have to undergo a period of quarantine.

That had been twelve hours ago.

"I hope he's all right," Austin finally said, staring at the deck.

"I don't know what he's been through," Nubern admitted, "but I know it wasn't good. You need to be there for him, son. I know what this galaxy can throw at someone. I know the horrors. Josh has undoubtedly seen it, stared a grim reality in the face he probably didn't believe existed, except in nightmares. He'll need you, more than you can probably comprehend."

Austin forced a lump down his throat. "What do you think happened?"

"I'd rather not guess. I don't want to disillusion you as to what's out there." Nubern looked at him. "But I promise you that you have only just scratched the surface."

He leaned forward. "What's next for me, sir?"

"You need to take your leave," he said with a smile. "I think this one was a little, uh, stressful."

Austin laughed and turned as a nurse walked up to check the screens surrounding Nubern. "He going to live?"

She flashed a grin. "Looks like it."

His tablet beeped. He pulled it from his satchel and opened the message.

"Looks like EIF has released Josh," he said. "He's in his quarters and will be departing for Base Prime this afternoon."

"Go see him," Nubern said. "I'll see you before you leave."

Austin rushed out of the infirmary, passing through the rebuilding efforts of Atlantis. Crew covered the command center, men and women hovering over the workstations like concerned parents. A pair of workers descended from the dome, apparently having checked the integrity of the largest Atlantis structure.

In the distance, Brannen and Wallace were locked into a discussion. Wallace, his head wrapped in a white bandage, stared at a tablet while Brannen spoke. Austin watched the Legion crew working, noticing the sense of clockwork efficiency descending over Atlantis once again.

Austin worked his way through the reconstruction efforts, nodding at other Star Runners and officers. He stepped in front of the temporary quarters assigned to Josh and pressed the bell. When no one responded, he assumed Josh had not arrived. He looked down both sides of the corridor. Apparently no one had been staying in the temporary quarters.

Imagine that, he thought. *Who would want to visit Atlantis after what happened?*

Trying one last time, he pressed the bell. He started to turn away when someone finally answered.

"Yes?" the intercom hissed, a weak voice behind the speaker.

"Ah, I'm sorry." Austin shifted his weight. "I'm looking for Lieutenant Morris's room."

"Come in."

The hatch slid open. Josh sat on the bed, facing away from the opening, wearing only his green Lobera Squadron pants. His ribs poked out his back as if he were a painted skeleton. Wounds and scars mixed across his body.

"Good Lord," Austin breathed, stepping inside and keying for the hatch to shut. "Josh?"

He muttered something.

Austin took one step toward the bed. He looked around the room. Josh had the top part of his uniform hanging in the closet, the shirt neatly pressed and packed with enough starch it could have been cardboard. His new wings glistened in the low light.

"I can't," Josh whispered, so soft Austin had to guess he heard correctly.

"Can't what, man?" Austin took another step, holding his hand over his friend's naked and battered shoulder before pulling it back. "Tell me what to do, buddy. Please."

With a groan, Josh stood and faced Austin. His cheeks were damp with tears, his eyes bloodshot. He pointed to the uniform in the closet.

"I can't. I never thought I'd be back here to see any of this."

Austin glanced at the uniform. "You've done so much to earn it. Listen, I know—"

"Stop!"

Austin recoiled as Josh lunged toward him.

"You know nothing," he sneered, grabbing Austin's shoulders, his voice quivering. "You don't know what I've been through."

"Tell me then."

Josh's face crumpled. He tried to speak, but a sentence did not form. When he finally spoke, the words came in gasps like he convulsed.

"It...It was supposed to be...a game." He collapsed onto Austin's shoulder, sobbing. "It was supposed to be a game. Oh, God."

Austin embraced his friend, listening to him weep.

THE ATLANTIS MESS hall reminded Austin of Tarton's Junction. Instead of the nebula, the viewport revealed lighted rows of rocks of different shapes and sizes. Strange and otherworldly fish twinkled by the massive window. He slid his finger around the lid of his coffee. Moving his hand from the cup to his shoulder, he felt the fabric's dampness where Josh had cried.

Josh said little else before Austin left his quarters, other than mentioning his destination. He said Command had ordered him back to Base Prime for more questioning and a thorough debriefing of his situation. After that, he would undergo counseling and said he planned to turn in his wings.

Austin had no words of comfort to offer. Josh was right; he had no idea what his friend had been through. It wasn't right for him to pretend he did.

"May I join you?"

He looked up, his mouth hanging open. "Hey, Sky."

Skylar slid into the seat in front of him, graceful as always. Her Tizona uniform impeccable, she looked just as the Legion would want any junior officer to appear. She had her blonde hair pulled back, revealing her flawless skin.

"You okay?" she asked after a pause.

Austin pressed his lips together, staring at the cup of coffee. "Sure."

"Liar."

"Yep." When he looked up, his eyes brimmed and he swayed. "What happened to my friend?"

He collapsed onto the table. Skylar's hands descended over him, one caressing his hand while the other rubbed his head. The recent events stacked up in his mind. The Phantoms' attack. His mother. Kadyn. Death tugging at his elbow with every step of the way.

"Is this really what being a Star Runner is?" he asked, raising his head. "Is it going to be *this* dangerous?"

Skylar tilted her head as she studied his face. "It's just life, Austin. There are no guarantees."

He sat up. "I'm sorry. I shouldn't have said that. Thanks for being here."

"Hey," she said, squeezing his hand, "what are friends for?"

"True."

She looked him with a crooked grin. "Wanna go for a run?"

He laughed. "Right."

Taking a deep breath, she sat back still holding his hand. "After what we did in yesterday's battle, they're saying the rest of us are going to be promoted to flight status. We're getting our wings. Looks like we caught up with your greatness."

Austin placed his other hand over hers. "I'm very proud. You deserve this."

"Want to come with me?"

He blinked. "What?"

"I stopped by to see Nubern. He's doing good. Anyway, he said you were going on your leave. I, well, I wanted to know if you wanted to come see me—I mean the rest of us, get our wings on Tarton's Junction."

Austin nearly said he would, but thought of Ryker sitting in a hospital bed in between hours of rehabilitation. "I don't know."

"Afterward, I'll get *my* leave and..." She looked away. "I thought you might want to, ah, I wanted to take you to Florida to see where I'm from. I know you got tired of hearing about it back at the academy, right? I thought you might want to see it, though. Unless you want to go home to see your mom. I completely would understand that."

He smiled. "My mom's in the orientation training. She's going to be part of a medical frigate or something. I need to check in with her, let her know I'm okay."

He paused. It hadn't really occurred to him before, but there would be nothing left on Earth for him after his mother shipped out. Earth would be a memory. His home would be elsewhere.

"Hey," Skylar said when he paused. She leaned forward and touched his cheek. "I didn't want to freak you out or anything, Austin. I'm sorry. It's just, well, being in the dogfight yesterday...I realized we aren't going to live forever and I thought you should know how I feel."

She kissed him on the forehead as she stood. "Tell you what." She glanced at her watch. "Our freighter for the Junction leaves in thirty minutes. I'll save you a seat."

She grabbed his hand, squeezed it, and smiled. Then she marched out.

Austin gazed at the wonders of the ocean habitat, his mind lost in the thought.

"Lieutenant?"

He sighed and turned to the door. Captain Braddock stood near the entrance. He raised to stand, but Braddock held him at bay with a quick hand gesture.

"At ease," he said, strolling in with his hands behind his back. "How are you?"

"I'm okay, sir."

Braddock stepped to the window and took a deep breath, peering into the depths. "Your planet has a very unique beauty."

He looked at the water. "I agree, sir."

Braddock folded his arms over his chest. "All of Atlantis is talking about you, Stone."

Warmth rushed to his face. "Thank you, sir."

"It wasn't a compliment," he snapped. "It shows how boring things are on this backwater planet."

"Sir?"

"The reason these people are talking about this incident is because they have become complacent. Most of the staff here comes to Earth to get away from the action or they're shipped here to be isolated. What happened over the past week has been the most excitement Earth has seen in a long time."

"I don't understand, sir."

Braddock turned to face him. "I don't want you getting a big head over this, Lieutenant. Get cocky out there and you'll die. While you certainly did some fancy flying yesterday, this Atlantis incident is nothing more than a blip on the Legion's radar. It was a skirmish. A lowly pirate commander with delusions of grandeur thought he'd make a stab at taking a backwater world. You helped prevent that. Nothing more, nothing less."

"May I ask why you're telling me this, sir?"

Braddock stepped toward him. "I respect what you did, but Earth is nothing. I'm talking about the rest of the Legion. We need you, Lieutenant. If you were offered assignment on a Legion carrier, could you do it?"

Austin thought about Ryan Bean and his opinion of carrier life. Of course, Bean still had a life here on Earth. With his mother leaving, he had no reason to return.

"I would be honored, sir."

For the first time since entering the mess hall, Braddock smiled. "With the current events unfolding and tensions rising, I've been told

I'll be taking a squadron on a carrier tour near the Zahl border. I'm going to request you come with me."

"Thank you, sir."

"The fact is, Dax Rodon had support. I know you don't know, yet, what I'm about to tell you. Your friend Lieutenant Morris saw more than he thought."

"What do you mean?"

He lowered his voice. "What I'm about to tell you is top secret. If I'm asked about it, I'll deny it. If the evidence can be trusted, Rodon was receiving his support from the Zahl Empire. Josh witnessed it. This is going to be a scandal if and when this gets back to the capital worlds."

His jaw dropped. "I thought the Zahl Empire wasn't at war with the Legion."

"They aren't." Braddock gazed back at the water. "But tensions have been growing for some time. These orders to transfer to a carrier task force wouldn't come otherwise. Brass is taking this seriously.

He stared unfocused at the table. "Will there be a war?"

"That's the real question, isn't it?" He sighed. "If these orders come through, I want you to take your leave, sign your five-year papers, and be ready to report to wherever they assign me. Are you up to it?"

He stood and saluted. "Absolutely, sir."

Braddock shook his hand. "I look forward to it."

FREIGHTERS STRETCHED out in the only operational hangar of Atlantis. The ships packed in tight as possible, crews and staff falling into tremendous lines as they moved into the station to help the rebuilding operation. Austin glanced at his tablet. One of the many freighters would depart in twenty minutes for Oma where Ryker was undergoing rehabilitation. Another would depart shortly after for Tarton's Junction and the promotion ceremony.

He watched people cram into the hangar.

"Amazing, isn't it?" Nubern said, stepping next to Austin, his arm still in a sling. "The perseverance of the human spirit. Support is coming in from all over Quadrant Eight. Other planets have heard of the attack. There's more aid coming than we can handle. And to imagine yesterday, I heard some officers say Atlantis would never be rebuilt. Now look."

"Amazing."

Nubern eyed him. "You ready for your leave?"

He nodded. "Yes, sir. Very ready."

"Decided where you're going?"

He smiled. "Off world." He adjusted his satchel on his shoulder and studied the bustling hangar. "It makes me very proud."

Nubern turned to him. "How do you mean?"

"I'm proud to be a Legion officer," he said, looking at the freighters. He turned to Nubern and smiled. "Very proud, sir."

"You know, I'm glad to hear you say that. After our conversation a while back...I hope you mean it."

He frowned. "Of course, sir. Why?"

"I've heard scuttlebutt about some of what your friend has been through."

"And?"

He winced. "Well, he apparently witnessed a Zahl capital ship destroy Rodon and his primary base in the Zine System."

Austin remembered Braddock's warning about keeping quiet. "Zahl? Are you sure?"

"That's all I know and that's all I've heard. If that's true, it would explain a great deal. It's why Lieutenant Morris left for Base Prime. Command needs to verify this."

He bit his lip. "But what does that explain?"

"Explains why the Tyral Pirates have been so well-equipped, why we've been having so much trouble with them the past couple years." He moved as a pair of workers pushed a cart between them. "For the sake of the Legion, I hope it's not true."

Austin thought back to his introductory classes on the history of the Galactic Legion and its contentious relationship with the Zahl Empire. There hadn't been a full-scale galactic war in a generation. If the Zahl Empire had supported a pirate organization to spread dissent in the Quadrant Eight worlds so far from the border, what else would they be capable of doing?

"So do I," he said.

They stood in silence for a moment.

"A message came through regarding Lieutenant Zyan's status," Nubern said. "She's recovering well and rehabilitation is nearly complete. Her leg was shattered pretty badly."

Austin thought of Ryker, her smile and her laugh. Her voice as she tried to speak English.

"I'm very glad to hear it, sir. She's very special."

"That she is." Nubern cleared his throat. "So I've heard you might be assigned to a carrier task force?"

"Nothing's sure, yet."

"You'll do a great job wherever you go."

"Thank you, sir."

"I would like to say something else," Nubern said. "I heard Josh may turn in his wings."

He nodded. "Yes. What will happen to him?"

Nubern chewed on his lip. "With what he's been through, the Legion will take care of him no matter what he decides. Maybe desk work, who knows? It's made me concerned about your future as well."

"How so?"

"You've been through a great deal since you received your wings, son. A great deal. I wouldn't blame you if you decided to take a different path. If you also considered turning in your wings, I wouldn't try to stop you—not after what you've been through. I don't want you flying just for me."

Austin looked at him, then turned to the freighters. He took a few steps toward the hangar. A clump of blue Tizona uniforms boarded a freighter two hundred yards away, moving through the ocean of people.

He took a deep breath.

"I'll never quit, sir." He turned around, looking Nubern in the eye and gesturing to the wings on his chest. "This is what I do."

Swinging the satchel over his shoulder, Austin strolled toward the line of departing freighters.

EPILOGUE

He wore a simple hunter-green shirt and old blue jeans as he stood at the edge of the room full of patients in white robes. Finally, he trudged toward the front desk, where he produced his identification.

The nurse nodded, her knowing glance telling him she knew his story. "Lieutenant Morris."

"Ma'am."

Josh squinted at the high windows revealing a view of the Golden Gate Bridge. After the past forty-eight hours of questioning by the EIF and top Legion officers regarding his incident, the bright sunlight burned his eyes. He was tired and didn't want to think any further about Zahlian ARCs, the vessel's offensive capabilities, and the response times of the Interceptors. The Legion agents repeated the same questions in different forms, all with the goal of discovering more about this mysterious vessel.

His eyes came to rest on the woman in the chair closest to the window.

"How is she?" he asked the nurse, his eyes still on the patient.

The nurse stared at the woman as she paused. "She has come to grips with the situation and will be going home tomorrow to see her parents. This has been very...difficult for her."

Josh recalled the file he had read about the incident with the Phantoms. Her parents' house had nearly burned down in the ensuing firefight in the neighborhood. "Are they okay?"

"Her parents? Yes. Revelation Protocol was carried out on the entire family," the nurse said with a nod. "They are waiting for her in Savannah. I was told they've spent the past few hours at the Tizona Campus in Georgia."

"I see." He looked over at her again, trying to accept it was real. After all this time, she sat just on the other side of the room. "And her counseling?"

The nurse glanced at her tablet. "She has recovered from the initial shock, but has been very quiet since she was told she would be going back to school."

Josh swallowed, his mouth dry. "May I see her?"

"Of course. She was told she was receiving a special guest today."

He gestured to the room. "Now?"

"Sure."

He strolled past the tables covered in chess and checker boards, around the people pouring their feelings out to the counselors. Some spoke in grim tones, others spit out sentences between bouts of sobbing.

He paused behind her chair. Reaching out with one hand, he froze.

"Kadyn?" he asked.

She spun around, her hair falling over her shoulder. "Josh?" She blinked. "Oh my God, *Josh*?"

He held out his hand, stopping her from standing. Moving around in front of her, he knelt on one knee.

"What are you doing here?" she asked, her voice soft.

He reached out, caressing her arm. He gazed into her brown eyes for a long, precious moment. If he spoke, if he said anything, he knew it could end like a dream interrupted by an alarm, and he wanted to feel the softness of her skin, wanted it to last.

"Josh," she said, leaning forward. Darkness had formed under her eyes. She looked tired. "What are you doing here?"

He smiled and squeezed her hand. He'd been waiting for this moment for a very long time. "There's something I need to tell you."

Read more for a sneak peek into the next adventure in the Star Runners Universe!

Fadre Gree was not his real name.

He continued every day as if he were one of the Zahlian engineers. The staff dressed in their civilian clothing lined up in pairs behind the shiny black elevator doors. A nearby man cleared his throat. Gree kept his gaze on the polished obsidian floor to avoid eye contact.

After a minute, the elevator pinged, and the dark reflective doors opened. Two Zahlian Marines, in their crisp crimson uniforms, held repeating laser rifles over their chests. They stepped out of the elevator, their ice-like eyes steady on the engineers.

Behind the Marines stood an officer with a silver tablet in one hand and a blinking metallic wand in the other. He swept the metallic device over two engineers at the front of the group and glanced at his tablet. The wand beeped and flashed green, signaling the first engineers could pass into the elevator. The Marines motioned with their laser rifles for the next pair to step forward. Their fingertips rapped on the rifles as they glared at each waiting person.

A muscle in Gree's cheek twitched. The security to access the bowels of Zone Ninety was far more extensive than he'd anticipated. After seven months on Claria, he still had his movements monitored, and his correspondence surveyed. He hadn't risked checking in with his superiors for two weeks. Now that he was about to descend into the depths of the complex, he wouldn't be able to send or receive any communications. The building blocked all incoming or outgoing transmissions to maintain the operation's security.

The Zahlian agents didn't realize he knew about the surveillance or the blocked transmissions. He spent what little free time he had to try to appear like a bored employee. But the agents had reason to keep a watchful eye on the engineers working on this project for Baron Industries.

The Marines allowed the next pair to pass. They turned and gestured for Gree and the woman next to him to step forward. Her name was Ula Mara, an engineer from a local town on Claria. He had tried to get close to her in the past few months, but she kept to herself. During their one after-work drink in the company lounge, he discovered Ula had received accolades for her revolutionary designs in spacecraft hull plating. His cover story proclaimed him as a genius for optimizing the Lutimite Drive utilized by all spacecraft traveling within the Zahlian space lanes. The project supervisor charged him with advancing the engines on a Zahlian Interceptor, and he had wondered why.

Today, he hoped to find out.

The wand passed over his head, down his back, and touched the back of his legs. Gree sighed and looked up at the ceiling. The officer's device flashed green, and Gree stepped into the elevator. The engineers packed into the rapidly shrinking elevator causing Ula to press against him, her eyes on the wall.

The final two engineers shoved into the elevator. The officer stood at the edge of the door, surveying the group. He nodded while counting the number of employees packed inside. He keyed for the level, and the entry hissed shut.

Gree couldn't believe the length of the ride down. When the doors parted, guards escorted workers from the first elevator to the locker room where they changed into black lab coats. They had locked personal items into blue, plastic bins before ordered to another elevator. He marveled at the silence—the methodical efficiency of the Zahlian operation.

But he could see it in the eyes of the Marines and officer. Today would not be another day of calculations and study. Excitement radiated from their faces as they ushered the staff into another lift and proceeded with the descent.

The second elevator slowed, bounced once, and came to a stop. With a snap-hiss of servos, the doors parted to reveal an expanse substantial enough to fit a Zahlian capital ship. White fluorescent lights buzzed in the ceiling several stories above the floor. Other technicians and engineers, all in black lab coats, worked at stations around the room. Some carried tablets while others labored on equipment. The lighting increased in intensity at the center of the space where the floor lowered into a bowl shape.

"All right, move it," the officer barked from near the elevator.

The engineers stepped forward with caution, surveying the bustling area. Ula leaned back, her eyes on the ceiling high above their heads. A solid red line stretched across the length of the room's upper limit. Zahlian guards dispersed the newly arrived pack, escorting them to workstations. Gree watched them lead Ula away while he remained with engineers he didn't know and hadn't seen during his months in the Zone.

A Marine guard led him and the other engineers through various workstations. At one table, engineers focused on dissecting the inner workings of a laser canon. At another, designers wearing red goggles studied the microscopic variations of a piece of metal.

His pulse quickened, but he tried to control his breathing. After months of being Fadre Gree, trying to work his way into a project so secret it existed hundreds of marks below the surface, he now walked into an underground operations laboratory on Claria. His Legion contacts were not going to believe his report...if he would ever be able to give it.

Acting as if his upper arm itched, he scratched just behind his elbow and gently pressed the activation switch embedded under his skin. As he did so, his vision shifted and blurred like static for an instant. Implants attached to his retina warmed and activated, the images he saw now being recorded and saved into the thumb-sized device placed just under the skin on his arm. If all went well, and he could trust the Legion agent he met on the edge of the Fringe two years ago, he had thirty minutes of recording time. He hoped the image captured clear and true—especially when he recalled the pain of the initial procedure. He hoped the years of planning and execution would be worth it.

He rounded a line of lofty cubicles. Before him stretched a pair of engines connected to computer terminals and colorful wires. He nodded at the guard and stepped in front of the engine he had thus far seen only in schematics. When the trials were complete, it would be the fastest ship in the known galaxy. Nothing in the Legion even compared, but the Zahl project was still far from test flights.

Folding his arms across his chest, Gree turned his head to the side and walked around the engines. No matter who you were or where you were from, you had to be impressed with this technology. It was no wonder the Legion wanted him to get a look at the prototype. In a couple of years, this spacecraft could render the Zahlian Navy invincible.

He picked up a tablet and started reading his assignments for the day. Zahlian command wanted him to begin tests for engine optimization. They planned on installing the advanced engines in...two months? No, that couldn't be possible. This project had barely advanced beyond the preliminary stages, right?

Two attendants moved a lengthy line of diagnostic equipment in front of his station on shiny metal carts. The instruments moved out of his view, revealing a sleek object in the distance.

Gree's jaw dropped, the tablet lowering to his side. In the center of the laboratory, parked like it would blast through the ceiling at any moment, was the *Wraith*.

It couldn't be.

He stepped forward, drawn to the spacecraft as if it had a magnetic pull. The ship's stabilizers looked like the fins of a sea creature. He shook his head, studying the smooth ebony hull and curved arching nose coming together in the shape of a horseshoe crab. Up until that moment, many in Legion intelligence had discounted the rumor of an advanced Zahlian Interceptor code-named *Wraith*. If he could trust the reports, this Interceptor could fly completely undetected by sensors, avoiding missile lock, and operate unaffected by stunners or system disruptors of any kind. A fighter with such abilities would tilt the balance in the Legion-Imperial Cold War. With the work his team had completed on the engine enhancements, the stealth ship would also become the fastest in the galaxy.

"Dr. Gree, isn't it?"

Gree spun around, facing the younger engineer. "Yes?"

"Sir, aren't we supposed to begin working on the engines?"

"Right," he said, turning back to the *Wraith*, "we are. I just, well, I hadn't seen her up close."

"No one has." He stepped next to Gree. From the smooth skin around his eyes, the fellow engineer had to be ten years his junior, or he had received some genetic enhancement—probably on a world like Claria. "She's beautiful."

Gree blinked, appearing to bring himself back to the task at hand but hoping his eye implant focused and captured a clear shot of the first known image of the *Wraith*.

"We had better get to work, Doctor..."

"I'm Sarta Bren, but everyone calls me 'Popper.'"

Gree nodded, his eyes still on the *Wraith* looming like a silent sentinel. He opened the tablet to access his files on engine specifications, pulling his gaze away from the design perfection of the *Wraith*.

"Okay, Dr. Bren," he said, "we need to start by testing if our engine can endure the modifications we made last week."

"Right."

Gree stopped listening as Bren launched into his expectations. Instead, he focused on the dread penetrating his stomach. The Zahl Empire would kill to acquire the images he just recorded. He had actual proof the rumors of the *Wraith* were true.

He needed to get topside after his shift, away from the building's jamming, and send the video off world before it was too late.

As the shift ended, the laboratory lights turned off. One spotlight remained on the *Wraith*. Gree stared at the ship for a moment longer. Smaller than the Legion's Trident, the Interceptor design looked less militaristic and more organic, almost as if the Zahlian craft had been born, not created. It had an elegant design. The smooth surface of the hull glistened like polished marble, the remaining light in the room rippling on the craft like a pond in the moonlight.

Gree sat his tablet next to the engines and, even though his recording device had filled hours ago, took one last look at the *Wraith*. He needed to get this information back to the Legion.

He filed out with the other engineers. Bren was babbling something about his evening plans when Gree came back to the conversation.

"I'm sorry," he said, "what's that now? I zoned out for a second."

Bren snorted. "Glad you find me so interesting. Anyway, some people I know wanted to go to the Jouncy game later tonight, but I'm *so* over sports. Seriously, what's the point? You know? Your team wins, or they lose—your life is the same the next day, right?"

Gree said nothing.

Bren continued his rant on the elevator ride back to the surface, launching into a tirade over a guy he knew who lost next month's rent betting on a game.

Ula rode in silence at the elevator's front, her arms behind her back. Gree stared at her, noticing the wisps of blonde hair stretching out like golden spider webs. He didn't know much about her side of the project, but he knew it was her brilliance enabling the *Wraith* to remain invisible from sensors. Her advancements and dedication would serve the project well.

And she was beautiful.

Shorter than him and fit. He'd admitted a long time ago she was the best part of the daily elevator rides. Perhaps in another place and time, something could have...

Instead, he had to listen to Bren talking about the upcoming tournament he claimed not to care about.

They retrieved their belongings, including Gree's bag with the crucial bit of technology, from the locker room, and changed into the civilian clothes they had worn when they arrived sixteen hours ago. With the schedule requiring them to return in six hours, he knew he had limited time to launch his remote Whisper carrying the *Wraith* video into space, away from the jamming, and back to his Legion contacts.

Wearing his light blue shirt and dark pants, he passed through the locker room door. It felt better to be out of the lab coat. He glanced at his watch and stopped, nearly crashing into Ula standing near the locker room entrance.

"Oh, I'm sorry," she said, her voice soft. "I didn't mean to frighten you."

Gree adjusted his shirt. "Not at all. I was just leaving."

"Dr. Gree," she said, tilting her head. "Mind if I call you Fadre?"

"Sure."

"You asked me a few weeks ago if I would like to go for a drink after work." She stared at the floor. "I feel I owe you an apology."

Shifting his weight, he shook his head and moved around her. "No apology needed. I understand not mixing business with pleasure. I really should be—"

Pushing a strand of her blonde hair over her right ear, Ula held her arm in front of him. "I'm trying to say I was interested. I shouldn't have shot you down that day." She fiddled with her hands. "I really need to talk to someone. I'm in some trouble and, well, I don't really know where I can turn."

The clock was ticking. He needed to send the images stored in his implant. But avoiding a coworker might seem suspicious, and he didn't need any reason to draw attention to himself.

"Okay, Ula," he said, trying to sound like he cared. "Where would you like to go?"

"There's a bar here in this installation. Street side, though. What do you think?"

"I think it sounds great." He raised his hand toward the door. "Lead the way."

She strolled through the brightly lit corridors of the Zahlian research facility. She nodded as they passed other engineers and scientists still wearing black lab coats. Marine guards stood at two doors they passed, their cold stares sending a shiver through his core.

If they only knew what I had stored in my implant.

Shaking away thoughts of capture and torture, Gree feigned a pleasant smile as he passed two Marines and followed Ula into the elevator. She grinned sheepishly, pressing an elevator button. The door pinged and started to slide shut.

"Hold it! *Please*!" a voice yelled from the corridor.

Gree looked up. Dr. Bren, or Popper, sprinted down the hall, his skin glistening with sweat. He burst into the elevator like a gust of the wind in a storm, collapsing against the wall.

"Thanks!" he gasped. "I didn't want to have to wait another twenty minutes for the next elevator, and I'm ready to get out of here."

"No problem," Ula said in a soft voice, "what floor?"

Bren glanced at both of them. "Am I interrupting something?"

She shook her head. "Of course not."

He sighed, appearing relieved. "I'm heading topside."

"Very well."

Ula pressed the button, and the doors slid shut. After a moment, the elevator deep inside Claria accelerated, traveling away from the hidden research station. Gree stared at the levels changing on the LED display above the door, lost in thought.

So, Legion Intelligence had been right to send him here. Rumors of the Zahlian war faction were true. More than that, the war faction had created an advanced prototype fighter with potentially deadly consequences to the Legion fleet. From what he knew of the Legion's naval abilities, the *Wraith* would be able to render the Tridents obsolete. He had the only evidence this prototype fighter existed. He *had* to send this information.

Gree sighed, bouncing on his heels. Couldn't this elevator move faster?

He closed his eyes and rolled his head around, relishing in the feeling of release as the joints popped.

A blunt force struck his face.

Gree tumbled back against the wall then slid to the floor, his nose gushing. His eyes blurred with water. He brought his hands to his face, confused as to what had just happened. He saw Ula attacking Bren. Her body spun, hands and feet pummeling the doctor into the wall. She grabbed the back of his head and smashed it against the door. At the same time, she punched the emergency stop. The lights shifted to a blood red. The elevator halted.

Shaking his head, Gree sat up. Before he knew it, Ula grabbed him by the collar and yanked him to his feet. She pulled a spray bottle from her bag, launching a concentrated neon-yellow mist into two corners of the elevator car. The walls dripped with a bright mix of red and vibrant golden streams.

Gree glanced at Bren's crumpled body—still and bloodied.

Ula pulled him close, so close her breath warmed his face as she spoke.

"They know," she hissed.

Ice shot through his chest. "What do—"

"Don't," she said, placing her finger over his mouth. She glanced at Bren's body. "He came here to kill you. It took them time to trace the signal, but they detected your implant when you activated it near the ship."

"I don't know—"

"You're wasting time!" Ula snapped. She jumped up, grabbing a handle on the ceiling. When she dropped, the elevator's service hatch unlatched and a ladder descended. "I've disabled the cameras, but we need to move. *Now*!"

Gree stared at her, his heart thumping.

"I understand," he said, pulling the ladder to the floor. He slipped his bag around his back. "What's the plan?"

"It won't take them long to override the emergency stop. We need to switch elevators and go to the roof."

"All the way to the top?" he asked, reaching the hatch and turning around to Ula.

"You have a launcher to take your images off world, yes?" She gestured at the ceiling. "Away from this jamming?"

Gree nodded, helping her through the hatch, his mind racing at the fact this woman knew about his mission. "How do you know all this? Who *are* you?"

"Your backup," she said, searching the elevator tube. She peered over the edge. "One's coming. Get ready to jump."

"Are you crazy?"

She stared at him, her black eyes cold. "You'd rather wait for them to find you?"

Shaking his head, peered down the elevator shaft, saw the other car coming. "What's our exit strategy?"

"There is none."

Gree shot her a glance, but she didn't look back. He opened his mouth to object but realized she was right. Whatever his mission had been, whatever he had hoped to accomplish, had ended the moment Bren attacked him.

The elevator car neared, moving faster than he thought they could handle.

"Maybe we should—"

"*Jump*!"

They leaped across the shaft onto the car. The collision shocked him, the metal crashing against his body. He shook his head as his vision darkened. He rolled over on his back. Wind touched his face as the car accelerated upward. Lights played across the roof as they passed the building's levels.

"Are you okay?" Ula asked.

Gree looked at her. A vicious gash above her left eye spilt blood down her cheek. "Are you?"

She touched her face. "Yeah."

He probed his forehead and felt a lump growing, courtesy of the metal roof.

Ula surveyed her surroundings. "I don't think they knew about me, but I knew they had you when Bren charged into our elevator."

"I was told the implant couldn't be detected."

"You were told wrong."

"Are we all there is?"

"I believe there is another." She shook her head. "It doesn't matter now."

Ula pulled up her pant leg, exposing her calf. She squeezed the skin. The muscle glowed an emerald-green and opened. Pulling out a pistol not much bigger than a pen, she grinned. "When we get to the top, your job is to launch that image into space. No gamma wave will transmit from this building—it *has* to be sent into space."

"I know." Gree gripped his bag. "What are you going to do?"

"Give you the time."

He gestured toward the tiny weapon in her hand. "With that? You won't last long."

She offered a lopsided grin. "You better hurry, then."

They traveled for thirty seconds. Gree looked up. He'd just seen the metal rafters above when the elevator screeched to a halt.

"What happened?" he asked, standing as if the elevator would resume its sudden ascent.

Ula glanced around, her small pistol in hand. She nodded behind him. "Jump off. We walk the rest of the way."

Gree turned. A steel staircase inside the shaft led the remaining distance to the roof. He jumped to the stairs, his boots clanging on the grating. He turned around to help Ula. She waved him off.

"Just move!" she snapped, glancing back. "No matter what happens—you get that message sent!"

Gree started to ask what she meant but noticed movement below.

Another elevator car sped toward them. Fast.

Spinning around, he tightened the bag's strap and ran. He heard Ula's quick footsteps behind him. He skipped a step, then two, his leg muscles burning as he increased his speed. He rounded a floor, ascending closer to the roof.

A laser blast flashed by him, illuminating the shaft like a strobe. Two shots followed.

Sweat poured down his face and dripped off his nose. He rounded another floor and paused. Blocking his path was a metal door with red lettering: AUTHORIZED PERSONNEL ENTRY ONLY.

The roof.

He clutched his bag's strap and sprinted forward. Lowering his shoulder, he lunged for the door. His shoulder flashed with pain as he bounced back from the immovable barrier. He pounded on the door and kicked the steel.

"Move!"

Gree turned. Ula stood at the pinnacle of the stairs, a fresh laser burn sizzling into her upper arm. She held out the small weapon, aiming at the top of the door. She fired, the laser's light flashing in the dim corridor. Sparks flew down on his head. She fired twice more. He flinched but saw the hinges had melted.

He stood, reared back, and kicked.

The door fell forward. A gust of wind howled through the opening.

"Hurry!" Ula yelled. "Go!"

He sprinted onto the roof and into the daylight. Claria's space station dominated the heavens, visible even on a cloudless day. A massive Zahlian capital ship orbited the installation.

Zone Ninety's urban cityscape surrounded the building on all sides, the skyline stretching to the distant sea. Wind blasts nearly knocked him off his feet as he ran across the rooftop. As an explosion boomed from behind him, he tried to ignore the realization of being more than three thousand feet above the ground and looked for a spot to set up the launcher.

He crouched behind an junction box, whipping the bag around and opening it in one motion.

Ula limped next to him and fell with her back against the box. "How long do you need?"

He pulled the cylinder apart like a telescope. "A few minutes."

She coughed. "I can give you that."

Gree glanced at her and saw laser wounds on her arm and leg, sweat drenching her shirt. He bit his lip, trying to focus on the launcher. Just as he had practiced countless times in training, the four-foot device extended from the rooftop, the silver missile glistening in the light. He reached to touch his elbow, found the implant, and squeezed hard.

His skin burned and sizzled. The odor of burning flesh filled the air. He winced. Once he heard the loud buzzing alarm, he ripped back his skin and screamed, freeing the implant from his arm. Ignoring the pain, he opened the transmission pocket on the launcher and keyed in the coordinates. Once the missile traveled beyond the building's jamming effects and reached the upper atmosphere, the message would begin its transmission via Whisper to the closest Legion post.

Ula fired her laser and crouched. "You done already?"

"Twenty seconds to launch!"

She smiled. "You did good, Dr. Gree."

Their eyes met. He touched her knee and patted it once.

Laser fire splattered against the junction box. Sparks erupted skyward. Ula stood to return fire. Bolts exploded into her chest, spinning her around like a top. Her body crumpled to the roof, lifeless.

Keeping low, Gree crawled to her. He turned her over and saw tiny fires burning into her body. She wasn't breathing. He grabbed her pistol and glanced back.

Two Marines emerged from the charred doorway, their blaster rifles trained in his direction.

Here we go, Gree thought.

He turned back to the launcher, rechecking the coordinates. A few more seconds and he would finish the launch prep.

Gripping the compact pistol, he leaned against the box. He panted as cold sweat covered his clammy skin. He glanced at the brilliant blue sky. Fighting back nausea, he emerged from his cover and fired.

He squeezed off two shots, one striking an attacker in the leg before the return blasts hit him. His chest flashed with pain, the force knocking him to the rooftop. He remained on his back, the sound around him muffling. The missile's hiss transformed into a roar. With a whoosh, it propelled high into the air.

He smiled, watching it soar. Laser fire filled the sky, but the bolts didn't find their mark. After another two seconds, the missile vanished, leaving only a white trail behind it.

"We did it," he said, rising from the rooftop. "Ula."

He dragged himself to her, ignoring the fact he'd left his cover. Her eyes remained focused on the heavens.

Gree looked to the door as more armed Marines poured from the elevator shaft. Their red armor reflected the light, splintering flashes of crimson across the rooftop. There was only one thing he could do.

He raised the pistol and fired.

The rooftop ignited, filling his vision with sparks, lethal fire, and darkness.

The compact missile reached supersonic speeds as it ascended away from Zone Ninety and through the atmosphere. The air thinned, and the temperature dropped as the projectile transitioned into deep orbit.

No one saw the tiny missile as it passed Claria's spaceport.

A sensor operator aboard the Zahlian All-purpose Response

Cruiser, *Dauntless,* momentarily detected it, but could not achieve a lock. As a result, Regional Governor Knox Tulin, who utilized the *Dauntless* as his flagship, was not told of the incident until hours later.

The Legion agent's missile surpassed the final patrolling Zahlian Interceptors and ran out of fuel. Away from any electronic jamming pumped into the air by Zahlian forces, the video transmission started and repeated until the missile ran out of battery power hours later.

Light years away, a Legion listening post awaited information from their team. Video captured of the *Wraith* was downloaded, copied, and sent to the highest levels of Legion Command.

ABOUT THE AUTHOR

L.E. Thomas lives in the Appalachian Mountains of North America with his wife and rescued dog where he is currently working on his next novel.

www.starrunners.net
info@starrunners.net

Made in the USA
Middletown, DE
28 May 2021

40592358R00201